THE PICKERING MASTERS

THE WORKS OF ELIZABETH GASKELL
VOLUME 2

THE WORKS OF
ELIZABETH GASKELL

VOLUME 2

Novellas and Shorter Fiction I

The Moorland Cottage,
Cranford
and
Related Writings

Edited by
Alan Shelston

LONDON AND NEW YORK

First published 2005 by Pickering & Chatto (Publishers) Limited

2 Park Square, Milton Park, Abingdon, Oxon OX14 4RN
711 Third Avenue, New York, NY 10017, USA

Routledge is an imprint of the Taylor & Francis Group, an informa business

First issued in paperback 2017

BRITISH LIBRARY CATALOGUING IN PUBLICATION DATA
Gaskell, Elizabeth Cleghorn, 1810–1865
    The works of Elizabeth Gaskell
    Vols. 1–3, 5, 7. – (The Pickering masters)
    1. Gaskell, Elizabeth Cleghorn, 1810–1865 – Criticism and interpretation
    I. Title II. Shattock, Joanne
    823.8

LIBRARY OF CONGRESS CATALOGING-IN-PUBLICATION DATA
A catalogue record for this title is available from the Library of Congress.

ISBN-13: 978-1-85196-777-3 (set)
ISBN-13: 978-1-1387-6399-9 (hbk)
ISBN-13: 978-1-138-11151-6 (pbk)

New material typeset by
P&C

CONTENTS

ACKNOWLEDGEMENTS

I wish to acknowledge the help given to me by Christine Lingard, Coordinator of Language and Literature Services at the City of Manchester Central Library; by Emma Marigliano, Librarian at the Portico Library and Gallery, Manchester; by the special collections librarians at the John Rylands University Library, Manchester; and the staff at the Knutsford Public Library. All of these institutions readily made texts and other material available to me from their specialist collections. I am especially grateful to Mr John Geoffrey Sharps for letting me have his copy of the 1864 edition of *Cranford* on a very extended loan. Only those who have worked in the field know the full extent to which Gaskell studies are indebted to Geoffrey Sharps, and I should like to take this opportunity to express my appreciation of both his work and his companionship over many years. In the same spirit I record my indebtedness to Professor John Chapple, friend and colleague of many years, who has willingly responded to a sequence of queries. Dr Roger Holdsworth helped me with matters bibliographical. Professor Joanne Shattock was an understanding general editor whose invaluable advice was always available, as was that of Marian Olney of Pickering & Chatto. Finally, to those too numerous to identify by name with whom I have discussed queries and points of detail I again extend my thanks. They will know who they are.

Alan Shelston

INTRODUCTION

Elizabeth Gaskell's first full-scale appearance as a professional author was both late and successful. When *Mary Barton* was published in 1848 she was thirty-eight years of age: its reception saw her immediate recognition as an author of distinction, most notably of course by Charles Dickens, himself at something of a turning point in his own career. The experience of seeing the book through the press had quickly taught her how the publishing industry conducted itself, and it had given her the important initial contact with the firm of Chapman and Hall, who were to be her publisher for most of the next decade. Chapman and Hall had until recently been Dickens's publisher also, and they would in all probability have been eager to encourage a new and perhaps more malleable talent. From the outset Gaskell's letters to Edward Chapman reveal her as confident and indeed sometimes demanding in her contact with his firm, but of *Mary Barton* she was able to note that 'Not the least agreeable part of yr letter is that in which you speak of the book "being a source of profit to the publisher."'[1] She was thus fully appreciative of the economic dimension of her new profession. Contacts too, with generous commentators like Thomas Carlyle, and John Forster, later to be a much relied upon adviser and friend, meant that with the publication of *Mary Barton*, Gaskell became increasingly involved with the Victorian publishing establishment. With the exception of *The Cage at Cranford*, her late and very limited return to Cranford, the works collected in this volume all show her extending her range as she established herself on the Victorian literary scene at the turning point of the half-century.

★ ★ ★

Mary Barton, Gaskell's 'Tale of Manchester Life', identified her as a novelist of the industrial city but, as she wrote to Lady Kay-Shuttleworth, 'the work appointed for my husband & me lies in Manchester. I would fain be in the country'.[2] Gaskell's loss of her parents at an early age meant that she was remarkably well travelled during her formative years. As a girl she lived first with her Aunt Lumb, in Knutsford; she was educated for probably five years at the Miss Byerleys' school, originally at Barford in Warwickshire and then

1. *Letters*, p. 69.
2. *Letters*, p. 139.

at Stratford-upon-Avon. Following this she returned to Knutsford but spent periods of time with her extended family in Liverpool, in North Wales, and with Unitarian connections in Newcastle. J. A. V. Chapple has detailed this extensive experience of English provincial life in his magisterial *Elizabeth Gaskell: The Early Years* (Manchester: Manchester University Press, 1997). Knutsford and its surrounding countryside always remained her emotional home, and in the stories in this volume 'the country' means either 'Cranford' – the fictionalised version of the Knutsford of her early life – or, in the case of *The Moorland Cottage*, the 'rocky moorland' of the north Lancashire and Yorkshire borders. According to Gaskell, *The Moorland Cottage* was written at Silverdale, the Gaskells' summer retreat on the North Lancashire coast, from which they often visited the Lake District. 'I tried,' she writes, 'to convey the impressions made upon me by that wild Moorland scenery, with the Lake and the Yorkshire hills girding it round'.[1] The region was to provide her with the setting for a number of her early stories and the austerity of its landscapes seems to have had a special emotional resonance for her. As Old Alice Wilson, who in her early life has come south to Manchester in search of work, says in *Mary Barton*, Chapter VI, 'Eh, lasses! Ye don't know what rocks are in Manchester'. *The Moorland Cottage* was perhaps Gaskell's first opportunity, after the success of her industrial novel, to return to a landscape with real rocks: it is permeated with her affection for a landscape of which she had direct personal experience and to which, throughout her Manchester life, she often returned, in fiction as well as in person.

The Moorland Cottage was commissioned by Chapman and Hall as a Christmas story, and its physical format – a small octavo volume with its illustrations by Birket Foster inserted directly into the text – is not unlike that of some of Dickens's Christmas stories, for example *The Chimes* (1845) or *The Battle of Life* (1846). Its published price was five shillings, the price of Dickens's Christmas books, although this was later reduced to two shillings and sixpence.[2] Gaskell herself described her story as being 'about the length of Mr Dickens' Christmas Stories' when considering the possibility of its translation into French[3] and she would certainly have been conscious of the Dickens model. She herself was sceptical about her ability to write to the Christmas formula – 'I cannot write a Xmas book', she wrote to Chapman, and to her friend Eliza Fox she described the project as 'a *very foolish* engagement of mine'.[4] In its general tone *The Moorland Cottage* would have satisfied Chapman's request for a story '"recommending benevolence, charity, etc"',[5]

---

1. *Further Letters*, p. 53.

2. Clarke S. Northup, 'Bibliography' in G. De Witt Sanders, *Elizabeth Gaskell* (New Haven: Yale University Press for Cornell University), p. 171; *Smith*, p. 46.

3. *Further Letters*, pp. 134. 169. Initially she was sceptical about such a translation, but she later included it in a list of her works to be considered (*Further Letters*, pp. 134, 169).

4. *Letters*, pp. 104, 130.

5. *Letters*, p. 132.

but it certainly lacks the optimistic dimension, not to say the comedy of Dickens's stories. The timescale of the narrative is arranged to allow for direct references to the Christmas season, and its Christian sentiment, notably in the utterances of its heroine, Maggie Browne, is explicit. It is fair to say that the story is one of Christian virtue rewarded. But for Gaskell, who always seems to have had mixed feelings about her story (it was never reprinted, but it crops up later in her career as a matter for concern over copyright), *The Moorland Cottage* was 'simply a little country love-story'.

The Moorland Cottage is as much a story of its setting as it is of its characters. It is a distinctly Wordsworthian exercise: at its opening we are taken, just as we are in William Wordsworth's *Michael*, from a situation already remote to a location even more so. Stephen Gill has described Gaskell as 'Wordsworth's ideal reader' and documented the extent to which his influence pervades her work. In the case of *The Moorland Cottage* he notes the allusions to the Lucy poems, while arguing that 'Maggie is not Lucy'.[1] Perhaps not, but in fact Maggie Browne does dwell 'amongst th'untrodden ways' and there are none to praise and few to love her. Her favourite resting place is by an isolated thorn on a rocky crest – another Wordsworthian echo – and she rejects the attractions of social and city life. Just how conscious Gaskell would have been of these associations cannot be calculated, but she had met the widowed Mrs Wordsworth in her old age and she was acquainted with the Lake District group – the Davys and the Arnolds – at Ambleside. Wordsworth himself had congratulated William Gaskell on his 'Temperance Rhymes'[2] and clearly Gaskell had absorbed the Wordsworthian ethos. As *The Moorland Cottage* develops however, the melodramatic narrative surrounding Edward Browne's malfeasance brings it very much into the Victorian period. Financial failure, and in particular fraud and the shame associated with it, inspired a particular horror amongst Victorian novelists and their readers. Furthermore the story of the over-privileged brother and the sister constrained by her secondary status is one which was to recur – in Dickens's *Hard Times* for example, with the Bounderby children, and again for Dickens in the case of Lizzie and Charlie Hexham in *Our Mutual Friend*. But the most notable example is that of Maggie and Tom Tulliver in *The Mill on the Floss*. Tom Tulliver does not go spectacularly to the bad as does Edward Browne, but in Eliot's novel, as in Gaskell's story, the way in which the seeds of the distinction between male and female roles are established in childhood is the source of the adult histories. *The Moorland Cottage* is outspoken in this respect: the 'little country love-story' is consistent and emphatic about the factors which constrain female development. And when Gaskell refers to her heroine as one of 'those whose names will never be blazoned on earth', and then, in the

1. Stephen Gill, *Wordsworth and the Victorians* (Oxford: Clarendon Press, 1998), pp. 119, 128.
2. *Further Letters*, p. 24.

next breath, identifies piano-playing as 'the very head and front of a genteel education' (p. 25), it is not inappropriate to think forward to *Middlemarch*. A number of Gaskell's early stories reflect the pastoral setting of *The Moorland Cottage*: 'The Sexton's Hero' (1847), for example, set on the shores of More-cambe Bay; 'Martha Preston' (1850), later revised as 'The Half-Brothers' (1859) in Cumberland, and 'The Heart of John Middleton' (1850), whose action is located near Pendle in Lancashire. She was to add North Wales as the setting for several stories, and also for the initiating action in *Ruth*. In all of these, the rural location is as much a contribution to the moral climate as the characters and their actions: the inference seems to be that the rural world brings its own therapeutic blessings to human experience. To Gaskell these were all familiar environments; but she always retained her affection for her childhood home at Knutsford in the softer rural surroundings of Cheshire, some fourteen miles from Manchester. In August 1838 she wrote to William and Mary Howitt: 'I was brought up in a country town, and my lot is now to live in or rather on the borders of a great manufacturing town, but when spring days first come … I feel a stirring instinct and long to be off into the grassy solitudes of the country'.[1] She describes the 'country town' as 'clean' and 'kindly', and in a second letter to Mary Howitt she identifies it as 'my dear *adoptive native* town, Knutsford'.[2] It was in and around Knutsford that so many of Gaskell's maternal relations lived, and it was there that from the age of two until going away to boarding school at about the age of eleven, she lived. It was to Knutsford too that she frequently returned after her marriage in 1832 for breaks from the domestic and social duties of Manchester. Its fictionalisation as Cranford has always been accepted, and with sound reason. The remaining material in this volume consists of three *Cranford*-related shorter pieces – an autobiographical essay, *The Last Generation in England* (1849); two stories, *Mr. Harrison's Confessions* (1851) and *The Cage at Cranford* (1863); and finally *Cranford* itself (1852–3).

★ ★ ★

The Last Generation in England is something of a curiosity amongst Gaskell's work. First published anonymously in 1849 through the agency of Mary Howitt in the short-lived American journal *Sartain's Union Magazine*, it was not identified as Gaskell's until 1935.[3] It remained unpublished in England until it was reprinted in Watson's edition of *Cranford* (1972). Despite this inauspicious history the essay forms a valuable link in establishing Knutsford as the origin of Cranford. Neither Knutsford nor its fictional counterpart is named in the essay, but it is described as 'an Amazonian town'

---

1. *Letters*, p. 14.

2. *Letters*, p. 28.

3. Ross D. Waller, 'Articles by Mrs. Gaskell', letter in *The Times Literary Supplement* (25 July 1935), p. 477.

and the essay is clearly a directly autobiographical reminiscence. As Gaskell says, she is putting on record, 'some of the details of country town life, either observed by myself or handed down to me by older relations', and 'every circumstance and occurrence which I shall relate is strictly and truthfully told without exaggeration' (p. 91). In her essay, stories which were later recounted in the fictional context of *Cranford*, appear as straight autobiography – the stories of the cow in flannel drawers for example, of the cat which swallowed the lace, and of the tea tray concealed under the sofa. The first of these was cited as a Knutsford anecdote as early as 1859 by Henry Green, a friend of Gaskell's and Unitarian minister of Knutsford's Brook Street Chapel,[1] and its appearance in *The Last Generation in England* from Gaskell's own hand, suggests that she knew of it before Green gave it circulation. From *The Last Generation in England* we can identify with greater certainty Knutsford figures who, if they do not appear directly in the fictional work, contribute significantly to its ethos of 'etiquette and precedence' (p. 91): the aristocratic Lady Jane Stanley, for example, an unmarried daughter of the eleventh Earl of Derby, who provides the precedent for the social position of *Cranford*'s Honorable Mrs Jamieson, 'sister-in-law to the late Earl of Glenmire'. Gaskell's title, *The Last Generation in England* embodies a nice ambiguity – are we to read 'last' in the sense of 'previous' or, more emphatically, of 'final'? – and it is one perhaps to appeal to an American audience, with its implications of a world now lost. Much later in the century *Cranford* was to prove easily the most popular of Gaskell's works in the United States, and there is thus a certain appropriateness in its forerunner making its first appearance there.

★ ★ ★

Mr. Harrison's Confessions, published in *The Ladies Companion* in 1851, anticipates *Cranford* more by its choice of subject than by its setting. The country town on this occasion is fictionalised as 'Duncombe', and there is little of substance to connect it with Knutsford itself. With one exception the description of both the town and its surroundings has little specifically in common with the Knutsford Gaskell knew. What does anticipate *Cranford* is the statement at the outset that 'five-sixths of our householders of a certain rank in Duncombe are women' (p. 105). In *Cranford*, as the opening sentence tells us, 'all the holders of houses, above a certain rent, are women' (p. 165). This provides the basis for the central and very simple joke of the story – unattached females, whether unmarried or widowed, will have matrimonial designs on (usually) younger bachelors. There are

---

1. Henry Green, *Knutsford: Its Traditions and History* (London: Smith, Elder & Co., 1859), p. 114. Green's work was published by Smith, Elder at the point in time when Gaskell had moved from Chapman and Hall to Smith, Elder. Green was minister of Knutsford's Brook Street chapel; his wife, Mary Green, was an intimate friend of Gaskell.

variations on this theme: thus Mrs Bullock is trying to marry off her daughter who herself resents the process, and in the course of the story develops a character of her own; the widowed Mrs Rose will ultimately marry the established doctor in the practice and not Mr Harrison, his younger assistant, but in this story of the eccentricities of single ladies there is little of the generosity of *Cranford*, either in the characterisation or the handling of the narrative. Characters are effectively identified but, unusually for Gaskell, sometimes less than kindly observed. It is enough that Mrs Munton is deaf, Miss Tomkinson overbearing, Mrs Bullock a bully and Mrs Rose obsessive in her grief for her long-dead husband. The problem is compounded by the fact that it is the eponymous male narrator who is the target of the ladies' attentions. There is some attempt to place his somewhat superior mode of utterance, but the overall impression is of a masculine and somewhat privileged narrator amusing himself at the expense of female folly. There is too an uneasy link between the comic, the romantic and the serious elements of the story. While the ladies are plotting their designs on Mr Harrison he falls in love with Sophy Hutton, the vicar's daughter. But early in the story her little brother dies of croup, with neither doctor able to save him, while later Sophy herself nearly dies of a potentially fatal illness. These more serious moments are interspersed with comedy that sometimes approaches farce, and while Gaskell tries to adjust her tone accordingly – as in the incident of the injury and illness of the farm-labourer threatened with the amputation of his arm – for much of the story the mixture is less than successful.

In two instances direct links with Gaskell's earlier life can be detected. In the first, in Chapters V and VI, she takes her characters on a picnic to an old country hall. The account of the event is very similar to that of an outing recalled from Gaskell's past in her letter to the Howitts, quoted earlier. There she writes, 'Here, on summer mornings did we often come, a merry young party, on donkey, or pony, or even in a cart with sacks swung across – each with our favourite book, some with sketch-books, and one or two baskets filled with eatables. Here we rambled, lounged and meditated; some stretched on the grass in indolent repose ...'[1] It is an attractive picture of young people enjoying themselves. The venue is described in her letter as 'an old house with a moat within a park called Old Tabley'. Tabley Hall is only a few miles from Knutsford, and this allows us to make the larger identification of the setting of *Mr. Harrison's Confessions* with that known to Gaskell in her early life. The description of the picnic in the story is similarly idyllic to that of the letter, with its appeal to the beauty of nature, its moated manor house, and the sense of holiday for all the participants. But the idyll is interrupted by the importunities to which the narrator is

1. *Letters*, p. 15.

exposed by the female members of the party and, as he says: 'I became so irritable before I reached home, that I thought it was the most disagreeable day of pleasure I ever had' (p. 118). The interruption of the reminiscence by the demands of the story's theme epitomises the limitations of the story as a whole. Shifts of mood were to be much more subtle in *Cranford*. Secondly, and in more serious mode, in the account of the death of the Vicar's son, we can sense Gaskell's memory of the death by scarlet fever of Willie Gaskell, her own much younger child. Mr Harrison reflects that his presence at the death had made him 'one of the "Peculiar people, whom Death had made dear"' (p. 120). This is exactly the attitude that Gaskell took towards her nurse, Barbara Fergusson, who had been with her at Willie's deathbed.[1] Personal experience thus filters into the story in ways which, in Gaskell's failure to distance herself from it, are not always to its benefit.

★ ★ ★

In the last year of her life Gaskell wrote to John Ruskin thanking him for some unspecified help that she had requested. In a letter to her, cited by A. W. Ward in the 'Knutsford' edition of *Cranford*, Ruskin had written that he had been reading *Cranford* to his mother, who had read it 'about 5 times'. He continues, 'I do not know when I have read a more finished little piece of human nature … Nor was I ever more sorry to come to a book's end.'[2] Gaskell was equally generous in her reply:

> And then again about 'Cranford'. I am so pleased you like it. It is the only one of my own books that I can read again; but whenever I am ailing or ill, I take 'Cranford' and – I was going to say *'enjoy'* it but that would not be pretty, – laugh over it afresh. And it is true too, for I have seen the cow that wore the grey flannel jacket, and I knew the cat that swallowed the lace, that belonged to the lady, that sent for the doctor, that gave the emetic &c &c.
> I am so glad that your mother likes it too.[3]

Ruskin's enthusiasm for *Cranford*, evoking Gaskell's own affection for it, was confirmed by many of its contemporary readers, and for many readers today it remains Gaskell's representative work. Gaskell's own laughter, too, is a timely reminder that above all *Cranford* is a work of comedy. In his bibiliography, Clark S. Northup records twenty separate published versions of *Cranford* in Britain, and twenty in the United States, between Gaskell's death in 1865 and the end of the nineteenth century. In the United States eight editions appeared in 1892 alone and this popularity continued well into the twentieth century.[4] With the revival of critical interest in Gaskell's work in

---

1.   'I can not keep down the feeling … that it is ungrateful to part with one who was *so tender* to my poor darling boy' (*Further Letters*, p. 34). Gaskell repeated the reference to 'peculiar people' in the sense of watchers at a death-bed in *North and South*.

2.   Quoted in *Knutsford*, vol. ii, p. xxiv.

3.   *Further Letters*, p. 268.

4.   Northup, 'Bibliography', pp. 163–267.

the 1960s and 70s this enthusiasm tended to be superseded by an often politicised concern with the industrial fiction, but in more recent years feminist criticism has given a new dimension to *Cranford's* status.[1] In terms of genre *Cranford* has always been difficult to define, but not the least of its attractions is perhaps that it has proved to be an infinitely adaptable work to its readership.

Cranford, according to Gaskell, in her letter to Ruskin, began as '*one* paper in *Household Words*'. There she continues: 'I never meant to write more; so killed poor Captain Brown, – very much against my will.'[2] She was responding to Ruskin's objection to Captain Brown's death, and his observation that 'you're fond of killing nice people'.[3] That '*one* paper', 'Our Society at Cranford', appeared in *Household Words* on 13 December 1851. It was already with the printer by 5 December, since on that date Dickens wrote apologising to Gaskell that he had been unable to inform her in time of changes he had made involving the removal of references to his own works from her text. Gaskell's account of the origins of her story has always been accepted at face value, but in a letter to Eliza Fox, also written in December 1851 (day unspecified), she refers to having written 'a couple of tales about Cranford in Household Words.'[4] This must refer to the first two instalments, originally entitled 'Our Society at Cranford' (13 December 1851) and 'A Love Affair at Cranford' (3 January 1852), since Dickens wrote to Gaskell, thanking her for the latter, 'in the purest metal of praise', and announcing the title he had given it, in a letter of 21 December.[5] Furthermore, the first instalment, ending with the anticipation of Miss Deborah Jenkyns's death, is clearly conceived as one 'tale' and is printed as such in the *Household Words* text; the second instalment which concludes with the death of another of Gaskell's 'nice people', Mr Holbrook, Miss Matty's one-time suitor, is another. There is thus an inconsistency here with Gaskell's reference in her letter to Ruskin to 'one paper', and to her having been obliged to engineer the death of Captain Brown to bring that original 'paper' to an end. Furthermore, despite Gaskell's 'I never meant more', four instalments had appeared by 5 April 1852; any change of plan, whenever it took place, must therefore have been speedily acted upon.

The nine *Household Words* instalments that make up the finished work appeared irregularly between December 1851 and 21 May 1853. After the

1. Raymond Williams's *Culture and Society* (London: Chatto & Windus, 1958), initiated a sequence of socio-historical readings of *Mary Barton* and *North and South*; more recent feminist readings of *Cranford* can be found in Patsy Stoneman, *Elizabeth Gaskell* (Brighton: Harvester Press, 1987), and Hilary M. Schor, *Sceherezade in the Market-Place* (Oxford: Oxford University Press, 1992).

2. *Further Letters*, p. 268.

3. *Knutsford*, vol. ii, p. xxiv.

4. *Letters*, p. 174.

5. *CD Letters*, vol. vi, 1850–2 p. 558.

first four instalments had appeared there was a long gap between 3 April
1852 and 8 January 1853. Unfortunately, where *Cranford* is concerned, we
have little detailed information about the writing and publishing process in
the correspondence of either Gaskell or Dickens, but undoubtedly Gaskell's
other commitments at this time will have interrupted her progress. As well
as the *Cranford* stories, in 1852 she was writing *Ruth* (published in three vol-
umes in January 1853). Two essays, 'The Schah's English Gardener' and
'Cumberland Sheep-Shearers' appeared in *Household Words* on 19 June 1852
and 22 January 1853 respectively, and at the end of the year she fulfilled a
commission by Dickens to write a Christmas story ('The Old Nurse's
Story') for the *Household Words* Christmas number. It is hardly surprising
that in February 1852 Gaskell should have written to her daughter Marianne
that she 'had writing to do *without end*, till my wrist actually swelled with it'.[1]
The publication of *Cranford* at such irregular intervals will have suited
Gaskell, and Dickens so much admired the stories that he seems to have
been more than usually tolerant of the procedure, although at one point we
find him adding 'Cranford???' as a postscript to one of his letters to her.[2] It is
interesting incidentally that, despite his enthusiasm, Dickens should have
found the episode in which Peter Jenkyns imitates his unmarried sister Deb-
orah by dressing up as a woman, and carrying a baby, 'ill-considered': ever-
conscious of his family readership perhaps, he seems on this occasion to
have been more decorous in such matters than his contributor.[3]

The single-volume edition of *Cranford* was published by Chapman and
Hall on 18 June 1853, just one month after the final instalment in *Household
Words*. This left Gaskell with little time for revision and apart from some
alterations to the names of characters, the addition of chapter titles, and
some textual corrections and adjustments (these are indicated in the Textual
and Explanatory Notes to this edition), she altered nothing of substance.
What is remarkable about the finalised narrative is the way in which it devel-
ops a coherence of its own out of the original episodes. Thus from the
opening two chapters, located in the *Cranford* of the late 1830s, she moves
back in time with first the 'Love Affair of Long Ago' and then Miss Matty's
reminiscences as she burns her family letters. This allows for the introduc-
tion of Peter Jenkyns, whose reappearance at the end of the narrative will
resolve the plot. The appearance of Samuel Brown, aka Signor Brugnoni,
brings the story back to the present day, while further relating to the material
about the subcontinent and leading into the account of the Cranford ladies
in 'The Panic', the marriage of Lady Glenmire to Mr Hoggins, and the final
sequence of events involving Miss Matty's bravery in the face of financial

1. *Letters*, p. 846.
2. *CD Letters*, vol. vi, 1850–2, p. 812.
3. *CD Letters*, vol. vi, 1850–2, p. 623.

disaster, and her rescue by her long-lost brother. Holding all this together, we have the emergence of Miss Matty as the heroine of the tale after the death of her imperious sister, unstated between Chapters II and III, but beautifully prepared for by the final paragraph of Chapter II. Finally there is the developing and coordinating awareness of the narrator as she comes to realise the strengths of Cranford and its values. What had been presented episodically to the readership of *Household Words* thus presents itself as a remarkably coherent narrative in its final form. For all the occasional nature of the original publication, and despite Gaskell's own account of its origins, it is arguable that she must have come increasingly to see her separate stories as a single developing narrative as she prepared them for *Household Words*.

The reputation of *Cranford* as the whimsical record of a gentler and now departed world has dogged it from at least the end of the nineteenth-century. For this the edition published by Macmillan in 1891, introduced by Anne Thackeray Ritchie, and with illustrations by Hugh Thomson and in a variety of decorated bindings, has much to answer for, not only in its own terms but also because it set a precedent for further reprints in a similar style. Like Ritchie's is the edition of 1898, with illustrations by H. M. Brock, while in 1904 G. A. Payne's *Knutsford*, an elegantly illustrated little volume in the 'Temple Topographies', reinforced the connection between the town itself and its fictional equivalent, as they had come to be perceived. Not only had 'Cranford' come to be identified with Knutsford, but Knutsford with 'Cranford'. More than anything such productions have been responsible for a very partial view of Gaskell's work, emphasising to an exaggerated degree its appeal as a story of old-world charm at the expense of the more contemporary dimension that would have recommended it to Dickens for *Household Words*. Popular editions continued to proliferate well into the twentieth century: *Cranford* appeared for successive generations in the guises of school text, dramatic adaptation, selection and gift book, and in the process became more and more distanced from its origins.

To be fair, Ritchie's introductory essay is very specific in contextualising the work in the time when it was written, insisting on 'the difference between the world of Cranford and that of Miss Austen.'[1] Other commentators have not been so particular: the association with Austen is one that was increasingly made in the early years of the twentieth century, with Austen being defined as the sharper spirit and Gaskell the more benevolent. C. K. Shorter's 'Introduction' to the Cranford volume in the 'World's Classics' series is very much of its time: it speaks of the 'kindliness' of Mrs Gaskell's humour, whereas 'Jane Austen's humour was always tart'.[2] For A.

---

1. Anne Thackeray Ritchie, 'Introduction' to *Cranford*, with Illustrations by Hugh Thompson (London: Macmillan, 1891), p. xviii.

2. *Shorter*, vol. iii, p. xii.

Stanton Whitfield, 'quiet comedy and irony walk hand-in-hand through her radiant and alert pages, and there is a verity in their presentation which would have delighted Jane Austen', while for Lord David Cecil the comparison with Austen was one which not only had to be made, but made to Gaskell's disadvantage. According to Cecil, 'It is true Mrs.Gaskell lived a narrow life, but Jane Austen, living a life just as narrow, was able to make major works of art out of it.'[1] About the narrowness of the life, at least, it would be difficult to be more wrong.

Such comparisons do little to identify the quality of Gaskell's work. The 'Amazons' of *Cranford* are not living in a time-warp; they are living in a small town in England in the 1830s and 40s and the message they bear is one for the newly developing industrial and commercial culture that encroaches upon them. The chronology of the story is not entirely consistent but the first and last paragraphs are written in the present tense, and they are the words of a young woman very much of her own day. The literary works that are identified – *Pickwick Papers,* the early poems of Tennyson – are those of the new reign of Queen Victoria; it is Dr Johnson who has to make way for them. Furthermore, and remarkably in this study of provincial life, there are the references to British colonial rule on the sub-continent. Some four years later Gaskell was to lose two close friends in the massacre at Cawnpore.[2] This event can hardly be foreseen in *Cranford*'s pages, but the story of the wife of Samuel Brown, wife of the 'serjeant in the 31st' in Chapter XI gives substance to the context – the history of British administration in India – of the story of Peter Jenkyns on which the larger narrative depends. But above all it is Drumble – modern-day Manchester – that has much to learn from *Cranford*. *Cranford* was, for its first readers, a very contemporary story, and both in its record of human behaviour and attitudes and in its frame of reference it was a tale that met Dickens's criteria for his periodical. Anne Lohrli has identified the contents of *Household Words* as falling into three categories – 'material of social import, informational articles, and material for entertainment'.[3] In its own way *Cranford* embodies all of these, and it does so in a manner that is uniquely its own.

★ ★ ★

The story of Cranford having been concluded, Gaskell would seem not to have intended to return there. But surprisingly, in 1863, she made one more visit when she wrote a single episode, *The Cage at Cranford*, for *All The Year Round*, Dickens's successor to *Household Words*. By this time, due to various factors, Gaskell's relationship with Dickens had cooled; she had also been

---

1. A. Stanton Whitfield, *Mrs Gaskell* (London: Routledge, 1929), p. 176; Lord David Cecil, *Early Victorian Novelists* (London: Constable, 1934), p. 201.

2. See *Further Letters*, pp. 177–8.

3. *Lohrli*, p. 4.

very unhappy about Dickens's deliberately public separation from his wife. On the inception of *All The Year Round* Gaskell had wanted to keep her distance from the new title, referring to it, not intending flattery, as 'Dickensy'.[1] In March 1859 she wrote in the same letter to Charles Eliot Norton:

> I am afraid he [Dickens's sub-editor, Wills] is making some arrangement by which they *can* take my story; as Mr Dickens happens to be extremely unpopular just now, – (owing to the well-grounded feeling of dislike to the publicity he has given to his domestic affairs,) & I think they would be glad to announce my name on their list of contributors. And I would much rather they did *not*.[2]

The story in question was *Lois the Witch*, which was in fact published in *All the Year Round*, in 1859. But her further contributions to *All The Year Round* were few in number, although she was to use it for her serialised novella, *A Dark Night's Work* in 1863. The distancing was not all on one side: such comments as we have from Dickens from this period in their relationship show his frequent exasperation with his now much more experienced contributor.

The Cage at Cranford is at best an occasional piece about whose origins we know very little. There is no reference to it in Gaskell's correspondence, nor apparently in that of Dickens. It consists of a rather heavy-handed joke whereby the residents of Cranford mistake a 'cage' – as in the form of a frame for a petticoat – for a birdcage. The narrator is the same Miss Smith of the original work but she is now over thirty, so that the contrast between youth and age is, if not nullified, less effective. Characters from the earlier stories make their appearance, but Miss Matty is this time only a marginal figure, and it is Miss Pole who takes centre stage. According to Chadwick, Gaskell regretted having published the story; certainly she never attempted to repeat it. It was not included in Ward's 'Knutsford' edition and and most of Gaskell's commentators, both early and more recent, have been happy to ignore it.[3] J. G. Sharps has said of the work that 'literary successes can rarely be repeated, and Mrs Gaskell rarely endeavoured to do so'[4] and this would seem to be the view of such of Gaskell's commentators who have troubled to refer to it.[5]

1. *Letters*, p. 538.
2. *Letters*, p. 535.
3. Mrs Ellis H. Chadwick, *Mrs. Gaskell: Haunts, Homes and Stories*, 'New and Revised Edition' (London: Pitman, 1913), p. 296.
4. *Sharps*, p. 443.
5. For Jenny Uglow it is one of a number of 'short pieces for quick money' (Uglow, *Elizabeth Gaskell: A Habit of Stories* (London: Faber and Faber, 1993), p. 553). A dissentient voice is A. B. Hopkins, who describes the story as ' the most striking instance of the author's genius for recapturing the tones of her story' (*Elizabeth Gaskell* (London: John Lehmann, 1952), p. 108). For Angus Easson, the story 'remains a good-humoured and ineffective joke' (*Elizabeth Gaskell* (London: Routledge and Kegan Paul, 1979), p.108).

The Cage at Cranford is in fact a story out of its time. At this point in her career Gaskell was preparing and writing what were to be her final works, all written for George Smith, an editor and publisher very different from Dickens. The shift to Smith had occurred with *The Life of Charlotte Brontë*, and it took Gaskell into a different publishing environment. Smith, Elder & Co. were to publish *Sylvia's Lovers* in 1863, *Cousin Phillis* in 1864 and *Wives and Daughters*, posthumously in 1866. The last two of these made their first appearance in the *Cornhill Magazine*, a journal with very different social and literary pretensions from those edited by Dickens. In 1864 also, Smith published an 'illustrated edition' of *Cranford*, the illustrations being by George Du Maurier, one of the *Cornhill*'s distinguished group of artists. This was the third single-volume edition of the work to appear in Gaskell's lifetime; it appeared in a larger format and it was the first to be illustrated. There is a sense in which it can be said to have marked the beginning of *Cranford*'s movement away from its more humble origins. Given all that Gaskell had on her hands it is not surprising that she seems not to have made any alterations to her text and for that, given the perfection of the work as it stands, it is right to be thankful.

BIBLIOGRAPHY

All The Year Round, 10 (1863)

Bagley, J. J., *The Earls of Derby, 1485–1985* (London: Sidgwick and Jackson, 1985)

Cecil, Lord David, *Early Victorian Novelists: Essays in Revaluation* (London: Constable, 1934)

Chadwick, Mrs Ellis H., *Mrs Gaskell: Haunts Homes and Stories*, 'New and Revised Edition' (London: Pitman, 1913)

Chapple, J. A. V., *Elizabeth Gaskell: The Early Years* (Manchester and New York: Manchester University Press, 1997)

Chapple, J. A. V. and Arthur Pollard (eds), *The Letters of Mrs Gaskell* (Manchester: Manchester University Press, 1966, new edn 1997)

Chapple, John and Alan Shelston (eds), *Further Letters of Mrs Gaskell* (Manchester: Manchester University Press, 2000)

Collin, Dorothy, 'The Composition and Publication of Elizabeth Gaskell's *Cranford*', *BJRL*, 69:1 (Autumn 1986), pp. 59–95

Cundall, H. M., *Birket Foster, R. W. S.* (London: A. and C. Black, 1906)

Easson, Angus, *Elizabeth Gaskell* (London: Routledge and Kegan Paul, 1979)

—, (ed.), *Elizabeth Gaskell: The Critical Heritage* (London: Routledge, 1991)

Gaskell, Elizabeth, *The Moorland Cottage.* By the Author of *Mary Barton.* With Illustrations by Birkett [*sic*] Foster (London: Chapman and Hall, 1850)

—, *Cranford.* By the Author of *Mary Barton, Ruth*, &c. (London: Chapman and Hall, 1853)

—, *Cranford.* By the Author of *Mary Barton, Ruth, North and South*, &c. Cheap Edition (London: Chapman and Hall, 1855)

—, *Cranford.* By the Author of *Mary Barton, Ruth*, etc. (London: Chapman and Hall, 'Select Library' edn, n. d. [c. 1863–4])

—, *Cranford*. By Mrs Gaskell, Author of *Sylvia's Lovers, Cousin Phillis, Mary Barton, A Dark Night's Work*, etc. Illustrated Edition (London: Smith, Elder & Co., 1864)

—, *Cranford*. By Mrs Gaskell, with a Preface by Anne Thackeray Ritchie and Illustrations by Hugh Thompson (London: Macmillan, 1891)

—, *Cranford*, ed. by Elizabeth Porges Watson, 'Oxford English Novels' (London: Oxford University Press, 1972)

—, *Cranford*, ed. by Charlotte Mitchell, 'Oxford World's Classics' (Oxford: Oxford University Press, 1998)

—, *Lizzie Leigh and Other Tales*. By the Author of *Mary Barton, Ruth*, &c. Cheap Edition (London: Chapman and Hall, 1855)

—, *'My Lady Ludlow' and Other Stories*, ed. by Edgar Wright, 'The World's Classics' (Oxford: Oxford University Press, 1989)

—, *The Moorland Cottage and Other Stories*, ed. by Suzanne Lewis, 'The World's Classics' (Oxford: Oxford University Press, 1995)

Gill, Stephen, *Wordsworth and the Victorians* (Oxford: Clarendon Press, 1998)

Green, Henry, *Knutsford: Its Traditions and History* (London: Smith, Elder & Co., 1859)

Haldane, Elizabeth, *Mrs. Gaskell and Her Friends* (London: Hodder and Stoughton, 1930)

Hopkins, Annette B., *Elizabeth Gaskell* (London: John Lehmann, 1952)

House, M., G. Storey et al (eds), *The Pilgrim Edition of the Letters of Charles Dickens*, 12 vols (Oxford: Oxford University Press, 1965–2002)

Household Words (1850–9)

Howitt, Margaret (ed.), *Mary Howitt: An Autobiography*, 2 vols (London: Isbister, 1889)

Hughes, Linda K. and Michael Lund, *Victorian Publishing and Mrs Gaskell's Work* (Charlottesville and London: University Press of Virginia, 1999)

The Ladies' Companion and Monthly Magazine (1850–1)

Lohrli, Anne (compiler), *Household Words: A Weekly Journal 1850–1859 Conducted by Charles Dickens*: A Table of Contents, List of Contributors and their Contributions based on the *Household Words* Office Book (Toronto: University of Toronto Press, 1973)

Northup, Clark S., 'Bibliography' in G. De Witt Sanders, *Elizabeth Gaskell* (New Haven: Yale University Press for Cornell University, 1929), pp. 163–262

Payne, G. A., *Knutsford,* with Illustrations by Edmund H. New (London: Dent, 1904)

Sanders, G. De Witt, *Elizabeth Gaskell* (New Haven: Yale University Press for Cornell University, 1929)

Sartain's Union Magazine (1849–50)

Schor, Hilary M., *Scheherezade in the Marketplace* (New York and Oxford: Oxford University Press, 1992)

Sharps, J. G., *Mrs Gaskell's Observation and Invention: A Study of her Non-Biographic Works* (Fontwell: Linden Press, 1970)

Shelston, Alan, '*The Moorland Cottage*: Elizabeth Gaskell and Myles Birket Foster', *GSJ*, 2 (1998), pp. 41–58

Shorter, C. K. (ed.), *The Novels and Tales of Mrs. Gaskell*, 'World's Classics', 11 vols (London: Oxford University Press, 1906–19)

Skrine, Peter, 'Mrs Gaskell and Germany', *GSJ*, 7 (1993), p. 43

Stoneman, Patsy, *Elizabeth Gaskell* (Brighton: Harvester Press, 1987)

Waller, R. D., 'Articles by Mrs Gaskell', *The Times Literary Supplement* (25 July 1935), p. 477

—, 'Letters Addressed to Mrs Gaskell by Celebrated Contemporaries' (Manchester: Manchester University Press, 1935). Rptd from *BJRL*, 19:1 (January 1935), pp. 102–69

Ward, A. W. (ed.), *The Works of Mrs. Gaskell*, The 'Knutsford' Edition, 8 vols (London: Smith, Elder & Co., 1906)

Whitfield, A. Stanton, *Mrs Gaskell* (London: Routledge, 1929)

Uglow, Jenny, *Elizabeth Gaskell: A Habit of Stories* (London: Faber and Faber, 1993)

ABBREVIATIONS

AYR	*All the Year Round*
BJRL	*Bulletin of the John Rylands University Library of Manchester*
C	*Cranford*
CDLetters	*The Pilgrim Edition of the Letters of Charles Dickens*, ed. by M. House, G. Storey et al, 12 vols (Oxford: Oxford University Press, 1965–2002)
CH	*Elizabeth Gaskell: The Critical Heritage*, ed. by Angus Easson (London: Routledge, 1991)
CM	*Cornhill Magazine*
Collin	Dorothy Collin, 'The Composition and Publication of Elizabeth Gaskell's *Cranford*', *BJRL*, 69:1 (Autumn 1986), pp. 59–95
DNB	*Dictionary of National Biography*
Easson	Angus Easson, *Elizabeth Gaskell* (London: Routledge and Kegan Paul, 1979)
EG	Elizabeth Gaskell
Further Letters	*Further Letters of Mrs Gaskell*, ed. by John Chapple and Alan Shelston (Manchester: Manchester University Press, 2000)
GSJ	*Gaskell Society Journal*
HW	*Household Words*
Knutsford	*The Works of Mrs Gaskell*, ed. by A. W. Ward, The 'Knutsford' Edition, 8 vols (London: Smith, Elder & Co., 1906)
LC	*The Ladies' Companion and Monthly Magazine* (1850–1)
Letters	*The Letters of Mrs Gaskell,* ed. by J. A. V. Chapple and Arthur Pollard (Manchester: Manchester University Press, 1966, new edn 1997)
Lewis	Suzanne Lewis (ed.), *The Moorland Cottage and Other Stories* 'The World's Classics' (Oxford: Oxford University Press, 1995)

Lohrli   Anne Lohrli (compiler), *Household Words: A Weekly Journal 1850–1859 Conducted by Charles Dickens*: A Table of Contents, List of Contributors and their Contributions based on the *Household Words* Office Book (Toronto: University of Toronto Press, 1973)

MB   *Mary Barton*

MC   *The Moorland Cottage*

Mitchell   Charlotte Mitchell (ed.), *Elizabeth Gaskell: 'Cranford'* (Oxford: 'World's Classics' Oxford University Press, 1998)

Northup   Clark S. Northup, 'Bibliography' in G. De Witt Sanders, *Elizabeth Gaskell* (New Haven: Yale University Press for Cornell University, 1929), pp. 163–262

OED   *Oxford English Dictionary*

Selig   R. L. Selig (ed.), *Elizabeth Gaskell: A Reference Guide* (Boston: G. K. Hall, 1977)

Sharps   J. G. Sharps, *Mrs Gaskell's Observation and Invention: A Study of her Non-Biographic Works* (Fontwell: Linden Press, 1970)

Shorter   *The Novels and Tales of Mrs Gaskell*, ed by C. K. Shorter, World's Classics edn, 11 vols (London: Oxford University Press, 1906–19)

Smith   Walter E. Smith, *Elizabeth Gaskell: A Bibliographical Catalogue* (Los Angeles: Heritage Bookshop Inc., 1997)

SUM   *Sartain's Union Magazine*

Uglow   Jenny Uglow, *Elizabeth Gaskell: a Habit of Stories* (London: Faber and Faber, 1993)

Watson   Elizabeth Porges Watson (ed.), *Elizabeth Gaskell; 'Cranford'* (Oxford: Oxford University Press 1972)

Welch   J. E. Welch, *Elizabeth Gaskell: an Annotated Bibliography 1929–1975* (New York: Garland, 1977)

Weyant 1994   Nancy S. Weyant, *Elizabeth Gaskell: An Annotated Bibliography of English-Language Sources 1976–1991* (Metuchen, NJ: The Scarecrow Press, 1994)

Weyant 2004   Nancy S. Weyant, *Elizabeth Gaskell: An Annotated Guide to English Language Sources 1992–2001* (Lanham, Maryland, Toronto, Oxford: The Scarecrow Press, 2004)

THE MOORLAND COTTAGE

The Moorland Cottage was published as a Christmas book by Chapman and Hall on 14 December 1850 at the price of five shillings. It was illustrated by Myles Birket Foster (1825–1905). It was EG's only publication in this format, although she was later to write for the Christmas numbers of both *Household Words* and *All the Year Round*. In format, as well as in length, *The Moorland Cottage* is similar to Dickens's Christmas stories, notably *The Chimes* and *The Battle of Life*. In EG's story, as in Dickens's, the illustrations appear at appropriate moments in the narrative, and are interwoven with the text.

EG herself seems to have had misgivings about *The Moorland Cottage*, both during the writing process and after its publication. 'I cannot write a Xmas book', she wrote to Edward Chapman in a letter which Chapple and Pollard date as c. early 1850: this would seem to be in response to his approach to her. Having accepted the commission she complains that 'it was a very foolish engagement of mine' (*Letters*, p. 81), a sentiment she repeats when writing to Lady Kay-Shuttleworth in September [1850]: 'Mr Chapman asked me to write a Xmas story, "recommending benevolence, charity, etc", to which I agreed, why I cannot think now, for it was very foolish indeed.' (*Letters*, p. 132). As with other EG works there were to be disagreements over the title. In her letter to Lady Kay-Shuttleworth the story is referred to as 'Rosemary', and this is confirmed by a letter from her illustrator to his brother-in-law:

> The author of Mary Barton is a Mrs Gaskill [sic] I don't know her although she writes a good deal about me to Chapman – indeed wanted me to entitle her new book. She first called it 'Rosemary for Remembrance' but said it was only something for me to shoot at – we then had it called 'A Fagot for Xmas' – however that did not do so we called it *The Moorland Cottage* – it is a nice little tale.[1]

'The Fagot' was the publisher's suggestion, while EG requested 'December Days' (*Letters*, p. 140). The title as it stands would seem to have been a last-minute compromise, but given the setting it was nonetheless an appropriate one.

1. Jan Reynolds, *Birket Foster* (London, Batsford, 1984, p. 40)

EG's uncertainty about her story did not inhibit her from keeping an eye on its financial success. Her correspondence with Chapman and Hall testifies to her concern that she may not have been fully paid according to her contract (*Letters*, p. 382; *Further Letters*, p. 208) and when she moved to Smith, Elder & Co. in 1857 it was one of the stories whose copyright she was concerned to transfer. In 1861 she was still trying to get information from Frederick Chapman about the copyright position, since she planned to include it in a collection of her stories, perhaps *My Lady Ludlow and Other Tales* which appeared in that year. For whatever reason, *The Moorland Cottage* did not appear in any of EG's later collections, and it was not in fact reprinted in her lifetime. The text reprinted here is therefore that of the first edition of 1850.

Illustration was a feature of Chapman and Hall's Christmas productions. Like the Howitts, to whom he was known, Birket Foster had Quaker origins. In the later 1840s he had illustrated Christmas numbers of the *Illustrated London News* and this may have recommended him to Chapman and Hall as a suitable artist for EG's story. In the case of *The Moorland Cottage* his illustrations (included in Appendix A) can fairly be said to add a dimension to the tale. Delicately drawn and carefully set within the text, they reinforce selected moments of the narrative. In its review the *Standard* found them 'beautiful', while the *Morning Chronicle* referred to them as 'exceedingly clever and pretty designs' (Reynolds, *Birket Foster*, p. 40). Birket Foster – his name is misspelt Birkett Foster on the title-page of the first edition – operated within a naturalist tradition of engraving going back to Bewick. His later work, mostly in watercolour, with which he achieved enormous popularity, concentrated almost entirely on the English rural scene. In *The Moorland Cottage* his identification of character and surroundings is exactly appropriate to EG's tale. Pastoral was his forte, and the sense in the book of a world remote from the Manchester of EG's other fiction at this time is successfully reflected in both narrative and illustration.

On Myles Birket Foster see H. M. Cundall, *Birket Foster, R. W. S.* (London: A. and C. Black, 1906), and Jan Reynolds, *Birket Foster*. On the illustration of *The Moorland Cottage* see Alan Shelston, 'The Moorland Cottage: Elizabeth Gaskell and Myles Birket Foster', *GSJ*, 2 (1998), pp. 41–58.

In my explanatory notes I have been helped by having the 'World's Classics' edition of *The Moorland Cottage and other Stories*, ed. by Suzanne Lewis (Oxford: Oxford University Press, 1995) to hand. Specific instances of indebtedness are acknowledged as *Lewis*.

THE

MOORLAND COTTAGE.

BY

THE AUTHOR OF MARY BARTON

with ILLUSTRATIONS BY BIRKETT FOSTER

LONDON:

CHAPMAN AND HALL, 193, PICCADILLY

1850

LONDON:
BRADBURY AND EVANS, PRINTERS, WHITEFRIARS.

The Moorland Cottage.

CHAPTER I.

IF you take the turn to the left, after you pass the lyke-gate[1] at Combehurst Church, you will come to the wooden bridge over the brook; keep along the field-path which mounts higher and higher, and, in half a mile or so, you will be in a breezy upland field, almost large enough to be called a down, where sheep pasture on the short, fine, elastic turf. You look down on Combehurst and its beautiful church-spire. After the field is crossed, you come to a common, richly coloured with the golden gorse and the purple heather, which in summer-time send out their warm scents into the quiet air. The swelling waves of the upland make a near horizon against the sky; the line is only broken in one place by a small grove of Scotch firs, which always look black and shadowed even at mid-day, when all the rest of the landscape seems bathed in sunlight. The lark quivers and sings high up in the air; too high – in too dazzling a region, for you to see her. Look! she drops into sight; – but, as if loth to leave the heavenly radiance, she balances herself and floats in the ether. Now she falls suddenly right into her nest, hidden among the ling, unseen except by the eyes of Heaven, and the small bright insects that run hither and thither on the elastic flower-stalks. With something like the sudden drop of the lark, the path goes down a green abrupt descent; and in a basin, surrounded by the grassy hills, there stands a dwelling, which is neither cottage nor house, but something between the two in size. Nor yet is it a farm, though surrounded by living things. It is, or rather it was, at the time of which I speak, the dwelling of Mrs. Browne, the widow of the late curate of Combehurst. There she lived with her faithful old servant and her only children, a boy and girl. They were as secluded in their green hollow as the households in the German forest-tales.[2] Once a week they emerged and crossed the common, catching on its summit the first sounds of the sweet-toned bells, calling them to church. Mrs. Browne walked first, holding Edward's hand. Old Nanny followed with Maggie; but they were all one party and all talked together in a subdued and quiet tone, as beseemed the day. They had not much to say, their lives were too unbroken; for, excepting on Sundays, the widow and her children never went to Combehurst. Most people would have thought the little town a quiet, dreamy place; but to those two children it seemed the world; and after they had crossed the bridge, they each clasped more tightly the hands which they held, and looked shyly up from beneath their drooped eyelids when spoken to by any of their mother's friends. Mrs. Browne was regularly asked by some one to stay to dinner after morning church, and as regularly declined, rather to the timid children's relief; although in the week-days they sometimes spoke together in a low voice of the pleasure it would be to them if mama would go and dine at Mr. Buxton's, where the little girl in white and that great tall boy lived. Instead of staying there, or anywhere else, on Sundays, Mrs. Browne thought it her duty to go and cry over her husband's grave. The custom had arisen out of true sorrow for his loss, for a kinder husband, and more worthy man, had never lived; but the simplicity of her sorrow had been destroyed by the observation of others on the mode of its manifestation. They made way for her to cross the grass towards his grave; and she, fancying that it was expected of her, fell into the habit I have mentioned. Her children, holding each a hand, felt awed and uncomfortable, and were sensitively conscious how often they were pointed out, as a mourning group, to observation.

'I wish it would always rain on Sundays,' said Edward one day to Maggie, in a garden-conference.

'Why?' asked she.

'Because then we bustle out of church, and get home as fast as we can, to save mama's crape; and we have not to go and cry over papa.'

'I don't cry,' said Maggie. 'Do you?'

Edward looked round before he answered, to see if they were quite alone, and then said:

'No; I was sorry a long time about papa, but one can't go on being sorry for ever. Perhaps grown-up people can.'

'Mama can,' said little Maggie. 'Sometimes I am very sorry too; when I am by myself, or playing with you, or when I am wakened up by the moonlight in our room. Do you ever waken and fancy you heard papa calling you? I do sometimes; and then I am very sorry to think we shall never hear him calling us again.'

'Ah, it's different with me, you know. He used to call me to lessons.'

'Sometimes he called me when he was displeased with me. But I always dream that he was calling us in his own kind voice, as he used to do when he wanted us to walk with him, or to show us something pretty.'

Edward was silent, playing with something on the ground. At last he looked round again, and, having convinced himself that they could not be overheard, he whispered –

'Maggie, – sometimes I don't think I'm sorry that papa is dead – when I'm naughty, you know; he would have been so angry with me if he had been here; and I think, – only sometimes, you know, – I'm rather glad he is not.'

'Oh, Edward! you don't mean to say so, I know. Don't let us talk about him. We can't talk rightly, we're such little children. Don't, Edward, please.'

Poor little Maggie's eyes filled with tears; and she never spoke again to Edward, or indeed to any one, about her dead father. As she grew older, her life became more actively busy. The cottage and small outbuildings, and the garden and field, were their own; and on the produce they depended for much of their support. The cow, the pig, and the poultry took up much of Nancy's time. Mrs. Browne and Maggie had to do a great deal of the house-work; and when the beds were made, and the rooms swept and dusted, and the preparations for dinner ready, then, if there was any time, Maggie sat down to her lessons. Ned, who prided himself considerably on his sex, had been sitting all the morning, in his father's arm-chair, in the little book-room, 'studying,' as he chose to call it. Sometimes Maggie would pop her head in, with a request that he would help her to carry the great pitcher of water upstairs, or do some other little household service; with which request he occasionally complied, but with so many complaints about the interruption, that at last she told him she would never ask him again. Gently as this was said, he yet felt it as a reproach, and tried to excuse himself.

'You see, Maggie, a man must be educated to be a gentleman. Now, if a woman knows how to keep a house, that's all that is wanted from her. So my time is of more consequence than yours. Mama says I'm to go to college, and be a clergyman; so I must get on with my Latin.'

Maggie submitted in silence; and almost felt it as an act of gracious con-descension when, a morning or two afterwards, he came to meet her as she was toiling in from the well, carrying the great brown jug full of spring-water ready for dinner. 'Here,' said he, 'let us put it in the shade behind the horse-mount. Oh, Maggie! look what you've done! Spilt it all, with not turning quickly enough when I told you. Now you may fetch it again for yourself, for I'll have nothing to do with it.'

'I did not understand you in time,' said she, softly. But he had turned away, and gone back in offended dignity to the house. Maggie had nothing to do but return to the well, and fill it again. The spring was some distance off, in a little rocky dell. It was so cool after her hot walk, that she sat down in the shadow of the grey lime-stone rock, and looked at the ferns, wet with the dripping water. She felt sad, she knew not why. 'I think Ned is some-times very cross,' thought she. 'I did not understand he was carrying it there. Perhaps I am clumsy. Mama says I am; and Ned says I am. Nancy never says so, and papa never said so. I wish I could help being clumsy and stupid. Ned says all women are so. I wish I was not a woman. It must be a fine thing to be a man. Oh dear! I must go up the field again with this heavy pitcher, and my arms do so ache!' She rose and climbed the steep brae. As she went she heard her mother's voice.

'Maggie! Maggie! there's no water for dinner, and the potatoes are quite boiled. Where is *that* child?'

They had begun dinner, before she came down from brushing her hair and washing her hands. She was hurried and tired.

'Mother,' said Ned, 'mayn't I have some butter to these potatoes, as there is cold meat? They are so dry.'

'Certainly, my dear. Maggie, go and fetch a pat of butter out of the dairy.'

Maggie went from her untouched dinner without speaking.

'Here, stop, you child!' said Nancy, turning her back in the passage. 'You go to your dinner, – I'll fetch the butter. You've been running about enough to-day.'

Maggie durst not go back without it, but she stood in the passage till Nancy returned; and then she put up her mouth to be kissed by the kind rough old servant.

'Thou'rt a sweet one,' said Nancy to herself, as she turned into the kitchen; and Maggie went back to her dinner with a soothed and lightened heart.

When the meal was ended, she helped her mother to wash up the old-fashioned glasses and spoons, which were treated with tender care and exquisite cleanliness in that house of decent frugality; and then, exchanging her pinafore for a black silk apron, the little maiden was wont to sit down to some useful piece of needlework, in doing which her mother enforced the most dainty neatness of stitches. Thus every hour in its circle brought a duty to be fulfilled; but duties fulfilled are as pleasures to the memory, and little Maggie always thought those early childish days most happy, and remembered them only as filled with careless contentment.

Yet, at the time, they had their cares.

In fine summer days Maggie sat out of doors at her work. Just beyond the court lay the rocky moorland, almost as gay as that with its profusion of flowers. If the court had its clustering noisettes, and fraxinellas, and sweet-briar, and great tall white lilies, the moorland had its little creeping scented rose, its straggling honeysuckle, and an abundance of yellow cistus; and here and there a grey rock cropped out of the ground, and over it the yellow stone-crop and scarlet-leaved crane's-bill[3] grew luxuriantly. Such a rock was Maggie's seat. I believe she considered it her own, and loved it accordingly; although its real owner was a great lord, who lived far away, and had never seen the moor, much less the piece of grey rock, in his life.

The afternoon of the day which I have begun to tell you about, she was sitting there, and singing to herself as she worked: she was within call of home, and could hear all home sounds, with their shrillness softened down. Between her and it, Edward was amusing himself; he often called upon her for sympathy, which she as readily gave.

'I wonder how men make their boats steady; I have taken mine to the pond, and she has toppled over every time I sent her in.'

'Has it? – that's very tiresome! Would it do to put a little weight in it, to keep it down?'

'How often must I tell you to call a ship "her;" and there you will go on saying – it, – it!'

After this correction of his sister, Master Edward did not like the condescension of acknowledging her suggestion to be a good one; so he went silently to the house in search of the requisite ballast; but not being able to find anything suitable, he came back to his turfy hillock, littered round with chips of wood, and tried to insert some pebbles into his vessel; but they stuck fast, and he was obliged to ask again.

'Supposing it was a good thing to weight her, what could I put in?'

Maggie thought a moment.

'Would shot do?' asked she.

'It would be the very thing; but where can I get any?'

'There is some that was left of papa's. It is in the right-hand corner of the second drawer of the bureau, wrapped up in a newspaper.'

'What a plague! I can't remember your "seconds," and "right-hands," and fiddle-faddles.' He worked on at his pebbles. They would not do.

'I think if you were good-natured, Maggie, you might go for me.'

'Oh, Ned! I 've all this long seam to do. Mama said I must finish it before tea; and that I might play a little if I had done it first,' said Maggie, rather plaintively; for it was a real pain to her to refuse a request.

'It would not take you five minutes.'

Maggie thought a little. The time would only be taken out of her playing, which, after all, did not signify; while Edward was really busy about his ship She rose, and clambered up the steep grassy slope, slippery with the heat.

Before she had found the paper of shot, she heard her mother's voice calling, in a sort of hushed hurried loudness, as if anxious to be heard by one person, yet not by another – 'Edward, Edward, come home quickly. Here's Mr. Buxton coming along the Fell-Lane; – he's coming here, as sure as sixpence; come, Edward, – come.'

Maggie saw Edward put down his ship and come. At his mother's bidding it certainly was; but he strove to make this as little apparent as he could, by sauntering up the slope, with his hands in his pockets, in a very independent and *négligé* style. Maggie had no time to watch longer; for now she was called too and down stairs she ran.

'Here, Maggie,' said her mother, in a nervous hurry; – 'help Nancy to get a tray ready all in a minute. I do believe here's Mr. Buxton coming to call. Oh, Edward! go and brush your hair, and put on your Sunday jacket; here's Mr. Buxton just coming round. I'll only run up and change my cap; and you say you'll come up and tell me, Nancy; all proper, you know.'

'To be sure, ma'am. I've lived in families afore now,' said Nancy, gruffly.

'Oh, yes, I know you have. Be sure you bring in the cowslip wine. I wish I could have stayed to decant some port.'

Nancy and Maggie bustled about, in and out of the kitchen and dairy; and were so deep in their preparations for Mr. Buxton's reception that they were not aware of the very presence of that gentleman himself on the scene. He had found the front door open, as is the wont in country places, and had walked in; first stopping at the empty parlour, and then finding his way to the place where voices and sounds proclaimed that there were inhabitants. So he stood there, stooping a little under the low-browed lintels of the kitchen door, and looking large, and red, and warm, but with a pleased and almost amused expression of face.

'Lord bless me, sir! what a start you gave me!' said Nancy, as she suddenly caught sight of him. 'I'll go and tell my missus in a minute that you 're come.'

Off she went, leaving Maggie alone with the great, tall, broad gentleman, smiling at her from his frame in the door-way, but never speaking. She went on dusting a wine-glass most assiduously.

'Well done, little girl,' came out a fine strong voice at last. 'Now I think that will do. Come and show me the parlour where I may sit down, for I've had a long walk, and am very tired.'

Maggie took him into the parlour, which was always cool and fresh in the hottest weather. It was scented by a great beau-pot[4] filled with roses; and, besides, the casement was open to the fragrant court. Mr. Buxton was so large, and the parlour so small, that when he was once in, Maggie thought, when he went away, he would carry the room on his back, as a snail does its house.

'And so, you are a notable little woman, are you?' said he, after he had stretched himself (a very unnecessary proceeding), and unbuttoned his waistcoat. Maggie stood near the door, uncertain whether to go or to stay. 'How bright and clean you were making that glass! Do you think you could get me some water to fill it? Mind, it must be that very glass I saw you pol- ishing. I shall know it again.'

Maggie was thankful to escape out of the room; and in the passage she met her mother, who had made time to change her gown as well as her cap. Before Nancy would allow the little girl to return with the glass of water, she smoothed her short cut glossy hair; it was all that was needed to make her look delicately neat. Maggie was conscientious in trying to find out the iden- tical glass; but I am afraid Nancy was not quite so truthful in avouching that one of the six, exactly similar, which were now placed on the tray, was the same she had found on the dresser, when she came back from telling her mistress of Mr. Buxton's arrival.

Maggie carried in the water, with a shy pride in the clearness of the glass. Her mother was sitting on the edge of her chair, speaking in unusually fine language, and with a higher pitched voice than common. Edward, in all his Sunday glory, was standing by Mr. Buxton, looking happy and conscious. But when Maggie came in, Mr. Buxton made room for her between Edward and himself, and, while he went on talking, lifted her on to his knee. She sat there as on a pinnacle of honour; but as she durst not nestle up to him, a chair would have been the more comfortable seat.

'As founder's line, I have a right of presentation;[5] and for my dear old friend's sake' (here Mrs. Browne wiped her eyes), 'I am truly glad of it; my young friend will have a little form of examination to go through; and then we shall see him carrying every prize before him, I have no doubt. Thank you, – just a little of your sparkling cowslip wine. Ah! this gingerbread is like the gingerbread I had when I was a boy. My little lady here must learn the receipt, and make me some. Will she?'

'Speak to Mr. Buxton, child, who is kind to your brother. You will make him some gingerbread, I am sure.'

'If I may,' said Maggie, hanging down her head.

'Or, I'll tell you what. Suppose you come to my house, and teach us how to make it there; and then, you know, we could always be making gingerbread when we were not eating it. That would be best, I think. Must I ask mama to bring you down to Combehurst, and let us all get acquainted together? I have a great boy and a little girl at home, who will like to see you, I'm sure. And we have got a pony for you to ride on, and a peacock and guinea fowls, and I don't know what all. Come, madam, let me persuade you. School begins in three weeks. Let us fix a day before then.'

'Do, mama,' said Edward.

'I am not in spirits for visiting,' Mrs. Browne answered. But the quick children detected a hesitation in her manner of saying the oft spoken words, and had hopes, if only Mr. Buxton would persevere in his invitation.

'Your not visiting is the very reason why you are not in spirits. A little change, and a few neighbourly faces, would do you good, I'll be bound. Besides, for the children's sake you should not live too secluded a life. Young people should see a little of the world.'

Mrs. Browne was much obliged to Mr. Buxton for giving her so decent an excuse for following her inclination, which, it must be owned, tended to the acceptance of the invitation. So, 'for the children's sake,' she consented. But she sighed, as if making a sacrifice.

'That's right,' said Mr. Buxton. 'Now for the day.'

It was fixed that they should go on that day week; and after some further conversation about the school at which Edward was to be placed, and some more jokes about Maggie's notability, and an inquiry if she would come and live with him the next time he wanted a housemaid, Mr. Buxton took his leave.

His visit had been an event; and they made no great attempt at settling again that day to any of their usual employments. In the first place, Nancy came in to hear and discuss all the proposed plans, Ned, who was uncertain whether to like or dislike the prospect of school, was very much offended by the old servant's remark, on first hearing of the project.

'It's time for him. He 'll learn his place there, which, it strikes me, he and others too are apt to forget at home.'

Then followed discussions and arrangements respecting his clothes. And then they came to the plan of spending a day at Mr. Buxton's, which Mrs. Browne was rather shy of mentioning, having a sort of an idea of inconstancy and guilt connected with the thought of mingling with the world again. However, Nancy approved: 'It was quite right,' and 'just as it should be,' and 'good for the children.'

'Yes; it was on their account I did it, Nancy,' said Mrs. Browne.

'How many children has Mr. Buxton?' asked Edward.

'Only one. Frank, I think, they call him. But you must say Master Buxton; be sure.'

'Who is the little girl, then,' asked Maggie, 'who sits with them in church?'

'Oh! that's little Miss Harvey, his niece, and a great fortune.'

'They do say he never forgave her mother till the day of her death,' remarked Nancy.

'Then they tell stories, Nancy!' replied Mrs. Browne (it was she herself who had said it; but that was before Mr. Buxton's call). 'For d'ye think his sister would have left him guardian to her child, if they were not on good terms?'

'Well! I only know what folks say. And, for sure, he took a spite at Mr. Harvey for no reason on earth; and every one knows he never spoke to him.'

'He speaks very kindly and pleasantly,' put in Maggie.

'Ay; and I'm not saying but what he is a very good, kind man in the main. But he has his whims, and keeps hold on 'em when he's got 'em. There's them pies burning, and I'm talking here!'

When Nancy had returned to her kitchen, Mrs. Browne called Maggie up stairs, to examine what clothes would be needed for Edward. And when they were up, she tried on the black satin gown, which had been her visiting dress ever since she was married, and which she intended should replace the old, worn-out bombazine on the day of the visit to Combehurst.

'For Mrs. Buxton is a real born lady,' said she; 'and I should like to be well dressed, to do her honour.'

'I did not know there was a Mrs. Buxton,' said Maggie. 'She is never at church.'

'No; she is but delicate and weakly, and never leaves the house. I think her maid told me she never left her room now.'

The Buxton family, root and branch, formed the *pièce de résistance* in the conversation between Mrs. Browne and her children for the next week. As the day drew near, Maggie almost wished to stay at home, so impressed was she with the awfulness of the visit. Edward felt bold in the idea of a new suit of clothes, which had been ordered for the occasion, and for school afterwards. Mrs. Browne remembered having heard the rector say, 'A woman never looked so lady-like as when she wore black satin,' and kept her spirits up with that observation; but when she saw how worn it was at the elbows, she felt rather depressed, and unequal to visiting. Still, for her children's sake, she would do much.

After her long day's work was ended, Nancy sat up at her sewing. She had found out that among all the preparations, none were going on for Margaret; and she had used her influence over her mistress (who half-liked and half-feared, and entirely depended upon her) to obtain from her an old gown, which she had taken to pieces, and washed and scoured, and was now making up, in a way a little old-fashioned to be sure; but, on the whole, it looked so nice when completed and put on, that Mrs. Browne gave Maggie a strict lecture about taking great care of such a handsome frock, and forgot that she had considered the gown from which it had been made as worn out and done for.

CHAPTER II.

AT length they were dressed, and Nancy stood on the court-stops, shading her eyes, and looking after them, as they climbed the heathery slope leading to Combehurst.

'I wish she 'd take her hand sometimes, just to let her know the feel of her mother's hand. Perhaps she will, at least after Master Edward goes to school.'

As they went along, Mrs. Browne gave the children a few rules respecting manners and etiquette.

'Maggie! you must sit as upright as ever you can; make your back flat, child, and don't poke. If I cough, you must draw up. I shall cough whenever I see you do anything wrong, and I shall be looking at you all day; so remember. You hold yourself very well, Edward. If Mr. Buxton asks you, you may have a glass of wine, because you're a boy. But mind and say, "Your good health, sir," before you drink it.'

'I'd rather not have the wine if I'm to say that,' said Edward, bluntly.

'Oh, nonsense! my dear. You'd wish to be like a gentleman, I'm sure.'

Edward muttered something which was inaudible. His mother went on –

'Of course you'll never think of being helped more than twice. Twice of meat, twice of pudding, is the genteel thing. You may take less, but never more.'

'Oh, mama! how beautiful Combehurst spire is, with that dark cloud behind it!' exclaimed Maggie, as they came in sight of the town.

'You've no business with Combehurst spire when I'm speaking to you. I'm talking myself out of breath to teach you how to behave, and there you go looking after clouds, and such like rubbish. I'm ashamed of you.'

Although Maggie walked quietly by her mother's side all the rest of the way, Mrs. Browne was too much offended to resume her instructions on good-breeding. Maggie might be helped three times if she liked: she had done with her.

They were very early. When they drew near the bridge, they were met by a tall, fine-looking boy, leading a beautiful little Shetland pony, with a side-saddle on it. He came up to Mrs. Browne, and addressed her.

'My father thought your little girl would be tired, and he told me to bring my cousin Erminia's pony for her. It's as quiet as can be.'

Now this was rather provoking to Mrs. Browne, as she chose to consider Maggie in disgrace. However, there was no help for it: all she could do was to spoil the enjoyment as far as possible, by looking and speaking in a cold manner, which often chilled Maggie's little heart, and took all the zest out of the pleasure now. It was in vain that Frank Buxton made the pony trot and canter; she still looked sad and grave.

'Little dull thing!' he thought; but he was as kind and considerate as a gentlemanly boy could be.

At last they reached Mr. Buxton's house. It was in the main street, and the front door opened upon it by a flight of steps. Wide on each side extended the stone-coped windows. It was in reality a mansion, and needed not the neighbouring contrast of the cottages on either side to make it look impos-ing. When they went in, they entered a large hall, cool even on that burning July day, with a black and white flag floor, and old settees round the walls, and great jars of curious china, which were filled with pot-pourrie. The dusky gloom was pleasant, after the glare of the street outside; and the requi-site light and cheerfulness were given by the peep into the garden, framed, as it were, by the large doorway that opened into it. There were roses, and sweet-peas, and poppies, – a rich mass of colour, which looked well, set in the somewhat sombre coolness of the hall. All the house told of wealth – wealth which had accumulated for generations, and which was shown in a sort of comfortable, grand, unostentatious way. Mr. Buxton's ancestors had been yeomen; but, two or three generations back, they might, if ambitious, have taken their place as county gentry, so much had the value of their prop-erty increased, and so great had been the amount of their savings. They, however, continued to live in the old farm till Mr. Buxton's grandfather built the house in Combehurst of which I am speaking, and then he felt rather ashamed of what he had done; it seemed like stepping out of his posi-tion. He and his wife always sat in the best kitchen; and it was only after his son's marriage that the entertaining rooms were furnished. Even then they were kept with closed shutters and bagged-up furniture during the lifetime of the old couple, who, nevertheless, took a pride in adding to the rich-fash-ioned ornaments and grand old china of the apartments. But they died, and were gathered to their fathers, and young Mr. and Mrs. Buxton (aged respectively fifty-one and forty-five) reigned in their stead. They had the good taste to make no sudden change; but gradually the rooms assumed an inhabited appearance, and their son and daughter grew up in the enjoyment of great wealth, and no small degree of refinement. But as yet they held back modestly from putting themselves in any way on a level with the county people. Lawrence Buxton was sent to the same school as his father had been before him; and the notion of his going to college to complete his education was, after some deliberation, negatived. In process of time he succeeded his father, and married a sweet gentle lady, of a decayed and very poor county family, by whom he had one boy before she fell into delicate health. His sister had married a man whose character was worse than his fortune, and had been left a widow. Everybody thought her husband's death a blessing; but she loved him, in spite of negligence and many grosser faults; and so, not many years after, she died, leaving her little daughter to her brother's care, with many a broken-voiced entreaty that he would never speak a word against the dead father of her child. So the little Erminia was taken home by her self-reproaching uncle, who felt now how hardly he had acted towards his sister in breaking off all communication with her on her ill-starred marriage.

'Where is Erminia, Frank?' asked his father, speaking over Maggie's shoulder, while he still held her hand. 'I want to take Mrs. Browne to your mother. I told Erminia to be here to welcome this little girl.'

'I'll take her to Minnie; I think she's in the garden. I'll come back to you,' nodding to Edward, 'directly, and then we will go to the rabbits.'

So Frank and Maggie left the great lofty room, full of strange rare things, and rich with books, and went into the sunny scented garden, which stretched far and wide behind the house. Down one of the walks, with a hedge of roses on either side, came a little tripping fairy, with long golden ringlets, and a complexion like a china rose. With the deep blue of the summer sky behind her, Maggie thought she looked like an angel. She neither hastened nor slackened her pace when she saw them, but came on with the same dainty light prancing step.

'Make haste, Minnie,' cried Frank.

But Minnie stopped to gather a rose.

'Don't stay with me,' said Maggie, softly, although she had held his hand like that of a friend, and did not feel that the little fairy's manner was particularly cordial or gracious. Frank took her at her word, and ran off to Edward.

Erminia came a little quicker when she saw that Maggie was left alone; but for some time after they were together, they had nothing to say to each other. Erminia was easily impressed by the pomps and vanities of the world; and Maggie's new handsome frock seemed to her made of old ironed brown silk. And though Maggie's voice was soft, with a silver ringing sound in it, she pronounced her words in Nancy's broad country way. Her hair was cut short all round; her shoes were thick, and clumped as she walked. Erminia patronised her, and thought herself very kind and condescending; but they were not particularly friendly. The visit promised to be more honourable than agreeable, and Maggie almost wished herself at home again. Dinner-time came. Mrs. Buxton dined in her own room. Mr. Buxton was hearty, and jovial, and pressing; he almost scolded Maggie because she would not take more than twice of his favourite pudding; but she remembered what her mother had said, and that she would be watched all day; and this gave her a little prim, quaint manner, very different from her usual soft charming unconsciousness. She fancied that Edward and Master Buxton were just as little at their ease with each other as she and Miss Harvey. Perhaps this feeling on the part of the boys made all four children unite after dinner.

'Let us go to the swing in the shrubbery,' said Frank, after a little consideration; and off they ran. Frank proposed that he and Edward should swing the two little girls; and for a time all went on very well. But by-and-by Edward thought that Maggie had had enough, and that he should like a turn; and Maggie, at his first word, got out.

'Don't you like swinging?' asked Erminia.

'Yes! but Edward would like it now.' And Edward accordingly took her place. Frank turned away, and would not swing him. Maggie strove hard to do it, but he was heavy, and the swing bent unevenly. He scolded her for what she could not help, and at last jumped out so roughly, that the seat hit Maggie's face, and knocked her down. When she got up, her lips quivered with pain, but she did not cry; she only looked anxiously at her frock. There was a great rent across the front breadth. Then she did shed tears, – tears of fright. What would her mother say?

Erminia saw her crying.

'Are you hurt?' said she, kindly. 'Oh, how your cheek is swelled! What a rude, cross boy your brother is!'

'I did not know he was going to jump out. I am not crying because I am hurt, but because of this great rent in my nice new frock. Mama will be so displeased.'

'Is it a new frock?' asked Erminia.

'It is a new one for me. Nancy has sat up several nights to make it. Oh! what shall I do?'

Erminia's little heart was softened by such excessive poverty. A best frock made of shabby old silk! She put her arms round Maggie's neck, and said –

'Come with me; we will go to my aunt's dressing-room, and Dawson will give me some silk, and I'll help you to mend it.'

'That's a kind little Minnie,' said Frank. Ned had turned sulkily away. I do not think the boys were ever cordial again that day; for, as Frank said to his mother, 'Ned might have said he was sorry; but he is a regular tyrant to that little brown mouse of a sister of his.'

Erminia and Maggie went, with their arms round each other's necks, to Mrs. Buxton's dressing-room. The misfortune had made them friends. Mrs. Buxton lay on the sofa; so fair and white and colourless, in her muslin dressing-gown, that when Maggie first saw the lady lying with her eyes shut, her heart gave a start, for she thought she was dead. But she opened her large languid eyes, and called them to her, and listened to their story with interest.

'Dawson is at tea. Look, Minnie, in my work-box; there is some silk there. Take off your frock, my dear, and bring it here, and let me see how it can be mended.'

'Aunt Buxton,' whispered Erminia, 'do let me give her one of my frocks. This is such an old thing.'

'No, love. I'll tell you why afterwards,' answered Mrs. Buxton.

She looked at the rent, and arranged it nicely for the little girls to mend. Erminia helped Maggie with right good will. As they sat on the floor, Mrs. Buxton thought what a pretty contrast they made; Erminia, dazzlingly fair, with her golden ringlets, and her pale-blue frock: Maggie's little round white shoulders peeping out of her petticoat; her brown hair as glossy and smooth as the nuts that it resembled in colour; her long black eye-lashes drooping over her clear smooth cheek, which would have given the idea of delicacy, but for the coral lips that spoke of perfect health: and when she glanced up, she showed long, liquid, dark-grey eyes. The deep red of the curtain behind, threw out these two little figures well.

Dawson came up. She was a grave elderly person, of whom Erminia was far more afraid than she was of her aunt; but at Mrs. Buxton's desire she finished mending the frock for Maggie.

'Mr. Buxton has asked some of your mama's old friends to tea, as I am not able to go down. But I think, Dawson, I must have these two little girls to tea with me. Can you be very quiet, my dears; or shall you think it dull?'

They gladly accepted the invitation; and Erminia promised all sorts of fanciful promises as to quietness; and went about on her tiptoes in such a laboured manner, that Mrs. Buxton begged her at last not to try and be quiet, as she made much less noise when she did not. It was the happiest part of the day to Maggie. Something in herself was so much in harmony with Mrs. Buxton's sweet resigned gentleness, that it answered like an echo, and the two understood each other strangely well. They seemed like old friends. Maggie, who was reserved at home because no one cared to hear what she had to say, opened out, and told Erminia and Mrs. Buxton all about her way of spending her day, and described her home.

'How odd!' said Erminia. 'I have ridden that way on Abdel-Kadr,[6] and never seen your house.'

'It is like the place the Sleeping Beauty lived in; people sometimes seem to go round it and round it, and never find it. But unless you follow a little sheep-track, which seems to end at a grey piece of rock, you may come within a stone's throw of the chimneys and never see them. I think you would think it so pretty. Do you ever come that way, ma'am?'

'No, love,' answered Mrs. Buxton.

'But will you some time?'

'I am afraid I shall never be able to go out again,' said Mrs. Buxton, in a voice which, though low, was very cheerful. Maggie thought how sad a lot was here before her; and by-and-by she took a little stool, and sat by Mrs. Buxton's sofa, and stole her hand into hers.

Mrs. Browne was in full tide of pride and happiness down stairs. Mr. Buxton had a number of jokes, which would have become dull from repetition (for he worked a merry idea threadbare before he would let it go), had it not been for his jovial blandness and good-nature. He liked to make people happy, and, as far as bodily wants went, he had a quick perception of what was required. He sat like a king (for, excepting the rector, there was not another gentleman of his standing at Combehurst), among six or seven ladies, who laughed merrily at all his sayings, and evidently thought Mrs. Browne had been highly honoured in having been asked to dinner as well as to tea. In the evening, the carriage was ordered to take her as far as a carriage could go; and there was a little mysterious hand-shaking between her host and herself on taking leave, which made her very curious for the lights of home by which to examine a bit of rustling paper that had been put in her hand with some stammered-out words about Edward

When every one had gone, there was a little gathering in Mrs. Buxton's dressing-room. Husband, son and niece, all came to give her their opinions on the day and the visitors.

'Good Mrs. Browne is a little tiresome,' said Mr. Buxton, yawning. 'Living in that moorland hole, I suppose. However, I think she has enjoyed her day; and we'll ask her down now and then, for Browne's sake. Poor Browne! what a good man he was!'

'I don't like that boy at all,' said Frank. 'I beg you'll not ask him again while I'm at home: he is so selfish and self-important; and yet he's a bit snobbish now and then. Mother! I know what you mean by that look. Well! if I am self-important sometimes, I'm not a snob.'

'Little Maggie is very nice,' said Erminia. 'What a pity she has not a new frock! Was not she good about it, Frank, when she tore it?'

'Yes, she's a nice little thing enough, if she does not get all spirit cowed out of her by that brother. I'm thankful that he is going to school.'

When Mrs. Browne heard where Maggie had drank tea, she was offended. She had only sat with Mrs. Buxton for an hour before dinner. If Mrs. Buxton could bear the noise of children, she could not think why she shut herself up in that room, and gave herself such airs. She supposed it was because she was the grand-daughter of Sir Henry Biddulph that she took upon herself to have such whims, and not sit at the head of her table, or make tea for her company in a civil decent way. Poor Mr. Buxton! What a sad life for a merry light-hearted man to have such a wife! It was a good thing for him to have agreeable society sometimes. She thought he looked a deal better for seeing his friends. He must be sadly moped with that sickly wife.

(If she had been clairvoyante at that moment, she might have seen Mr. Buxton tenderly chafing his wife's hands, and feeling in his innermost soul a wonder how one so saint-like could ever have learnt to love such a boor as he was; it was the wonderful mysterious blessing of his life. So little do we know of the inner truths of the households, where we come and go like intimate guests!)

Maggie could not bear to hear Mrs. Buxton spoken of as a fine lady assuming illness. Her heart beat hard as she spoke. 'Mama! I am sure she is really ill. Her lips kept going so white; and her hand was so burning hot all the time that I held it.'

'Have you been holding Mrs. Buxton's hand? Where were your manners? You are a little forward creature, and ever were. But don't pretend to know better than your elders. It is no use telling me Mrs. Buxton is ill, and she able to bear the noise of children.'

'I think they are all a pack of set-up people, and that Frank Buxton is the worst of all,' said Edward.

Maggie's heart sank within her to hear this cold unkind way of talking over the friends who had done so much to make their day happy. She had never before ventured into the world, and did not know how common and universal is the custom of picking to pieces those with whom we have just been associating; and so it pained her. She was a little depressed too with the idea that she should never see Mrs. Buxton and the lovely Erminia again, Because no future visit or intercourse had been spoken about, she fancied it would never take place; and she felt like the man in the Arabian Nights, who caught a glimpse of the precious stones and dazzling glories of the cavern, which was immediately after closed, and shut up into the semblance of hard, barren rock.[7] She tried to recall the house. Deep blue, crimson red, warm brown draperies, were so striking after the light chintzes of her own house; and the effect of a suite of rooms opening out of each other was something quite new to the little girl; the apartments seemed to melt away into vague distance, like the dim endings of the arched aisles in church. But most of all she tried to recall Mrs. Buxton's face; and Nancy had at last to put away her work, and come to bed, in order to soothe the poor child, who was crying at the thought that Mrs. Buxton would soon die, and that she should never see her again. Nancy loved Maggie dearly, and felt no jealousy of this warm admiration of the unknown lady. She listened to her story and her fears till the sobs were hushed; and the moon fell through the casement on the white closed eyelids of one, who still sighed in her sleep.

CHAPTER III.

IN three weeks, the day came for Edward's departure. A great cake and a parcel of gingerbread soothed his sorrows on leaving home.

'Don't cry, Maggie!' said he to her on the last morning; 'you see I don't. Christmas will soon be here, and I dare say I shall find time to write to you now and then. Did Nancy put any citron in the cake?'

Maggie wished she might accompany her mother to Combehurst to see Edward off by the coach; but it was not to be. She went with them, without her bonnet, as far as her mother would allow her; and then she sat down, and watched their progress for a long, long way. She was startled by the sound of a horse's feet, softly trampling through the long heather. It was Frank Buxton's.

'My father thought Mrs. Browne would like to see the Woodchester Herald. Is Edward gone?' said he, noticing her sad face.

'Yes! he is just gone down the hill to the coach. I dare say you can see him crossing the bridge, soon. I did so want to have gone with him,' answered she, looking wistfully towards the town.

Frank felt sorry for her, left alone to gaze after her brother, whom, strange as it was, she evidently regretted. After a minute's silence, he said –

'You liked riding the other day. Would you like a ride now? Rhoda is very gentle, if you can sit on my saddle. Look! I'll shorten the stirrup. There now; there's a brave little girl! I'll lead her very carefully. Why, Erminia durst not ride without a side-saddle! I'll tell you what; I'll bring the newspaper every Wednesday till I go to school, and you shall have a ride. Only I wish we had a side-saddle for Rhoda. Or, if Erminia will let me, I'll bring Abdel-Kadr, the little Shetland you rode the other day.'

'But will Mr. Buxton let you?' asked Maggie, half delighted – half afraid.

'Oh, my father! to be sure he will. I have him in very good order.'

Maggie was rather puzzled by this way of speaking.

'When do you go to school?' asked she.

'Towards the end of August; I don't know the day.'

'Does Erminia go to school?'

'No. I believe she will soon though, if mama does not get better.' Maggie liked the change of voice, as he spoke of his mother.

'There, little lady! now jump down. Famous! you've a deal of spirit, you little brown mouse.'

Nancy came out, with a wondering look, to receive Maggie.

'It is Mr. Frank Buxton,' said she, by way of an introduction. 'He has brought mama the newspaper.'

'Will you walk in, sir, and rest? I can tie up your horse.'

'No, thank you,' said he. 'I must be off. Don't forget, little Mousey, that you are to be ready for another ride next Wednesday.' And away he went.

It needed a good deal of Nancy's diplomacy to procure Maggie this pleasure; although I don't know why Mrs. Browne should have denied it, for the circle they went was always within sight of the knoll in front of the house, if any one cared enough about the matter to mount it, and look after them. Frank and Maggie got great friends in these rides. Her fearlessness delighted and surprised him, she had seemed so cowed and timid at first. But she was only so with people, as he found out before his holidays ended. He saw her shrink from particular looks and inflexions of voice of her mother's; and learnt to read them, and dislike Mrs. Browne accordingly, notwithstanding all her sugary manner towards himself. The result of his observations he communicated to his mother, and in consequence, he was the bearer of a most civil and ceremonious message from Mrs. Buxton to Mrs. Browne, to the effect that the former would be much obliged to the latter if she would allow Maggie to ride down occasionally with the groom, who would bring the newspapers on the Wednesdays (now Frank was going to school), and to spend the afternoon with Erminia. Mrs. Browne consented, proud of the honour, and yet a little annoyed that no mention was made of herself. When Frank had bid good-bye, and fairly disappeared, she turned to Maggie.

'You must not set yourself up if you go amongst these fine folks. It is their way of showing attention to your father and myself. And you must mind and work doubly hard on Thursdays to make up for playing on Wednesdays.'

Maggie was in a flush of sudden colour, and a happy palpitation of her fluttering little heart. She could hardly feel any sorrow that the kind Frank was going away, so brimful was she of the thoughts of seeing his mother; who had grown strangely associated in her dreams, both sleeping and waking, with the still calm marble effigies that lay for ever clasping their hands in prayer on the altar-tombs in Combehurst church. All the week was one happy season of anticipation. She was afraid her mother was secretly irritated at her natural rejoicing; and so she did not speak to her about it, but she kept awake till Nancy came to bed, and poured into her sympathising ears every detail, real or imaginary, of her past or future intercourse with Mrs. Buxton. And the old servant listened with interest, and fell into the custom of picturing the future with the ease and simplicity of a child.

'Suppose, Nancy! only suppose, you know, that she did die. I don't mean really die, but go into a trance like death; she looked as if she was in one when I first saw her; I would not leave her, but I would sit by her, and watch her, and watch her.'

'Her lips would be always fresh and red,' interrupted Nancy.

'Yes, I know; you've told me before how they keep red, – I should look at them quite steadily; I would try never to go to sleep.'

'The great thing would be to have air-holes left in the coffin.' But Nancy felt the little girl creep close to her at the grim suggestion, and, with the tact of love, she changed the subject.

'Or supposing we could hear of a doctor who could charm away illness. There were such in my young days; but I don't think people are so knowledgeable now. Peggy Jackson, that lived near us when I was a girl, was cured of a waste by a charm.'[8]

'What is a waste, Nancy?'

'It is just a pining away. Food does not nourish, nor drink strengthen them, but they just fade off, and grow thinner and thinner, till their shadow looks grey instead of black at noon day; but he cured her in no time by a charm.'

'Oh, if we could find him.'

'Lass, he's dead, and she's dead, too, long ago!'

While Maggie was in imagination going over moor and fell, into the hollows of the distant mysterious hills, where she imagined all strange beasts and weird people to haunt, she fell asleep.

Such were the fanciful thoughts which were engendered in the little girl's mind by her secluded and solitary life. It was more solitary than ever, now that Edward was gone to school. The house missed his loud cheerful voice, and bursting presence. There seemed much less to be done, now that his numerous wants no longer called for ministration and attendance. Maggie did her task of work on her own grey rock; but as it was sooner finished, now that he was not there to interrupt and call her off, she used to stray up the Fell Lane at the back of the house; a little steep stony lane, more like stairs cut in the rock than what we, in the level land, call a lane: it reached on to the wide and open moor, and near its termination there was a knotted thorn-tree; the only tree for apparent miles. Here the sheep crouched under the storms, or stood and shaded themselves in the noontide heat. The ground was brown with their cleft round foot-marks; and tufts of wool were hung on the lower part of the stem, like votive offerings on some shrine. Here Maggie used to come and sit and dream in any scarce half-hour of leisure. Here she came to cry, when her little heart was overfull at her mother's sharp fault-finding, or when bidden to keep out of the way, and not be troublesome. She used to look over the swelling expanse of moor, and the tears were dried up by the soft low-blowing wind which came sighing along it. She forgot her little home griefs to wonder why a brown-purple shadow always streaked one particular part in the fullest sunlight; why the cloud-shadows always seemed to be wafted with a sidelong motion; or she would imagine what lay beyond those old grey holy hills, which seemed to bear up the white clouds of Heaven on which the angels flew abroad. Or she would look straight up through the quivering air, as long as she could bear its white dazzling, to try and see God's throne in that unfathomable and infinite depth of blue. She thought she should see it blaze forth sudden and glorious, if she were but full of faith. She always came down from the thorn, comforted, and meekly gentle.

But there was danger of the child becoming dreamy, and finding her pleasure in life in reverie, not in action, or endurance, or the holy rest which comes after both, and prepares for further striving or bearing. Mrs. Buxton's kindness prevented this danger just in time. It was partly out of interest in Maggie, but also partly to give Erminia a companion, that she wished the former to come down to Combehurst.

When she was on these visits, she received no regular instruction; and yet all the knowledge, and most of the strength of her character, was derived from these occasional hours. It is true her mother had given her daily lessons in reading, writing, and arithmetic; but both teacher and taught felt these more as painful duties to be gone through, than understood them as means to an end. The 'There! child; now that's done with,' of relief, from Mrs. Browne, was heartily echoed in Maggie's breast, as the dull routine was concluded.

Mrs. Buxton did not make a set labour of teaching; I suppose she felt that much was learned from her superintendence, but she never thought of doing or saying anything with a latent idea of its indirect effect upon the little girls, her companions. She was simply, herself; she even confessed (where the confession was called for) to short-comings, to faults, and never denied the force of temptations, either of those which beset little children, or of those which occasionally assailed herself. Pure, simple, and truthful to the heart's core, her life, in its uneventful hours and days, spoke many homilies. Maggie, who was grave, imaginative, and somewhat quaint, took pains in finding words to express the thoughts to which her solitary life had given rise, secure of Mrs. Buxton's ready understanding and sympathy.

'You are so like a cloud,' said she to Mrs. Buxton. 'Up at the Thorn-tree, it was quite curious how the clouds used to shape themselves, just according as I was glad or sorry. I have seen the same clouds, that, when I came up first, looked like a heap of little snow-hillocks over babies' graves, turn, as soon as I grew happier, to a sort of long bright row of angels. And you seem always to have had some sorrow when I am sad, and to turn bright and hopeful as soon as I grow glad. Dear Mrs. Buxton! I wish Nancy knew you.'

The gay, volatile, wilful, warm-hearted Erminia was less earnest in all things. Her childhood had been passed amid the distractions of wealth; and passionately bent upon the attainment of some object at one moment, the next found her angry at being reminded of the vanished anxiety she had shown but a moment before. Her life was a shattered mirror; every part dazzling and brilliant, but wanting the coherency and perfection of a whole. Mrs. Buxton strove to bring her to a sense of the beauty of completeness, and the relation which qualities and objects bear to each other; but in all her striving she retained hold of the golden clue of sympathy. She would enter into Erminia's eagerness, if the object of it varied twenty times a day; but by-and-by, in her own mild, sweet, suggestive way, she would place all these objects in their right and fitting places, as they were worthy of desire. I do not know how it was, but all discords, and disordered fragments, seemed to fall into harmony and order before her presence.

She had no wish to make the two little girls into the same kind of pattern character. They were diverse as the lily and the rose. But she tried to give stability and earnestness to Erminia; while she aimed to direct Maggie's imagination, so as to make it a great minister to high ends, instead of simply contributing to the vividness and duration of a reverie.

She told her tales of saints and martyrs, and all holy heroines, who forgot themselves, and strove only to be 'ministers of Him, to do His pleasure.'[9] The tears glistened in the eyes of hearer and speaker, while she spoke in her low, faint voice, which was almost choked at times when she came to the noblest part of all.

But when she found that Maggie was in danger of becoming too little a dweller in the present, from the habit of anticipating the occasion for some great heroic action, she spoke of other heroines. She told her how, though the lives of these women of old were only known to us through some strik-ing glorious deed, they yet must have built up the temple of their perfection by many noiseless stories; how, by small daily offerings laid on the altar, they must have obtained their beautiful strength for the crowning sacrifice. And then she would turn and speak of those whose names will never be blazoned on earth – some poor maid-servant, or hard-worked artisan, or weary gov-erness – who have gone on through life quietly, with holy purposes in their hearts, to which they gave up pleasure and ease, in a soft, still, succession of resolute days. She quoted those lines of George Herbert's,

'All may have,
If they dare choose, a glorious life, or grave.'[10]

And Maggie's mother was disappointed because Mrs. Buxton had never offered to teach her 'to play on the piano,' which was to her the very head and front of a genteel education.[11] Maggie, in all her time of yearning to become Joan of Arc, or some great heroine, was unconscious that she herself showed no little heroism, in bearing meekly what she did every day from her mother. It was hard to be questioned about Mrs. Buxton, and then to have her answers turned into subjects for contempt, and faultfinding with that sweet lady's ways.

When Ned came home for the holidays, he had much to tell. His mother listened for hours to his tales; and proudly marked all that she could note of his progress in learning. His copy-books and writing-flourishes were a sight to behold; and his account-books contained towers and pyramids of figures.

'Ay, ay!' said Mr. Buxton, when they were shown to him; 'this is grand! when I was a boy I could make a flying eagle with one stroke of my pen, but I never could do all this. And yet I thought myself a fine fellow, I warrant you. And these sums! why man! I must make you my agent. I need one, I'm sure; for though I get an accountant every two or three years to do up my books, they somehow have the knack of getting wrong again. Those quarries, Mrs. Browne, which every one says are so valuable, and for the stone out of which I receive orders amounting to hundreds of pounds, what d'ye think was the profit I made last year, according to my books?'

'I'm sure I don't know, sir; something very great, I've no doubt.'

'Just seven-pence three farthings,' said he, bursting into a fit of merry laughter, such as another man would have kept for the announcement of enormous profits. 'But I must manage things differently soon. Frank will want money when he goes to Oxford, and he shall have it. I'm but a rough sort of fellow, but Frank shall take his place as a gentleman. Aha, Miss Maggie! and where's my gingerbread? There you go, creeping up to Mrs. Buxton on a Wednesday, and have never taught Cook how to make gingerbread yet. Well, Ned! and how are the classics going on? Fine fellow, that Virgil! Let me see, how does it begin?

"Arma, virumque cano, Trojæ qui primus ab oris."[12]

'That's pretty well, I think, considering I've never opened him since I left school, thirty years ago. To be sure, I spent six hours a day at it when I was there. Come now, I'll puzzle you. Can you construe this?

"Infir dealis, inoak noneis; inmud eelis, inclay noneis."'[13]

'To be sure I can,' said Edward, with a little contempt in his tone. 'Can you do this, sir?

'"Apud in is almi des ire,
Mimis tres i neve require,
Alo veri findit a gestis,
His miseri ne ver at restis."'[14]

But though Edward had made much progress, and gained three prizes, his moral training had been little attended to. He was more tyrannical than ever, both to his mother and Maggie. It was a drawn battle between him and Nancy, and they kept aloof from each other as much as possible. Maggie fell into her old humble way of submitting to his will, as long as it did not go against her conscience; but that, being daily enlightened by her habits of pious aspiring thought, would not allow her to be so utterly obedient as formerly. In addition to his imperiousness, he had learned to affix the idea of cleverness to various artifices and subterfuges, which utterly revolted her by their meanness.

'You are so set up, by being intimate with Erminia, that you won't do a thing I tell you; you're as selfish and self-willed as –' he made a pause. Maggie was ready to cry.

'I will do anything, Ned, that is right.'

'Well! and I tell you this is right.'

'How can it be?' said she, sadly, almost wishing to be convinced.

'How – why it is, and that's enough for you. You must always have a reason for everything now. You're not half so nice as you were. Unless one chops logic with you, and convinces you by a long argument, you'll do nothing. Be obedient, I tell you. That is what a woman has to be.'

'I could be obedient to some people, without knowing their reasons, even though they told me to do silly things,' said Maggie, half to herself.

'I should like to know to whom,' said Edward, scornfully.

'To Don Quixote,'[15] answered she, seriously; for, indeed, he was present in her mind just then, and his noble, tender, melancholy character had made a strong impression there.

Edward stared at her for a moment, and then burst into a loud fit of laughter. It had the good effect of restoring him to a better frame of mind. He had such an excellent joke against his sister, that he could not be angry with her. He called her Sancho Panza all the rest of the holidays, though she protested against it, saying she could not bear the Squire, and disliked being called by his name.

Frank and Edward seemed to have a mutual antipathy to each other, and the coldness between them was rather increased than diminished by all Mr. Buxton's efforts to bring them together. 'Come, Frank, my lad!' said he, 'don't be so stiff with Ned. His father was a dear friend of mine, and I've set my heart on seeing you friends. You'll have it in your power to help him on in the world.'

But Frank answered, 'He is not quite honourable, sir. I can't bear a boy who is not quite honourable. Boys brought up at those private schools are so full of tricks!'

'Nay, my lad, there thou'rt wrong. I was brought up at a private school, and no one can say I ever dirtied my hands with a trick in my life. Good old Mr. Thomson would have flogged the life out of a boy who did anything mean or underhand.'

CHAPTER IV.

SUMMERS and winters came and went, with little to mark them, except the growth of the trees, and the quiet progress of young creatures. Erminia was sent to school somewhere in France, to receive more regular instruction than she could have in the house with her invalid aunt. But she came home once a year, more lovely and elegant and dainty than ever; and Maggie thought, with truth, that ripening years were softening down her volatility, and that her aunt's dewlike sayings had quietly sunk deep, and fertilised the soil. That aunt was fading away. Maggie's devotion added materially to her happiness; and both she and Maggie never forgot that this devotion was to be in all things subservient to the duty which she owed to her mother.

'My love,' Mrs. Buxton had more than once said, 'you must always recollect that your first duty is towards your mother. You know how glad I am to see you; but I shall always understand how it is, if you do not come. She may often want you when neither you nor I can anticipate it.'

Mrs. Browne had no great wish to keep Maggie at home, though she liked to grumble at her going. Still she felt that it was best, in every way, to keep on good terms with such valuable friends; and she appreciated, in some small degree, the advantage which her intimacy at the house was to Maggie. But yet she could not restrain a few complaints, nor withhold from her, on her return, a recapitulation of all the things which might have been done if she had only been at home, and the number of times that she had been wanted; but when she found that Maggie quietly gave up her next Wednesday's visit as soon as she was made aware of any necessity for her presence at home, her mother left off grumbling, and took little or no notice of her absence.

When the time came for Edward to leave school, he announced that he had no intention of taking orders, but meant to become an attorney.

'It's such slow work,' said he to his mother. 'One toils away for four or five years, and then one gets a curacy of seventy pounds a-year, and no end of work to do for the money. Now the work is not much harder in a lawyer's office, and if one has one's wits about one, there are hundreds and thousands a-year to be picked up with mighty little trouble.'

Mrs. Browne was very sorry for this determination. She had a great desire to see her son a clergyman, like his father. She did not consider whether his character was fitted for so sacred an office; she rather thought that the profession itself, when once assumed, would purify the character; but, in fact, his fitness or unfitness for holy orders entered little into her mind. She had a respect for the profession, and his father had belonged to it.

'I had rather see you a curate at seventy pounds a-year, than an attorney with seven hundred,' replied she. 'And you know your father was always asked to dine everywhere, – to places where I know they would not have asked Mr. Bish, of Woodchester, and he makes his thousand a-year. Besides, Mr. Buxton has the next presentation to Combehurst, and you would stand a good chance for your father's sake. And in the meantime you should live here, if your curacy was any way near.'

'I dare say! Catch me burying myself here again. My dear mother, it's a very respectable place for you and Maggie to live in, and I dare say you don't find it dull; but the idea of my quietly sitting down here, is something too absurd!'

'Papa did, and was very happy,' said Maggie.

'Yes! after he had been at Oxford,' replied Edward, a little nonplussed by this reference to one whose memory even the most selfish and thoughtless must have held in respect.

'Well! and you know you would have to go to Oxford first.'

'Maggie! I wish you would not interfere between my mother and me. I want to have it settled and done with, and that it will never be if you keep meddling. Now, mother, don't you see how much better it will be for me to go into Mr. Bish's office? Harry Bish has spoken to his father about it.'

Mrs. Browne sighed.

'What will Mr. Buxton say?' asked she, dolefully.

'Say! Why don't you see it was he who first put it into my head, by telling me, that first Christmas holidays, that I should be his agent. That would be something, would it not? Harry Bish says he thinks a thousand a-year might be made of it.'

His loud, decided, rapid talking overpowered Mrs. Browne; but she resigned herself to his wishes with more regret than she had ever done before. It was not the first case in which fluent declamation has taken the place of argument.

Edward was articled to Mr. Bish, and thus gained his point. There was no one with power to resist his wishes, except his mother and Mr. Buxton. The former had long acknowledged her son's will as her law; and the latter, though surprised and almost disappointed at a change of purpose which he had never anticipated in his plans for Edward's benefit, gave his consent, and even advanced some of the money requisite for the premium.

Maggie looked upon this change with mingled feelings. She had always from a child pictured Edward to herself as taking her father's place. When she had thought of him as a man, it was as contemplative, grave, and gentle, as she remembered her father. With all a child's deficiency of reasoning power, she had never considered how impossible it was that a selfish, vain, and impatient boy could become a meek, humble, and pious man, merely by adopting a profession in which such qualities are required. But now, at sixteen, she was beginning to understand all this. Not by any process of thought, but by something more like a correct feeling, she perceived that Edward would never be the true minister of Christ. So, more glad and thankful than sorry, though sorrow mingled with her sentiments, she learned the decision that he was to be an attorney.

Frank Buxton all this time was growing up into a young man. The hopes both of father and mother were bound up in him; and, according to the difference in their characters was the difference in their hopes. It seemed, indeed, probable that Mr. Buxton, who was singularly void of worldliness or ambition for himself, would become worldly and ambitious for his son. His hopes for Frank were all for honour and distinction here. Mrs. Buxton's hopes were prayers. She was fading away, as light fades into darkness on a summer evening. No one seemed to remark the gradual progress; but she was fully conscious of it herself. The last time that Frank was at home from college before her death, she knew that she should never see him again; and when he gaily left the house, with a cheerfulness, which was partly assumed, she dragged herself with languid steps into a room at the front of the house, from which she could watch him down the long, straggling little street, that led to the inn from which the coach started. As he went along, he turned to look back at his home; and there he saw his mother's white figure gazing after him. He could not see her wistful eyes, but he made her poor heart give a leap of joy by turning round and running back for one more kiss and one more blessing.

When he next came home, it was at the sudden summons of her death.

His father was as one distracted. He could not speak of the lost angel without sudden bursts of tears, and oftentimes of self-upbraiding, which disturbed the calm, still, holy ideas, which Frank liked to associate with her. He ceased speaking to him, therefore, about their mutual loss; and it was a certain kind of relief to both when he did so; but he longed for some one to whom he might talk of his mother, with the quiet reverence of intense and trustful affection. He thought of Maggie, of whom he had seen but little of late; for when he had been at Combehurst, she had felt that Mrs. Buxton required her presence less, and had remained more at home. Possibly Mrs. Buxton regretted this; but she never said anything. She, far-looking, as one who was near death, foresaw that, probably, if Maggie and her son met often in her sick-room, feelings might arise which would militate against her husband's hopes and plans, and which, therefore, she ought not to allow to spring up. But she had been unable to refrain from expressing her gratitude to Maggie for many hours of tranquil happiness, and had unconsciously dropped many sentences which made Frank feel, that, in the little brown mouse of former years, he was likely to meet with one who could tell him much of the inner history of his mother in her last days, and to whom he could speak of her without calling out the passionate sorrow which was so little in unison with her memory.

Accordingly, one afternoon, late in the autumn, he rode up to Mrs. Browne's. The air on the heights was so still, that nothing seemed to stir. Now and then a yellow leaf came floating down from the trees, detached from no outward violence, but only because its life had reached its full limit, and then ceased. Looking down on the distant sheltered woods, they were gorgeous in orange and crimson, but their splendour was felt to be the sign of the decaying and dying year. Even without an inward sorrow, there was a grand solemnity in the season which impressed the mind, and hushed it into tranquil thought. Frank rode slowly along, and quietly dismounted at the old horse-mount, beside which there was an iron bridle-ring fixed in the grey stone wall. He saw the casement of the parlour-window open, and Maggie's head bent down over her work. She looked up as he entered the court, and his footsteps sounded on the flag-walk. She came round and opened the door. As she stood in the door-way, speaking, he was struck by her resemblance to some old painting. He had seen her young, calm face, shining out with great peacefulness, and the large, grave, thoughtful eyes, giving the character to the features which otherwise they might, from their very regularity, have wanted. Her brown dress had the exact tint which a painter would have admired. The slanting mellow sunlight fell upon her as she stood; and the vine-leaves, already frost-tinted, made a rich, warm border, as they hung over the old house-door.

'Mama is not well; she is gone to lie down. How are you? How is Mr. Buxton?'

'We are both pretty well; quite well, in fact, as far as regards health. May I come in? I want to talk to you, Maggie!'

She opened the little parlour-door, and they went in; but for a time they were both silent. They could not speak of her who was with them, present in their thoughts, Maggie shut the casement, and put a log of wood on the fire. She sat down with her back to the window; but as the flame sprang up, and blazed at the touch of the dry wood, Frank saw that her face was wet with quiet tears. Still her voice was even and gentle, as she answered his questions. She seemed to understand what were the very things he would care most to hear. She spoke of his mother's last days; and without any word of praise (which, indeed, would have been impertinence), she showed such a just and true appreciation of her who was dead and gone, that he felt as if he could listen for ever to the sweet-dropping words. They were balm to his sore heart. He had thought it possible that the suddenness of her death might have made her life incomplete, in that she might have departed without being able to express wishes and projects, which would now have the sacred force of commands. But he found that Maggie, though she had never intruded herself as such, had been the depositary of many little thoughts and plans; or, if they were not expressed to her, she knew that Mr. Buxton or Dawson was aware of what they were, though, in their violence of early grief, they had forgotten to name them. The flickering brightness of the flame had died away; the gloom of evening had gathered into the room, through the open door of which the kitchen fire sent a ruddy glow, distinctly marked against carpet and wall. Frank still sat, with his head buried in his hands against the table, listening.

'Tell me more,' he said, at every pause.

'I think I have told you all now,' said Maggie, at last. 'At least, it is all I recollect at present; but if I think of anything more, I will be sure and tell you.'

'Thank you; do.' He was silent for some time.

'Erminia is coming home at Christmas. She is not to go back to Paris again. She will live with us. I hope you and she will be great friends, Maggie.'

'Oh yes,' replied she. 'I think we are already. At least we were last Christmas. You know it is a year since I have seen her.'

'Yes; she went to Switzerland with Mademoiselle Michel, instead of coming home the last time, Maggie, I must go, now. My father will be waiting dinner for me.'

'Dinner! I was going to ask if you would not stay to tea. I hear mama stirring about in her room. And Nancy is getting things ready, I see. Let me go and tell mama. She will not be pleased unless she sees you. She has been very sorry for you all,' added she, dropping her voice.

Before he could answer, she ran up stairs.

Mrs. Browne came down.

'Oh, Mr. Frank! Have you been sitting in the dark? Maggie, you ought to have rung for candles! Ah! Mr. Frank, you've had a sad loss since I saw you here – let me see – in the last week of September. But she was always a sad invalid; and no doubt your loss is her gain. Poor Mr. Buxton, too! How is he? When one thinks of him, and of her years of illness, it seems like a happy release.'

She could have gone on for any length of time, but Frank could not bear this ruffling up of his soothed grief, and told her that his father was expecting him home to dinner.

'Ah! I am sure you must not disappoint him. He'll want a little cheerful company more than ever now. You must not let him dwell on it, Mr. Frank, but turn his thoughts another way by always talking of other things. I am sure if I had some one to speak to me in a cheerful, pleasant way, when poor dear Mr. Browne died, I should never have fretted after him as I did; but the children were too young, and there was no one to come and divert me with any news. If I'd been living in Combehurst, I am sure I should not have let my grief get the better of me as I did. Could you get up a quiet rubber in the evenings, do you think?'

But Frank had shaken hands and was gone. As he rode home he thought much of sorrow, and the different ways of bearing it. He decided that it was sent by God for some holy purpose, and to call out into existence some higher good; and he thought that if it were faithfully taken as His decree, there would be no passionate, despairing resistance to it; not yet, if it were trustfully acknowledged to have some wise end, should we dare to baulk it, and defraud it by putting it on one side, and, by seeking the distractions of worldly things, not let it do its full work. And then he returned to his conversation with Maggie. That had been real comfort to him. What an advantage it would be to Erminia to have such a girl for a friend and companion!

It was rather strange that, having this thought, and having been struck, as I said, with Maggie's appearance while she stood in the doorway (and I may add that this impression of her unobtrusive beauty had been deepened by several succeeding interviews), he should reply as he did to Erminia's remark, on first seeing Maggie after her return from France.

'How lovely Maggie is growing! Why, I had no idea she would ever turn out pretty. Sweet-looking she always was; but now her style of beauty makes her positively distinguished. Frank! speak! is not she beautiful?'

'Do you think so?' answered he, with a kind of lazy indifference, exceedingly gratifying to his father, who was listening with some eagerness to his answer. That day, after dinner, Mr. Buxton began to ask his opinion of Erminia's appearance.

Frank answered at once –

'She is a dazzling little creature. Her complexion looks as if it were made of cherries and milk; and, it must be owned, the little lady has studied the art of dress to some purpose in Paris.'

Mr. Buxton was nearer happiness at this reply than he had ever been since his wife's death; for the only way he could devise to satisfy his reproachful conscience towards his neglected and unhappy sister, was to plan a marriage between his son and her child. He rubbed his hands, and drank two extra glasses of wine.

'We'll have the Brownes to dinner, as usual, next Thursday,' said he. 'I am sure your mother would have been hurt if we had omitted it; it is now nine years since they began to come, and they have never missed one Christmas since. Do you see any objection, Frank?'

'None at all, sir,' answered he. 'I intend to go up to town soon after Christmas, for a week or ten days, on my way to Cambridge. Can I do anything for you?'

'Well, I don't know. I think I shall go up myself some day soon. I can't understand all these lawyer's letters, about the purchase of the Newbridge estate; and I fancy I could make more sense out of it all, if I saw Mr. Hodgson.'

'I wish you would adopt my plan, of having an agent, sir. Your affairs are really so complicated now, that they would take up the time of an expert man of business. I am sure all those tenants at Dumford ought to be seen after.'

'I do see after them. There's never a one that dares cheat me, or that would cheat me if they could. Most of them have lived under the Buxtons for generations. They know that if they dared to take advantage of me, I should come down upon them pretty smartly.'

'Do you rely upon their attachment to your family, – or on their idea of your severity?'

'On both. They stand me instead of much trouble in account-keeping, and those eternal lawyers' letters some people are always despatching to their tenants. When I'm cheated, Frank, I give you leave to make me have an agent, but not till then. There's my little Erminia singing away, and nobody to hear her.'

CHAPTER V.

CHRISTMAS-DAY was strange and sad. Mrs. Buxton had always contrived to be in the drawing-room, ready to receive them all after dinner. Mr. Buxton tried to do away with his thoughts of her by much talking; but every now and then he looked wistfully towards the door. Erminia exerted herself to be as lively as she could, in order, if possible, to fill up the vacuum. Edward, who had come over from Woodchester for a walk, had a good deal to say; and was, unconsciously, a great assistance with his never-ending flow of rather clever small-talk. His mother felt proud of her son, and his new waistcoat, which was far more conspicuously of the latest fashion than Frank's could be said to be. After dinner, when Mr. Buxton and the two young men were left alone, Edward launched out still more. He thought he was impressing Frank with his knowledge of the world, and the world's ways. But he was doing all in his power to repel one who had never been much attracted towards him. Worldly success was his standard of merit. The end seemed with him to justify the means; if a man prospered, it was not necessary to scrutinise his conduct too closely. The law was viewed in its lowest aspect; and yet with a certain cleverness, which preserved Edward from being intellectually contemptible. Frank had entertained some idea of studying for a barrister himself; not so much as a means of livelihood as to gain some idea of the code which makes and shows a nation's conscience: but Edward's details of the ways in which the letter so often baffles the spirit, made him recoil. With some anger against himself, for viewing the profession with disgust, because it was degraded by those who embraced it, instead of looking upon it as what might be ennobled and purified into a vast intelligence by high and pureminded men, he got up abruptly and left the room.

The girls were sitting over the drawing-room fire, with unlighted candles on the table, talking, he felt, about his mother; but when he came in they rose, and changed their tone. Erminia went to the piano, and sang her newest and choicest French airs. Frank was gloomy and silent; but when she changed into more solemn music his mood was softened. Maggie's simple and hearty admiration, untinged by the slightest shade of envy for Erminia's accomplishments, charmed him. The one appeared to him the perfection of elegant art, the other of graceful nature. When he looked at Maggie, and thought of the moorland home from which she had never wandered, the mysteriously beautiful lines of Wordsworth seemed to become sunclear to him.

> 'And she shall lean her ear
> In many a secret place
> Where rivulets dance their wayward round,
> And beauty born of murmuring sound
> Shall pass into her face.'[16]

Mr. Buxton, in the dining-room, was really getting to take an interest in Edward's puzzling cases. They were like tricks at cards. A quick motion, and out of the unpromising heap, all confused together, presto! the right card turned up. Edward stated his case, so that there did not seem a loophole for the desired verdict; but, through some conjuration, it always came uppermost at last. He had a graphic way of relating things; and, as he did not spare epithets in his designation of the opposing party, Mr. Buxton took it upon trust that the defendant or the prosecutor (as it might happen) was a 'pettifogging knave,' or a 'miserly curmudgeon,' and rejoiced accordingly in the triumph over him gained by the ready wit of 'our governor,' Mr. Bish. At last he became so deeply impressed with Edward's knowledge of law, as to consult him about some cottage property he had in Woodchester.

'I rather think there are twenty-one cottages, and they don't bring me in four pounds a-year; and out of that I have to pay for collecting. Would there be any chance of selling them? They are in Doughty-street; a bad neighbourhood, I fear.'

'Very bad,' was Edward's prompt reply. 'But if you are really anxious to effect a sale, I have no doubt I could find a purchaser in a short time.'

'I should be very much obliged to you,' said Mr. Buxton. 'You would be doing me a kindness. If you meet with a purchaser, and can manage the affair, I would rather that you drew out the deeds for the transfer of the property. It would be the beginning of business for you; and I only hope I should bring you good luck.'

Of course Edward could do this; and when they left the table, it was with a feeling on his side that he was a step nearer to the agency which he coveted; and with a happy consciousness on Mr. Buxton's of having put a few pounds in the way of a deserving and remarkably clever young man.

Since Edward had left home, Maggie had gradually, but surely, been gaining in importance. Her judgment and her untiring unselfishness could not fail to make way. Her mother had some respect for, and great dependence on her; but still it was hardly affection that she felt for her; or if it was, it was a dull and torpid kind of feeling, compared with the fond love and exulting pride which she took in Edward. When he came back for occasional holidays, his mother's face was radiant with happiness, and her manner towards him was even more caressing than he approved of. When Maggie saw him repel the hand that fain would have stroked his hair as in childish days, a longing came into her heart for some of these uncared-for tokens of her mother's love. Otherwise she meekly sank back into her old secondary place, content to have her judgment slighted and her wishes unasked as long as he stayed. At times she was now beginning to disapprove and regret some things in him; his flashiness of manner jarred against her taste; and a deeper, graver feeling was called out by his evident want of quick moral perception. 'Smart and clever,' or 'slow and dull,' took with him the place of 'right and wrong.' Little as he thought it, he was himself narrow-minded and dull; slow and blind to perceive the beauty and eternal wisdom of simple goodness.

Erminia and Maggie became great friends. Erminia used to beg for Maggie, until she herself put a stop to the practice; as she saw her mother yielded more frequently than was convenient, for the honour of having her daughter a visitor at Mr. Buxton's, about which she could talk to her few acquaintances who persevered in calling at the cottage. Then Erminia volunteered a visit of some days to Maggie, and Mrs. Browne's pride was redoubled; but she made so many preparations, and so much fuss, and gave herself so much trouble, that she was positively ill during Erminia's stay; and Maggie felt that she must henceforward deny herself the pleasure of having her friend for a guest, as her mother could not be persuaded from attempting to provide things in the same abundance and style as that to which Erminia was accustomed at home; whereas, as Nancy shrewdly observed, the young lady did not know if she was eating jelly, or porridge, or whether the plates were common delf or the best China,[17] so long as she was with her dear Miss Maggie. Spring went, and summer came. Frank had gone to and fro between Cambridge and Combehurst, drawn by motives of which he felt the force, but into which he did not care to examine. Edward had sold the property of Mr. Buxton; and he, pleased with the possession of half the purchase money (the remainder of which was to be paid by instalments), and happy in the idea that his son came over so frequently to see Erminia, had amply rewarded the young attorney for his services.

One summer's day, as hot as day could be, Maggie had been busy all morning; for the weather was so sultry that she would not allow either Nancy or her mother to exert themselves much. She had gone down with the old brown pitcher, coeval with herself, to the spring for water; and while it was trickling, and making a tinkling music, she sat down on the ground. The air was so still that she heard the distant wood-pigeons cooing; and round about her the bees were murmuring busily among the clustering heath. From some little touch of sympathy with these low sounds of pleasant harmony, she began to try and hum some of Erminia's airs. She never sang out loud, or put words to her songs; but her voice was very sweet, and it was a great pleasure to herself to let it go into music. Just as her jug was filled, she was startled by Frank's sudden appearance. She had thought he was at Cambridge, and, from some cause or other, her face, usually so faint in colour, became the most vivid scarlet. They were both too conscious to speak. Maggie stooped (murmuring some words of surprise) to take up her pitcher.

'Don't go yet, Maggie,' said he, putting his hand on hers to stop her; but, somehow, when that purpose was effected, he forgot to take it off again. 'I have come all the way from Cambridge to see you. I could not bear suspense any longer. I grew so impatient for certainty of some kind, that I went up to town last night, in order to feel myself on my way to you, even though I knew I could not be here a bit earlier to-day for doing so. Maggie, – dear Maggie! how you are trembling! Have I frightened you? Nancy told me you were here; but it was very thoughtless to come so suddenly upon you.'

It was not the suddenness of his coming; it was the suddenness of her own heart, which leaped up with the feelings called out by his words. She went very white, and sat down on the ground as before. But she rose again immediately, and stood, with drooping, averted head. He had dropped her hand, but now sought to take it again.

'Maggie, darling, may I speak?' Her lips moved, he saw, but he could not hear. A pang of affright ran through him that, perhaps, she did not wish to listen. 'May I speak to you?' he asked again, quite timidly. She tried to make her voice sound, but it would not; so she looked round. Her soft grey eyes were eloquent in that one glance. And, happier than his words, passionate and tender as they were, could tell, he spoke till her trembling was changed into bright flashing blushes, and even a shy smile hovered about her lips, and dimpled her cheeks.

The water bubbled over the pitcher unheeded. At last she remembered all the work-a-day world. She lifted up the jug, and would have hurried home, but Frank decidedly took it from her.

'Henceforward,' said he, 'I have a right to carry your burdens.' So with one arm round her waist, and with the other carrying the water, they climbed the steep turfy slope. Near the top she wanted to take it again.

'Mama will not like it. Mama will think it so strange.'

'Why, dearest, if I saw Nancy carrying it up this slope I would take it from her. It would be strange if a man did not carry it for any woman. But you must let me tell your mother of my right to help you. It is your dinner-time, is it not? I may come in to dinner as one of the family, may not I, Maggie?'

'No,' she said softly. For she longed to be alone; and she dreaded being overwhelmed by the expression of her mother's feelings, weak and agitated as she felt herself. 'Not to-day.'

'Not to-day!' said he, reproachfully. 'You are very hard upon me. Let me come to tea, If you will, I will leave you now. Let me come to early tea. I must speak to my father. He does not know I am here. I may come to tea. At what time is it? Three o'clock. Oh, I know you drink tea at some strange early hour; perhaps it is at two. I will take care to be in time.'

'Don't come till five, please. I must tell mama; and I want some time to think. It does seem so like a dream. Do go, please.'

'Well! if I must, I must. But I don't feel as if I were in a dream, but in some real blessed heaven, so long as I see you.'

At last he went. Nancy was awaiting Maggie, at the side-gate.

'Bless us and save us, bairn! what a time it has taken thee to get the water. Is the spring dry with the hot weather?'

Maggie ran past her. All dinner-time she heard her mother's voice in long-continued lamentation about something. She answered at random, and startled her mother by asserting that she thought 'it' was very good; the said 'it' being milk turned sour by thunder. Mrs. Browne spoke quite sharply, 'No one is so particular as you, Maggie. I have known you drink water, day after day, for breakfast, when you were a little girl, because your cup of milk had a drowned fly in it; and now you tell me you don't care for this, and don't mind that, just as if you could eat up all the things which are spoiled by the heat. I declare my head aches so, I shall go and lie down as soon as ever dinner is over.'

If this was her plan, Maggie thought she had no time to lose in making her confession. Frank would be here before her mother got up again to tea. But she dreaded speaking about her happiness; it seemed as yet so cobweb-like, as if a touch would spoil its beauty.

'Mama, just wait one minute. Just sit down in your chair while I tell you something. Please, dear mama.' She took a stool, and sat at her mother's feet; and then she began to turn the wedding-ring on Mrs. Browne's hand, looking down and never speaking, till the latter became impatient.

'What is it you have got to say, child? Do make haste, for I want to go up-stairs.'

With a great jerk of resolution, Maggie said –

'Mama, Frank Buxton has asked me to marry him.'

She hid her face in her mother's lap for an instant; and then she lifted it up, as brimful of the light of happiness as is the cup of a water-lily of the sun's radiance.

'Maggie – you don't say so,' said her mother, half incredulously. 'It can't be, for he's at Cambridge, and it's not post-day.[18] What do you mean?'

'He came this morning, mother, when I was down at the well; and we fixed that I was to speak to you; and he asked if he might come again for tea.'

'Dear! dear! and the milk all gone sour! We should have had milk of our own, if Edward had not persuaded me against buying another cow.'

'I don't think Mr. Buxton will mind it much,' said Maggie, dimpling up, as she remembered, half-unconsciously, how little he had seemed to care for anything but herself.

'Why, what a thing it is for you!' said Mrs. Browne, quite roused up from her languor and her head-ache. 'Everybody said he was engaged to Miss

Erminia. Are you quite sure you made no mistake, child? What did he say? Young men are so fond of making fine speeches; and young women are so silly in fancying they mean something. I once knew a girl who thought that a gentleman who sent her mother a present of a sucking-pig, did it as a delicate way of making her an offer. Tell me his exact words.'

But Maggie blushed, and either would not or could not. So Mrs. Browne began again,

'Well, if you're sure, you're sure. I wonder how he brought his father round. So long as he and Erminia have been planned for each other! That very first day we ever dined there after your father's death, Mr. Buxton as good as told me all about it. I fancied they were only waiting till they were out of mourning.'

All this was news to Maggie. She had never thought that either Erminia or Frank was particularly fond of the other; still less had she had any idea of Mr. Buxton's plans for them. Her mother's surprise at her engagement jarred a little upon her too: it had become so natural, even in these last two hours, to feel that she belonged to *him*. But there were more discords to come. Mrs. Browne began again, half in soliloquy:

'I should think he would have four thousand a-year. He did not tell you, love, did he, if they had still that bad property in the canal, that his father complained about? But he will have four thousand. Why you'll have your carriage, Maggie. Well! I hope Mr. Buxton has taken it kindly, because he'll have a deal to do with the settlements. I'm sure I thought he was engaged to Erminia.'

Ringing changes on these subjects all the afternoon, Mrs. Browne sat with Maggie. She occasionally wandered off to speak about Edward, and how favourably his future prospects would be advanced by the engagement.

'Let me see – there's the house in Combehurst; the rent of that would be a hundred and fifty a year, but we'll not reckon that. But there's the quarries' (she was reckoning upon her fingers in default of a slate, for which she had vainly searched), 'we'll call them two hundred a-year, for I don't believe Mr. Buxton's stories about their only bringing him in sevenpence; and there's Newbridge, that's certainly thirteen hundred, – where had I got to, Maggie?'

'Dear mama, do go and lie down for a little; you look quite flushed,' said Maggie, softly.

Was this the manner to view her betrothal with such a man as Frank? Her mother's remarks depressed her more than she could have thought it possible; the excitement of the morning was having its reaction, and she longed to go up to the solitude under the thorn-tree, where she had hoped to spend a quiet, thoughtful afternoon.

Nancy came in to replace glasses and spoons in the cupboard. By some accident, the careful old servant broke one of the former. She looked up quickly at her mistress, who usually visited all such offences with no small portion of rebuke.

'Never mind, Nancy,' said Mrs. Browne. 'It's only an old tumbler; and Maggie's going to be married, and we must buy a new set for the wedding-dinner.'

Nancy looked at both, bewildered; at last a light dawned into her mind, and her face looked shrewdly and knowingly back at Mrs. Browne. Then she said, very quietly.

'I think I'll take the next pitcher to the well myself, and try my luck. To think how sorry I was for Miss Maggie this morning! "Poor thing," says I to myself, "to be kept all this time at that confounded well" (for I'll not deny that I swear a bit to myself at times – it sweetens the blood), "and she so tired." I e'en thought I'd go help her; but I reckon she'd some other help. May I take a guess at the young man?'

'Four thousand a-year! Nancy;' said Mrs. Browne exultingly.

'And a blithe look, and a warm, kind heart, – and a free step, – and a noble way with him to rich and poor, – aye, aye, I know the name. No need to alter all my neat M.B.'s., done in turkey red cotton.[19] Well, well! every one's turn comes sometime, but mine's rather long a-coming.'

The faithful old servant came up to Maggie, and put her hand caressingly on her shoulder. Maggie threw her arms round her neck, and kissed the brown, withered face.

'God bless thee, bairn,' said Nancy, solemnly. It brought the low music of peace back into the still recesses of Maggie's heart. She began to look out for her lover; half-hidden behind the muslin window curtain, which waved gently to and fro in the afternoon breezes. She heard a firm, buoyant step, and had only time to catch one glimpse of his face, before moving away. But that one glance made her think that the hours which had elapsed since she saw him had not been serene to him any more than to her.

When he entered the parlour, his face was glad and bright. He went up in a frank, rejoicing way to Mrs. Browne; who was evidently rather puzzled how to receive him – whether as Maggie's betrothed, or as the son of the greatest man of her acquaintance.

'I am sure, sir,' said she, 'we are all very much obliged to you for the honour you have done our family!'

He looked rather perplexed as to the nature of the honour which he had conferred without knowing it; but as the light dawned upon him, he made answer in a frank, merry way, which was yet full of respect for his future mother-in-law –

'And I am sure I am truly grateful for the honour one of your family has done me.'

When Nancy brought in tea she was dressed in her fine-weather Sunday gown; the first time it had ever been worn out of church, and the walk to and fro.

After tea, Frank asked Maggie if she would walk out with him; and accordingly they climbed the Fell-Lane and went out upon the moors, which seemed vast and boundless as their love.

'Have you told your father?' asked Maggie; a dim anxiety lurking in her heart.

'Yes,' said Frank. He did not go on; and she feared to ask, although she longed to know, how Mr. Buxton had received the intelligence.

'What did he say? at length she inquired.

'Oh! it was evidently a new idea to him that I was attached to you; and he does not take up a new idea speedily. He has had some notion, it seems, that Erminia and I were to make a match of it; but she and I agreed, when we talked it over, that we should never have fallen in love with each other if there had not been another human being in the world. Erminia is a little sensible creature, and says she does not wonder at any man falling in love with you. Nay, Maggie, don't hang your head so down; let me have a glimpse of your face.'

'I am sorry your father does not like it,' said Maggie, sorrowfully.

'So am I. But we must give him time to get reconciled. Never fear but he will like it in the long run; he has too much good taste and good feeling. He must like you.'

Frank did not choose to tell even Maggie how violently his father had set himself against their engagement. He was surprised and annoyed at first to find how decidedly his father was possessed with the idea that he was to marry his cousin, and that she, at any rate, was attached to him, whatever his feelings might be towards her; but after he had gone frankly to Erminia and told her all, he found that she was as ignorant of her uncle's plans for her as he had been; and almost as glad at any event which should frustrate them.

Indeed she came to the moorland cottage on the following day, after Frank had returned to Cambridge. She had left her horse in charge of the groom, near the fir-trees on the heights, and came running down the slope in her habit. Maggie went out to meet her, with just a little wonder at her heart if what Frank had said could possibly be true; and that Erminia, living in the house with him, could have remained indifferent to him. Erminia threw her arms round her neck, and they sat down together on the court-steps.

'I durst not ride down that hill; and Jem is holding my horse, so I may not stay very long; now begin, Maggie, at once, and go into a rhapsody about Frank. Is not he a charming fellow? Oh! I am so glad. Now don't sit smiling and blushing there to yourself; but tell me a great deal about it. I have so wanted to know somebody that was in love, that I might hear what it was like; and the minute I could, I came off here. Frank is only just gone. He has had another long talk with my uncle, since he came back from you this morning; but I am afraid he has not made much way yet.'

Maggie sighed. 'I don't wonder at his not thinking me good enough for Frank.'

'No! the difficulty would be to find any one he did think fit for his paragon of a son.'

'He thought you were, dearest Erminia.'

'So Frank has told you that, has he? I suppose we shall have no more family secrets now,' said Erminia, laughing. 'But I can assure you I had a strong rival in Lady Adela Castlemayne, the Duke of Wight's daughter; she was the most beautiful lady my uncle had ever seen (he only saw her in the Grand Stand at Woodchester races, and never spoke a word to her in his life). And if she would have had Frank, my uncle would still have been dissatisfied as long as the Princess Victoria was unmarried,[20] none would have been good enough while a better remained. But Maggie,' said she, smiling up into her friend's face, 'I think it would have made you laugh, for all you look as if a kiss would shake the tears out of your eyes, if you could have seen my uncle's manner to me all day. He will have it that I am suffering from an unrequited attachment; so he watched me and watched me over breakfast; and at last, when I had eaten a whole nest-full of eggs, and I don't know how many pieces of toast, he rang the bell and asked for some potted charr.[21] I was quite unconscious that it was for me, and I did not want it when it came; so he sighed in a most melancholy manner, and said, "My poor Erminia!" If Frank had not been there, and looking dreadfully miserable, I am sure I should have laughed out.'

'Did Frank look miserable?' said Maggie, anxiously.

'There now! you don't care for anything but the mention of his name.'

'But did he look unhappy?' persisted Maggie.

'I can't say he looked happy, dear Mousey; but it was quite different when he came back from seeing you. You know you always had the art of stilling any person's trouble. You and my aunt Buxton are the only two I ever knew with that gift.'

'I am so sorry he has any trouble to be stilled,' said Maggie.

'And I think it will do him a world of good. Think how successful his life has been! the honours he got at Eton! his picture taken, and I don't know what! and at Cambridge just the same way of going on. He would be insufferably imperious in a few years, if he did not meet with a few crosses.'

'Imperious! – oh, Erminia, how can you say so?'

'Because it's the truth. He happens to have very good dispositions; and therefore his strong will is not either disagreeable, or offensive; but once let him become possessed by a wrong wish, and you would then see how vehement and imperious he would be. Depend upon it, my uncle's resistance is a capital thing for him. As dear sweet Aunt Buxton would have said, "There is a holy purpose in it;" and as Aunt Buxton would not have said, but as I, a "fool, rush in where angels fear to tread,"[22] I decide that the purpose is to teach Master Frank patience and submission.'

'Erminia – how could you help –' and there Maggie stopped.

'I know what you mean; how could I help falling in love with him? I think he has not mystery and reserve enough for me. I should like a man with some deep, impenetrable darkness round him; something one could always keep wondering about. Besides, think what clashing of wills there would have been! My uncle was very short-sighted in his plan; but I don't think he thought so much about the fitness of our characters and ways, as the fitness of our fortunes!'

'For shame, Erminia! No one cares less for money than Mr. Buxton!'

'There's a good little daughter-in-law elect! But seriously, I do think he is beginning to care for money; not in the least for himself, but as a means of aggrandizement for Frank. I have observed, since I came home at Christmas, a growing anxiety to make the most of his property; a thing he never cared about before. I don't think he is aware of it himself; but from one or two little things I have noticed, I should not wonder if he ends in being avaricious in his old age.' Erminia sighed.

Maggie had almost a sympathy with the father, who sought what he imagined to be for the good of his son, and that son, Frank. Although she was as convinced as Erminia, that money could not really help any one to happiness, she could not at the instant resist saying –

'Oh! how I wish I had a fortune! I should so like to give it all to him.'

'Now Maggie! don't be silly! I never heard you wish for anything different from what *was,* before, so I shall take this opportunity of lecturing you on your folly. No! I won't either, for you look sadly tired with all your agitation; and besides I must go, or Jem will be wondering what has become of me. Dearest cousin-in-law, I shall come very often to see you; and perhaps I shall give you my lecture yet.'

CHAPTER VI.

IT was true of Mr. Buxton, as well as of his son, that he had the seeds of imperiousness in him. His life had not been such as to call them out into view. With more wealth than he required; with a gentle wife, who if she ruled him never showed it, or was conscious of the fact herself; looked up to by his neighbours, a simple affectionate set of people, whose fathers had lived near his father and grandfather in the same kindly relation, receiving benefits cordially given, and requiting them with good will and respectful attention: such had been the circumstances surrounding him; and until his son grew out of childhood, there had not seemed a wish which he had it not in his power to gratify as soon as formed. Again, when Frank was at school and at college, all went on prosperously; he gained honours enough to satisfy a far more ambitious father. Indeed, it was the honours he gained that stimulated his father's ambition. He received letters from tutors, and headmasters, prophesying that, if Frank chose, he might rise to the 'highest honours in church or state;' and the idea thus suggested, vague as it was, remained, and filled Mr. Buxton's mind; and, for the first time in his life, made him wish that his own career had been such as would have led him to form connexions among the great and powerful. But, as it was, his shyness and *gêne,*[23] from being unaccustomed to society, had made him averse to Frank's occasional requests that he might bring such and such a schoolfellow, or college-chum, home on a visit. Now he regretted this, on account of the want of those connexions which might thus have been formed; and, in his visions, he turned to marriage as the best way of remedying this. Erminia was right in saying that her uncle had thought of Lady Adela Castlemayne for an instant; though how the little witch had found it out I cannot say, as the idea had been dismissed immediately from his mind. He was wise enough to see its utter vanity, as long as his son remained undistinguished. But his hope was this. If Frank married Erminia, their united property (she being her father's heiress) would justify him in standing for the shire;[24] or if he could marry the daughter of some leading personage in the county, it might lead to the same step; and thus at once he would obtain a position in parliament, where his great talents would have scope and verge enough. Of these two visions, the favourite one (for his sister's sake) was that of marriage with Erminia.

And, in the midst of all this, fell, like a bomb-shell, the intelligence of his engagement with Maggie Browne; a good sweet little girl enough, but without fortune or connexion, – without, as far as Mr. Buxton knew, the least power, or capability, or spirit, with which to help Frank on in his career to eminence in the land! He resolved to consider it as a boyish fancy, easily to be suppressed; and pooh-poohed it down, to Frank, accordingly. He remarked his son's set lips, and quiet determined brow, although he never spoke in a more respectful tone, than while thus steadily opposing his father. If he had shown more violence of manner, he would have irritated him less; but, as it was, it was the most miserable interview that had ever taken place between the father and son.

Mr. Buxton tried to calm himself down with believing that Frank would change his mind, if he saw more of the world; but, somehow, he had a prophesying distrust of this idea internally. The worst was, there was no fault to be found with Maggie herself, although she might want the accomplishments he desired to see in his son's wife. Her connexions, too, were so perfectly respectable (though humble enough in comparison with Mr. Buxton's soaring wishes), that there was nothing to be objected to on that score; her position was the great offence. In proportion to his want of any reason but this one, for disapproving of the engagement, was his annoyance under it. He assumed a reserve towards Frank; which was so unusual a restraint upon his open genial disposition, that it seemed to make him irritable towards all others in contact with him, excepting Erminia. He found it difficult to behave rightly to Maggie. Like all habitually cordial persons, he went into the opposite extreme, when he wanted to show a little coolness. However angry he might be with the events of which she was the cause, she was too innocent and meek to justify him in being more than cool; but his awkwardness was so great, that many a man of the world has met his greatest enemy, each knowing the other's hatred, with less freezing distance of manner than Mr. Buxton's to Maggie. While she went simply on in her own path, loving him the more through all, for old kindness' sake, and because he was Frank's father, he shunned meeting her with such evident and painful anxiety, that at last she tried to spare him the encounter, and hurried out of church, or lingered behind all, in order to avoid the only chance they now had of being forced to speak; for she no longer went to the dear house in Combehurst, though Erminia came to see her more than ever.

Mrs. Browne was perplexed and annoyed beyond measure. She upbraided Mr. Buxton to every one but Maggie. To her she said, – 'Any one in their senses might have foreseen what had happened, and would have thought well about it, before they went and fell in love with a young man of such expectations as Mr. Frank Buxton.'

In the middle of all this dismay, Edward came over from Woodchester for a day or two. He had been told of the engagement, in a letter from Maggie herself; but it was too sacred a subject for her to enlarge upon to him; and Mrs. Browne was no letter-writer. So this was his first greeting to Maggie, after kissing her –

'Well, Sancho, you've done famously for yourself. As soon as I got your letter I said to Harry Bish, – "Still waters run deep; here's my little sister Maggie, as quiet a creature as ever lived, has managed to catch young Buxton, who has five thousand a-year if he's a penny." Don't go so red, Maggie. Harry was sure to hear of it soon from some one, and I see no use in keeping it secret, for it gives consequence to us all.'

'Mr. Buxton is quite put out about it,' said Mrs. Browne, querulously; 'and I'm sure he need not be, for he's enough of money, if that's what he wants; and Maggie's father was a clergyman, and I've seen "yeoman," with my own eyes, on old Mr. Buxton's (Mr. Lawrence's father's) carts; and a clergyman is above a yeoman any day. But if Maggie had had any thought for other people, she'd never have gone and engaged herself, when she might have been sure it would give offence. We are never asked down to dinner now. I've never broken bread there since last Christmas.'

'Whew' – said Edward to this. It was a disappointed whistle; but he soon cheered up. 'I thought I could have lent a hand in screwing old Buxton up about the settlements; but I see it's not come to that yet. Still I'll go and see the old gentleman. I'm a bit of a favourite of his, and I've no doubt I can turn him round.'

'Pray, Edward, don't go,' said Maggie. 'Frank and I are content to wait; and I'm sure we would rather not have any one speak to Mr. Buxton, upon a subject which evidently gives him so much pain; please, Edward, don't!'

'Well, well. Only I must go about this property of his. Besides, I don't mean to get into disgrace; so I shan't seem to know anything about it, if it would make him angry. I want to keep on good terms, because of the agency. So, perhaps, I shall shake my head, and think it great presumption in you, Maggie, to have thought of becoming his daughter-in-law. If I can do you no good, I may as well do myself some.'

'I hope you won't mention me at all,' she replied.

One comfort (and almost the only one arising from Edward's visit) was, that she could now often be spared to go up to the thorn-tree, and calm down her anxiety, and bring all discords into peace, under the sweet influences of nature. Mrs. Buxton had tried to teach her the force of the lovely truth, that the 'melodies of the everlasting chime'[25] may abide in the hearts of those who ply their daily task in towns, and crowded populous places; and that solitude is not needed by the faithful for them to feel the immediate presence of God; nor utter stillness of human sound necessary, before they can hear the music of His angels' footsteps: but, as yet, her soul was a young disciple; and she felt it easier to speak to Him, and come to Him for help, sitting lonely, with wild moors swelling and darkening around her, and not a creature in sight but the white specks of distant sheep, and the birds that shun the haunts of men, floating in the still mid-air.

She sometimes longed to go to Mr. Buxton and tell him how much she could sympathise with him, if his dislike to her engagement arose from his thinking her unworthy of his son. Frank's character seemed to her grand in its promise. With vehement impulses, and natural gifts, craving worthy employment, his will sat supreme over all, like a young emperor calmly seated on his throne, whose fiery generals and wise counsellors stand alike ready to obey him. But if marriage were to be made by due measurement and balance of character, and if others, with their scales, were to be the judges, what would become of all the beautiful services rendered by the loyalty of true love? Where would be the raising up of the weak by the strong? or the patient endurance? or the gracious trust of her –

> 'Whose faith is fixt and cannot move;
> She darkly feels him great and wise,
> She dwells on him with faithful eyes,
> "I cannot understand: I love."'[26]

Edward's manners and conduct caused her more real anxiety than anything else. Indeed, no other thoughtfulness could be called anxiety compared to this, His faults, she could not but perceive, were strengthening with his strength,' and growing with his growth. She could not help wondering whence he obtained the money to pay for his dress, which she thought was of a very expensive kind. She heard him also incidentally allude to 'runs up to town,' of which, at the time, neither she nor her mother had been made aware. He seemed confused when she questioned him about these, although he tried to laugh it off; and asked her how she, a country girl, cooped up among one set of people, could have any idea of the life it was necessary for a man to lead who 'had any hope of getting on in the world.' He must have acquaintances and connexions, and see something of life, and make an appearance. She was silenced, but not satisfied. Nor was she at ease with regard to his health. He looked ill, and worn; and when he was not rattling and laughing, his face fell into a shape of anxiety and uneasiness, which was new to her in it. He reminded her painfully of an old German engraving she had seen in Mrs. Buxton's portfolio, called, 'Pleasure digging a Grave;'[27] Pleasure being represented by a ghastly figure of a young man, eagerly industrious over his dismal work.

A few days after he went away, Nancy came to her in her bed-room.

'Miss Maggie,' said she, 'may I just speak a word?' But when the permission was given, she hesitated.

'It's none of my business, to be sure,' said she at last: 'only, you see, I've lived with your mother ever since she was married; and I care a deal for both you and Master Edward. And I think he drains Missus of her money; and it makes me not easy in my mind. You did not know of it, but he had his father's old watch when he was over last time but one; I thought he was of an age to have a watch, and that it was all natural. But, I reckon, he's sold it, and got that gimcrack one instead. That's perhaps natural too. Young folks like young fashions. But, this time, I think he has taken away your mother's watch; at least, I've never seen it since he went. And this morning she spoke to me about my wages. I'm sure I've never asked for them, nor troubled her; but I'll own it's now near on to twelve months since she paid me; and she was as regular as clock-work till then. Now, Miss Maggie, don't look so sorry, or I shall wish I had never spoken. Poor Missus seemed sadly put about, and said something as I did not try to hear; for I was so vexed she should think I needed apologies, and them sort of things. I'd rather live with you without wage than have her look so shame-faced as she did this morning. I don't want a bit for money, my dear; I've a deal in the bank. But I'm afeard Master Edward is spending too much, and pinching Missus.'

Maggie was very sorry indeed. Her mother had never told her anything of all this, so it was evidently a painful subject to her; and Maggie determined (after lying awake half the night) that she would write to Edward, and remonstrate with him; and that in every personal and household expense, she would be, more than ever, rigidly economical.

The full, free, natural intercourse between her lover and herself, could not fail to be checked by Mr. Buxton's aversion to the engagement. Frank came over for some time in the early autumn. He had left Cambridge, and intended to enter himself at the Temple as soon as the vacation was ended.[28] He had not been very long at home before Maggie was made aware, partly through Erminia, who had no notion of discreet silence on any point, and partly by her own observation, of the increasing estrangement between father and son. Mr. Buxton was reserved with Frank for the first time in his life; and Frank was depressed and annoyed at his father's obstinate repetition of the same sentence, in answer to all his arguments in favour of his engagement – arguments which were overwhelming to himself, and which it required an effort of patience on his part to go over and recapitulate, so obvious was the conclusion: and then to have the same answer for ever, the same words even, –

'Frank! it's no use talking. I don't approve of the engagement; and never shall.'

He would snatch up his hat, and hurry off to Maggie to be soothed. His father knew where he was gone without being told; and was jealous of her influence over the son who had long been his first and paramount object in life.

He needed not have been jealous. However angry and indignant Frank was when he went up to the moorland cottage, Maggie almost persuaded him, before half an hour had elapsed, that his father was but unreasonable from his extreme affection. Still she saw that such frequent differences would weaken the bond between father and son; and, accordingly, she urged Frank to accept an invitation into Scotland.

'You told me,' said she, 'that Mr. Buxton will have it, it is but a boy's attachment; and that when you have seen other people, you will change your mind; now do try how far you can stand the effects of absence.' She said it playfully, but he was in a humour to be vexed.

'What nonsense, Maggie! You don't care for all this delay yourself; and you take up my father's bad reasons as if you believed them.'

'I don't believe them; but still they may be true.'

'How should you like it, Maggie, if I urged you to go about and see something of society, and try if you could not find some one you liked better? It is more probable in your case than in mine; for you have never been from home, and I have been half over Europe.'

'You are very much afraid, are not you, Frank?' said she, her face bright with blushes, and her grey eyes smiling up at him. 'I have a great idea that if I could see that Harry Bish that Edward is always talking about, I should be charmed. He must wear such beautiful waistcoats! Don't you think I had better see him before our engagement is quite, quite final?'

But Frank would not smile. In fact, like all angry persons, he found fresh matter for offence in every sentence. She did not consider the engagement as quite final: thus he chose to understand her playful speech. He would not answer. She spoke again:

'Dear Frank, you are not angry with me, are you? It is nonsense to think that we are to go about the world, picking and choosing men and women, as if they were fruit, and we were to gather the best; as if there was not something in our own hearts which, if we listen to it conscientiously, will tell us at once when we have met the one of all others. There now, am I sensible? I suppose I am, for your grim features are relaxing into a smile. That's right. But now listen to this. I think your father would come round sooner, if he were not irritated every day by the knowledge of your visits to me. If you went away, he would know that we should write to each other, yet he would forget the exact time when; but now he knows as well as I do where you are when you are up here; and I fancy, from what Erminia says, it makes him angry the whole time you are away.'

Frank was silent. At last he said: 'It is rather provoking to be obliged to acknowledge that there is some truth in what you say. But even if I would, I am not sure that I could go. My father does not speak to me about his affairs, as he used to do; so I was rather surprised yesterday to hear him say to Erminia (though I'm sure he meant the information for me), that he had engaged an agent.'

'Then there will be the less occasion for you to be at home. He won't want your help in his accounts.'

'I've given him little enough of that. I have long wanted him to have somebody to look after his affairs. They are very complicated, and he is very careless. But I believe my signature will be wanted for some new leases; at least he told me so.'

'That need not take you long,' said Maggie.

'Not the mere signing. But I want to know something more about the property, and the proposed tenants. I believe this Mr. Henry that my father has engaged, is a very hard sort of man. He is what is called scrupulously honest and honourable; but I fear a little too much inclined to drive hard bargains for his client. Now I want to be convinced to the contrary, if I can, before I leave my father in his hands. So, you cruel judge, you won't transport me yet, will you?'

'No,' said Maggie, over-joyed at her own decision, and blushing her delight that her reason was convinced it was right for Frank to stay a little longer.

The next day's post brought her a letter from Edward. There was not a word in it about her enquiry or remonstrance; it might never have been written, or never received; but a few hurried anxious lines, asking her to write by return of post, and say if it was really true that Mr. Buxton had engaged an agent. 'It's a confounded shabby trick if he has, after what he said to me long ago. I cannot tell you how much I depend on your complying with my request. Once more, *write directly*. If Nancy cannot take the letter to the post, run down to Combehurst with it yourself. I must have an answer to-morrow, and every particular as to who, – when to be appointed, &c. But I can't believe the report to be true.'

Maggie asked Frank if she might name what he had told her the day before to her brother. He said: –

'Oh, yes, certainly, if he cares to know. Of course, you will not say anything about my own opinion of Mr. Henry. He is coming to-morrow, and I shall be able to judge how far I am right.'

CHAPTER VII.

THE next day Mr. Henry came. He was a quiet, stern-looking man, of considerable intelligence and refinement, and so much taste for music as to charm Erminia, who had rather dreaded his visit. But all the amenities of life were put aside when he entered Mr. Buxton's sanctum – his 'office,' as he called the room where he received his tenants and business-people. Frank thought Mr. Henry was scarce commonly civil in the open evidence of his surprise and contempt for the habits, of which the disorderly books and ledgers were but too visible signs. Mr. Buxton himself felt more like a school-boy, bringing up an imperfect lesson, than he had ever done since he was thirteen.

'The only wonder, my good sir, is that you have any property left; that you have not been cheated out of every farthing.'

'I'll answer for it,' said Mr. Buxton, in reply, 'that you'll not find any cheating has been going on. They dared not, sir; they know I should make an example of the first rogue I found out.'

Mr. Henry lifted up his eyebrows, but did not speak.

'Besides, sir, most of these men have lived for generations under the Buxtons. I'd give you my life, they would not cheat me.'

Mr. Henry coldly said:

'I imagine a close examination of these books by some accountant will be the best proof of the honesty of these said tenants. If you will allow me, I will write to a clever fellow I know, and desire him to come down and try and regulate this mass of papers.'

'Anything – anything you like,' said Mr. Buxton, only too glad to escape from the lawyer's cold, contemptuous way of treating the subject.

The accountant came; and he and Mr. Henry were deeply engaged in the office for several days. Mr. Buxton was bewildered by the questions they asked him. Mr. Henry examined him in the worrying way in which an unwilling witness is made to give evidence. Many a time and oft did he heartily wish he had gone on in the old course to the end of his life, instead of putting himself into an agent's hands; but he comforted himself by thinking that, at any rate, they would be convinced he had never allowed himself to be cheated or imposed upon, although he did not make any parade of exactitude.

What was his dismay when, one morning, Mr. Henry sent to request his presence, and, with a cold, clear voice, read aloud an admirably drawn up statement, informing the poor landlord of the defalcations, nay more, the impositions of those whom he had trusted. If he had been alone, he would have burst into tears, to find how his confidence had been abused. But as it was, he became passionately angry.

'I'll prosecute them, sir. Not a man shall escape. I'll make them pay back every farthing, I will. And damages, too. Crayston, did you say, sir? Was that one of the names? Why, that is the very Crayston who was bailiff under my father for years. The scoundrel! And I set him up in my best farm when he married. And he's been swindling me, has he?'

Mr. Henry ran over the items of the account, – '421*l*. 13*s*. 4 3/4*d*. Part of this I fear we cannot recover –'

He was going on, but Mr. Buxton broke in: 'But I will recover it. I'll have every farthing of it. I'll go to law with the viper. I don't care for money, but I hate ingratitude.'

'If you like, I will take counsel's opinion on the case,' said Mr. Henry, coolly.

'Take anything you please, sir. Why, this Crayston was the first man that set me on a horse, – and to think of his cheating me!'

A few days after this conversation, Frank came on his usual visit to Maggie.

'Can you come up to the thorn-tree, dearest?' said he. 'It is a lovely day, and I want the solace of a quiet hour's talk with you.'

So they went, and sat in silence some time, looking at the calm and still blue air about the summits of the hills, where never tumult of the world came to disturb the peace, and the quiet of whose heights was never broken by the loud passionate cries of men.

'I am glad you like my thorn-tree,' said Maggie.

'I like the view from it. The thought of the solitude which must be among the hollows of those hills pleases me particularly to-day. Oh, Maggie! it is one of the times when I get depressed about men and the world. We have had such sorrow, and such revelations, and remorse, and passion at home to-day. Crayston (my father's old tenant) has come over. It seems, – I am afraid there is no doubt of it, – he has been peculating to a large amount. My father has been too careless, and has placed his dependants in great temptation; and Crayston – he is an old man, with a large extravagant family – has yielded. He has been served with notice of my father's intention to prosecute him; and came over to confess all, and ask for forgiveness, and time to pay back what he could. A month ago, my father would have listened to him, I think; but now, he is stung by Mr. Henry's sayings, and gave way to a furious passion. It has been a most distressing morning. The worst side of everybody seems to have come out. Even Crayston, with all his penitence and appearance of candour, had to be questioned closely by Mr. Henry before he would tell the whole truth. Good God! that money should have such power to corrupt men. It was all for money, and money's worth, that this degradation has taken place. As for Mr. Henry, to save his client money, and to protect money, he does not care, – he does not even perceive, – how he induces deterioration of character. He has been encouraging my father in measures which I cannot call anything but vindictive. Crayston is to be made an example of, they say. As if my father had not half the sin on his own head! As if he had rightly discharged his duties as a rich man! Money was as dross to him; but he ought to have remembered how it might be as life itself to many, and be craved after, and coveted, till the black longing got the better of principle, as it has done with this poor Crayston. They say the man was once so truthful, and now his self-respect is gone; and he has evidently lost the very nature of truth. I dread riches. I dread the responsibility of them. At any rate, I wish I had begun life as a poor boy, and worked my way up to competence. Then I could understand and remember the temptations of poverty. I am afraid of my own heart becoming hardened as my father's is. You have no notion of his passionate severity to-day, Maggie! It was quite a new thing even to me!'

'It will only be for a short time,' said she. 'He must be much grieved about this man.'

'If I thought I could ever grow as hard and indifferent to the abject entreaties of a criminal as my father has been this morning, – one whom he has helped to make, too, – I would go off to Australia at once. Indeed, Maggie, I think it would be the best thing we could do. My heart aches about the mysterious corruptions and evils of an old state of society such as we have in England. – What do you say, Maggie? Would you go?'

She was silent, – thinking.

'I would go with you directly, if it were right,' said she, at last. 'But would it be? I think it would be rather cowardly. I feel what you say; but don't you think it would be braver to stay, and endure much depression and anxiety of mind, for the sake of the good those always can do who see evils clearly. I am speaking all this time as if neither you nor I had any home duties, but were free to do as we liked.'

'What can you or I do? We are less than drops in the ocean, as far as our influence can go to re-model a nation?'

'As for that,' said Maggie, laughing, 'I can't remodel Nancy's old-fashioned ways; so I've never yet planned how to remodel a nation.'

'Then what did you mean by the good those always can do who see evils clearly? The evils I see are those of a nation whose god is money.'

'That is just because you have come away from a distressing scene. To-morrow you will hear or read of some heroic action meeting with a nation's sympathy, and you will rejoice and be proud of your country.'

'Still I shall feel the evils of her complex state of society keenly; and where is the good I can do?'

'Oh! I can't tell in a minute. But cannot you bravely face these evils, and learn their nature and causes; and then has God given you no powers to apply to the discovery of their remedy? Dear Frank, think! It may be very little you can do, – and you may never see the effect of it, any more than the widow saw the world-wide effect of her mite.[29] Then, if all the good and thoughtful men run away from us to some new country, what are we to do with our poor, dear Old England?'

'Oh, you must run away with the good thoughtful men – (I mean to consider that as a compliment to myself, Maggie!). Will you let me wish I had been born poor, if I am to stay in England? I should not then be liable to this fault into which I see the rich men fall, of forgetting the trials of the poor.'

'I am not sure whether, if you had been poor, you might not have fallen into an exactly parallel fault, and forgotten the trials of the rich. It is so difficult to understand the errors into which their position makes all men liable to fall. Do you remember a story in "Evenings at Home," called the Transmigrations of Indra?[30] Well! when I was a child, I used to wish I might be transmigrated (is that the right word?) into an American slave-owner for a little while, just that I might understand how he must suffer, and be sorely puzzled, and pray and long to be freed from his odious wealth, till at last he grew hardened to its nature; – and since then, I have wished to be the Emperor of Russia, for the same reason, Ah! you may laugh; but that is only because I have not explained myself properly.'

'I was only smiling to think how ambitious any one might suppose you were who did not know you.'

'I don't see any ambition in it – I don't think of the station – I only want sorely to see the "What's resisted" of Burns, in order that I may have more charity for those who seem to me to have been the cause of such infinite woe and misery.'

> '"What's done we partly may compute;
> But know not what's resisted,"'[31]

repeated Frank, musingly. After some time he began again:

'But, Maggie, I don't give up this wish of mine to go to Australia, – Canada, if you like it better, – anywhere where there is a newer and purer state of society.'

'The great objection seems to be your duty, as an only child, to your father. It is different to the case of one out of a large family.'

'I wish I were one in twenty, then I might marry where I liked to-morrow.'

'It would take two people's consent to such a rapid measure,' said Maggie, laughing. 'But now I am going to wish a wish, which it won't require a fairy godmother to gratify. Look, Frank, do you see in the middle of that dark brown purple streak of moor a yellow gleam of light? It is a pond, I think, that at this time of the year catches a slanting beam of the sun. It can't be very far off. I have wished to go to it every autumn. Will you go with me now? We shall have time before tea.'

Frank's dissatisfaction with the stern measures that, urged on by Mr. Henry, his father took against all who had imposed upon his carelessness as a landlord, increased rather than diminished. He spoke warmly to him on the subject, but without avail. He remonstrated with Mr. Henry, and told him how he felt that, had his father controlled his careless nature, and been an exact, vigilant landlord, these tenantry would never have had the great temptation to do him wrong; and that therefore he considered some allowance should be made for them, and some opportunity given them to redeem their characters, which would be blasted and hardened for ever by the publicity of a law-suit. But Mr. Henry only raised his eyebrows and made answer:

'I like to see these notions in a young man, sir. I had them myself at your age. I believe I had great ideas then, on the subject of temptation and the force of circumstances; and was as Quixotic as any one about reforming rogues. But my experience has convinced me that roguery is innate. Nothing but outward force can control it, and keep it within bounds. The terrors of the law must be that outward force. I admire your kindness of heart; and in three-and-twenty we do not look for the wisdom and experience of forty or fifty.'

Frank was indignant at being set aside as an unripe youth. He disapproved so strongly of all these measures, and of so much that was now going on at home under Mr. Henry's influence, that he determined to pay his long promised visit to Scotland; and Maggie, sad at heart to see how he was suffering, encouraged him in his determination.

CHAPTER VIII.

AFTER he was gone, there came a November of the most dreary and characteristic kind. There was incessant rain, and closing-in mists, without a gleam of sunshine to light up the drops of water, and make the wet stems and branches of the trees glisten. Every colour seemed dimmed and darkened; and the crisp autumnal glory of leaves fell soddened to the ground. The latest flowers rotted away without ever coming to their bloom; and it looked as if the heavy monotonous sky had drawn closer and closer, and shut in the little moorland cottage as with a shroud. In doors, things were no more cheerful. Maggie saw that her mother was depressed, and she thought that Edward's extravagance must be the occasion. Oftentimes she wondered how far she might speak on the subject; and once or twice she drew near it in conversation; but her mother winced away, and Maggie could not as yet see any decided good to be gained from encountering such pain. To herself it would have been a relief to have known the truth, – the worst, as far as her mother knew it; but she was not in the habit of thinking of herself. She only tried, by long tender attention, to cheer and comfort her mother; and she and Nancy strove in every way to reduce the household expenditure, for there was little ready money to meet it. Maggie wrote regularly to Edward; but since the note inquiring about the agency, she had never heard from him. Whether her mother received letters she did not know; but at any rate she did not express anxiety, though her looks and manner betrayed that she was ill at ease. It was almost a relief to Maggie when some change was given to her thoughts by Nancy's becoming ill. The damp gloomy weather brought on some kind of rheumatic attack, which obliged the old servant to keep her bed. Formerly, in such an emergency, they would have engaged some cottager's wife to come and do the house-work; but now it seemed tacitly understood that they could not afford it. Even when Nancy grew worse, and required attendance in the night, Maggie still persisted in her daily occupations. She was wise enough to rest when and how she could; and, with a little forethought, she hoped to be able to go through this weary time without any bad effect. One morning (it was on the second of December; and even the change of name in the month, although it brought no change of circumstances or weather, was a relief, – December brought glad tidings even in its very name), one morning, dim and dreary, Maggie had looked at the clock on leaving Nancy's room, and finding it was not yet half-past five, and knowing that her mother and Nancy were both asleep, she determined to lie down and rest for an hour before getting up to light the fires. She did not mean to go to sleep; but she was tired out, and fell into a sound slumber. When she awoke it was with a start. It was still dark; but she had a clear idea of being wakened by some distinct, rattling noise. There it was once more – against the window, like a shower of shot. She went to the lattice, and opened it to look out. She had that strange consciousness, not to be described, of the near neighbourhood of some human creature, although she neither saw nor heard any one for the first instant. Then Edward spoke in a hoarse whisper, right below the window, standing on the flower-beds.

'Maggie! Maggie! Come down and let me in. For your life, don't make any noise. No one must know.'

Maggie turned sick. Something was wrong, evidently; and she was weak and weary. However, she stole down the old creaking stairs, and undid the heavy bolt, and let her brother in. She felt that his dress was quite wet, and she led him, with cautious steps, into the kitchen, and shut the door, and stirred the fire, before she spoke. He sank into a chair, as if worn out with fatigue. She stood, expecting some explanation. But when she saw he could not speak, she hastened to make him a cup of tea; and, stooping down, took off his wet boots, and helped him off with his coat, and brought her own plaid to wrap round him. All this time her heart sunk lower and lower. He allowed her to do what she liked, as if he were an automaton; his head and his arms hung loosely down, and his eyes were fixed, in a glaring way, on the fire. When she brought him some tea, he spoke for the first time; she could not hear what he said till he repeated it, so husky was his voice.

'Have you no brandy?'

She had the key of the little wine-cellar, and fetched up some. But as she took a tea-spoon to measure it out, he tremblingly clutched at the bottle, and shook down a quantity into the empty tea-cup, and drank it off at one gulp. He fell back again in his chair; but in a few minutes he roused himself, and seemed stronger.

'Edward, dear Edward, what is the matter?' said Maggie, at last; for he got up, and was staggering towards the outer door, as if he were going once more into the rain, and dismal morning-twilight.

He looked at her fiercely, as she laid her hand on his arm.

'Confound you! Don't touch me. I'll not be kept here, to be caught and hung!'

For an instant she thought he was mad.

'Caught and hung!' she echoed. 'My poor Edward! what do you mean?'

He sat down suddenly on a chair, close by him, and covered his face with his hands. When he spoke, his voice was feeble and imploring.

'The police are after me, Maggie! What must I do? Oh! can you hide me? Can you save me?'

He looked wild, like a hunted creature. Maggie stood aghast. He went on:

'My mother! – Nancy! Where are they? I was wet through and starving, and I came here. Don't let them take me, Maggie, 'till I'm stronger, and can give battle.'

'Oh! Edward! Edward! What are you saying?' said Maggie, sitting down on the dresser, in absolute, bewildered despair. 'What have you done?'

'I hardly know. I'm in a horrid dream, I see you think I'm mad; I wish I were. Won't Nancy come down soon? You must hide me.'

'Poor Nancy is ill in bed!' said Maggie.

'Thank God,' said he. 'There's one less. But my mother will be up soon, will she not?'

'Not yet,' replied Maggie. 'Edward, dear, do try and tell me what you have done. Why should the police be after you?'

'Why, Maggie,' said he with a kind of forced, unnatural laugh, 'they say I've forged.'

'And have you?' asked Maggie, in a still, low tone of quiet agony.

He did not answer for some time, but sat, looking on the floor with unwinking eyes. At last he said, as if speaking to himself: –

'If I have, it's no more than others have done before, and never been found out. I was but borrowing money. I meant to repay it. If I had asked Mr. Buxton, he would have lent it me.'

'Mr. Buxton!' said Maggie.

'Yes!' answered he, looking sharply and suddenly up at her. 'Your future father-in-law. My father's old friend. It is he that is hunting me to death! No need to look so white and horror-struck, Maggie! It's the way of the world, as I might have known, if I had not been a blind fool.'

'Mr. Buxton!' she whispered, faintly.

'Oh, Maggie!' said he, suddenly throwing himself at her feet, 'save me! You can do it. Write to Frank, and make him induce his father to let me off. I came to see you, my sweet, merciful sister! I knew you would save me. Good God! What noise is that? There are steps in the yard!'

And before she could speak, he had rushed into the little china closet, which opened out of the parlour, and crouched down in the darkness. It was only the man who brought their morning's supply of milk from a neighbouring farm. But when Maggie opened the kitchen door, she saw how the cold, pale light of a winter's day had filled the air.

'You're late with your shutters to-day, miss,' said the man. 'I hope Nancy has not been giving you all a bad night. Says I to Thomas, who came with me to the gate, "It's many a year since I saw them parlour shutters barred up at half-past eight."'

Maggie went, as soon as he was gone, and opened all the low windows, in order that they might look as usual. She wondered at her own outward composure, while she felt so dead and sick at heart. Her mother would soon get up; must she be told? Edward spoke to her now and then from his hiding-place. He dared not go back into the kitchen, into which the few neighbours they had were apt to come, on their morning's way to Combehurst, to ask if they could do any errands there for Mrs. Browne or Nancy. Perhaps a quarter of an hour or so had elapsed since the first alarm, when, as Maggie was trying to light the parlour fire, in order that the doctor, when he came, might find all as usual, she heard the click of the garden gate, and a man's step coming along the walk. She ran up stairs to wash away the traces of the tears which had been streaming down her face as she went about her work, before she opened the door. There, against the watery light of the rainy day without, stood Mr. Buxton. He hardly spoke to her, but pushed past her, and entered the parlour. He sat down, looking as if he did not know what he was doing. Maggie tried to keep down her shivering alarm. It was long since she had seen him; and the old idea of his kind, genial disposition, had been sadly disturbed by what she had heard from Frank, of his severe proceedings against his unworthy tenantry; and now, if he was setting the police in search of Edward, he was indeed to be dreaded; and with Edward so close at hand, within earshot! If the china fell! He would suspect nothing from that; it would only be her own terror. If her mother came down! But, with all these thoughts, she was very still, outwardly, as she sat waiting for him to speak.

'Have you heard from your brother lately?' asked he, looking up in an angry and disturbed manner. 'But I'll answer for it he has not been writing home for some time. He could not, with the guilt he has had on his mind. I'll not believe in gratitude again. There perhaps was such a thing once; but now-a-days the more you do for a person, the surer they are to turn against you, and cheat you. Now, don't go white and pale. I know you're a good girl in the main; and I've been lying awake all night, and I've a deal to say to you. That scoundrel of a brother of yours!'

Maggie could not ask (as would have been natural, if she had been ignorant) what Edward had done. She knew too well. But Mr. Buxton was too full of his own thoughts and feelings to notice her much.

'Do you know he has been like the rest? Do you know he has been cheating me – forging my name? I don't know what besides. It's well for him that they've altered the laws, and he can't be hung for it' (a dead heavy weight was removed from Maggie's mind), 'but Mr. Henry is going to transport him. It's worse than Crayston. Crayston only ploughed up the turf, and did not pay rent, and sold the timber, thinking I should never miss it. But your brother has gone and forged my name. He had received all the purchase-money, while he only gave me half, and said the rest was to come afterwards. And the ungrateful scoundrel has gone and given a forged receipt! You might have knocked me down with a straw when Mr. Henry told me about it all last night. 'Never talk to me of virtue and such humbug again,' I said, 'I'll never believe in them. Every one is for what he can get.' However, Mr.

Henry wrote to the superintendent of police at Woodchester; and has gone over himself this morning to see after it. But to think of your father having such a son!'

'Oh, my poor father!' sobbed out Maggie. 'How glad I am you are dead before this disgrace came upon us!'

'You may well say disgrace. You're a good girl yourself, Maggie. I have always said that. How Edward has turned out as he has done, I cannot conceive. But now, Maggie, I've something to say to you.' He moved uneasily about, as if he did not know how to begin. Maggie was standing leaning her head against the chimney-piece, longing for her visitor to go, dreading the next minute, and wishing to shrink into some dark corner of oblivion where she might forget all for a time, till she regained a small portion of the bodily strength that had been sorely tried of late. Mr. Buxton saw her white look of anguish, and read it in part, but not wholly. He was too intent on what he was going to say.

'I've been lying awake all night, thinking. You see the disgrace it is to you, though you are innocent; and I'm sure you can't think of involving Frank in it.'

Maggie went to the little sofa, and, kneeling down by it, hid her face in the cushions. He did not go on, for he thought she was not listening to him. At last he said,

'Come now, be a sensible girl, and face it out. I've a plan to propose.'

'I hear,' said she, in a dull veiled voice.

'Why, you know how against this engagement I have always been. Frank is but three-and-twenty, and does not know his own mind, as I tell him. Besides, he might marry any one he chose.'

'He has chosen me,' murmured Maggie.

'Of course, of course. But you'll not think of keeping him to it, after what has passed. You would not have such a fine fellow as Frank pointed at as the brother-in-law of a forger, would you? It was far from what I wished for him before; but now! Why you're glad your father is dead, rather than he should have lived to see this day; and rightly too, I think. And you'll not go and disgrace Frank. – From what Mr. Henry hears, Edward has been a discredit to you in many ways. Mr. Henry was at Woodchester yesterday, and he says if Edward has been fairly entered as an attorney, his name may be struck off the Rolls for many a thing he has done. Think of my Frank having his bright name tarnished by any connexion with such a man! Mr. Henry says, even in a court of law what has come out about Edward would be excuse enough for a breach of promise of marriage.'[32]

Maggie lifted up her wan face; the pupils of her eyes were dilated, her lips were dead white. She looked straight at Mr. Buxton with indignant impatience –

'Mr. Henry! Mr. Henry! What has Mr. Henry to do with me?'

Mr. Buxton was staggered by the wild, imperious look, so new upon her mild, sweet face. But he was resolute for Frank's sake, and returned to the charge after a moment's pause.

'Mr. Henry is a good friend of mine, who has my interest at heart. He has known what a subject of regret your engagement has been to me; though really my repugnance to it was without cause formerly, compared to what it is now. Now be reasonable, my dear. I'm willing to do something for you if you will do something for me. You must see what a stop this sad affair has put to any thoughts between you and Frank. And you must see what cause I have to wish to punish Edward for his ungrateful behaviour, to say nothing of the forgery. Well now! I don't know what Mr. Henry will say to me, but I have thought of this. If you'll write a letter to Frank, just saying distinctly that, for reasons which must for ever remain a secret –'

'Remain a secret from Frank?' said Maggie, again lifting up her head. 'Why?'

'Why? my dear! You startle me with that manner of yours – just let me finish out my sentence. If you'll say that, for reasons which must for ever remain a secret, you decidedly and unchangeably give up all connexion, all engagement with him (which, in fact, Edward's conduct has as good as put an end to), I'll go over to Woodchester and tell Mr. Henry and the police that they need not make further search after Edward, for that I won't appear against him. You can save your brother; and you'll do yourself no harm by writing this letter, for of course you see your engagement is broken off. For you never would wish to disgrace Frank.'

He paused, anxiously awaiting her reply. She did not speak.

'I'm sure, if I appear against him, he is as good as transported,' he put in, after a while.

Just at this time there was a little sound of displaced china in the closet. Mr. Buxton did not attend to it, but Maggie heard it. She got up, and stood quite calm before Mr. Buxton.

'You must go,' said she. 'I know you; and I know you are not aware of the cruel way in which you have spoken to me, while asking me to give up the very hope and marrow of my life, –' she could not go on for a moment; she was choked up with anguish.

'It was the truth, Maggie,' said he, somewhat abashed.

'It was the truth that made the cruelty of it. But you did not mean to speak cruelly to me, I know. Only it is hard all at once to be called upon to face the shame and blasted character of one who was once an innocent child at the same father's knee.'

'I may have spoken too plainly,' said Mr. Buxton, 'but it was necessary to set the plain truth before you, for my son's sake. You will write the letter I ask?'

Her look was wandering and uncertain. Her attention was distracted by sounds which to him had no meaning; and her judgment she felt was wavering and disturbed.

'I cannot tell. Give me time to think; you will do that, I'm sure. Go now, and leave me alone. If it is right, God will give me strength to do it, and perhaps He will comfort me in my desolation. But I do not know – I cannot tell. I must have time to think. Go now, if you please, sir,' said she, imploringly.

'I am sure you will see it is a right thing I ask of you,' he persisted.

'Go now,' she repeated.

'Very well. In two hours, I will come back again; for your sake, time is precious. Even while we speak he may be arrested. At eleven, I will come back.'

He went away, leaving her sick and dizzy with the effort to be calm and collected enough to think. She had forgotten for the moment how near Edward was; and started when she saw the closet-door open, and his face put out.

'Is he gone? I thought he never would go. What a time you kept him, Maggie! I was so afraid, once, you might sit down to write the letter in this room; and then I knew he would stop and worry you with interruptions and advice, so that it would never be ended; and my back was almost broken. But you sent him off famously. Why, Maggie! Maggie! – you're not going to faint, surely!'

His sudden burst out of a whisper into a loud exclamation of surprise, made her rally; but she could not stand. She tried to smile, for he really looked frightened.

'I have been sitting up for many nights, – and now this sorrow!' Her smile died away into a wailing, feeble cry.

'Well, well! it's over now, you see. I was frightened enough myself this morning, I own; and then you were brave and kind. But I knew you could save me, all along.'

At this moment the door opened, and Mrs. Browne came in.

'Why, Edward, dear! who would have thought of seeing you! This is good of you; what a pleasant surprise! I often said, you might come over for a day from Woodchester. What's the matter, Maggie, you look so fagged? She's losing all her beauty, is not she, Edward? Where's breakfast? I thought I should find all ready. What's the matter? Why don't you speak?' said she, growing anxious at their silence. Maggie left the explanation to Edward.

'Mother,' said he, 'I've been rather a naughty boy, and got into some trouble; but Maggie is going to help me out of it, like a good sister.'

'What is it?' said Mrs. Browne, looking bewildered and uneasy.

'Oh – I took a little liberty with our friend Mr. Buxton's name; and wrote it down to a receipt – that was all.'

Mrs. Browne's face showed that the light came but slowly into her mind.

'But that's forgery – is not it?' asked she at length, in terror.

'People call it so,' said Edward; 'I call it borrowing from an old friend, who was always willing to lend.'

'Does he know? – is he angry?' asked Mrs. Browne.

'Yes, he knows; and he blusters a deal. He was working himself up grandly at first. Maggie! I was getting rarely frightened, I can tell you.'

'Has he been here?' said Mrs. Browne, in bewildered fright.

'Oh, yes! he and Maggie have been having a long talk, while I was hid in the china-closet. I would not go over that half-hour again for any money. However, he and Maggie came to terms, at last.'

'No, Edward, we did not!' said Maggie, in a low quivering voice.

'Very nearly. She's to give up her engagement, and then he will let me off.'

'Do you mean that Maggie is to give up her engagement to Mr. Frank Buxton?' asked his mother.'

'Yes, It would never have come to anything, one might see that. Old Buxton would have held out against it till doomsday. And sooner or later, Frank would have grown weary. If Maggie had had any spirit, she might have worked him up to marry her before now; and then I should have been spared even this fright, for they would never have set the police after Mrs. Frank Buxton's brother.'

'Why, dearest Edward, the police are not after you, are they?' said Mrs. Browne, for the first time alive to the urgency of the case.

'I believe they are, though,' said Edward. 'But after what Mr. Buxton promised this morning, it does not signify.'

'He did not promise anything,' said Maggie.

Edward turned sharply to her, and looked at her. Then he went and took hold of her wrists with no gentle grasp, and spoke to her through his set teeth.

'What do you mean, Maggie – what do you mean?' (giving her a little shake). 'Do you mean that you'll stick to your lover, through thick and thin, and leave your brother to be transported? Speak, can't you?'

She looked up at him, and tried to speak, but no words came out of her dry throat. At last she made a strong effort.

'You must give me time to think. I will do what is right, by God's help.'

'As if it was not right, – and such cant, – to save your brother,' said he, throwing her hands away in a passionate manner.

'I must be alone,' said Maggie, rising, and trying to stand steadily in the reeling room. She heard her mother and Edward speaking, but their words gave her no meaning, and she went out. She was leaving the house by the kitchen door, when she remembered Nancy, left alone and helpless all through this long morning; and, ill as she could endure detention from the solitude she longed to seek, she patiently fulfilled her small duties, and sought out some breakfast for the poor old woman.

When she carried it upstairs, Nancy said:

'There's something up. You've trouble in your sweet face, my darling. Never mind telling me, – only don't sob so. I'll pray for you, bairn, and God will help you.'

'Thank you, Nancy. Do!' and she left the room.

CHAPTER IX.

WHEN she opened the kitchen-door, there was the same small, mizzling rain that had obscured the light for weeks, and now it seemed to obscure hope. She clambered slowly (for indeed she was very feeble,) up the Fell Lane, and threw herself under the leafless thorn, every small branch and twig of which was loaded with rain-drops. She did not see the well-beloved and familiar landscape, for her tears; and did not miss the hills in the distance that were hidden behind the rain-clouds, and sweeping showers.

Mrs. Browne and Edward sat over the fire. He told her his own story: making the temptation, strong; the crime a mere trifling, venial error, which he had been led into, through his idea that he was to become Mr. Buxton's agent.

'But if it is only that,' said Mrs. Browne, 'surely Mr. Buxton will not think of going to law with you?'

'It's not merely going to law that he will think of, but trying and transporting me. That Henry he has got for his agent is as sharp as a needle, and as hard as a nether mill-stone.[33] And the fellow has obtained such a hold over Mr. Buxton, that he dare but do what he tells him. I can't imagine how he had so much free-will left as to come with his proposal to Maggie; unless, indeed, Henry knows of it, – or, what is most likely of all, has put him up to it. Between them, they have given that poor fool Crayston a pretty dose of it; and I should have come yet worse off, if it had not been for Maggie. Let me get clear this time, and I will keep to windward of the law for the future.'

'If we sold the cottage we could repay it,' said Mrs. Browne, meditating. 'Maggie and I could live on very little. But you see this property is held in trust for you two.'

'Nay mother! you must not talk of repaying it. Depend upon it he will be so glad to have Frank free from his engagement, that he won't think of asking for the money. And if Mr. Henry says anything about it, we can tell him it's not half the damages they would have had to have given Maggie, if Frank had been extricated in any other way.[34] I wish she would come back; I would prime her a little as to what to say. Keep a look out, mother, lest Mr. Buxton return and find me here.'

'I wish Maggie would come in too,' said Mrs. Browne. 'I'm afraid she'll catch cold this damp day, and then I shall have two to nurse. You think she'll give it up, don't you, Edward? If she does not, I'm afraid of harm coming to you. Had you not better keep out of the way?'

'It's fine talking. Where am I to go out of sight of the police, this wet day: without a shilling in the world, too? If you'll give me some money I'll be off fast enough, and make assurance doubly sure.[35] I'm not much afraid of Maggie. She's a little yea-nay thing, and I can always bend her round to what we want. She had better take care, too,' said he, with a desperate look on his face, 'for by G— I'll make her give up all thoughts of Frank, rather than be taken and tried. Why! it's my chance for all my life; and do you think I'll have it frustrated for a girl's whim!'

'I think it's rather hard upon her too,' pleaded his mother. 'She's very fond of him; and it would have been such a good match for her.'

'Pooh! she's not nineteen yet, and has plenty of time before her to pick up somebody else; while, don't you see, if I'm caught and transported, I'm done for for life. Besides, I've a notion Frank had already begun to be tired of the affair; it would have been broken off in a month or two, without her gaining anything by it.'

'Well, if you think so,' replied Mrs. Browne. 'But I'm sorry for her. I always told her she was foolish to think so much about him; but I know she'll fret a deal if it's given up.'

'Oh! she'll soon comfort herself with thinking that she has saved me. I wish she'd come. It must be near eleven. I do wish she would come. Hark! is not that the kitchen-door?' said he, turning white, and betaking himself once more to the china-closet. He held it ajar, till he heard Maggie stepping softly and slowly across the floor. She opened the parlour-door; and stood looking in, with the strange imperceptive gaze of a sleep-walker. Then she roused herself, and saw that he was not there; so she came in a step or two, and sat down in her dripping cloak on a chair near the door.

Edward returned, bold, now there was no danger.

'Maggie!' said he, 'what have you fixed to say to Mr. Buxton?'

She sighed deeply; and then lifted up her large innocent eyes to his face.

'I cannot give up Frank,' said she, in a low, quiet voice.

Mrs. Browne threw up her hands and exclaimed in terror:

'Oh Edward, Edward! go away – I will give you all the plate I have; you can sell it – my darling, go!'

'Not till I have brought Maggie to reason,' said he, in a manner as quiet as her own; but with a subdued ferocity in it, which she saw, but which did not intimidate her.

He went up to her, and spoke below his breath.

'Maggie, we were children together, – we two, – brother and sister of one blood! Do you give me up to be put in prison, – in the hulks, – among the basest of criminals, – I don't know where, – all for the sake of your own selfish happiness?'

She trembled very much; but did not speak, or cry, or make any noise.

'You were always selfish. You always thought of yourself. But this time I did think you would have shown how different you could be. But it's self – self – paramount above all.'

'Oh, Maggie! how can you be so hard-hearted and selfish?' echoed Mrs. Browne, crying and sobbing.

'Mother!' said Maggie, 'I know that I think too often and too much of myself. But this time I thought only of Frank. He loves me; it would break his heart if I wrote as Mr. Buxton wishes, cutting our lives asunder, and giving no reason for it.'

'He loves you so!' said Edward, tauntingly, 'A man's love break his heart! You've got some pretty notions! Who told you that he loved you so desperately? How do you know it?'

'Because I love him so,' said she, in a quiet earnest voice. 'I do not know of any other reason; but that is quite sufficient to me. I believe him when he says he loves me; and I have no right to cause him the infinite – the terrible pain, which my own heart tells me he would feel, if I did what Mr. Buxton wishes me.'

Her manner was so simple and utterly truthful, that it was as quiet and fearless as a child's; her brother's fierce looks of anger had no power over her; and his blustering died away before her, into something of the frightened cowardliness he had shown in the morning. But Mrs. Browne came up to Maggie; and took her hand between both of hers, which were trembling. 'Maggie, you can save Edward. I know I have not loved you as I should have done; but I will love and comfort you for ever, if you will but write as Mr. Buxton says. Think! Perhaps Mr. Frank may not take you at your word, but may come over and see you, and all may be right, and yet Edward may be saved. It is only writing this letter; you need not stick to it.'

'No!' said Edward. 'A signature, if you can prove compulsion, is not valid. We will all prove that you write this letter under compulsion; and if Frank loves you so desperately, he won't give you up without a trial to make you change your mind.'

'No!' said Maggie, firmly. 'If I write the letter I abide by it. I will not quibble with my conscience. Edward! I will not marry, – I will go, and live near you, and come to you whenever I may, – and give up my life to you if you are sent to prison; – my mother and I will go, if need be; – I do not know yet what I can do, or cannot do, for you, but all I can, I will; – but this one thing I cannot.'

'Then I'm off!' said Edward. 'On your death-bed may you remember this hour, and how you denied your only brother's request. May you ask my forgiveness with your dying breath, and may I be there to deny it you.'

'Wait a minute!' said Maggie, springing up, rapidly. 'Edward, don't curse me with such terrible words till all is done. Mother, I implore you to keep him here. Hide him, – do what you can to conceal him. I will have one more trial.' She snatched up her bonnet, and was gone, before they had time to think or speak to arrest her.

On she flew along the Combehurst road. As she went, the tears fell like rain down her face, and she talked to herself.

'He should not have said so. No! he should not have said so. We were the only two.' But still she pressed on, over the thick, wet, brown heather. She saw Mr. Buxton coming; and she went still quicker. The rain had cleared off, and a yellow watery gleam of sunshine was struggling out. She stopped him, or he would have passed her unheeded; little expecting to meet her there.

'I wanted to see you,' said she, all at once resuming her composure, and almost assuming a dignified manner. 'You must not go down to our house; we have sorrow enough there. Come under these fir-trees, and let me speak to you.'

'I hope you have thought of what I said, and are willing to do what I asked you.'

'No!' said she. 'I have thought and thought. I did not think in a selfish spirit, though they say I did. I prayed first. I could not do that earnestly, and be selfish, I think. I cannot give up Frank. I know the disgrace; and if he, knowing all, thinks fit to give me up, I shall never say a word, but bow my head, and try and live out my appointed days quietly and cheerfully. But he is the judge, not you; nor have I any right to do what you ask me.' She stopped, because the agitation took away her breath.

He began in a cold manner: 'I am very sorry. The law must take its course. I would have saved my son from the pain of all this knowledge, and that which he will of course feel in the necessity of giving up his engagement. I would have refused to appear against your brother, shamefully ungrateful as he has been. Now, you cannot wonder that I act according to my agent's advice; and prosecute your brother as if he were a stranger.'

He turned to go away. He was so cold and determined that for a moment Maggie was timid. But she then laid her hand on his arm.

'Mr. Buxton,' said she, 'you will not do what you threaten. I know you better. Think! My father was your old friend. That claim is, perhaps, done away with by Edward's conduct. But I do not believe you can forget it always. If you did fulfil the menace you uttered just now, there would come times as you grew older, and life grew fainter and fainter before you, – quiet times of thought, when you remembered the days of your youth, and the friends you then had and knew; – you would recollect that one of them had left an only son, who had done wrong; who had sinned; sinned against you in his weakness; – and you would think then – you could not help it – how you had forgotten mercy in justice; and, as justice required he should be treated as a felon, you threw him among felons; where every glimmering of goodness was darkened for ever. Edward is, after all, more weak than wicked; – but he will become wicked if you put him in prison, and have him transported. God is merciful, – we cannot tell or think how merciful. Oh, sir, I am so sure you will be merciful, and give my brother – my poor sinning brother – a chance, that I will tell you all. I will throw myself upon your pity. Edward is even now at home, – miserable and desperate; – my mother is too much stunned to understand all our wretchedness, – for very wretched we are in our shame.'

As she spoke, the wind arose and shivered in the wiry leaves of the fir-trees, and there was a moaning sound as of some Ariel imprisoned in the thick branches[36] that, tangled over-head, made a shelter for them. Either the noise, or Mr. Buxton's fancy called up an echo to Maggie's voice – a pleading with her pleading – a sad tone of regret, distinct yet blending with her speech, and a falling, dying sound, as her voice died away in miserable suspense.

It might be that, formed as she was by Mrs. Buxton's care and love, her accents and words were such as that lady, now at rest from all sorrow, would have used; – somehow, at any rate, the thought flashed into Mr. Buxton's mind, that as Maggie spoke, his dead wife's voice was heard, imploring mercy in a clear distinct tone, though faint, as if separated from him by an infinite distance of space. At least, this is the account Mr. Buxton would have given of the manner in which the idea of his wife became present to him, and what she would have wished him to do a powerful motive in his conduct. Words of hers, long ago spoken, and merciful forgiving expressions, made use of in former days to soften him in some angry mood, were clearly remembered while Maggie spoke; and their influence was perceptible in the change of his tone, and the wavering of his manner henceforward.

'And yet you will not save Frank from being involved in your disgrace,' said he; but more as if weighing and deliberating on the case than he had ever spoken before.

'If Frank wishes it, I will quietly withdraw myself out of his sight for ever; – I give you my promise, before God, to do so. I shall not utter one word of entreaty or complaint. I will try not to wonder or feel surprise; – I will bless him in every action of his future life; – but think how different would be the disgrace he would voluntarily incur, to my poor mother's shame, when she wakens up to know what her child has done! Her very torpor about it now is more painful than words can tell.'

'What could Edward do?' asked Mr. Buxton. 'Mr. Henry won't hear of my passing over any frauds.'

'Oh, you relent!' said Maggie, taking his hand, and pressing it. 'What could he do? He could do the same, whatever it was, as you thought of his doing, if I had written that terrible letter.'

'And you'll be willing to give it up, if Frank wishes, when he knows all?' asked Mr. Buxton.

She crossed her hands and drooped her head, but answered steadily:

'Whatever Frank wishes, when he knows all, I will gladly do. I will speak the truth. I do not believe that any shame surrounding me, and not in me, will alter Frank's love one tittle.'

'We shall see,' said Mr. Buxton. 'But what I thought of Edward's doing, in case – Well, never mind!' (seeing how she shrunk back from all mention of the letter he had asked her to write) – 'was to go to America, out of the way. Then Mr. Henry would think he had escaped, and need never be told of my connivance. I think he would throw up the agency, if he were; and he's a very clever man. If Ned is in England, Mr. Henry will ferret him out. And, besides, this affair is so blown, I don't think he could return to his profession. What do you say to this, Maggie?'

'I will tell my mother. I must ask her. To me it seems most desirable. Only, I fear he is very ill; and it seems lonely; but never mind! We ought to be thankful to you for ever. I cannot tell you how I hope and trust he will live to show you what your goodness has made him.'

'But you must lose no time. If Mr. Henry traces him, I can't answer for myself. I shall have no good reason to give, as I should have had, if I could have told him that Frank and you were to be as strangers to each other. And even then I should have been afraid, he is such a determined fellow; but uncommonly clever. Stay!' said he, yielding to a sudden and inexplicable desire to see Edward, and discover if his criminality had in any way changed his outward appearance. 'I'll go with you. I can hasten things. If Edward goes, he must be off, as soon as possible, to Liverpool,[37] and leave no trace. The next packet sails the day after to-morrow. I noted it down from the *Times*.'

Maggie and he sped along the road. He spoke his thoughts aloud:

'I wonder if he will be grateful to me for this. Not that I ever mean to look for gratitude again. I mean to try, not to care for anybody but Frank. 'Govern men by outward force,' says Mr. Henry. He is an uncommonly clever man, and he says, the longer he lives, the more he is convinced of the badness of men. He always looks for it now, even in those who are the best, apparently.'

Maggie was too anxious to answer, or even to attend to him. At the top of the slope she asked him to wait while she ran down, and told the result of her conversation with him. Her mother was alone, looking white and sick. She told her that Edward had gone into the hay-loft, above the old, disused shippen.[38]

Maggie related the substance of her interview with Mr. Buxton, and his wish that Edward should go to America.

'To America!' said Mrs. Browne. 'Why that's as far as Botany Bay.[39] It's just like transporting him. I thought you'd done something for us, you looked so glad.'

'Dearest mother, it *is* something. He is not to be subjected to imprison-
ment nor trial. I must go and tell him, only I must beckon to Mr. Buxton
first. But when he comes, do show him how thankful we are for his mercy
to Edward.'

Mrs. Browne's murmurings, whatever was their meaning, were lost upon
Maggie. She ran through the court, and up the slope, with the lightness of a
fawn; for though she was tired in body to an excess she had never been
before in her life, the opening beam of hope in the dark sky made her spirit
conquer her flesh for the time.

She did not stop to speak, but turned again as soon as she had signed to
Mr. Buxton to follow her, She left the house-door open for his entrance, and
passed out again through the kitchen into the space behind, which was partly
an unenclosed yard, and partly rocky common. She ran across the little
green to the shippen, and mounted the ladder into the dimly-lighted loft.
Up in a dark corner Edward stood, with an old rake in his hand.

'I thought it was you, Maggie!' said he, heaving a deep breath of relief.
'What have you done? Have you agreed to write the letter? You've done
something for me, I see by your looks.'

'Yes! I have told Mr. Buxton all. He is waiting for you in the parlour. Oh!
I knew he could not be so hard!' She was out of breath.

'I don't understand you!' said he. You've never been such a fool as to go
and tell him where I am?'

'Yes, I have. I felt I might trust him. He has promised not to prosecute
you. The worst is, he says you must go to America. But come down, Ned,
and speak to him. You owe him thanks, and he wants to see you.'

'I can't go through a scene. I'm not up to it. Besides, are you sure he is not
entrapping me to the police? If I had a farthing of money I would not trust
him, but be off to the moors.'

'Oh, Edward! How do you think he would do anything so treacherous
and mean! I beg you not to lose time in distrust. He says himself, if Mr.
Henry comes before you are off, he does not know what will be the conse-
quence. The packet sails for America in two days. It is sad for you to have to
go. Perhaps even yet he may think of something better, though I don't know
how we can ask or expect it.'

'I don't want anything better,' replied he, 'than that I should have money
enough to carry me to America. I'm in more scrapes than this (though none
so bad) in England; and in America there's many an opening to fortune.'

He followed her down the steps while he spoke. Once in the yellow light
of the watery day, she was struck by his ghastly look. Sharp lines of suspicion
and cunning seemed to have been stamped upon his face, making it look
older by many years than his age warranted. His jaunty evening dress, all
weather-stained and dirty, added to his forlorn and disreputable appearance;
but most of all – deepest of all – was the impression she received that he was

not long for this world; and Oh! how unfit for the next! Still if time was given – if he were placed far away from temptation – she thought that her father's son might yet repent, and be saved. She took his hand, for he was hanging back as they came near the parlour-door, and led him in. She looked like some guardian angel, with her face that beamed out trust, and hope, and thankfulness. He, on the contrary, hung his head in angry, awkward shame; and half wished he had trusted to his own wits, and tried to evade the police, rather than have been forced into this interview.

His mother came to him; for she loved him all the more fondly, now he seemed degraded and friendless. She could not, or would not, comprehend the extent of his guilt; and had upbraided Mr. Buxton to the top of her bent for thinking of sending him away to America. There was a silence when he came in which was insupportable to him. He looked up with clouded eyes, that dared not meet Mr.Buxton's.

'I am here, sir, to learn what you wish me to do. Maggie says I am to go to America: if that is where you want to send me, I'm ready.'

Mr. Buxton wished himself away as heartily as Edward. Mrs. Browne's upbraidings, just when he felt that he had done a kind action, and yielded, against his judgment, to Maggie's entreaties, had made him think himself very ill used. And now here was Edward speaking in a sullen, savage kind of way, instead of showing any gratitude. The idea of Mr. Henry's stern displeasure loomed in the background.

'Yes!' said he, 'I'm glad to find you come into the idea of going to America. It's the only place for you. The sooner you can go, and the better.'

'I can't go without money,' said Edward, doggedly. 'If I had money, I need not have come here.'

'Oh, Ned! would you have gone without seeing me?' said Mrs. Browne, bursting into tears. 'Mr. Buxton, I cannot let him go to America. Look how ill he is. He'll die if you send him there.'

'Mother, don't give way so,' said Edward, kindly, taking her hand. 'I'm not ill, at least not to signify. Mr. Buxton is right: America is the only place for me. To tell the truth, even if Mr. Buxton is good enough' (he said this as if unwilling to express any word of thankfulness) 'not to prosecute me, there are others who may – and will. I'm safer out of the country. Give me money enough to get to Liverpool and pay my passage, and I'll be off this minute.'

'You shall not,' said Mrs. Browne, holding him tightly. 'You told me this morning you were led into temptation, and went wrong because you had no comfortable home, nor any one to care for you, and make you happy. It will be worse in America. You'll get wrong again, and be away from all who can help you. Or you'll die all by yourself, in some back-wood or other. Maggie! you might speak and help me – how can you stand so still, and let him go to America without a word!'

Maggie looked up bright and steadfast, as if she saw something beyond the material present. Here was the opportunity for self-sacrifice of which Mrs. Buxton had spoken to her in her childish days – the time which comes to all, but comes unheeded and unseen to those whose eyes are not trained to watching.'

'Mother! could you do without me for a time? If you could, and it would make you easier, and help Edward to –' The word on her lips died away; for it seemed to imply a reproach on one who stood in his shame among them all.

'You would go!' said Mrs. Browne, catching at the unfinished sentence. 'Oh! Maggie, that's the best thing you've ever said or done since you were born. Edward, would not you like to have Maggie with you?'

'Yes,' said he, 'well enough. It would be far better for me than going all alone; though I dare say I could make my way pretty well after a time. If she went, she might stay till I felt settled, and had made some friends, and then she could come back.'

Mr. Buxton was astonished at first by this proposal of Maggie's. He could not all at once understand the difference between what she now offered to do, and what he had urged upon her only this very morning. But as he thought about it, he perceived that what was her own she was willing to sacrifice; but that Frank's heart once given into her faithful keeping, she was answerable for it to him and to God. This light came down upon him slowly; but when he understood, he admired with almost a wondering admiration. That little timid girl brave enough to cross the ocean and go to a foreign land, if she could only help to save her brother!

'I'm sure, Maggie,' said he, turning towards her, 'you are a good, thoughtful little creature. It may be the saving of Edward – I believe it will. I think God will bless you for being so devoted.'

'The expense will be doubled,' said Edward.

'My dear boy! never mind the money. I can get it advanced upon this cottage.'

'As for that, I'll advance it,' said Mr. Buxton.

'Could we not,' said Maggie, hesitating from her want of knowledge, 'make over the furniture, papa's books, and what little plate we have, to Mr.Buxton – something like pawning them – if he would advance the requisite money? He, strange as it may seem, is the only person you can ask in this great strait.'

And so it was arranged, after some demur on Mr. Buxton's part. But Maggie kept steadily to her point as soon as she found that it was attainable; and Mrs. Browne was equally inflexible, though from a different feeling. She regarded Mr. Buxton as the cause of her son's banishment, and refused to accept of any favour from him. If there had been time, indeed, she would have preferred obtaining the money in the same manner from any one else.

Edward brightened up a little when he heard the sum could be procured; he was almost indifferent how; and, strangely callous, as Maggie thought, he even proposed to draw up a legal form of assignment. Mr. Buxton only thought of hurrying on the departure; but he could not refrain from expressing his approval and admiration of Maggie whenever he came near her. Before he went, he called her aside.

'My dear, I'm not sure if Frank can do better than marry you, after all. Mind! I've not given it as much thought as I should like. But if you come back as we plan, next autumn, and he is steady to you till then, – and Edward is going on well (if he can but keep good, he'll do, for he is very sharp – yon is a knowing paper he drew up), – why, I'll think about it. Only let Frank see a bit of the world first. I'd rather you did not tell him I've any thoughts of coming round, that he may have a fair trial; and I'll keep it from Erminia if I can, or she will let it all out to him. I shall see you to-morrow at the coach. God bless you, my girl, and keep you on the great wide sea.' He was absolutely in tears when he went away – tears of admiring regret over Maggie.

       CHAPTER X.
          ———•———

THE more Maggie thought, the more she felt sure that the impulse on which she had acted in proposing to go with her brother was right. She feared there was little hope for his character, whatever there might be for his worldly fortune, if he were thrown, in the condition of mind in which he was now, among the set of adventurous men who are continually going over to America in search of an El Dorado[40] to be discovered by their wits. She knew she had but little influence over him at present; but she would not doubt or waver in her hope that patience and love might work him right at last. She meant to get some employment – in teaching – in needlework – in a shop – no matter how humble – and be no burden to him, and make him a happy home, from which he should feel no wish to wander. Her chief anxiety was about her mother. She did not dwell more than she could help on her long absence from Frank; it was too sad, and yet too necessary. She meant to write and tell him all about herself and Edward. The only thing which she would keep for some happy future, should be the possible revelation of the proposal which Mr. Buxton had made, that she should give up her engagement as a condition of his not prosecuting Edward.

There was much sorrowful bustle in the moorland cottage that day. Erminia brought up a portion of the money Mr. Buxton was to advance, with an entreaty that Edward would not show himself out of his home; and an account of a letter from Mr. Henry, stating that the Woodchester police believed him to be in London, and that search was being made for him there.

Erminia looked very grave and pale. She gave her message to Mrs. Browne, speaking little beyond what was absolutely necessary. Then she took Maggie aside, and suddenly burst into tears.

'Maggie, darling – what is this going to America? You've always and always been sacrificing yourself to your family, and now you're setting off, nobody knows where, in some vain hope of reforming Edward. I wish he was not your brother, that I might speak of him as I should like.'

'He has been doing what is very wrong,' said Maggie. 'But you – none of you – know his good points, – nor how he has been exposed to all sorts of bad influences. I am sure; and never had the advantage of a father's training and friendship, which are so inestimable to a son. Oh! Minnie, when I remember how we two used to kneel down in the evenings at my father's knee, and say our prayers; and then listen in awe-struck silence to his earnest blessing, which grew more like a prayer for us as his life waned away; I would do anything for Edward rather than that wrestling agony of supplication should have been in vain. I think of him as the little innocent boy, whose arm was round me as if to support me in the Awful Presence, whose true name of Love we had not learned. Minnie! he has had no proper training – no training, I mean, to enable him to resist temptation; and he has been thrown into it without warning or advice. Now he knows what it is; and I must try, though I am but an unknowing girl, to warn and to strengthen him. Don't weaken my faith. Who can do right if we lose faith in them?'

'And Frank!' said Erminia, after a pause. 'Poor Frank!'

'Dear Frank!' replied Maggie, looking up, and trying to smile; but, in spite of herself, her eyes filled with tears. 'If I could have asked him, I know he would approve of what I am going to do. He would feel it to be right that I should make every effort – I don't mean,' said she, as the tears would fall down her cheeks in spite of her quivering effort at a smile, 'that I should not have liked to have seen him. But it is no use talking of what one would have liked. I am writing a long letter to him at every pause of leisure.'

'And I'm keeping you all this time,' said Erminia, getting up, yet loth to go. 'When do you intend to come back? Let us feel there is a fixed time. America! Why, it's thousands of miles away. Oh, Maggie! Maggie!'

'I shall come back the next autumn, I trust,' said Maggie, comforting her friend with many a soft caress. 'Edward will be settled then, I hope. You were longer in France, Minnie. Frank was longer away, that time he wintered in Italy with Mr. Monro.'

Erminia went slowly to the door. Then she turned, right facing Maggie.

'Maggie! tell the truth. Has my uncle been urging you to go? Because if he has, don't trust him; it is only to break off your engagement.'

'No, he has not, indeed. It was my own thought at first. Then in a moment I saw the relief it was to my mother – my poor mother! Erminia, the thought of her grief at Edward's absence is the trial; for my sake, you will come often and often, and comfort her in every way you can.'

'Yes! that I will; tell me everything I can do for you.' Kissing each other, with long lingering delay they parted.

Nancy would be informed of the cause of the commotion in the house; and when she had in some degree ascertained its nature, she wasted no time in asking further questions, but quietly got up and dressed herself; and appeared among them, weak and trembling indeed, but so calm and thoughtful, that her presence was an infinite help to Maggie.

When day closed in, Edward stole down to the house once more. He was haggard enough to have been in anxiety and concealment for a month. But when his body was refreshed, his spirits rose in a way inconceivable to Maggie. The Spaniards who went out with Pizarro[41] were not lured on by more fantastic notions of the wealth to be acquired in the New World than he was. He dwelt on these visions in so brisk and vivid a manner, that he even made his mother cease her weary weeping (which had lasted the livelong day, despite all Maggie's efforts), to look up and listen to him.

'I'll answer for it,' said he: 'before long I'll be an American judge, with miles of cotton plantations.'

'But in America,' sighed out his mother.

'Never mind, mother!' said he, with a tenderness which made Maggie's heart glad. 'If you won't come over to America to me, why I'll sell them all, and come back to live in England. People will forget the scrapes that the rich American got into in his youth.'

'You can pay back Mr. Buxton then,' said his mother.

'Oh, yes – of course,' replied he, as if falling into a new and trivial idea.

Thus the evening whiled away. The mother and son sat, hand in hand, before the little glinting blazing parlour fire, with the unlighted candles on the table behind. Maggie, busy in preparations, passed softly in and out. And when all was done that could be done before going to Liverpool, where she hoped to have two days to prepare their outfit more completely, she stole back to her mother's side. But her thoughts would wander off to Frank, 'working his way south through all the hunting-counties,'[42] as he had written her word. If she had not urged his absence, he would have been here for her to see his noble face once more; but then, perhaps, she might never have had the strength to go.

Late, late in the night, they separated. Maggie could not rest, and stole into her mother's room. Mrs. Browne had cried herself to sleep, like a child. Maggie stood and looked at her face, and then knelt down by the bed and prayed. When she arose, she saw that her mother was awake, and had been looking at her.

'Maggie dear! you're a good girl, and I think God will hear your prayer whatever it was for. I cannot tell you what a relief it is to me to think you're going with him. It would have broken my heart else. If I've sometimes not been as kind as I might have been, I ask your forgiveness, now, my dear; and I bless you and thank you for going out with him; for I'm sure he's not well and strong, and will need somebody to take care of him. And you shan't lose with Mr. Frank, for as sure as I see him I'll tell him what a good daughter and sister you've been; and I shall say, for all he is so rich, I think he may look long before he finds a wife for him like our Maggie. I do wish Ned had got that new great coat he says he left behind him at Woodchester.'

Her mind reverted to her darling son; but Maggie took her short slumber by her mother's side, with her mother's arms around her; and awoke and felt that her sleep had been blessed. At the coach-office the next morning they met Mr. Buxton, all ready as if for a journey, but glancing about him as if in fear of some coming enemy.

'I'm going with you to Liverpool,' said he. 'Don't make any ado about it, please. I shall like to see you off; and I may be of some use to you, and Erminia begged it of me; and, besides, it will keep me out of Mr. Henry's way for a little time, and I'm afraid he will find it all out, and think me very weak; but you see he made me too hard upon Crayston, so I may take it out in a little soft-heartedness towards the son of an old friend.'

Just at this moment Erminia came running through the white morning mist all glowing with haste.

'Maggie,' said she, 'I'm come to take care of your mother. My uncle says she and Nancy must come to us for a long, long visit. Or if she would rather go home, I'll go with her till she feels able to come to us, and do anything I can think of for her. I will try to be a daughter till you come back, Maggie; only don't be long, or Frank and I shall break our hearts.'

Maggie waited till her mother had ended her long clasping embrace of Edward, who was subdued enough this morning; and then with something like Esau's craving for a blessing,[43] she came to bid her mother good-bye, and received the warm caress she had longed for for years. In another moment the coach was away; and before half an hour had elapsed, Combehurst church-spire had been lost in a turn of the road.

Edward and Mr. Buxton did not speak to each other, and Maggie was nearly silent. They reached Liverpool in the afternoon; and Mr. Buxton, who had been there once or twice before, took them directly to some quiet hotel. He was far more anxious that Edward should not expose himself to any chance of recognition, than Edward himself. He went down to the Docks to secure berths in the vessel about to sail the next day, and on his return he took Maggie out to make the requisite purchases.

'Did you pay for us, sir?' said Maggie, anxious to ascertain the amount of money she had left, after defraying the passage.

'Yes,' replied he, rather confused. 'Erminia begged me not to tell you about it, but I can't manage a secret well. You see she did not like the idea of your going as steerage-passengers[44] as you meant to do; and she desired me to take you cabin places for her. It is no doing of mine, my dear. I did not think of it; but now I have seen how crowded the steerage is, I am very glad Erminia had so much thought. Edward might have roughed it well enough there, but it would never have done for you.'

'It was very kind of Erminia,' said Maggie, touched at this consideration of her friend; 'but –'

'Now don't "but" about it,' interrupted he. 'Erminia is very rich, and has more money than she knows what to do with. I'm only vexed I did not think of it myself. For, Maggie, though I may have my own ways of thinking on some points, I can't be blind to your goodness.'

All evening Mr. Buxton was busy, and busy on their behalf. Even Edward, when he saw the attention that was being paid to his physical comfort, felt a kind of penitence; and, after choking once or twice in the attempt, conquered his pride (such I call it for want of a better word) so far as to express some regret for his past conduct, and some gratitude for Mr. Buxton's present kindness. He did it awkwardly enough, but it pleased Mr. Buxton.

'Well – well – that's all very right,' said he, reddening from his own uncomfortableness of feeling. 'Now don't say any more about it, but do your best in America; don't let me feel I've been a fool in letting you off. I know Mr. Henry will think me so. And, above all, take care of Maggie, Mind what she says, and you're sure to go right.'

He asked them to go on board early the next day, as he had promised Erminia to see them there, and yet wished to return as soon as he could. It was evident that he hoped, by making his absence as short as possible, to prevent Mr. Henry's ever knowing that he had left home, or in any way connived at Edward's escape.

So, although the vessel was not to sail till the afternoon's tide, they left the hotel soon after breakfast, and went to the 'Anna-Maria.' They were among the first passengers on board. Mr. Buxton took Maggie down to her cabin. She then saw the reason of his business the evening before. Every store that could be provided was there. A number of books lay on the little table – books just suited to Maggie's taste. 'There!' said he, rubbing his hands. 'Don't thank me. It's all Erminia's doing. She gave me the list of books. I've not got all; but I think they'll be enough. Just write me one line, Maggie, to say I've done my best.'

Maggie wrote with tears in her eyes – tears of love towards the generous Erminia. A few minutes more and Mr. Buxton was gone. Maggie watched him as long as she could see him; and as his portly figure disappeared among the crowd on the pier, her heart sank within her.

Edward's, on the contrary, rose at his absence. The only one, cognisant of his shame and ill-doing, was gone. A new life lay before him, the opening of which was made agreeable to him, by the position in which he found himself placed, as a cabin-passenger; with many comforts provided for him; for although Maggie's wants had been the principal object of Mr. Buxton's attention, Edward was not forgotten.

He was soon among the sailors, talking away in a rather consequential manner. He grew acquainted with the remainder of the cabin-passengers, at least those who arrived before the final bustle began; and kept bringing his sister such little pieces of news as he could collect.

'Maggie, they say we are likely to have a good start, and a fine moon-light night.' Away again he went.

'I say, Maggie, there's an uncommonly pretty girl come on board, with those old people in black. Gone down into the cabin, now; I wish you would scrape up an acquaintance with her, and give me a chance.'

CHAPTER XI.

MAGGIE sat on deck, wrapped in her duffel-cloak; the old familiar cloak, which had been her wrap in many a happy walk in the haunts near her moorland home. The weather was not cold for the time of year, but still it was chilly to any one that was stationary. But she wanted to look her last on the shoals of English people, who crowded backwards and forwards, like ants, on the pier. Happy people! who might stay among their loved ones. The mocking dæmons gathered round her, as they gather round all who sacrifice self, tempting. A crowd of suggestive doubts pressed upon her. 'Was it really necessary that she should go with Edward? Could she do him any real good? Would he be in any way influenced by her?' Then the dæmon tried another description of doubt. 'Had it ever been her duty to go? She was leaving her mother alone. She was giving Frank much present sorrow. It was not even yet too late!' She could not endure longer; and replied to her own tempting heart.

'I was right to hope for Edward; I am right to give him the chance of steadiness which my presence will give. I am doing what my mother earnestly wished me to do; and what to the last she felt relieved by my doing. I know Frank will feel sorrow, because I myself have such an aching heart; but if I had asked him whether I was not right in going, he would have been too truthful not to have said yes. I have tried to do right, and though I may fail, and evil may seem to arise rather than good out of my endeavour, yet still I will submit to my failure, and try and say "God's will be done!" If only I might have seen Frank once more, and told him all face to face!'

To do away with such thoughts, she determined no longer to sit gazing, and tempted by the shore; and, giving one look to the land which contained her lover, she went down below, and busied herself, even through her blinding tears, in trying to arrange her own cabin, and Edward's. She heard boat after boat arrive, loaded with passengers. She learnt from Edward, who came down to tell her the fact, that there were upwards of two hundred steerage passengers. She felt the tremulous shake which announced that the ship was loosed from her moorings, and being tugged down the river. She wrapped herself up once more, and came on deck, and sat down among the many who were looking their last look at England. The early winter evening was darkening in, and shutting out the Welsh coast, the hills of which were like the hills of home. She was thankful when she became too ill to think and remember.

Exhausted and still, she did not know whether she was sleeping or waking; or whether she had slept, since she had thrown herself down on her cot; when suddenly, there was a great rush, and then Edward stood like lightning by her, pulling her up by the arm.

'The ship is on fire, – to the deck, Maggie! Fire! Fire!' he shouted, like a maniac, while he dragged her up the stairs – as if the cry of Fire could summon human aid on the great deep. And the cry was echoed up to heaven by all that crowd, in an accent of despair.

They stood huddled together, dressed and undressed; now in red lurid light, showing ghastly faces of terror, – now in white wreaths of smoke, – as far away from the steerage as they could press; for there, up from the hold, rose columns of smoke, and now and then a fierce blaze leaped out, exulting – higher and higher every time; while from each crevice on that part of the deck, issued harbingers of the terrible destruction that awaited them.

The sailors were lowering the boats; and above them stood the captain, as calm as if he were on his own hearth at home – his home where he never more should be. His voice was low – was lower; but as clear as a bell in its distinctness; as wise in its directions as collected thought could make it. Some of the steerage passengers were helping; but more were dumb and motionless with affright. In that dead silence was heard a low wail of sorrow, as of numbers whose power was crushed out of them by that awful terror. Edward still held his clutch of Margaret's arm.

'Be ready!' said he, in a fierce whisper.

The fire sprung up along the main-mast, and did not sink or disappear again. They knew, then, that all the mad efforts made by some few below to extinguish it were in vain; and then went up the prayers of hundreds, in mortal agony of fear:

'Lord! have mercy upon us!'

Not in quiet calm of village church did ever such a pitiful cry go up to heaven; it was like one voice – like the day of judgment in the presence of the Lord.

And after that there was no more silence; but a confusion of terrible farewells, and wild cries of affright, and purposeless rushes hither and thither.

The boats were down, rocking on the sea. The captain spoke:

'Put the children in first; they are the most helpless.'

One or two stout sailors stood in the boats to receive them. Edward drew nearer and nearer to the gangway, pulling Maggie with him. She was almost pressed to death, and stifled. Close in her ear, she heard a woman praying to herself. She, poor creature, knew of no presence but God's in that awful hour, and spoke in a low voice to Him.

'My heart's darlings are taken away from me. Faith! faith! Oh, my great God! I will die in peace, if Thou wilt but grant me faith in this terrible hour, to feel that Thou wilt take care of my poor orphans. Hush! dearest Billy,' she cried out shrill to a little fellow in the boat, waiting for his mother; and the change in her voice, from despair to a kind of cheerfulness, showed what a mother's love can do. 'Mother will come soon. Hide his face, Anne, and wrap your shawl tight round him.' And then her voice sank down again, in the same low, wild prayer for faith. Maggie could not turn to see her face, but took the hand which hung near her. The woman clutched at it with the grasp of a vice; but went on praying, as if unconscious. Just then the crowd gave way a little. The captain had said, that the women were to go next; but they were too frenzied to obey his directions, and now pressed backward and forward. The sailors, with mute, stern obedience, strove to follow out the captain's directions. Edward pulled Maggie, and she kept her hold on the mother. The mate, at the head of the gangway, pushed him back.

'Only women are to go!'

'There are men there.'

'Three, to manage the boat.'

'Come on, Maggie! while there's room for us,' said he, unheeding. But Maggie drew back, and put the mother's hand into the mate's. 'Save her first!' said she. The woman did not know of anything, but that her children were there; it was only in after days, and quiet hours, that she remembered the young creature who pushed her forwards to join her fatherless children, and, by losing her place in the crowd, was jostled – where, she did not know; but dreamed until her dying day. Edward pressed on, unaware that Maggie was not close behind him. He was deaf to reproaches; and, heedless of the hand stretched out to hold him back, sprang towards the boat. The men there pushed her off – full, and more than full, as she was; and overboard he fell into the sullen heaving waters.

His last shout had been on Maggie's name – a name she never thought to hear again on earth, as she was pressed back, sick and suffocating. But suddenly a voice rang out above all confused voices and moaning hungry waves, and above the roaring fire.

'Maggie, Maggie! My Maggie!'

Out of the steerage side of the crowd a tall figure issued forth, begrimed with smoke. She could not see, but she knew. As a tame bird flutters to the human breast of its protector when affrighted by some mortal foe, so Maggie fluttered and cowered into his arms. And, for a moment, there was no more terror or thought of danger in the hearts of those twain, but only infinite and absolute peace. She had no wonder how he came there: it was enough that he was there. He first thought of the destruction that was present with them. He was as calm and composed as if they sat beneath the thorn-tree on the still moorlands, far away. He took her, without a word, to the end of the quarter-deck. He lashed her to a piece of spar. She never spoke.

'Maggie,' he said, 'my only chance is to throw you overboard. This spar will keep you floating. At first, you will go down – deep, deep down. Keep your mouth and eyes shut. I shall be there when you come up. By God's help, I will struggle bravely for you.'

She looked up; and by the flashing light he could see a trusting, loving smile upon her face. And he smiled back at her; a grave, beautiful look, fit to wear on his face in heaven. He helped her to the side of the vessel, away from the falling burning pieces of mast. Then for a moment he paused.

'If – Maggie, I may be throwing you in to death.' He put his hand before his eyes. The strong man lost courage. Then she spoke.

'I am not afraid; God is with us, whether we live or die!' She looked as quiet and happy as a child on its mother's breast; and so before he lost heart again, he heaved her up, and threw her as far as he could over into the glaring, dizzying water; and straight leaped after her. She came up with an involuntary look of terror on her face; but when she saw him by the red glare of the burning ship, close by her side, she shut her eyes, and looked as if peacefully going to sleep. He swam, guiding the spar.

'I think we are near Llandudno. I know we have passed the little Ormes' head.'[45] That was all he said; but she did not speak.

He swam out of the heat and fierce blaze of light into the quiet dark waters; and then into the moon's path. It might be half an hour before he got into that silver stream. When the beams fell down upon them, he looked at Maggie. Her head rested on the spar, quite still. He could not bear it. 'Maggie, – dear heart! speak!'

With a great effort she was called back from the borders of death by that voice, and opened her filmy eyes, which looked abroad as if she could see nothing nearer than the gleaming lights of Heaven. She let the lids fall softly again. He was as if alone in the wide world with God.

'A quarter of an hour more and all is over,' thought he. 'The people at Llandudno must see our burning ship, and will come out in their boats.' He kept in the line of light, although it did not lead him direct to the shore, in order that they might be seen. He swam with desperation. One moment he thought he had heard her last gasp rattle through the rush of the waters; and all strength was gone, and he lay on the waves as if he himself must die, and go with her spirit straight through that purple lift to heaven; the next he heard the splash of oars, and raised himself and cried aloud. The boatmen took them in, – and examined her by the lantern, – and spoke in Welsh, – and shook their heads. Frank threw himself on his knees, and prayed them to take her to land. They did not know his words, but they understood his prayer. He kissed her lips, – he chafed her hands, – he wrung the water out of her hair, – he held her feet against his warm breast.

'She is not dead,' he kept saying to the men, as he saw their sorrowful pitying looks.

The kind people at Llandudno had made ready their own humble beds, with every appliance of comfort they could think of, as soon as they understood the nature of the calamity which had befallen the ship on their coasts. Frank walked, dripping, bareheaded, by the body of his Margaret, which was borne by some men along the rocky sloping shore.

'She is not dead!' he said. He stopped at the first house they came to. It belonged to a kind-hearted woman. They laid Maggie in her bed, and got the village doctor to come and see her.

'There is life still,' said he gravely.

'I knew it,' said Frank. But it felled him to the ground. He sank first in prayer, and then in insensibility. The doctor did everything. All that night long he passed to and fro from house to house; for several had swum to Llandudno. Others, it was thought, had gone to Abergele.

In the morning Frank was recovered enough to write to his father, by Maggie's bedside. He sent the letter off to Conway by a little bright-looking Welsh boy. Late in the afternoon she awoke.

In a moment or two she looked eagerly round her, as if gathering in her breath; and then she covered her head and sobbed.

'Where is Edward?' asked she.

'We do not know,' said Frank, gravely. 'I have been round the village, and seen every survivor here; he is not among them, but he may be at some other place along the coast.'

She was silent, reading in his eyes his fears, – his belief.

At last she asked again.

'I cannot understand it. My head is not clear. There are such rushing noises in it. How came you there?' She shuddered involuntarily as she recalled the terrible where.

For an instant he dreaded, for her sake, to recall the circumstances of the night before; but then he understood how her mind would dwell upon them until she was satisfied.

'You remember writing to me, love, telling me all. I got your letter – I don't know how long ago – yesterday, I think. Yes! in the evening. You could not think, Maggie, I would let you go alone to America. I won't speak against Edward, poor fellow! but we must both allow that he was not the person to watch over you, as such a treasure should be watched over. I thought I would go with you. I hardly know if I meant to make myself known to you all at once, for I had no wish to have much to do with your brother. I see now that it was selfish in me. Well! there was nothing to be done, after receiving your letter, but to set off for Liverpool straight, and join you. And after that decision was made, my spirits rose, for the old talks about Canada and Australia came to my mind, and this seemed like a realisation of them.

Besides, Maggie, I suspected – I even suspect now – that my father had something to do with your going with Edward?'

'Indeed, Frank!' said she earnestly, 'you are mistaken; I cannot tell you all now; but he was so good and kind at last. He never urged me to go; though, I believe, he did tell me it would be the saving of Edward.'

'Don't agitate yourself, love. I trust there will be time enough, some happy day at home, to tell me all. And till then, I will believe that my father did not in any way suggest this voyage. But you'll allow that, after all that has passed, it was not unnatural in me to suppose so. I only told Middleton I was obliged to leave him by the next train. It was not till I was fairly off, that I began to reckon up what money I had with me. I doubt even if I was sorry to find it was so little. I should have to put forth my energies and fight my way, as I had often wanted to do. I remember, I thought how happy you and I would be, striving together as poor people "in that new world which is the old."[46] Then you had told me you were going in the steerage; and that was all suitable to my desires for myself.'

'It was Erminia's kindness that prevented our going there. She asked your father to take us cabin places unknown to me.'

'Did she? Dear Erminia! it is just like her. I could almost laugh to remember the eagerness with which I doffed my signs of wealth, and put on those of poverty. I sold my watch when I got into Liverpool – yesterday, I believe – but it seems like months ago. And I rigged myself out at a slop-shop with suitable clothes for a steerage passenger. Maggie! you never told me the name of the vessel you were going to sail in!'

'I did not know it till I got to Liverpool. All Mr. Buxton said was, that some ship sailed on the 15th.'

'I concluded it must be the Anna-Maria (poor Anna-Maria!) and I had no time to lose. She had just heaved her anchor when I came on board. Don't you recollect a boat hailing her at the last moment? There were three of us in her.'

'No! I was below in my cabin – trying not to think,' said she, colouring a little.

'Well! as soon as I got on board it began to grow dark, or, perhaps, it was the fog on the river; at any rate, instead of being able to single out your figure at once, Maggie – it is one among a thousand – I had to go peering into every woman's face; and many were below. I went between decks, and by-and-by I was afraid I had mistaken the vessel; I sat down; I had no spirit to stand; and every time the door opened I roused up and looked, – but you never came. I was thinking what to do; whether to be put on shore in Ireland, or to go on to New York, and wait for you there; – it was the worst time of all, for I had nothing to do; and the suspense was horrible. I might have known,' said he, smiling, 'my little Emperor of Russia was not one to be a steerage passenger.'

But Maggie was too much shaken to smile; and the thought of Edward lay heavy upon her mind.

'Then the fire broke out; how, or why, I suppose, will never be ascertained. It was at our end of the vessel. I thanked God, then, that you were not there. The second mate wanted some one to go down with him to bring up the gunpowder, and throw it overboard. I had nothing to do, and I went. We wrapped it up in wet sails, but it was a ticklish piece of work, and took time. When we had got it over-board, the flames were gathering far and wide. I don't remember what I did until I heard Edward's voice speaking your name.'

It was decided that the next morning they should set off homewards, striving on their way to obtain tidings of Edward. Frank would have given his only valuable (his mother's diamond-guard,[47] which he wore constantly), as a pledge for some advance of money; but the kind Welsh people would not have it. They had not much spare cash, but what they had they readily lent to the survivors of the Anna-Maria. Dressed in the homely country garb of the people, Frank and Maggie set off in their car.[48] It was a clear, frosty morning; the first that winter. The road soon lay high up on the cliffs along the coast. They looked down on the sea rocking below. At every village they stopped, and Frank inquired, and made the driver inquire in Welsh; but no tidings gained they of Edward; though here and there Maggie watched Frank into some cottage or other, going to see a dead body, beloved by some one; and when he came out, solemn and grave, their sad eyes met, and she knew it was not he they sought, without needing words.

At Abergele they stopped to rest; and because, being a larger place, it would need a longer search, Maggie lay down on the sofa, for she was very weak, and shut her eyes, and tried not to see for ever and ever that mad struggling crowd lighted by the red flames.

Frank came back in an hour or so; and soft behind him, – laboriously treading on tiptoe, – Mr. Buxton followed. He was evidently choking down his sobs; but when he saw the white wan figure of Maggie, he held out his arms.

'My dear! my daughter!' he said, 'God bless you!' He could not speak more, – he was fairly crying; but he put her hand in Frank's, and kept holding them both.

'My father,' said Frank, speaking in a husky voice, while his eyes filled with tears, 'had heard of it before he received my letter. I might have known that the lighthouse signals would take it fast to Liverpool. I had written a few lines to him saying I was going to you; happily they never reached, – that was spared to my dear father.'

Maggie saw the look of restored confidence that passed between father and son.

'My mother?' said she at last.

'She is here,' said they both at once, with sad solemnity.

'Oh, where? Why did not you tell me?' exclaimed she, starting up. But their faces told her why.

'Edward is drowned, – is dead,' said she, reading their looks.

There was no answer.

'Let me go to my mother.'

'Maggie, she is with him. His body was washed ashore last night. My father and she heard of it as they came along. Can you bear to see her? She will not leave him.'

'Take me to her,' Maggie answered.

They led her into a bed-room. Stretched on the bed lay Edward, but now so full of hope and worldly plans.

Mrs. Browne looked round, and saw Maggie. She did not get up from her place by his head; nor did she long avert her gaze from his poor face. But she held Maggie's hand, as the girl knelt by her, and spoke to her in a hushed voice, undisturbed by tears. Her miserable heart could not find that relief.

'He is dead! – he is gone! – he will never come back again! If he had gone to America, – it might have been years first, – but he would have come back to me. But now he will never come back again; never, – never!'

Her voice died away, as the wailings of the night wind die in the distance; and there was silence, – silence more sad and hopeless than any passionate words of grief.

And to this day it is the same. She prizes her dead son more than a thousand living daughters, happy and prosperous as is Maggie now, – rich in the love of many. If Maggie did not show such reverence to her mother's faithful sorrows, others might wonder at her refusal to be comforted by that sweet daughter. But Maggie treats her with such tender sympathy, never thinking of herself or her own claims, that Frank, Erminia, Mr. Buxton, Nancy, and all, are reverent and sympathising too.

Over both old and young the memory of one who is dead broods like a dove, – of one who could do but little during her lifetime; who was doomed only to 'stand and wait;'[49] who was meekly content to be gentle, holy, patient, and undefiled, – the memory of the invalid Mrs. Buxton.

THE LAST GENERATION IN ENGLAND

The Last Generation in England, published in Philadelphia in *Sartain's Union Magazine* in July 1849 (5, pp. 45–68), was the first of two contributions by EG to this American journal. It then effectively disappeared and was not identified as Gaskell's until 1935, when R. D. Waller revealed its existence in a letter to *The Times Literary Supplement*. In his letter Waller reveals that Mary Howitt had passed on to EG 'a request for an article from the editor of *Sartain's Union Magazine*',[1] and that meanwhile the editor had sent through Mary Howitt a payment of £4 for an earlier article. This 'earlier article' was *The Last Generation in England*; the article requested was published as 'Martha Preston', a short story that was to appear in revised form in *Household Words* in 1855 under the title of 'Half a Life-Time Ago'. That EG had not entirely forgotten this American material is suggested by a letter (c. 16 February 1857) referring to a listing of her 'books' which she had given to the French publisher Louis Hachette: 'These stories are exclusive of the American publications' (*Further Letters*, p. 169). Nevertheless *The Last Generation in England* was not reprinted until it was added to Watson's 'Oxford English Novels' edition of *Cranford* in 1972.[2]

Sartain's Union Magazine, originally the New York periodical *The Union Magazine of Literature and Art*, was taken over in January 1849 by John Sartain (1809–1897), a London-born publisher and engraver, and his partner William Sloanaker who transferred it to Philadelphia. On its appearance in *Sartain's*, *The Last Generation in England* was attributed to 'the author of "Mary Barton"', with the sub-heading 'communicated for Sartain's magazine by Mary Howitt.'[3] As well as EG, Harriet Martineau published in the journal, and Mary Howitt's involvement suggests an attempt to establish an English connection. Although it published work by distinguished American authors, including Henry Wadsworth Longfellow, Henry David Thoreau and Edgar Allan Poe, *Sartain's* had only a short life, being discontinued in

---

1. Ross D. Waller, letter in *The Times Literary Supplement* (25 July 1935), p. 477. See also Ross D. Waller, *Letters Addressed to Mrs. Gaskell by Celebrated Contemporaries* (Manchester: Manchester University Press, 1935), and the note by Waller in *BJRL,* 20 (July 1936), pp. 25–7.

2. *Watson*, pp. 161–8.

3. *SUM*, 5 (July 1849), p. 45.

1852. Sartain himself, however, is an important figure in the development of middle-class American culture in the nineteenth century, his publishing activities being instrumental in promoting the visual arts as well as literature.

The Last Generation in England was EG's first attempt to recall the Knutsford environment of her early years. With so little information to go on, it is not possible to speculate on the writing origins of this short essay, but what is perhaps surprising about it in its anticipation of *Cranford* is not only the theme, but the detail. A number of well-known incidents in *Cranford* appear here for the first time, and characters who are fictionalised in the longer story appear in their own right. Clearly EG felt that with this first draft having been published only on the other side of the Atlantic she could recycle such material without embarrassment. The essay is both less sophisticated, and more explicitly autobiographical than *Cranford*, but it helps us to confirm the link between fiction and reportage in the full-length fiction that was ultimately developed from it.

THE LAST GENERATION IN ENGLAND.

BY THE AUTHOR OF 'MARY BARTON.'

COMMUNICATED FOR SARTAIN'S MAGAZINE BY MARY HOWITT.

I HAVE just taken up by chance an old number of the Edinburgh Review (April, 1848), in which it is said that Southey had proposed to himself to write a 'history of English domestic life.'[1] I will not enlarge upon the infinite loss we have had in the non-fulfilment of this plan; every one must in some degree feel its extent who has read those charming glimpses of home scenes contained in the early volumes of the 'Doctor, &c.'[2] This quarter of an hour's chance reading has created a wish in me to put upon record some of the details of country town life, either observed by myself, or handed down to me by older relations; for even in small towns, scarely removed from villages, the phases of society are rapidly changing; and much will appear strange, which yet occurred only in the generation immediately preceding ours. I must however say before going on, that although I choose to disguise my own identity, and to conceal the name of the town to which I refer, every circumstance and occurrence which I shall relate is strictly and truthfully told without exaggeration. As for classing the details with which I am acquainted under any heads, that will be impossible from their heterogeneous nature; I must write them down as they arise in my memory.

The town in which I once resided is situated in a district inhabited by large landed proprietors of a very old family. The daughters of these families,[3] if unmarried, retired to live in — on their annuities, and gave the ton to the society there; stately ladies they were, remembering etiquette and precedence in every occurrence of life, and having their genealogy at their tongue's end. Then there were the widows of the cadets of these same families;[4] also poor, and also proud, but I think more genial and less given to recounting their pedigrees than the former. Then came the professional men and their wives; who were more wealthy than the ladies I have named, but who always treated them with deference and respect, sometimes even amounting to obsequiousness; for was there not 'my brother, Sir John —,' and 'my uncle, Mr. —, of —,' to give employment and patronage to the doctor or the attorney? A grade lower came a class of single or widow ladies; and again it was possible, not to say probable, that their pecuniary circumstances were in better condition than those of the aristocratic dames, who nevertheless refused to meet in general society the *ci-devant*[5] housekeepers, or widows of stewards, who had been employed by their fathers and brothers, they would occasionally condescend to ask, 'Mason,' or 'that good Bentley,' to a private tea-drinking, at which I doubt not much gossip relating to former days at the hall would pass; but that was patronage; to associate with them at another person's house, would have been an acknowledgment of equality.

Below again came the shopkeepers, who dared to be original; who gave comfortable suppers after the very early dinners of that day, not checked by the honourable Mr. D—'s precedent of a seven o'clock tea on the most elegant and economical principles, and a supperless turn-out at nine. There were the usual respectable and disrespectable poor; and hanging on the outskirts of society were a set of young men, ready for mischief and brutality, and every now and then dropping off the pit's brink into crime. The habits of this class (about forty years ago) were much such as those of the Mohawks a century before.[6] They would stop ladies returning from the card-parties, which were the staple gaiety of the place, and who were only attended by a maid-servant bearing a lantern, and whip them; literally whip them as you whip a little child; until administering such chastisement to a good, precise old lady of high family, 'my brother, the magistrate,' came forward and put down such proceedings with a high hand.

Certainly there was more individuality of character in those days than now; no one even in a little town of two thousand inhabitants would now be found to drive out with a carriage full of dogs; each dressed in the male or female fashion of the day, as the case might be; each dog provided with a pair of house-shoes, for which his carriage boots were changed on his return. No old lady would be so oblivious of 'Mrs. Grundy's' existence[7] now as to dare to invest her favourite cow, after its unlucky fall into a lime-pit, in flannel waist-coat and drawers, in which the said cow paraded the streets of — to the day of its death.[8]

There were many regulations which were strictly attended to in the society of —, and which probably checked more manifestations of eccentricity. Before a certain hour in the morning calls were never paid, nor yet after a certain hour in the afternoon; the consequence was that everybody was out, calling on everybody at the same time, for it was *de rigueur* that morning calls should be returned within three days; and accordingly, making due allowance for our proportion of rain in England, every fine morning was given up to this employment. A quarter of an hour was the limit of a morning call.

Before the appointed hour of reception, I fancy the employment of many of the ladies was fitting up their laces and muslins (which, for the information of all those whom it may concern, were never ironed, but carefully stretched, and pinned, thread by thread, with most Lilliputian[9] pieces, on a board covered with flannel). Most of these scions of quality had many pounds' worth of valuable laces descended to them from mothers and grandmothers, which must be 'got up' by no hands, as you may guess, but those of Fairly Fair.[10] Indeed when muslin and net were a guinea a yard, this was not to be wondered at. The lace was washed in buttermilk, which gave rise to an odd little circumstance. One lady left her lace, basted up, in some not very sour buttermilk; and unluckily the cat lapped it up, lace and all (one would have thought the lace would have choked her, but so it was); the lace was too valuable to be lost, so a small dose of tartar emetic was administered to the poor cat; the lace returned to view was carefully darned, and decked the good old lady's best cap for many a year after; and many a time did she tell the story, gracefully bridling up in a prim sort of way, and giving a little cough, as if preliminary to a rather improper story. The first sentence of it was always, I remember, 'I do not think you can guess where the lace on my cap has been;' dropping her voice, 'in pussy's inside, my dear!'[11]

The dinner hour was three o'clock in all houses of any pretension to gentility; and a very late hour it was considered to be. Soon after four one or two inveterate card-players might be seen in calash and pattens,[12] picking their way along the streets to the house where the party of the evening was to be held. As soon as they arrived and had unpacked themselves, an operation of a good half-hour's duration in the dining-parlour, they were ushered into the drawing-room, where, unless in the very height of summer, it was considered a delicate attention to have the shutters closed, the curtains drawn, and the candles lighted. The card-tables were set out, each with two new packs of cards, for which it was customary to pay by each person placing a shilling under one of the candlesticks.

The ladies settled down to Preference,[13] and allowed of no interruption; even the tea-trays were placed on the middle of the card-tables, and tea hastily gulped down with a few remarks on the good or ill fortune of the evening. New arrivals were greeted with nods in the intervals of the game; and as people entered the room, they were pounced upon by the lady of the house to form another table. Cards were a business in those days, not a recreation. Their very names were to be treated with reverence. Some one came to — from a place where flippancy was in fashion; he called the knave 'Jack,' and everybody looked grave, and voted him vulgar;[14] but when he was over-heard calling Preference – the decorous, highly-respectable game of Preference, – Pref., why, what course remained for us but to cut him, and cut him we did.

About half-past eight, notices of servants having arrived for their respective mistresses were given: the games were concluded, accounts settled, a few parting squibs and crackers let off at careless or unlucky partners, and the party separated. By ten o'clock all — was in bed and asleep. I have made no mention of gentlemen at these parties, because if ever there was an Amazonian town in England it was —. Eleven widows of respectability at one time kept house there; besides spinsters innumerable. The doctor preferred his arm-chair and slippers to the forms of society, such as I have described, and so did the attorney, who was besides not insensible to the charms of a hot supper. Indeed, I suppose it was because of the small incomes of the more aristocratic portion of our little society not sufficing both for style and luxury, but it was a fact, that as gentility decreased good living increased in proportion. We had the honour and glory of looking at old plate and delicate china at the *comme il faut* tea-parties, but the slices of bread and butter were like wafers, and the sugar for coffee was rather of the brownest, still there was much gracious kindness among our *haute volée*.[15] In those times, good Mr. Rigmarole,[16] carriages were carriages, and there were not the infinite variety of broughams, droskys, &c., &c., down to a wheelbarrow, which now make locomotion easy; nor yet were there cars and cabs and flys ready for hire in our little town. A post-chaise was the only conveyance besides *the* sedan-chair, of which more anon. So the widow of an earl's son, who possessed a proper old-fashioned coach and pair, would, on rainy nights, send her carriage, the only private carriage of —, round the town, picking up all the dowagers and invalids, and conveying them dry and safe to and from their evening engagement. The various other ladies who, in virtue of their relations holding manors and maintaining game-keepers, had frequent presents, during the season, of partridges, pheasants, &c., &c., would daintily carve off the tid-bits, and putting them carefully into a hot basin, bid Betty or Molly cover it up quickly, and carry it to Mrs. or Miss So-and-so, whose appetite was but weakly and who required dainties to tempt it which she could not afford to purchase.

These poorer ladies had also their parties in turn; they were too proud to accept invitations if they might not return them, although various and amusing were their innocent make-shifts and imitations. To give you only one instance, I remember a card-party at one of these good ladies' lodgings; where, when tea-time arrived, the ladies sitting on the sofa had to be displaced for a minute, in order that the tea-trays, (plates of cake, bread and butter, and all,) might be extricated from their concealment under the valances of the couch.[17]

You may imagine the subjects of the conversation amongst these ladies; cards, servants, relations, pedigress, and last and best, much mutual interest about the poor of the town, to whom they were one and all kind and indefatigable benefactresses; cooking, sewing for, advising, doctoring, doing everything but educating them. One or two old ladies dwelt on the glories of former days; when – boasted of two earl's daughters as residents. Though it must be sixty years since they died, there are traces of their characters yet lingering about the place. Proud, precise, and generous; bitter tories were they. Their sister had married a General,[18] more distinguished for a successful comedy, than for his mode of conducting the war in America; and, consequently, his sisters-in-law held the name of Washington in deep abhorrence. I can fancy the way in which they must have spoken of him, from the shudder of abomination with which their devoted admirers spoke years afterwards of 'that man Washington.' Lady Jane[19] was moreover a benefactress to —. Before her day, the pavement of the foot-path was composed of loose round stones, placed so far apart that a delicate ankle might receive a severe wrench from slipping between; but she left a sum of money in her will to make and keep in repair a flag pavement, on condition that it should only be broad enough for one to walk abreast, in order 'to put a stop to the indecent custom coming into vogue, of ladies linking with gentlemen;' linking being the old-fashioned word for walking arm-in-arm. Lady Jane also left her sedan and money to pay the bearers for the use of the ladies of —, who were frequently like Adam and Eve in the weather-glass in consequence, the first arrival at a party having to commence the order of returning when the last lady was only just entering upon the gaieties of the evening.

The old ladies were living hoards of family tradition and old custom. One of them, a Shropshire woman, had been to school in London about the middle of the last century. The journey from Shropshire took her a week. At the school to which she was sent, besides fine work of innumerable descriptions, pastry, and the art of confectionary were taught to those whose parents desired it. The dancing-master gave his pupils instructions in the art of using a fan properly. Although an only child, she had never sat down in her parents' presence without leave until she was married; and spoke with infinite disgust of the modern familiarity with which children treated their parents. 'In my days,' said she, 'when we wrote to our fathers and mothers, we began "Honoured Sir," or "Honoured Madam," none of your "Dear Mamas," or "Dear Papas" would have been permitted; and we ruled off our margin before beginning our letters, instead of cramming writing into every corner of the paper; and when we ended our letters we asked our parents' blessing if we were writing to them; and if we wrote to a friend we were content to "remain your affectionate friend," instead of hunting up some new-fangled expression, such as "your attached, your loving," &c. Fanny, my dear! I got a letter to-day signed "Yours cordially," like a dram-shop! what will this world come to?'[20] Then she would tell how a gentleman having asked her to dance in her youth, never thought of such familiarity as offering her his arm to conduct her to her place, but taking up the flap of his silk-lined coat, he placed it over his open palm, and on it the lady daintily rested the tips of her fingers. To be sure, my dear old lady once confessed to a story neither so pretty nor so proper, namely, that one of the amusements of her youth was 'measuring noses' with some gentlemen, – not an uncommon thing in those days; and, as lips lie below noses, such measurements frequently ended in kisses. At her house there was a little silver basket-strainer, and once remarking on this, she showed me a silver saucer pierced through

with holes, and told me it was a relic of the times when tea was first intro-
duced into England; after it had been infused and the beverage drank, the
leaves were taken out of the teapot and placed on this strainer, and then
eaten by those who liked with sugar and butter, 'and very good they were,'
she added. Another relic which she possessed was an old receipt-book, dat-
ing back to the middle of the sixteenth century. Our grandmothers must
have been strong-headed women, for there were numerous receipts for
'ladies' beverages,' &c., generally beginning with 'Take a gallon of brandy, or
any other spirit.' The puddings, too, were no light matters: one receipt,
which I copied for the curiosity of the thing, begins with, 'Take thirty eggs,
two quarts of cream,' &c. These brobdignagian[21] puddings she explained by
saying that the afternoon meal, before the introduction of tea, generally con-
sisted of cakes and cold puddings, together with a glass of what we should
now call liqueur, but which was then denominated bitters.

The same old lady advocated strongly the manner in which marriages
were formerly often brought about. A young man went up to London to
study for the bar, to become a merchant, or what not, and arrived at middle
age without having thought about matrimony; when, finding himself rich
and desirous of being married, he would frequently write to some college
friend, or to the clergyman of his native place, asking him to recommend a
wife; whereupon the friend would send a list of suitable ladies; the bachelor
would make his selection, and empower his friend to wait upon the parents
of the chosen one, who accepted or refused without much consultation of
their daughter's wishes; often the first intelligence she had of the affair was
by being told by her mother to adorn herself in her best, as the gentleman
her parents proposed for her husband was expected by the night-coach to
supper.

'And very happy marriages they turned out, my dear – very,' my venerable
informant would add, sighing. I always suspected that her own had been of
this description.

MR. HARRISON'S CONFESSIONS

Mr. Harrison's Confessions first appeared in three instalments in the *Ladies' Companion and Monthly Magazine* (3:13 (1 February 1851), pp. 1–11; 3:14 (1 March 1851), pp. 49–56; and 3:15 (1 April 1851), pp. 97–106). In its account of a backward country town it has been seen by Gaskell commentators as an anticipation of *Cranford*, although the analogy should not be exaggerated. The *Ladies' Companion* was initially edited by Mrs Jane Loudon (1807–58), wife of John Claudius Loudon (1783–1843), the landscape-gardener and horticulturalist. Both Loudons were involved in periodical publishing. A letter from Mrs Loudon to EG of 20 October 1849 suggests that EG had rejected an invitation to write for the magazine (*Sharps*, p. 113, n. 1), but Loudon was succeeded as editor in May 1850 by Henry Fothergill Chorley, a writer who had reviewed EG's work and with whom she was on friendly terms. EG's story appeared anonymously under Chorley's editorship.[1] Despite Chorley's involvement with the *Ladies' Companion* it survived in its original format only until 1852. *Mr. Harrison's Confessions* was reprinted in *Lizzie Leigh and Other Tales* (1855), the only occasion on which the story reappeared in EG's lifetime. There are no substantive alterations to the text in the later reprint, and very few accidental differences. In a letter to Edward Chapman dated 25 April [1855] Gaskell asks whether she must seek permission for the re-printing of '"Mr. Harrison's confessions"? Or should you not think them worth reprinting?' (*Letters*, p. 340). The inference is that looking back on the story – and having reworked similar ground much more successfully in *Cranford* – she herself did not think highly of it, and it seems clear that she was not involved in any revision of the text for the 1855 collection.

In both the original *Ladies' Companion* text, and that of 1855, the character introduced as 'Ellen' (p. 112) later becomes 'Helen' (throughout in *1855*, but inconsistently in *LC*). I have followed 1855 in regularising to 'Helen'. All other differences between the texts are accidental and I have therefore reprinted the original *Ladies' Companion* text, making minor corrections to typographical errors (see Silent Corrections).

1. See *Sharps*, p. 113, n. 1; Margaret Howitt (ed.), *Mary Howitt: An Autobiography*, 2 vols (London: Isbister, 1889), vol. ii, p. 57.

MR. HARRISON'S CONFESSIONS.

CHAPTER I.

THE fire was burning gaily. My wife had just gone upstairs to put baby to bed. Charles sat opposite to me, looking very brown and handsome. It was pleasant enough that we should feel sure of spending some weeks under the same roof, a thing which we had never done since we were mere boys. I felt too lazy to talk, so I eat walnuts and looked into the fire. But Charles grew restless.

'Now that your wife is gone up-stairs, Will, you must tell me what I've wanted to ask you ever since I saw her this morning. Tell me all about the wooing and winning. I want to have the receipt for getting such a spicy little wife of my own. Your letters only gave the barest details. So set to, man, and tell me every particular.'

'If I tell you all, it will be a long story.'

'Never fear. If I get tired, I can go to sleep, and dream that I am back again, a lonely bachelor, in Ceylon; and I can waken up when you have done, to know that I am under your roof. Dash away, man! "Once upon a time, a gallant young bachelor –" There's a beginning for you!'

'Well, then, "once upon a time, a gallant young bachelor" was sorely puzzled where to settle, when he had completed his education as a surgeon. – I must speak in the first person; I cannot go on as a gallant young bachelor. – I had just finished walking the hospitals when you went to Ceylon, and, if you remember, I wanted to go abroad like you, and thought of offering myself as a ship-surgeon; but I found I should rather lose caste in my profession; so I hesitated, and, while I was hesitating, I received a letter from my father's cousin, Mr. Morgan, – that old gentleman who used to write such long letters of good advice to my mother, and who tipped me a five-pound note when I agreed to be bound apprentice to Mr. Howard, instead of going to sea. Well, it seems the old gentleman had all along thought of taking me as his partner, if I turned out pretty well; and as he heard a good account of me from an old friend of his, who was a surgeon at Guy's, he wrote to propose this arrangement: I was to have a third of the profits for five years; after that, half; and eventually I was to succeed to the whole. It was no bad offer for a penniless man like me, as Mr. Morgan had a capital country practice, and, though I did not know him personally, I had formed a pretty good idea of him, as an honourable, kind-hearted, fidgetty, meddlesome old bachelor; and a very correct notion it was, as I found out in the very first half-hour of seeing him. I had had some idea that I was to live in his house, as he was a bachelor and a kind of family friend; and I think he was afraid that I should expect this arrangement, for when I walked up to his door, with the porter carrying my portmanteau, he met me on the steps, and while he held my hand and shook it, he said to the porter, 'Jerry, if you 'll wait a moment, Mr. Harrison will be ready to go with you to his lodgings, at Jocelyn's, you know;' and then turning to me, he addressed his first words of welcome. I was a little inclined to think him inhospitable, but I got to understand him better afterwards. 'Jocelyn's,' said he, 'is the best place I have been able to hit upon in a hurry, and there is a good deal of fever about, which made me desirous that you should come this month, – a low kind of typhoid, in the oldest part of the town. I think you 'll be comfortable there for a week or two. I have taken the liberty of desiring my housekeeper to send down one or two things which give the place a little more of a home aspect, – an easy chair, a beautiful case of preparations,[1] and one or two little matters in the way of eatables; but if you'll take my advice, I've a plan in my head which we will talk about to-morrow morning. At present, I don't like to keep you standing out on the steps here, so I'll not detain you from your lodgings, where I rather think my housekeeper is gone to get tea ready for you.

'I thought I understood the old gentleman's anxiety for his own health, which he put upon care for mine, for he had on a kind of loose grey coat, and no hat on his head. But I wondered that he did not ask me in-doors, instead of keeping me on the steps. I believe, after all, I made a mistake in supposing he was afraid of taking cold; he was only afraid of being seen in *dishabille*.[2] And as for his apparent inhospitality, I had not been long in Duncombe before I understood the comfort of having one's house considered as a castle into which no one might intrude, and saw good reason for the practice Mr. Morgan had established of coming to his door to speak to every one. It was only the effect of habit that made him receive me so. Before long, I had the free run of his house.

'There was every sign of kind attention and forethought on the part of some one, whom I could not doubt to be Mr. Morgan, in my lodgings. I was too lazy to do much that evening, and sat in the little bow-window which projected over Jocelyn's shop, looking up and down the street. Duncombe calls itself a town, but I should call it a village. Really, looking from Jocelyn's, it is a very picturesque place. The houses are anything but regular; they may be mean in their details, but altogether they look well; they have not that flat unrelieved front, which many towns of far more pretensions present. Here and there a bow-window – every now and then a gable, cutting up against the sky – occasionally a projecting upper story – throws good effect of light and shadow along the street; and they have a queer fashion of their own of colouring the whitewash of some of the houses with a sort of pink blotting-paper tinge, more like the stone of which Mayence[3] is built than anything else. It may be very bad taste, but to my mind it gives a rich warmth to the colouring. Then, here and there a dwelling-house has a court in front, with a grass-plot on each side of the flagged walk, and a large tree or two – limes or horse-chestnuts – which send their great projecting upper branches over into the street, making round dry places of shelter on the pavement in the times of summer showers.

'While I was sitting in the bow-window, thinking of the contrast between this place and the lodgings in the heart of London, which I had left only twelve hours before, – the window open here, and, although in the centre of the town, admitting only scents from the mignonette boxes on the sill, instead of the dust and smoke of — Street, – the only sound heard in this, the principal street, being the voices of mothers calling their playing children home to bed, and the eight o'clock bell of the old parish church bim-bomming in remembrance of the curfew; – while I was sitting thus idly, the door opened, and the little maid-servant, dropping a courtesy, said –

'"Please, sir, Mrs. Munton's compliments, and she would be glad to know how you are after your journey."

'There! was not that hearty and kind? Would even the dearest chum I had at Guy's have thought of doing such a thing? while Mrs. Munton, whose name I had never heard of before, was doubtless suffering anxiety till I could relieve her mind by sending back word that I was pretty well.

'"My compliments to Mrs. Munton, and I am pretty well: much obliged to her." It was as well to say only "pretty well," for "very well" would have destroyed the interest Mrs. Munton evidently felt in me. Good Mrs. Munton! Kind Mrs. Munton! Perhaps, also, young, – handsome, – rich, – widowed Mrs. Munton! I rubbed my hands with delight and amusement, and, resuming my post of observation, began to wonder at which house Mrs. Munton lived.

'Again the little tap, and the little maid-servant:

'"Please, sir, Miss Tomkinsons' compliments; and they would be glad to know how you feel yourself after your journey."

'I don't know why, but Miss Tomkinsons' name had not such a halo about it as Mrs. Munton's. Still it was very pretty in Miss Tomkinsons to send and inquire. I only wished I did not feel so perfectly robust. I was almost ashamed that I could not send word I was quite exhausted by fatigue, and had fainted twice since my arrival. If I had but had a headache, at least! I heaved a deep breath: my chest was in perfect order; I had caught no cold; so I answered again –

'"Much obliged to the Miss Tomkinsons; I am not much fatigued; tolerably well; my compliments."

'Little Sally could hardly have got down-stairs, before she returned, bright and breathless: –

'"Mr. and Mrs. Bullock's compliments, sir; and they hope you are pretty well after your journey."

'Who would have expected such kindness from such an unpromising name? Mr. and Mrs. Bullock were less interesting, it is true, than their predecessors; but I graciously replied –

'"My compliments; a night's rest will perfectly recruit me."

'The same message was presently brought up from one or two more unknown kind hearts. I really wished I were not so ruddy-looking. I was afraid I should disappoint the tender-hearted town when they saw what a hale young fellow I was. And I was almost ashamed of confessing to a great appetite for supper when Sally came up to inquire what I would have. Beefsteaks were so tempting; but perhaps I ought rather to have water-gruel, and go to bed. The beef-steak carried the day, however. I need not have felt such a gentle elation of spirits, as this mark of the town's attention is paid to every one when they arrive after a journey. Many of the same people have sent to inquire after you, – great, hulking, brown fellow as you are, – only Sally spared you the infliction of devising interesting answers.

<hr>

CHAPTER II

'THE next morning Mr. Morgan came before I had finished breakfast. He was the most dapper little man I ever met. I see the affection with which people cling to the style of dress that was in vogue when they were beaux and belles, and received the most admiration. They are unwilling to believe that their youth and beauty are gone, and think that the prevailing mode is unbecoming. Mr. Morgan will inveigh by the hour together against frock-coats, for instance, and whiskers. He keeps his chin close shaven, wears a black dress-coat, and dark-grey pantaloons; and in his morning round to his town patients, he invariably wears the brightest and blackest of Hessian boots, with dangling silk tassels on each side. When he goes home, about ten o'clock, to prepare for his ride to see his country patients, he puts on the most dandy top-boots[4] I ever saw, which he gets from some wonderful boot-maker a hundred miles off. His appearance is what one calls "jemmy:"[5] there is no other word that will do for it. He was evidently a little discomfited when he saw me in my breakfast costume, with the habits which I brought with me from the fellows at Guy's; my feet against the fire-place, my chair balanced on its hind legs (a habit of sitting which I afterwards discovered he particularly abhorred), slippers on my feet (which, also, he considered a most ungentlemanly piece of untidiness "out of a bedroom"); in short, from what I afterwards learned, every prejudice he had was outraged by my appearance on this first visit of his. I put my book down, and sprang up to receive him. He stood, hat and cane in hand.

'"I came to inquire if it would be convenient for you to accompany me on my morning's round, and to be introduced to a few of our friends." I quite detected the little tone of coldness, induced by his disappointment at my appearance, though he never imagined that it was in any way perceptible. "I will be ready directly, sir," said I; and bolted into my bed room, only too happy to escape his scrutinising eye.

'When I returned, I was made aware, by sundry indescribable little coughs and hesitating noises, that my dress did not satisfy him. I stood ready, hat and gloves in hand; but still he did not offer to set off on our round. I grew very red and hot. At length he said –

'"Excuse me, my dear young friend, but may I ask if you have no other coat besides that – 'cut-away,'[6] I believe you call them? – We are rather sticklers for propriety, I believe, in Duncombe; and much depends on a first impression. Let it be professional, my dear sir. Black is the garb of our profession. Forgive my speaking so plainly, but I consider myself *in loco parentis.*"

'He was so kind, so bland, and, in truth, so friendly, that I felt it would be most childish to take offence; but I had a little resentment in my heart at this way of being treated. However, I mumbled, "Oh, certainly, sir, if you wish it!" and returned once more to change my coat – my poor cut-away.

'"Those coats, sir, give a man rather too much of a sporting appearance, not quite befitting the learned professions; more as if you came down here to hunt than to be the Galen or Hippocrates[7] of the neighbourhood." He smiled graciously, so I smothered a sigh; for, to tell you the truth, I had rather anticipated – and, in fact, had boasted at Guy's of the runs I hoped to have with the hounds; for Duncombe was in a famous hunting district. But all these ideas were quite dispersed when Mr. Morgan led me to the inn-yard, where there was a horse-dealer on his way to a neighbouring fair, and "strongly advised me," – which in our relative circumstances was equivalent to an injunction, – to purchase a little, useful, fast-trotting, brown cob, instead of a fine showy horse, "who would take any fence I put him to," as the horse-dealer assured me. Mr. Morgan was evidently pleased when I bowed to his decision, and gave up all hopes of an occasional hunt.

'He opened out a great deal more after this purchase. He told me his plan of establishing me in a house of my own, which looked more respectable, not to say professional, than being in lodgings; and then he went on to say that he had lately lost a friend, a brother surgeon in a neighbouring town, who had left a widow with a small income, who would be very glad to live with me, and act as mistress to my establishment; thus lessening the expense.

'"She is a lady-like woman," said Mr. Morgan, "to judge from the little I have seen of her; about forty-five or so; and may really be of some help to you in the little etiquettes of our profession; the slight delicate attentions which every man has to learn, if he wishes to get on in life. This is Mrs. Munton's, sir," said he, stopping short at a very unromantic-looking green door, with a brass knocker.

'I had no time to say, "Who is Mrs. Munton?" before we had heard Mrs. Munton was at home, and were following the tidy elderly servant up the narrow carpeted stairs into the drawing-room. Mrs. Munton was the widow of a former vicar, upwards of sixty, rather deaf; but like all the deaf people I have ever seen, very fond of talking; perhaps because she then knew the sub-ject, which passed out of her grasp when another began to speak. She was ill of a chronic complaint, which often incapacitated her from going out; and the kind people of the town were in the habit of coming to see her and sit with her, and of bringing her the newest, freshest, tid-bits of news; so that her room was the centre of the gossip of Duncombe; – not of scandal, mind; for I make a distinction between gossip and scandal. Now you can fancy the discrepancy between the ideal and the real Mrs. Munton. Instead of any foolish notion of a beautiful blooming widow, tenderly anxious about the health of the stranger, I saw a homely, talkative, elderly person, with a keen observant eye, and marks of suffering on her face; plain in manner and dress, but still unmistakeably a lady. She talked to Mr. Morgan, but she looked at me; and I saw that nothing I did escaped her notice. Mr. Morgan annoyed me by his anxiety to show me off; but he was kindly anxious to bring out every circumstance to my credit in Mrs. Munton's hearing, knowing well that the town-crier had not more opportunities to publish all about me than she had.

'"What was that remark you repeated to me of Sir Astley Cooper's?"[8] asked he. It had been the most trivial speech in the world that I had named as we walked along, and I felt ashamed of having to repeat it: but it answered Mr. Morgan's purpose, and before night all the town had heard that I was a favourite pupil of Sir Astley's (I had never seen him but twice in my life); and Mr. Morgan was afraid that as soon as he knew my full value I should be retained by Sir Astley to assist him in his duties as surgeon to the Royal Fam-ily. Every little circumstance was pressed into the conversation which could add to my importance.

'"As I once heard Sir Robert Peel[9] remark to Mr. Harrison, the father of our young friend here – 'The moons in August are remarkably full and bright.' – If you remember, Charles, my father was always proud of having sold a pair of gloves to Sir Robert, when he was staying at the Grange, near Biddicombe, and I suppose good Mr. Morgan had paid his only visit to my father at the time; but Mrs. Munton evidently looked at me with double respect after this incidental remark, which I was amused to meet with, a few months afterwards, disguised in the statement that my father was an intimate friend of the Premier's, and had, in fact, been the adviser of most of the measures taken by him in public life. I sat by, half indignant and half amused. Mr. Morgan looked so complacently pleased at the whole effect of the conversation, that I did not care to mar it by explanations; and, indeed, I had little idea at the time how small sayings were the seeds of great events in the town of Duncombe. When we left Mrs. Munton's he was in a blandly communicative mood.

'"You will find it a curious statistical fact, but five-sixths of our house-holders of a certain rank in Duncombe are women.[10] We have widows and old maids in rich abundance. In fact, my dear sir, I believe that you and I are almost the only gentlemen in the place – Mr. Bullock, of course, excepted. By gentlemen, I mean professional men. It behoves us to remember, sir, that so many of the female sex rely upon us for the kindness and protection which every man who is worthy of the name is always so happy to render."

'Miss Tomkinson, where we next called, did not strike me as remarkably requiring protection from any man. She was a tall, gaunt, masculine-looking woman, with an air of defiance about her, naturally; this, however, she softened and mitigated, as far as she was able, in favour of Mr. Morgan. He, it seemed to me, stood a little in awe of the lady, who was very *brusque* and plain-spoken, and evidently piqued herself on her decision of character and sincerity of speech.

'"So, this is the Mr. Harrison we have heard so much of from you, Mr. Morgan? I must say, from what I had heard, that I had expected something a little more – hum – hum! But he's young yet; he's young. We have been all anticipating an Apollo, Mr. Harrison, from Mr. Morgan's description, and an Æsculapius combined in one;[11] or, perhaps, I might confine myself to saying Apollo, as he, I believe, was the God of Medicine!"

'How could Mr. Morgan have described me without seeing me? I asked myself.

'Miss Tomkinson put on her spectacles, and adjusted them on her Roman nose. Suddenly relaxing from her severity of inspection, she said to Mr. Morgan –'But you must see Caroline. I had nearly forgotten it; she is busy with the girls, but I will send for her. She had a bad headache yesterday, and looked very pale; it made me very uncomfortable.'

'She rang the bell, and desired the servant to fetch Miss Caroline.

'Miss Caroline was the younger sister – younger by twenty years; and so considered as a child by Miss Tomkinson, who was fifty-five, at the very least. If she was considered as a child, she was also petted and caressed, and cared for as a child; for she had been left as a baby to the charge of her elder sister; and when the father died, and they had to set up a school, Miss Tomkinson took upon herself every difficult arrangement, and denied herself every pleasure, and made every sacrifice in order that "Carry" might not feel the change in their circumstances. My wife tells me she once knew the sisters purchase a piece of silk, enough, with management, to have made two gowns; but Carry wished for flounces, or some such fal-lals; and, without a word, Miss Tomkinson gave up her gown to have the whole made up as Carry wished, into one handsome one; and wore an old shabby affair herself as cheerfully as if it were Genoa velvet.[12] That tells the sort of relationship between the sisters as well as anything, and I consider myself very good to name it thus early, for it was long before I found out Miss Tomkinson's real goodness; and we had a great quarrel first. Miss Caroline looked very delicate and die-away when she came in; she was as soft and sentimental as Miss Tomkinson was hard and masculine; and had a way of saying, "Oh, sister, how can you?" at Miss Tomkinson's startling speeches, which I never liked, – especially as it was accompanied by a sort of protesting look at the company present, as if she wished to have it understood that she was shocked at her sister's *outré*[13] manners. Now, that was not faithful between sisters. A remonstrance in private might have done good, – though, for my own part, I have grown to like Miss Tomkinson's speeches and ways; but I don't like the way some people have of separating themselves from what may be unpopular in their relations. I know I spoke rather shortly to Miss Caroline when she asked me whether I could bear the change from "the great metropolis" to a little country village. In the first place, why could not she call it "London," or "town," and have done with it? And in the next place, why should she not love the place that was her home well enough to fancy that every one would like it when they came to know it as well as she did?

'I was conscious I was rather abrupt in my conversation with her, and I saw that Mr. Morgan was watching me, though he pretended to be listening to Miss Tomkinson's whispered account of her sister's symptoms. But when we were once more in the street, he began, "My dear young friend" –

'I winced; for all the morning I had noticed that when he was going to give a little unpalatable advice, he always began with "My dear young friend." He had done so about the horse.

'"My dear young friend, there are one or two hints I should like to give you about your manner. The great Sir Everard Home[14] used to say, 'a general practitioner should either have a very good manner, or a very bad one.' Now, in the latter case, he must be possessed of talents and acquirements sufficient to insure his being sought after, whatever his manner might be. But the rudeness will give notoriety to these qualifications. Abernethy[15] is a case in point. I rather, myself, question the taste of bad manners. I, therefore, have studied to acquire an attentive, anxious politeness, which combines ease and grace with a tender regard and interest. I am not aware whether I have succeeded (few men do) in coming up to my ideal; but I recommend you to strive after this manner, peculiarly befitting our profession. Identify yourself with your patients, my dear sir. You have sympathy in your good heart, I am sure, to really feel pain when listening to their account of their sufferings, and it soothes them to see the expression of this feeling in your manner. It is, in fact, sir, manners that make the man[16] in our profession. I don't set myself up as an example, far from it; – but – This is Mr. Hutton's, our vicar; one of the servants is indisposed, and I shall be glad of the opportunity of introducing you. We can resume our conversation at another time."

'I had not been aware that we had been holding a conversation, in which, I believe, the assistance of two persons is required. Why had not Mr. Hutton sent to ask after my health the evening before, according to the custom of the place? I felt rather offended.

CHAPTER III.

'THE vicarage was on the north side of the street, at the end opening towards the hills. It was a long low house, receding behind its neighbours; a court was between the door and the street, with a flag-walk and an old stone cistern on the right-hand side of the door; Solomon's seal[17] growing under the windows. Some one was watching from behind the window-curtain; for the door opened, as if by magic, as soon as we reached it; and we entered a low room, which served as hall, and was matted all over, with deep old-fashioned window-seats, and Dutch tiles in the fire-place; altogether it was very cool and refreshing, after the hot sun in the white and red street.

"'Bessy is not so well, Mr. Morgan," said the sweet little girl of eleven or so, who had opened the door. "Sophy wanted to send for you; but papa said he was sure you would come soon this morning, and we were to remember that there were other sick people wanting you."

"'Here's Mr. Morgan, Sophy," said she, opening the door into an inner room, to which we descended a step, as I remember well, – for I was nearly falling down it, I was so caught by the picture within. It was like a picture, – at least, seen through the door frame. A sort of mixture of crimson and sea-green in the room, and a sunny garden beyond; a very low casement window, open to the amber air; clusters of white roses peeping in, and Sophy sitting on a cushion on the ground, the light coming from above on her head, and a little sturdy round-eyed brother kneeling by her, to whom she was teaching the alphabet. It was a mighty relief to him when we came in, as I could see; and I am much mistaken if he was easily caught again to say his lesson, when he was once sent off to find papa. Sophy rose quietly, and of course we were just introduced, and that was all, before she took Mr. Morgan up-stairs to see her sick servant. I was left to myself in the room. It looked so like a home, that it at once made me know the full charm of the word. There were books and work about, and tokens of employment: there was a child's plaything on the floor; and against the sea-green walls there hung a likeness or two, done in water-colours; – one, I was sure, was that of Sophy's mother. The chairs and sofa were covered with a chintz, the same as the curtains – a little pretty red rose on a white ground. I don't know where the crimson came from, but I am sure there was crimson somewhere; perhaps in the carpet. There was a glass-door besides the window, and you went up a step into the garden. This was first, a grass plot, just under the windows, and beyond that, straight gravel walks, with box-borders and narrow flower-beds on each side, most brilliant and gay at the end of August, as it was then; and behind the flower-borders were fruit-trees, trained over wood-work, so as to shut out the beds of kitchen-garden within.

'While I was looking round, a gentleman came in, who, I was sure, was the vicar. It was rather awkward, for I had to account for my presence there.

'I came with Mr. Morgan; my name is Harrison,' said I, bowing. I could see he was not much enlightened by this explanation, but we sat down and talked about the time of year, or some such matter, till Sophy and Mr. Morgan came back. Then I saw Mr. Morgan to advantage. With a man whom he respected, as he did the vicar, he lost the prim artificial manner he had in general, and was calm and dignified; but not so dignified as the vicar. I never saw any one like him. He was very quiet and reserved, almost absent at times; his personal appearance was not striking; but he was altogether a man you would talk to with your hat off wherever you met him. It was his character that produced this effect – character that he never thought about, but that appeared in every word, and look, and motion.

'"Sophy," said he, "Mr. Morgan looks very warm; could you not gather a few jargonelle pears[18] off the south wall? I fancy there are some ripe there. Our jargonelle pears are remarkably early this year."

'Sophy went into the sunny garden, and I saw her take a rake and tilt at the pears, which were above her reach, apparently. The parlour had become chilly (I found out afterwards it had a flag floor, which accounts for its coldness), and I thought I should like to go into the warm sun. I said I would go and help the young lady; and without waiting for an answer, I went into the warm, scented garden, where the bees were rifling the flowers, and making a continual busy sound. I think Sophy had begun to despair of getting the fruit, and was glad of my assistance. I thought I was very senseless to have knocked them down so soon, when I found we were to go in as soon as they were gathered. I should have liked to have walked round the garden, but Sophy walked straight off with the pears, and I could do nothing but follow her. She took up her needlework while we ate them: they were very soon finished, and when the vicar had ended his conversation with Mr. Morgan about some poor people, we rose up to come away. I was thankful that Mr. Morgan had said so little about me. I could not have endured that he should have introduced Sir Astley Cooper or Sir Robert Peel at the vicarage; nor yet could I have brooked much mention of my "great opportunities for acquiring a through knowledge of my profession," which I had heard him describe to Miss Tomkinson, while her sister was talking to me. Luckily, however, he spared me all this at the vicar's. When we left, it was time to mount our horses and go the country rounds, and I was glad of it.

CHAPTER IV.

'By-and-by the inhabitants of Duncombe began to have parties in my honour. Mr. Morgan told me it was on my account, or I don't think I should have found it out. But he was pleased at every fresh invitation, and rubbed his hands, and chuckled, as if it was a compliment to himself, as in truth it was.

'Meanwhile, the arrangement with Mrs. Rose had been brought to a conclusion. She was to bring her furniture, and place it in a house, of which I was to pay the rent. She was to be the mistress, and in return, she was not to pay anything for her board. Mr. Morgan took the house, and delighted in advising, and settling all my affairs. I was partly indolent, and partly amused, and was altogether passive. The house he took for me was near his own: it had two sitting-rooms down-stairs, opening into each other by folding-doors, which were, however, kept shut in general. The back room was my consulting room ("the library," he advised me to call it), and he gave me a skull to put on the top of my bookcase, in which the medical books were all ranged on the conspicuous shelves; while Miss Austen, Dickens, and Thackeray were, by Mr. Morgan himself, skilfully placed in a careless way, upside down, or with their backs turned to the wall. The front parlour was to be the dining-room, and the room above was furnished with Mrs. Rose's drawing-room chairs and table, though I found she preferred sitting down-stairs in the dining-room, close to the window, where, between every stitch she could look up and see what was going on in the street. I felt rather queer to be the master of this house, filled with another person's furniture, before I had even seen the lady whose property it was.

'Presently she arrived. Mr. Morgan met her at the inn where the coach stopped, and accompanied her to my house. I could see them out of the drawing-room window, the little gentleman stepping daintily along, flourishing his cane, and evidently talking away. She was a little taller than he was, and in deep widow's mourning; such veils and falls, and capes and cloaks, that she looked like a black crape hay-cock. When we were introduced, she put up her thick veil, and looked around, and sighed.

'"Your appearance and circumstances, Mr. Harrison, remind me forcibly of the time when I was married to my dear husband, now at rest. He was then, like you, commencing practice as a surgeon. For twenty years I sympathised with him, and assisted him by every means in my power, even to making up pills when the young man was out. May we live together in like harmony for an equal length of time! May the regard between us be equally sincere, although, instead of being conjugal, it is to be maternal and filial!'

'I am sure she had been concocting this speech in the coach, for she afterwards told me she was the only passenger. When she had ended, I felt as if I ought to have had a glass of wine in my hand to drink, after the manner of toasts. And yet I doubt if I should have done it heartily, for I did not hope to live with her for twenty years; it had rather a dreary sound. However, I only bowed, and kept my thoughts to myself. I asked Mr. Morgan, while Mrs. Rose was up-stairs taking off her things, to stay to tea; to which he agreed, and kept rubbing his hands with satisfaction, saying –

"'Very fine woman, sir; very fine woman! And what a manner! How she will receive patients, who may wish to leave a message during your absence! Such a flow of words, to be sure!"

'Mr. Morgan could not stay long after tea, as there were one or two cases to be seen. I would willingly have gone, and had my hat on, indeed, for the purpose, when he said it would not be respectful, "not the thing," to leave Mrs. Rose the first evening of her arrival.

"'Tender deference to the sex, – to a widow in the first months of her loneliness, – requires this little consideration, my dear sir. I will leave that case at Miss Tomkinson's for you; you will perhaps call early to-morrow morning. Miss Tomkinson is rather particular, and is apt to speak plainly if she does not think herself properly attended to."

'I had often noticed that he shuffled off the visits to Miss Tomkinson's on me, and I suspect he was a little afraid of the lady.

'It was rather a long evening with Mrs. Rose. She had nothing to do, thinking it civil, I suppose, to stop in the parlour, and not to go up-stairs and unpack. I begged I might be no restraint upon her if she wished to do so; but (rather to my disappointment) she smiled in a measured, subdued way, and said it would be a pleasure to her to become better acquainted with me. She went up-stairs once, and my heart misgave me when I saw her come down with a clean folded pocket-handkerchief. Oh, my prophetic soul! – she was no sooner seated, than she began to give me an account of her late husband's illness, and symptoms, and death. It was a very common case, but she evidently seemed to think it had been peculiar. She had just a smattering of medical knowledge, and used the technical terms so very *mal-àpropos*[19] that I could hardly keep from smiling; but I would not have done it for the world, she was evidently in such deep and sincere distress. At last she said –

"'I have the 'dognoses' of my dear husband's complaint in my desk, Mr. Harrison, if you would like to draw up the case for the 'Lancet.'[20] I think he would have felt gratified, poor fellow, if he had been told such a compliment would be paid to his remains, and that his case should appear in those distinguished columns."

'It was rather awkward; for the case was of the very commonest, as I said before. However, I had not been even this short time in practice without having learnt a few of those noises which do not compromise one, and yet may bear a very significant construction if the listener chooses to exert a little imagination.

'Before the end of the evening, we were such friends that she brought me down the late Mr. Rose's picture to look at. She told me she could not bear, herself, to gaze upon the beloved features; but that if I would look upon the miniature, she would avert her face. I offered to take it into my own hands, but she seemed wounded at the proposal, and said she never, never could trust such a treasure out of her own possession; so she turned her head very much over her left shoulder, while I examined the likeness held by her extended right arm.

'The late Mr. Rose must have been rather a good-looking jolly man; and the artist had given him such a broad smile, and such a twinkle about the eyes, that it really was hard to help smiling back at him. However, I restrained myself.

'At first Mrs. Rose objected to accepting any of the invitations which were sent her to accompany me to the tea-parties in the town. She was so good and simple, that I was sure she had no other reason than the one which she alleged – the short time that had elapsed since her husband's death; or else, now that I had had some experience of the entertainments which she declined so pertinaciously, I might have suspected that she was glad of the excuse. I used sometimes to wish that I was a widow. I came home tired from a hard day's riding, and if I had but felt sure that Mr. Morgan would not come in, I should certainly have put on my slippers and my loose morning coat, and have indulged in a cigar in the garden. It seemed a cruel sacrifice to society to dress myself in tight boots, and a stiff coat, and go to a five o'clock tea. But Mr. Morgan read me such lectures upon the necessity of cultivating the good-will of the people among whom I was settled, and seemed so sorry, and almost hurt, when I once complained of the dulness of these parties, that I felt I could not be so selfish as to decline more than one out of three. Mr. Morgan, if he found that I had an invitation for the evening, would often take the longer round, and the more distant visits. I suspected him at first of the design, which I confess I often entertained, of shirking the parties; but I soon found out he was really making a sacrifice of his inclinations for what he considered to be my advantage.

CHAPTER V

'THERE was one invitation which seemed to promise a good deal of pleasure. Mr. Bullock (who is the attorney of Duncombe) was married a second

time to a lady from a large provincial town; she wished to lead the fashion, –
a thing very easy to do, for every one was willing to follow her. So instead of
giving a tea-party in my honour, she proposed a pic-nic to some old hall in
the neighbourhood; and really the arrangements sounded tempting enough.
Every patient we had seemed full of the subject; both those who were
invited and those who were not. There was a moat round the house, with a
boat on it; and there was a gallery in the hall, from which music sounded
delightfully. The family to whom the place belonged were abroad, and lived
at a newer and grander mansion when they were at home; there were only a
farmer and his wife in the old hall, and they were to have the charge of the
preparations. The little kind-hearted town was delighted when the sun
shone bright on the October morning of our pic-nic; the shopkeepers and
cottagers all looked pleased as they saw the cavalcade gathering at Mr. Bul-
lock's door. We were somewhere about twenty in number; a "silent few," she
called us; but I thought we were quite enough. There were the Miss Tom-
kinsons, and two of their young ladies – one of them belonged to a "country
family," Mrs. Bullock told me in a whisper; then came Mr. and Mrs. and
Miss Bullock, and a tribe of little children, the offspring of the present wife.
Miss Bullock was only a step-daughter. Mrs.Munton had accepted the invi-
tation to join our party, which was rather unexpected by the host and
hostess, I imagine, from little remarks that I overheard; but they made her
very welcome. Miss Horsman (a maiden lady who had been on a visit from
home till last week) was another. And last, there were the vicar and his chil-
dren. These, with Mr. Morgan and myself, made up the party. I was very
much pleased to see something more of the vicar's family. He had come in
occasionally to the evening parties, it is true; and spoken kindly to us all; but
it was not his habit to stay very long at them. And his daughter was, he said,
too young to visit. She had had the charge of her little sisters and brother
since her mother's death, which took up a good deal of her time, and she
was glad of the evenings to pursue her own studies. But to-day the case was
different; and Sophy, and Helen, and Lizzie, and even little Walter, were all
there, standing at Mrs. Bullock's door; for we none of us could be patient
enough to sit still in the parlour, with Mrs.Munton and the elder ones, qui-
etly waiting for the two chaises and the spring-cart, which were to have been
there by two o'clock, and now it was nearly a quarter past. "Shameful! the
brightness of the day would be gone." The sympathetic shopkeepers, stand-
ing at their respective doors with their hands in their pockets, had, one and
all, their heads turned in the direction from which the carriages (as Mrs.Bul-
lock called them) were to come. There was a rumble along the paved street;
and the shopkeepers turned and smiled, and bowed their heads congratulat-
ingly to us; all the mothers and all the little children of the place stood
clustering round the doors to see us set off. I had my horse waiting; and,
meanwhile, I assisted people into their vehicles. One sees a good deal of

management on such occasions. Mrs.Munton was handed first into one of the chaises; then there was a little hanging back, for most of the young people wished to go in the cart, – I don't know why. Miss Horsman, however, came forward, and as she was known to be the intimate friend of Mrs.Munton, so far was satisfactory. But who was to be third? – bodkin with two old ladies,[21] who liked the windows shut? I saw Sophy speaking to Helen; and then she came forward and offered to be the third. The two old ladies looked pleased and glad (as every one did near Sophy); so that chaise-full was arranged. Just as it was going off, however, the servant from the vicarage came running with a note for her master. When he had read it, he went to the chaise-door, and I suppose told Sophy, what I afterwards heard him say to Mrs.Bullock, that the clergyman of a neighbouring parish was ill, and unable to read the funeral-service for one of his parishioners who was to be buried that afternoon. The vicar was, of course, obliged to go, and said he should not return home that night. It seemed a relief to some, I perceived, to be without the little restraint of his dignified presence. Mr. Morgan came up just at the moment, having ridden hard all the morning to be in time to join our party; so we were resigned, on the whole, to the vicar's absence. His own family regretted him the most, I noticed, and I liked them all the better for it. I believe that I came next in being sorry for his departure; but I respected and admired him, and felt always the better for having been in his company. Miss Tomkinson, Mrs.Bullock, and the "county" young lady were in the next chaise. I think the last would rather have been in the cart with the younger and merrier set, but I imagine that was considered *infra dig.* The remainder of the party were to ride and tie;[22] and a most riotous laughing set they were. Mr. Morgan and I were on horseback; at least I led my horse, with little Walter riding on him; his fat, sturdy legs standing stiff out on each side of my cob's broad back. He was a little darling, and chattered all the way, his sister Sophy being the heroine of all his stories. I found he owed this day's excursion entirely to her begging papa to let him come; nurse was strongly against it – "cross old nurse!" he called her once, and then said, "No, not cross; kind nurse; Sophy tells Walter not to say cross nurse." I never saw so young a child so brave. The horse shied at a log of wood. Walter looked very red, and grasped the mane, but sat upright like a little man, and never spoke all the time the horse was dancing. When it was over, he looked at me, and smiled –

'"You would not let me be hurt, Mr. Harrison, would you?" He was the most winning little fellow I ever saw.

'There were frequent cries to me from the cart, "Oh, Mr. Harrison! do get us that branch of blackberries; you can reach it with your whip handle." – "Oh, Mr. Harrison! there were such splendid nuts on the other side of that hedge; would you just turn back for them?" Miss Caroline Tomkinson was once or twice rather faint with the motion of the cart, and asked me for my smelling-bottle, as she had forgotten hers. I was amused at the idea of my carrying such articles about with me. Then she thought she should like to walk, and got out, and came on my side of the road; but I found little Walter the pleasanter companion, and soon set the horse off into a trot, with which pace her tender constitution could not keep up.

'The road to the old hall was along a sandy lane, with high hedge-banks; the wych-elms almost met over-head. "Shocking farming!" Mr. Bullock called out; and so it might be, but it was very pleasant and picturesque-looking. The trees were gorgeous, in their orange and crimson hues, varied by great dark-green holly bushes, glistening in the autumn sun. I should have thought the colours too vivid, if I had seen them in a picture, especially when we wound up the brow, after crossing the little bridge over the brook – (what laughing and screaming there was as the cart splashed through the sparkling water!) – and I caught the purple hills beyond. We could see the old hall, too, from that point, with its warm rich woods billowing up behind, and the blue waters of the moat lying still under the sunlight.

'Laughing and talking is very hungry work, and there was a universal petition for dinner when we arrived at the lawn before the hall, where it had been arranged that we were to dine. I saw Miss Carry take Miss Tomkinson aside, and whisper to her; and presently the elder sister came up to me, where I was busy, rather apart, making a seat of hay, which I had fetched from the farmer's loft for my little friend Walter, who, I had noticed, was rather hoarse, and for whom I was afraid of a seat on the grass, dry as it appeared to be.

'"Mr. Harrison, Caroline tells me she has been feeling very faint, and she is afraid of a return of one of her attacks. She says she has more confidence in your medical powers than in Mr. Morgan's. I should not be sincere if I did not say that I differ from her; but as it is so, may I beg you to keep an eye upon her? I tell her she had better not have come if she did not feel well; but, poor girl, she had set her heart upon this day's pleasure. I have offered to go home with her; but she says, if she can only feel sure you are at hand, she would rather stay."

'Of course, I bowed, and promised all due attendance on Miss Caroline; and in the mean time, until she did require my services, I thought I might as well go and help the vicar's daughter, who looked so fresh and pretty, in her white muslin dress, here, there, and everywhere, now in the sunshine, now in the green shade, helping every one to be comfortable, and thinking of every one but herself.

'Presently Mr. Morgan came up.

'"Miss Caroline does not feel quite well. I have promised your services to her sister."

'"So have I, sir. But Miss Sophy cannot carry this heavy basket."

'I did not mean her to have heard this excuse; but she caught it up, and said –

'"Oh, yes I can! I can take the things out one by one. Go to poor Miss Caroline, pray, Mr. Harrison."

'I went; but very unwillingly, I must say. When I had once seated myself by her, I think she must have felt better. It was, probably, only a nervous fear, which was relieved when she knew she had assistance near at hand; for she made a capital dinner. I thought she would never end her modest requests for "just a little more pigeon-pie, or a merry-thought of chicken." Such a hearty meal would, I hoped, effectually revive her – and so it did; for she told me she thought she could manage to walk round the garden, and see the old peacock yews, if I would kindly give her my arm. It was very provoking; I had so set my heart upon being with the vicar's children. I advised Miss Caroline strongly to lie down a little, and rest before tea, on the sofa in the farmer's kitchen; you cannot think how persuasively I begged her to take care of herself. At last she consented, thanking me for my tender interest; she should never forget my kind attention to her. She little knew what was in my mind at the time. However, she was safely consigned to the farmer's wife, and I was rushing out in search of a white gown and a waving figure, when I encountered Mrs. Bullock at the door of the hall. She was a fine fierce-looking woman. I thought she had appeared a little displeased at my (unwilling) attentions to Miss Caroline at dinner-time; but now, seeing me alone, she was all smiles.

'"Oh, Mr. Harrison, all alone! How is that? What are the young ladies about to allow such churlishness? And, by the way, I have left a young lady who will be very glad of your assistance, I am sure – my daughter, Jemima (her step-daughter, she meant). Mr. Bullock is so particular, and so tender a father, that he would be frightened to death at the idea of her going into the boat on the moat unless she was with some one who could swim. He is gone to discuss the new wheel-plough with the farmer – (you know agriculture is his hobby, although law, horrid law, is his business). But the poor girl is pining on the bank, longing for my permission to join the others, which I dare not give, unless you will kindly accompany her, and promise, if any accident happens, to preserve her safe."

'Oh, Sophy, why was no one anxious about you?

CHAPTER VI.

'MISS BULLOCK was standing by the water-side, looking wistfully, as I thought, at the water-party; the sound of whose merry laughter came pleasantly enough from the boat which lay off (for, indeed, no one knew how to row, and she was of a clumsy flat-bottomed build,) about a hundred yards, "weather-bound," as they shouted out, among the long stalks of the water-lilies.

'Miss Bullock did not look up till I came close to her; and then, when I told her my errand, she lifted up her great heavy, sad eyes, and looked at me for a moment. It struck me, at the time, that she expected to find some expression on my face which was not there, and that its absence was a relief to her. She was a very pale, unhappy-looking girl, but very quiet, and, if not agreeable in manner, at any rate not forward or offensive. I called to the party in the boat, and they came slowly enough through the large, cool, green lily-leaves towards us. When they got near, we saw there was no room for us, and Miss Bullock said she would rather stay in the meadow and saunter about, if I would go into the boat; and I am certain from the look on her countenance that she spoke the truth; but Miss Horsman called out in a sharp voice, while she smiled in a very disagreeable knowing way,

'"Oh, mamma will be displeased if you don't come in, Miss Bullock, after all her trouble in making such a nice arrangement."

'At this speech the poor girl hesitated, and at last, in an undecided way, as if she was not sure whether she was doing right, she took Sophy's place in the boat. Helen and Lizzie landed with their sister, so that there was plenty of room for Miss Tomkinson, Miss Horsman, and all the little Bullocks; and the three vicarage girls went off strolling along the meadow side, and playing with Walter, who was in a high state of excitement. The sun was getting low, but the declining light was beautiful upon the water; and, to add to the charm of the time, Sophy and her sisters, standing on the green lawn in front of the hall, struck up the little German canon, which I had never heard before, –

'Oh wie wohl ist mir am abend,' &c.[23]

At last we were summoned to tug the boat to the landing-steps on the lawn, tea and a blazing wood fire being ready for us in the hall. I was offering my arm to Miss Horsman, as she was a little lame, when she said again, in her peculiar disagreeable way, 'Had you not better take Miss Bullock, Mr. Harrison? It will be more satisfactory.'

'I helped Miss Horsman up the steps, however, and then she repeated her advice; so, remembering that Miss Bullock was in fact the daughter of my entertainers, I went to her; but though she accepted my arm, I could perceive she was sorry that I had offered it.

'The hall was lighted by the glorious wood fire in the wide old grate; the daylight was dying away in the west; and the large windows admitted but little of what was left, through their small leaded frames, with coats of arms emblazoned upon them. The farmer's wife had set out a great long table, which was piled with good things; and a huge black kettle sang on the glowing fire, which sent a cheerful warmth through the room as it crackled and blazed. Mr. Morgan (who I found had been taking a little round in the neighbourhood among his patients) was there, smiling and rubbing his hands as usual. Mr. Bullock was holding a conversation with the farmer at the garden door on the nature of different manures, in which it struck me that if Mr. Bullock had the fine names and the theories on his side, the farmer had all the practical knowledge and the experience, and I knew which I would have trusted, I think Mr. Bullock rather liked to talk about Liebig[24] in my hearing; it sounded well, and was knowing. Mrs. Bullock was not particularly placid in her mood. In the first place, I wanted to sit by the vicar's daughter, and Miss Caroline as decidedly wanted to sit on my other side, being afraid of her fainting fits, I imagine. But Mrs. Bullock called me to a place near her daughter. Now I thought I had done enough civility to a girl who was evidently annoyed, rather than pleased, by my attentions, and I pretended to be busy stooping under the table for Miss Caroline's gloves, which were missing; but it was of no avail; Mrs. Bullock's fine severe eyes were awaiting my re-appearance, and she summoned me again.

"'I am keeping this place on my right hand for you, Mr. Harrison. Jemima; sit still!"

'I went up to the post of honour and tried to busy myself with pouring out coffee to hide my chagrin; but after forgetting to empty the water put in ("to warm the cups," Mrs. Bullock said), and omitting to add any sugar, the lady told me she would dispense with my services, and turn me over to my neighbour on the other side.

"'Talking to the younger lady was, no doubt, more Mr. Harrison's vocation than assisting the elder one." I dare say it was only the manner that made the words seem offensive. Miss Horsman sat opposite to me, smiling away. Miss Bullock did not speak, but seemed more depressed than ever. At length Miss Horsman and Mrs. Bullock got to a war of innuendoes, which were completely unintelligible to me; and I was very much displeased with my situation. While at the bottom of the table, Mr. Morgan and Mr. Bullock were making the young ones laugh most heartily. Part of the joke was Mr. Morgan's insisting upon making tea at that end; and Sophy and Helen were busy contriving every possible mistake for him. I thought honour was a very good thing, but merriment a better. Here was I in the the place of distinction, hearing nothing but cross words. At last the time came for us to go home. As the evening was damp; the seats in the chaises were the best and most to be desired. – And now Sophy offered to go in the cart; only she seemed anxious, and so was I, that Walter should be secured from the effects of the white wreaths of fog rolling up from the valley; but the little violent, affectionate fellow would not be separated from Sophy. She made a nest for him on her knee in one corner of the cart, and covered him with her own shawl; and I hoped that he would take no harm. Miss Tomkinson, Mr. Bullock, and some of the young ones walked; but I seemed chained to the windows of the chaise, for Miss Caroline begged me not to leave her, as she was dreadfully afraid of robbers; and Mrs. Bullock implored me to see that the man did not overturn them in the bad roads, as he had certainly had too much to drink.

'I became so irritable before I reached home, that I thought it was the most disagreeable day of pleasure I had ever had, and could hardly bear to answer Mrs. Rose's never-ending questions. She told me, however, that from my account the day was so charming that she thought she should relax in the rigour of her seclusion, and mingle a little more in the society of which I gave so tempting a description. She really thought her dear Mr. Rose would have wished it; and his will should be law to her after his death, as it had ever been during his life. In compliance, therefore, with his wishes, she would even do a little violence to her own feelings.

'She was very good and kind; not merely attentive to everything which she thought could conduce to my comfort, but willing to take any trouble in providing the broths and nourishing food which I often found it convenient to order, under the name of kitchen-physic, for my poorer patients; and I really did not see the use of her shutting herself up, in mere compliance with an etiquette, when she began to wish to mix in the little quiet society of Duncombe. Accordingly I urged her to begin to visit, and even when applied to as to what I imagined the late Mr. Rose's wishes on that subject would have been, answered for that worthy gentleman, and assured his widow that I was convinced he would have regretted deeply her giving way to immoderate grief, and would have been rather grateful than otherwise at seeing her endeavour to divert her thoughts by a few quiet visits. She cheered up, and said, "as I really thought so, she would sacrifice her own inclinations, and accept the very next invitation that came."

CHAPTER VII.

'I WAS roused from my sleep in the middle of the night by a messenger from the vicarage. Little Walter had got the croup,[25] and Mr. Morgan had been sent for into the country. I dressed myself hastily, and went through the quiet little street. There was a light burning upstairs at the vicarage. It was in the nursery. The servant, who opened the door the instant I knocked, was crying sadly, and could hardly answer my inquiries as I went up stairs, two steps at a time, to see my little favourite.

'The nursery was a great large room. At the farther end it was lighted by a common candle, which left the other end, where the door was, in shade, so I suppose the nurse did not see me come in, for she was speaking very crossly.

'"Miss Sophy!" said she, "I told you over and over again it was not fit for him to go, with the hoarseness that he had, and you would take him. It will break your papa's heart, I know; but it's none of my doing."

'Whatever Sophy felt, she did not speak in answer to this. She was on her knees by the warm bath, in which the little fellow was struggling to get his breath, with a look of terror on his face that I have often noticed in young children when smitten by a sudden and violent illness. It seems as if they recognised something infinite and invisible, at whose bidding the pain and the anguish come, from which no love can shield them. It is a very heart-rending look to observe, because it comes on the faces of those who are too young to receive comfort from the words of faith, or the promises of religion. Walter had his arms tight round Sophy's neck, as if she, hitherto his paradise-angel, could save him from the dread shadow of Death. Yes! of Death! I knelt down by him on the other side, and examined him. The very robustness of his little frame gave violence to the disease, which is always one of the most fearful by which children of his age can be attacked.

'"Don't tremble, Watty," said Sophy, in a soothing tone; "it's Mr. Harrison, darling, who let you ride on his horse." I could detect the quivering in the voice, which she tried to make so calm and soft to quiet the little fellow's fears. We took him out of the bath, and I went for leeches. While I was away, Mr. Morgan came. He loved the vicarage children as if he were their uncle; but he stood still and aghast at the sight of Walter, – so lately bright and strong, – and now hurrying alone to the awful change, – to the silent mysterious land, where, tended and cared for as he had been on earth, he must go – alone. The little fellow! the darling!

'We applied the leeches to his throat. He resisted at first; but Sophy, God bless her, put the agony of her grief on one side, and thought only of him, and began to sing the little songs he loved. We were all still. The gardener had gone to fetch the vicar; but he was twelve miles off, and we doubted if he would come in time. I don't know if they had any hope; but the first moment Mr. Morgan's eyes met mine, I saw that he, like me, had none. The ticking of the house-clock sounded through the dark quiet house. Walter was sleeping now, with the black leeches yet hanging to his fair, white throat. Still Sophy went on singing little lullabies, which she had sung under far different and happier circumstances. I remember one verse, because it struck me at the time as strangely applicable.

> 'Sleep, baby, sleep!
> Thy rest shall angels keep;
> While on the grass the lamb shall feed,
> And never suffer want or need.
> Sleep, baby, sleep.'[26]

The tears were in Mr. Morgan's eyes. I do not think either he or I could have spoken in our natural tones; but the brave girl went on, clear though low, She stopped at last, and looked up.

'"He is better, is he not, Mr. Morgan?"

'"No, my dear. He is – ahem" – he could not speak all at once. Then he said – "My dear! he will be better soon. Think of your mamma, my dear Miss Sophy. She will be very thankful to have one of her darlings safe with her, where she is."

'Still she did not cry. But she bent her head down on the little face, and kissed it long, and tenderly.

'"I will go for Helen and Lizzie. They will be sorry not to see him again.' She rose up and went for them. Poor girls, they came in in their dressing gowns, with eyes dilated with sudden emotion, pale with terror, stealing softly along, as if sound could disturb him. Sophy comforted them by gentle caresses. It was over soon.

'Mr. Morgan was fairly crying like a child. But he thought it necessary to apologise to me, for what I honoured him for. "I am a little overdone by yesterday's work, sir. I have had one or two bad nights, and they rather upset me. When I was your age I was as strong and manly as any one, and would have scorned to shed tears."

'Sophy came up to where we stood.

'"Mr. Morgan! I am so sorry for papa. How shall I tell him?" She was struggling against her own grief for her father's sake. Mr. Morgan offered to await his coming home; and she seemed thankful for the proposal. I, new friend, almost stranger, might stay no longer. The street was as quiet as ever; not a shadow was changed; for it was not yet four o'clock. But during the night a soul had departed.

'From all I could see, and all I could learn, the vicar and his daughter strove which should comfort the other the most. Each thought of the other's grief, – each prayed for the other rather than for themselves. We saw them walking out, countrywards; and we heard of them in the cottages of the poor. But it was some time before I happened to meet either of them again. And then I felt, from something indescribable in their manner towards me, that I was one of the

"Peculiar people, whom Death had made dear."[27]

That one day at the old hall had done this. I was, perhaps, the last person who had given the little fellow any unusual pleasure. Poor Walter! I wish I could have done more to make his short life happy!

(To be continued.)

𝕿𝖍𝖊 𝕷𝖆𝖉𝖎𝖊𝖘' 𝕮𝖔𝖒𝖕𝖆𝖓𝖎𝖔𝖓

No. 14.]　　　LONDON : SATURDAY, MARCH 1, 1851.　　　[PRICE 1*s.*

MR. HARRISON'S CONFESSIONS.

CHAPTER VIII.

THERE was a little lull, out of respect to the Vicar's grief, in the visiting. It gave time to Mrs. Rose to soften down the anguish of her weeds.

'At Christmas, Miss Tomkinson sent out invitations for a party. Miss Caroline had once or twice apologised to me because such an event had not taken place before; but, as she said, "the avocations of their daily life prevented their having such little *réunions* except in the vacations." And, sure enough, as soon as the holidays began, came the civil little note:

'"The Misses Tomkinson request the pleasure of Mrs. Rose's and Mr. Harrison's company at tea, on the evening of Monday, the 23rd inst. Tea at five o'clock."

'Mrs. Rose's spirit roused, like a war-horse at the sound of the trumpet,[28] at this. She was not of a repining disposition, but I do think she believed the party-giving population of Duncombe had given up inviting her, as soon as she had determined to relent, and accept the invitations, in compliance with the late Mr. Rose's wishes.

'Such snippings of white love-ribbon[29] as I found everywhere, making the carpet untidy! One day, too, unluckily, a small box was brought to me by mistake. I did not look at the direction, for I never doubted it was some hyosciamus[30] which I was expecting from London; so I tore it open, and saw inside a piece of paper, with "No more gray hair," in large letters, upon it. I folded it up in a hurry, and sealed it afresh, and gave it to Mrs. Rose; but I could not refrain from asking her, soon after, if she could recommend me anything to keep my hair from turning gray, adding that I thought prevention was better than cure. I think she made out the impression of my seal on the paper after that; for I learned that she had been crying, and that she talked about there being no sympathy left in the world for her since Mr. Rose's death; and that she counted the days until she could rejoin him in the better world. I think she counted the days to Miss Tomkinson's party, too; she talked so much about it.

'The covers were taken off Miss Tomkinson's chairs, and curtains, and sofas; and a great jar full of artificial flowers was placed in the centre of the table, which, as Miss Caroline told me, was all her doing, as she doated on the beautiful and artistic in life. Miss Tomkinson stood, erect as a grenadier, close to the door, receiving her friends, and heartily shaking them by the hands as they entered, she said she was truly glad to see them. And so she really was.

'We had just finished tea, and Miss Caroline had brought out a little pack of conversation cards –[31] sheaves of slips of card-board, with intellectual or sentimental questions on one set, and equally intellectual and sentimental answers on the other; and as the answers were to fit any and all the questions, you may think they were a characterless and "wersh"[32] set of things. I had just been asked by Miss Caroline,

'"*Can you tell what those dearest to you think of you at this present time?*" and had answered,

'"*How can you expect me to reveal such a secret to the present company!*" when the servant announced that a gentleman, a friend of mine, wished to speak to me down stairs.

'"Oh, show him up, Martha, show him up!" said Miss Tomkinson, in her hospitality.

'"Any friend of our friend's is welcome," said Miss Caroline, in an insinuating tone.

'I jumped up, however, thinking it might be some one on business; but I was so penned in by the spider-legged tables, stuck out on every side, that I could not make the haste I wished; and before I could prevent it, Martha had shown up Jack Marshland, who was on his road home for a day or two at Christmas.

'He came up in a hearty way, bowing to Miss Tomkinson, and explaining that he had found himself in my neighbourhood, and had come over to pass a night with me, and that my servant had directed him where I was.

'His voice, loud at all times, sounded like Stentor's[33] in that little room, where we all spoke in a kind of purring way. He had no swell in his tones; they were *forte* from the beginning. At first it seemed like the days of my youth come back again, to hear full manly speaking; and I felt proud of my friend, as he thanked Miss Tomkinson for her kindness in asking him to stay the evening. By-and-by he came up to me, and I dare say he thought he had lowered his voice, for he looked as if speaking confidentially, while in fact the whole room might have heard him.

'"Frank, my boy, when shall we have dinner at this good old lady's? I'm deuced hungry."

'Dinner! Why, we had had tea an hour ago! While he yet spoke, Martha came in with a little tray, on which was a single cup of coffee and three slices of wafer bread-and-butter. His dismay, and his evident submission to the decrees of Fate, tickled me so much, that I thought he should have a further taste of the life I led from month's end to month's end, and I gave up my plan of taking him home at once, and enjoyed the anticipation of the hearty laugh we should have together at the end of the evening. I was famously punished for my determination.

'"Shall we continue our game?" asked Miss Caroline, who had never relinquished her sheaf of questions.

'We went on questioning and answering, with little gain of information to either party.

'"No such thing as heavy betting in this game, eh Frank?" asked Jack, who had been watching us. "You don't lose ten pounds at a sitting, I guess, as you used to do at Short's.[34] Playing for love, I suppose you call it."

'Miss Caroline simpered, and looked down. Jack was not thinking of her. He was thinking of the days we had had at the Mermaid.[35] Suddenly he said, "Where were you this day last year, Frank?"

'"I don't remember!" said I.

'"Then I'll tell you. It's the 23rd – the day you were taken up for knocking down the fellow in Longacre, and that I had to bail you out ready for Christmas-day. You are in more agreeable quarters tonight."

'He did not intend this reminiscence to be heard, but was not in the least put out when Miss Tomkinson, with a face of dire surprise, asked,

'"Mr. Harrison taken up, sir?"

'"Oh, yes, ma'am; and you see it was so common an affair with him to be locked up that he can't remember the dates of his different imprisonments."

'He laughed heartily; and so should I, but that I saw the impression it made. The thing was, in fact, simple enough, and capable of easy explanation. I had been made angry by seeing a great hulking fellow, out of mere wantonness, break the crutch from under a cripple; and I struck the man more violently than I intended, and down he went, yelling out for the police, and I had to go before the magistrate to be released. I disdained giving this explanation at the time. It was no business of theirs what I had been doing a year ago; but still Jack might have held his tongue. However, that unruly member of his was set a-going, and he told me afterwards he was resolved to let the old ladies into a little of life; and accordingly he remembered every practical joke we had ever had, and talked and laughed, and roared again. I tried to converse with Miss Caroline – Mrs. Munton – any one; but Jack was the hero of the evening, and every one was listening to him.

'"Then he has never sent any hoaxing letters since he came here, has he? Good boy! He has turned over a new leaf. He was the deepest dog at that I ever met with. Such anonymous letters as he used to send! Do you remember that to Mrs. Walbrook, eh Frank? That was too bad!" (the wretch was laughing all the time) "No; I won't tell about it – don't be afraid. Such a shameful hoax!" (laughing again.)

'"Pray do tell," I called out; for he made it seem far worse than it was.

'Oh no, no; you've established a better character – I would not for the world nip your budding efforts. We'll bury the past in oblivion.'

'I tried to tell my neighbours the story to which he alluded; but they were attracted by the merriment of Jack's manner, and did not care to hear the plain matter of fact.

'Then came a pause; Jack was talking almost quietly to Miss Horsman, Suddenly he called across the room – "How many times have you been out with the hounds? The hedges were blind very late this year, but you must have had some good mild days since."

'"I have never been out," said I, shortly.

'"Never! – whew – ! Why I thought that was the great attraction to Duncombe."

'Now was not he provoking? He would condole with me, and fixed the subject in the minds of every one present.

'The supper-trays were brought in, and there was a shuffling of situations. He and I were close together again.

'"I say, Frank, what will you lay me that I don't clear that tray before people are ready for their second helping? I'm as hungry as a hound."

'"You shall have a round of beef and a raw leg of mutton when we get home. Only do behave yourself here."

'"Well, for your sake; but keep me away from those trays, or I'll not answer for myself. 'Hould me or I'll fight,' as the Irishman said. I'll go and talk to that little old lady in blue, and sit with my back to those ghosts of eatables."

'He sat down by Miss Caroline, who would not have liked his description of her; and began an earnest, tolerably quiet conversation. I tried to be as agreeable as I could, to do away with the impression he had given of me; but I found that every one drew up a little stiffly at my approach, and did not encourage me to make many remarks.

'In the middle of my attempts, I heard Miss Caroline beg Jack to take a glass of wine, and I saw him help himself to what appeared to be port; but in an instant he set it down from his lips, exclaiming – "Vinegar, by Jove!" He made the most horribly wry face; and Miss Tomkinson came up in a severe hurry to investigate the affair. It turned out it was some black currant wine, on which she particularly piqued herself; I drank two glasses of it to ingratiate myself with her, and can testify to its sourness. I don't think she noticed my exertions, she was so much engrossed in listening to Jack's excuses for his *mal-à-propos* observation. He told her with the gravest face that he had been a teetotaller so long that he had but a confused recollection of the distinction between wine and vinegar, particularly eschewing the latter, because it had been twice fermented; and that he had imagined Miss Caroline had asked him to take toast-and-water, or he should never have touched the decanter

CHAPTER IX.

'As we were walking home, Jack said, "Lord, Frank! I've had such fun with the little lady in blue. I told her you wrote to me every Saturday, telling me the events of the week. She took all in." He stopped to laugh; for he bubbled and chuckled so that he could not laugh and walk. "And I told her you were deeply in love," (another laugh); "and that I could not get you to tell me the name of the lady, but that she had light brown hair, – in short, I drew from life, and gave her an exact description of herself; and that I was most anxious to see her, and implore her to be merciful to you, for that you were a most timid, faint-hearted fellow with women." He laughed till I thought he would have fallen down. "I begged her, if she could guess who it was from my description – I'll answer for it, she did – I took care of that; for I said you described a mole on the left cheek, in the most poetical way, saying Venus had pinched it out of envy at seeing any one more lovely – Oh, hold me up, or I shall fall – laughing and hunger make me so weak: – well, I say, I begged her, if she knew who your fair one could be, to implore her to save you. I said I knew one of your lungs had gone after a former unfortunate love affair, and that I could not answer for the other if the lady here were cruel. She spoke of a respirator; but I told her that might do very well for the odd lung; but would it minister to a heart diseased![36] I really did talk fine; – I have found out the secret of eloquence – it's believing what you've got to say; and I worked myself well up with fancying you married to the little lady in blue."

'I got to laughing at last, angry as I had been; his impudence was irresistible. Mrs. Rose had come home in the sedan, and gone to bed; and he and I sat up over the round of beef and brandy-and-water till two o'clock in the morning.

'He told me I had got quite into the professional way of mousing about a room, and mewing and purring according as my patients were ill or well. He mimicked me, and made me laugh at myself. He left early the next morning.

'Mr. Morgan came at his usual hour; he and Marshland would never have agreed, and I should have been uncomfortable to see two friends of mine disliking and despising each other.

'Mr. Morgan was ruffled; but with his deferential manner to women, he smoothed himself down before Mrs. Rose, – regretted that he had not been able to come to Miss Tomkinson's the evening before, and consequently had not seen her in the society she was so well calculated to adorn. But when we were by ourselves, he said,

'"I was sent for to Mrs. Munton's this morning – the old spasms. May I ask what is this story she tells me about, – about prison, in fact? I trust, sir, she has made some little mistake, and that you never were – that it is an unfounded report." He could not get it out, – "that you were in Newgate for three months!" I burst out laughing; the story had grown like a mushroom indeed. Mr. Morgan looked grave. I told him the truth. Still he looked grave. "I've no doubt, sir, that you acted rightly; but it has an awkward sound. I imagined from your hilarity just now that there was no foundation whatever for the story. Unfortunately there is."

"'I was only a night at the police-station. I would go there again for the same cause, sir."

"'Very fine spirit, sir, – quite like Don Quixote; but don't you see you might as well have been to the hulks at once?"

"'No, sir; I don't."

"'Take my word, before long, the story will have grown to that. However, we won't anticipate evil. *Mens conscia recti,*[37] you remember, is the great thing. The part I regret is, that it may require some short time to overcome a little prejudice which the story may excite against you. However, we won't dwell on it. *Mens conscia recti!* Don't think about it, sir,"

'It was clear he was thinking a good deal about it.

CHAPTER X.

'Two or three days before this time, I had had an invitation from the Bullocks to dine with them on Christmas-day. Mrs. Rose was going to spend the week with friends in the town where she formerly lived; and I had been pleased at the notion of being received into a family, and of being a little with Mr. Bullock, who struck me as a bluff good-hearted fellow.

'But this Tuesday before Christmas-day, there came an invitation from the vicar to dine there; there were to be only their own family and Mr. Morgan. "Only their own family." It was getting to be all the world to me. I was in a passion with myself for having been so ready to accept Mr. Bullock's invitation, – coarse and ungentlemanly as he was; with his wife's airs of pretension, and Miss Bullock's stupidity. I turned it over in my mind. No! I could not have a bad headache, which should prevent my going to the place I did not care for, and yet leave me at liberty to go where I wished. All I could do was to join the vicarage girls after church, and walk by their side in a long country ramble. They were quiet; not sad, exactly; but it was evident that the thought of Walter was in their minds on this day. We went through a copse where there were a good number of evergreens planted as covers for game. The snow was on the ground; but the sky was clear and bright, and the sun glittered on the smooth holly leaves. Lizzie asked me to gather her some of the very bright red berries, and she was beginning a sentence with,

"'Do you remember –," when Helen said "*Hush,*" and looked towards Sophy, who was walking a little apart, and crying softly to herself. There was evidently some connection between Walter and the holly-berries, for Lizzie threw them away at once when she saw Sophy's tears. Soon we came to a stile which led to an open breezy common, half covered with gorse. I helped the little girls over it, and set them to run down the slope; but I took Sophy's arm in mine, and though I could not speak, I think she knew how I was feeling for her. I could hardly bear to bid her good-bye at the vicarage gate; it seemed as if I ought to go in and spend the day with her.

CHAPTER XI.

'I VENTED my ill-humour in being late for the Bullocks' dinner. There were one or two clerks, towards whom Mr. Bullock was patronising and pressing. Mrs. Bullock was decked out in extraordinary finery. Miss Bullock looked plainer than ever; but she had on some old gown or other, I think, for I heard Mrs. Bullock tell her she was always making a figure of herself. I began to-day to suspect that the mother would not be sorry if I took a fancy to the step-daughter. I was again placed near her at dinner, and when the little ones came in to dessert, I was made to notice how fond of children she was, and indeed when one of them nestled to her, her face did brighten; but the moment she caught this loud-whispered remark, the gloom came back again, with something even of anger in her look; and she was quite sullen and obstinate when urged to sing in the drawing-room. Mrs. Bullock turned to me –

'"Some young ladies won't sing unless they are asked by gentlemen." She spoke very crossly. "If you ask Jemima, she will probably sing. To oblige me, it is evident she will not."

'I thought the singing, when we got it, would probably be a great bore; however, I did as I was bid, and went with my request to the young lady, who was sitting a little apart. She looked up at me with eyes full of tears, and said in a decided tone (which, if I had not seen her eyes, I should have said was as cross as her mamma's), "No, sir, I will not." She got up, and left the room. I expected to hear Mrs. Bullock abuse her for her obstinacy. Instead of that, she began to tell me of the money that had been spent on her education; of what each separate accomplishment had cost. "She was timid," she said, "but very musical. Wherever her future home might be, there would be no want of music." She went on praising her till I hated her. If they thought I was going to marry that great lubberly girl, they were mistaken. Mr. Bullock and the clerks came up. He brought out Liebig, and called me to him.

'"I can understand a good deal of this Agricultural Chemistry," said he, "and have put it in practice – without much success, hitherto, I confess. But these unconnected letters puzzle me a little. I suppose they have some meaning, or else I should say it was mere book-making to put them in."

'"I think they give the page a very ragged appearance," said Mrs. Bullock, who had joined us. "I inherit a little of my late father's taste for books, and must say I like to see a good type, a broad margin, and an elegant binding. My father despised variety; how he would have held up his hands aghast at the cheap literature of these times! He did not require many books, but he would have twenty editions of those that he had; and he paid more for binding than he did for the books themselves. But elegance was everything with him. He would not have admitted your Liebig, Mr. Bullock; neither the nature of the subject, nor the common type, nor the common way in which your book is got up, would have suited him."

'"Go and make tea, my dear, and leave Mr. Harrison and me to talk over a few of these manures."

'We settled to it; I explained the meaning of the symbols, and the doctrine of chemical equivalents. At last he said, "Doctor! you're giving me too strong a dose of it at one time. Let's have a small quantity taken 'hodie;'[38] that's professional, as Mr. Morgan would call it. Come in and call when you have leisure, and give me a lesson in my alphabet. Of all you've been telling me I can only remember that C means carbon and O oxygen; and I see one must know the meaning of all these confounded letters before one can do much good with Liebig."

'"We dine at three," said Mrs. Bullock. "There will always be a knife and fork for Mr. Harrison. Bullock! don't confine your invitation to the evening!"

'"Why, you see, I've a nap always after dinner, so I could not be learning chemistry then."

'"Don't be so selfish, Mr. B. Think of the pleasure Jemima and I shall have in Mr. Harrison's society."

'I put a stop to the discussion by saying I would come in in the evenings occasionally, and give Mr. Bullock a lesson, but that my professional duties occupied me invariably until that time.

'I liked Mr. Bullock. He was simple, and shrewd; and to be with a man was a relief, after all the feminine society I went through every day.

CHAPTER XII.

'THE next morning I met Miss Horsman.

'"So you dined at Mr. Bullock's yesterday, Mr. Harrison? Quite a family party, I hear. They are quite charmed with you, and your knowledge of chemistry. Mr. Bullock told me so, in Hodgson's shop, just now. Miss Bullock is a nice girl, eh, Mr. Harrison?" She looked sharply at me. Of course, whatever I thought, I could do nothing but assent. "A nice little fortune, too, – three thousand pounds, Consols,[39] from her own mother."

'What did I care? She might have three millions, for me. I had begun to think a good deal about money, though, but not in connexion with her. I had been doing up our books ready to send out our Christmas bills, and had been wondering how far the Vicar would consider three hundred a year, with a prospect of increase, would justify me in thinking of Sophy. Think of her I could not help; and the more I thought of how good, and sweet, and pretty, she was, the more I felt that she ought to have far more than I could offer. Besides, my father was a shopkeeper, and I saw the Vicar had a sort of respect for family. I determined to try and be very attentive to my profession. I was as civil as could be to every one; and wore the nap off the brim of my hat by taking it off so often.

'I had my eyes open to every glimpse of Sophy. I am overstocked with gloves now that I bought at that time, by way of making errands into the shops where I saw her black gown. I bought pounds upon pounds of arrow-root, till I was tired of the eternal arrow-root puddings Mrs. Rose gave me. I asked her if she could not make bread of it, but she seemed to think that would be expensive; so I took to soap as a safe purchase. I believe soap improves by keeping.

CHAPTER XIII.

'THE more I knew of Mrs. Rose, the better I liked her. She was sweet, and kind, and motherly, and we never had any rubs. I hurt her once or twice, I think, by cutting her short in her long stories about Mr. Rose. But I found out that when she had plenty to do she did not think of him quite so much; so I expressed a wish for some Corazza shirts,[40] and in the puzzle of devising how they were to be cut out, she forgot Mr. Rose for some time. I was still more pleased by her way about some legacy her elder brother left her. I don't know the amount, but it was something handsome, and she might have set up housekeeping for herself; but instead, she told Mr. Morgan (who repeated it to me), that she should continue with me, as she had quite an elder sister's interest in me.

'The "country young lady," Miss Tyrrell, returned to Miss Tomkinson's after the holidays. She had an enlargement of the tonsils, which required to be frequently touched with caustic, so I often called to see her. Miss Caroline always received me, and kept me talking in her washed-out style, after I had seen my patient. One day she told me she thought she had a weakness about the heart, and would be glad if I would bring my stethoscope the next time, which I accordingly did; and while I was on my knees listening to the pulsations, one of the young ladies came in. She said:

'"Oh dear! I never! I beg your pardon, Ma'am," and scuttled out. There was not much the matter with Miss Caroline's heart; a little feeble in action or so, a mere matter of weakness and general languor. When I went down I saw two or three of the girls peeping out of the half-closed school-room door, but they shut it immediately, and I heard them laughing. The next time I called, Miss Tomkinson was sitting in state to receive me.

"'Miss Tyrrell's throat does not seem to make much progress. Do you understand the case, Mr. Harrison – or should we have further advice? I think Mr. Morgan would probably know more about it."

'I assured her it was the simplest thing in the world; that it always implied a little torpor in the constitution, and that we preferred working through the system, which of course was a slow process, and that the medicine the young lady was taking (iodide of iron) was sure to be successful, although the progress would not be rapid. She bent her head, and said, "It might be so; but she confessed she had more confidence in medicines which had some effect."

'She seemed to expect me to tell her something; but I had nothing to say, and accordingly I bade good-bye. Somehow Miss Tomkinson always managed to make me feel very small, by a succession of snubbings; and whenever I left her I had always to comfort myself under her contradictions by saying to myself, "Her saying it is so does not make it so." Or I invented good retorts which I might have made to her brusque speeches if I had but thought of them at the right time. But it was provoking that I had not had the presence of mind to recollect them just when they were wanted.

<hr>

CHAPTER XIV.

'ON the whole, things went on smoothly. Mr. Holden's legacy came in just about this time; and I felt quite rich. Five hundred pounds would furnish the house, I thought, when Mrs. Rose left and Sophy came. I was delighted, too, to imagine that Sophy perceived the difference of my manner to her from what it was to any one else, and that she was embarrassed and shy in consequence, but not displeased with me for it. All was so flourishing that I went about on wings instead of feet. We were very busy, without having anxious cases. My legacy was paid into Mr. Bullock's hands, who united a little banking business to his profession of law. In return for his advice about investments (which I never meant to take, having a more charming, if less profitable, mode in my head), I went pretty frequently to teach him his agricultural chemistry. I was so happy in Sophy's blushes that I was universally benevolent, and desirous of giving pleasure to every one. I went, at Mrs. Bullock's general invitation, to dinner there one day unexpectedly; but there was such a fuss of ill-concealed preparation consequent upon my coming, that I never went again. Her little boy came in, with an audibly-given message from the cook, to ask –

'"If this was the gentleman as she was to send in the best dinner-service and dessert for?"

'I looked deaf, but determined never to go again.

'Miss Bullock and I, meanwhile, became rather friendly. We found out that we mutually disliked each other; and were contented with the discovery. If people are worth anything, this sort of non-liking is a very good beginning of friendship. Every good quality is revealed naturally and slowly, and is a pleasant surprise. I found out that Miss Bullock was sensible, and even sweet-tempered, when not irritated by her stepmother's endeavours to show her off. But she would sulk for hours after Mrs. Bullock's offensive praise of her good points. And I never saw such a black passion as she went into when she suddenly came into the room when Mrs. Bullock was telling me of all the offers she had had.

'My legacy made me feel up to extravagance. I scoured the country for a glorious nosegay of camellias, which I sent to Sophy on Valentine's day. I durst not add a line, but I wished the flowers could speak, and tell her how I loved her.

'I called on Miss Tyrrell that day. Miss Caroline was more simpering and affected than ever; and full of allusions to the day.

'"Do you affix much sincerity of meaning to the little gallantries of this day, Mr. Harrison?" asked she in a languishing tone. I thought of my camellias, and how my heart had gone with them into Sophy's keeping; and I told her I thought one might often take advantage of such a time to hint at feelings one dared not fully express.

'I remembered afterwards the forced display she made, after Miss Tyrrell left the room, of a valentine. But I took no notice at the time; my head was full of Sophy.

'It was on that very day that John Brouncker, the gardener to all of us who had small gardens to keep in order, fell down and injured his wrist severely (I don't give you the details of the case, because they would not interest you, being too technical; if you've any curiosity, you will find them in the *Lancet* of August in that year). We all liked John, and this accident was felt like a town's misfortune. The gardens, too, just wanted doing up. Both Mr. Morgan and I went directly to him. It was a very awkward case, and his wife and children were crying sadly. He himself was in great distress at being thrown out of work. He begged us to do something that would cure him speedily, as he could not afford to be laid up, with six children depending on him for bread. We did not say much before him, but we both thought the arm would have to come off: and it was his right arm. We talked it over when we came out of the cottage. Mr. Morgan had no doubt of the necessity. I went back at dinner-time to see the poor fellow. He was feverish and anxious. He had caught up some expression of Mr. Morgan's in the morning, and had guessed the measure we had in contemplation. He bade his wife leave the room, and spoke to me by myself.

'"If you please, sir, I'd rather be done for at once than have my arm taken off, and be a burden to my family. I'm not afraid of dying, but I could not stand being a cripple for life, eating bread, and not able to earn it."

'The tears were in his eyes with earnestness. I had all along been more doubtful about the necessity of the amputation than Mr. Morgan. I knew the improved treatment of such cases. In his days there was much more of the rough and ready in surgical practice; so I gave the poor fellow some hope.

'In the afternoon I met Mr. Bullock.

'"So you're to try your hand at an amputation to-morrow, I hear. Poor John Brouncker! I used to tell him he was not careful enough about his ladders. Mr. Morgan is quite excited about it. He asked me to be present, and see how well a man from Guy's could operate; he says he is sure you'll do it beautifully. Pah! no such sights for me, thank you."

'Ruddy Mr. Bullock went a shade or two paler at the thought.

'"Curious! how professionally a man views these things. Here's Mr. Morgan, who has been all along as proud of you as if you were his own son, absolutely rubbing his hands at the idea of this crowning glory, this feather in your cap! He told me just now he knew he had always been too nervous to be a good operator; and had therefore preferred sending for White from Chesterton. But now any one might have a serious accident who liked, for you would be always at hand."

'I told Mr. Bullock, I really thought we might avoid the amputation; but his mind was pre-occupied with the idea of it, and he did not care to listen to me. The whole town was full of it. That is a charm in a little town, everybody is so sympathetically full of the same events. Even Miss Horsman stopped me to ask after John Brouncker with interest; but she threw cold water upon my intention of saving the arm.

'"As for the wife and family, we'll take care of them. Think what a fine opportunity you have of showing off, Mr. Harrison!"

'That was just like her. Always ready with her suggestions of ill-natured or interested motives.

'Mr. Morgan heard my proposal of a mode of treatment by which I thought it possible that the arm might be saved.

'"I differ from you, Mr. Harrison," said he. "I regret it, but I differ *in toto* from you. Your kind heart deceives you in this instance. There is no doubt that amputation must take place – not later than to-morrow morning, I should say. I have made myself at liberty to attend upon you, sir; I shall be happy to officiate as your assistant. Time was when I should have been proud to be principal, but a little trembling in my arm incapacitates me."

'I urged my reasons upon him again; but he was obstinate. He had, in fact, boasted so much of my acquirements as an operator, that he was unwilling I should lose this opportunity of displaying my skill. He could not see that there would be greater skill evinced in saving the arm; nor did I think of this at the time. I grew angry at his old-fashioned narrow-mindedness, as I thought it; and I became dogged in my resolution to adhere to my own course. We parted very coolly; and I went straight off to John Brouncker to tell him I believed that I could save the arm, if he would refuse to have it amputated. When I calmed myself a little, before going in and speaking to him, I could not help acknowledging that we should run some risk of locked jaw; but, on the whole, and after giving most earnest conscientious thought to the case, I was sure that my mode of treatment would be best.

'He was a sensible man. I told him the difference of opinion that existed between Mr. Morgan and myself. I said that there might be some little risk attending the non-amputation; but that I should guard against it, and I trusted that I should be able to preserve his arm.

'"Under God's blessing," said he, reverently. I bowed my head. I don't like to talk too frequently of the dependence which I always felt on that holy blessing, as to the result of my efforts; but I was glad to hear that speech of John's, because it showed a calm and faithful heart; and I had almost certain hopes of him from that time.

'We agreed that he should tell Mr. Morgan the reason of his objections to the amputation, and his reliance on my opinion. I determined to recur to every book I had relating to such cases, and to convince Mr. Morgan, if I could, of my wisdom. Unluckily, I found out afterwards that he had met Miss Horsman in the time that intervened before I saw him again at his own house that evening; and she had more than hinted that I shrunk from performing the operation, "for very good reasons, no doubt. She had heard that the medical students in London were a bad set, and were not remarkable for regular attendance in the hospitals. She might be mistaken; but she thought it was, perhaps, quite as well poor John Brouncker had not his arm cut off by — Was there not such a thing as mortification coming on after a clumsy operation? It was, perhaps, only a choice of deaths!'

'Mr. Morgan had been stung at all this. Perhaps I did not speak quite respectfully enough; I was a good deal excited. We only got more and more angry with each other; though he, to do him justice, was as civil as could be all the time, thinking that thereby he concealed his vexation and disappointment. He did not try to conceal his anxiety about poor John. I went home weary and dispirited. I made up, and took the necessary applications to John; and, promising to return with the dawn of day (I would fain have stayed, but I did not wish him to be alarmed about himself), I went home, and resolved to sit up and study the treatment of similar cases.

'Mrs. Rose knocked at the door.

'"Come in!" said I, sharply.

'She said she had seen I had something on my mind all day, and she could not go to bed without asking if there was nothing she could do. She was good and kind; and I could not help telling her a little of the truth. She listened pleasantly; and I shook her warmly by the hand, thinking that though she might not be very wise, her good heart made her worth a dozen keen, sharp, hard people like Miss Horsman.

'When I went at day-break, I saw John's wife for a few minutes outside of the door. She seemed to wish her husband had been in Mr. Morgan's hands rather than mine; but she gave me as good an account as I dared to hope for of the manner in which her husband had passed the night. This was confirmed by my own examination.

'When Mr. Morgan and I visited him together later on in the day, John said what we had agreed upon the day before; and I told Mr. Morgan openly that it was by my advice that amputation was declined. He did not speak to me till we had left the house. Then he said – "Now, sir, from this time, I consider this case entirely in your hands. Only remember the poor fellow has a wife and six children. In case you come round to my opinion, remember that Mr. White could come over, as he has done before, for the operation."

'So! Mr. Morgan believed I declined operating because I felt myself incapable. – Very well! – I was much mortified.

'An hour after we parted, I received a note to this effect: –

"'Dear Sir, – I will take the long round to-day, to leave you at liberty to attend to Brouncker's case, which I feel to be a very responsible one.

J. MORGAN."

'This was kindly done. I went back, as soon as I could, to John's cottage. While I was in the inner room with him, I heard the Miss Tomkinsons' voices outside. They had called to inquire. Miss Tomkinson came in, and evidently was poking and snuffing about. (Mrs. Brouncker told her that I was within; and within I resolved to be, till they had gone.)

"'What is this close smell?" asked she. "I am afraid you are not cleanly. Cheese! – cheese in this cupboard! No wonder there is an unpleasant smell. Don't you know how particular you should be about being clean when there is illness about?"

'Mrs. Brouncker was exquisitely clean in general, and was piqued at these remarks.

"'If you please, ma'am, I could not leave John yesterday to do any housework, and Jenny put the dinner-things away. She is but eight years old."

'But this did not satisfy Miss Tomkinson, who was evidently pursuing the course of her observations.

"'Fresh butter, I declare! Well now, Mrs. Brouncker, do you know I don't allow myself fresh butter at this time of the year? How can you save, indeed, with such extravagance!"

'"Please ma'am," answered Mrs. Brouncker, "you'd think it strange if I was to take such liberties in your house as you're taking here."

'I expected to hear a sharp answer. No! Miss Tomkinson liked true, plain-speaking. The only person in whom she would tolerate round-about ways of talking was her sister.

'"Well, that's true," she said. "Still, you must not be above taking advice. Fresh butter is extravagant at this time of the year. However, you're a good kind of woman, and I've a great respect for John. Send Jenny for some broth as soon as he can take it. Come, Caroline, we have got to go on to Williams's."

'But Miss Caroline said that she was tired, and would rest where she was till Miss Tomkinson came back. I was a prisoner for some time, I found. When she was alone with Mrs. Brouncker, she said –

'"You must not be hurt by my sister's abrupt manner. She means well. She has not much imagination or sympathy, and cannot understand the dis-traction of mind produced by the illness of a worshipped husband." I could hear the loud sigh of commiseration which followed this speech. Mrs. Brouncker said –

'"Please ma'am, I don't worship my husband. I would not be so wicked."

'"Goodness! – you don't think it wicked, do you? For my part, if ... I should worship, I should adore him. I thought she need not imagine such improbable cases. But sturdy Mrs. Brouncker said again –

'"I hope I know my duty better. I've not learned my Commandments for nothing. I know whom I ought to worship."

'Just then the children came in, dirty and unwashed, I have no doubt. And now Miss Caroline's real nature peeped out. She spoke sharply to them, and asked them if they had no manners, little pigs as they were, to come brushing against her silk gown in that way? She sweetened herself again; and was as sugary as love when Miss Tomkinson returned for her, accompanied by one whose voice, "like winds in summer sighing,"[41] I knew to be my dear Sophy's.

'She did not say much; but what she did say, and the manner in which she spoke, was tender and compassionate in the highest degree; and she came to take the four little ones back with her to the Vicarage, in order that they might be out of their mother's way; the older two might help at home. She offered to wash their hands and faces; and when I emerged from my inner chamber, after the Miss Tomkinsons had left, I found her with a chubby child on her knees, bubbling and sputtering against her white wet hand, with a face bright, rosy, and merry under the operation. Just as I came in, she said to him, "There, Jemmy, now I can kiss you with this nice clean face."

'She coloured when she saw me. I liked her speaking, and I liked her silence. She was silent now, and I "lo'ed a" the better.[42] I gave my directions to Mrs. Brouncker, and hastened to overtake Sophy and the children; but they had gone round by the lanes, I suppose, for I saw nothing of them.

'I was very anxious about the case. At night I went again. Miss Horsman had been there; I believe she was really kind among the poor, but she could not help leaving a sting behind her everywhere. She had been frightening Mrs. Brouncker about her husband; and been, I have no doubt, expressing her doubts of my skill; for Mrs. Brouncker began:

'"Oh, please sir, if you'll only let Mr. Morgan take off his arm. I will never think the worse of you for not being able to do it.

'I told her it was from no doubt of my own competency to perform the operation that I wished to save the arm; but that he himself was anxious to have it spared.

'"Aye, bless him! he frets about not earning enough to keep us, if he's crippled; but, sir, I don't care about that. I would work my fingers to the bone, and so would the children; I'm sure we'd be proud to do for him, and keep him; God bless him! It would be far better to have him only with one arm than to have him in the church-yard, Miss Horsman says" –

'"Confound Miss Horsman!" said I –

'"Thank you, Mr. Harrison," said her well-known voice behind me. She had come out, dark as it was, to bring some old linen to Mrs. Brouncker; for, as I said before, she was very kind to all the poor people of Duncombe.

'"I beg your pardon;" for I really was sorry for my speech, or, rather, that she had heard it.

'"There is no occasion for any apology," she replied, drawing herself up, and pinching her lips into a very venomous shape.

'John was doing pretty well; but of course the danger of locked jaw was not over. Before I left, his wife entreated me to take off the arm; – she wrung her hands in her passionate entreaty. "Spare him to me, Mr. Harrison," she implored. Miss Horsman stood by. It was mortifying enough; but I thought of the power which was in my hands, as I firmly believed, of saving the limb; and I was inflexible.

'You cannot think how pleasantly Mrs. Rose's sympathy came in on my return. To be sure she did not understand one word of the case which I detailed to her; but she listened with interest, and, as long as she held her tongue, I thought she was really taking it in; but her first remark was as *malapropos* as could be.

'"You are anxious to save the tibia, – I see completely how difficult that will be, My late husband had a case exactly similar, and I remember his anxiety; but you must not distress yourself too much, my dear Mr. Harrison; I have no doubt it will end well."

'I knew she had no grounds for this assurance, and yet it comforted me.

'However, as it happened, John did fully as well as I could hope – of course he was long in rallying his strength; and, indeed, sea-air was evidently so necessary for his complete restoration, that I accepted with gratitude Mrs. Rose's proposal of sending him to Highport for a fortnight or three weeks. Her kind generosity in this matter made me more desirous than ever of paying her every mark of respect and attention.

(*To be continued*)

MR. HARRISON'S CONFESSIONS.

CHAPTER XV.

ABOUT this time there was a sale at Ashmeadow, a pretty house in the neighbourhood of Duncombe. It was likewise an easy walk, and the spring days tempted many people thither, who had no intention of buying anything, but who liked the idea of rambling through the woods, gay with early primroses and wild daffodils, and of seeing the gardens and house, which till now had been shut up from the ingress of the town's people. Mrs. Rose had planned to go, but an unlucky cold prevented her. She begged me to bring her a very particular account, saying she delighted in details, and always questioned the late Mr. Rose as to the side dishes of the dinners to which he went. The late Mr. Rose's conduct was always held up as a model to me, by the way. I walked to Ashmeadow, pausing, or loitering with different parties of town's-people, all bound in the same direction. At last I found the vicar and Sophy, and with them I staid. I sat by Sophy, and talked and listened. A sale is a very pleasant gathering after all. The auctioneer, in a country place, is privileged to joke from his rostrum; and, having a personal knowledge of most of the people, can sometimes make a very keen hit at their circumstances, and turn the laugh against them. For instance, on the present occasion, there was a farmer present, with his wife, who was notoriously the grey mare. The auctioneer was selling some horse-cloths, and called out to recommend the article to her, telling her, with a knowing look at the company, that they would make her a dashing pair of trowsers if she was in want of such an article. She drew herself up with dignity, and said "Come, John, we've had enough of these." Whereupon there was a burst of laughter, and in the midst of it John meekly followed his wife out of the place. The furniture in the sitting-rooms was, I believe, very beautiful, but I did not notice it much. Suddenly I heard the auctioneer speaking to me, 'Mr. Harrison, won't you give me a bid for this table?'

'It was a very pretty little table of walnut-wood. I thought it would go into my study very well, so I gave him a bid. I saw Miss Horsman bidding against me, so I went off with full force, and at last it was knocked down to me. The auctioneer smiled, and congratulated me.

"'A most useful present for Mrs. Harrison, when that lady comes."

'Everybody laughed. They like a joke about marriage, it is so easy of comprehension. But the table which I had thought was for writing, turned out to be a work-table, scissors and thimble complete. No wonder I looked foolish. Sophy was not looking at me, that was one comfort. She was busy arranging a nosegay of wood-anemone and wild sorrel.

'Miss Horsman came up, with her curious eyes.

"'I had no idea things were far enough advanced for you to be purchasing a work-table, Mr. Harrison."

'I laughed off my awkwardness.

"'Did not you, Miss Horsman? You are very much behind-hand. You have not heard of my piano, then?"

"'No, indeed," said she, half uncertain whether I was serious or not. "Then it seems there is nothing wanting but the lady."

"'Perhaps she may not be wanting either," said I; for I wished to perplex her keen curiosity.

CHAPTER XVI.

'WHEN I got home from my round, I found Mrs. Rose in some sorrow.

"'Miss Horsman called after you left," said she. "Have you heard how John Brouncker is at Highport?"

"'Very well," replied I. "I called on his wife just now, and she had just got a letter from him. She had been anxious about him, for she had not heard for a week. However, all's right now; and she has pretty well of work at Mrs. Munton's, as her servant is ill. Oh, they'll do, never fear."

"'At Mrs. Munton's? Oh, that accounts for it, then. She is so deaf, and makes such blunders."

"'Accounts for what?" asked I.

"'Oh, perhaps I had better not tell you," hesitated Mrs. Rose.

"'Yes, tell me at once. I beg your pardon, but I hate mysteries."

"'You are so like my poor dear Mr. Rose. He used to speak to me just in that sharp, cross way. – It is only that Miss Horsman called. She had been making a collection for John Brouncker's widow, and" –

"'But the man's alive!" said I.

"'So it seems. But Mrs. Munton had told her that he was dead. And she has got Mr. Morgan's name down at the head of the list, and Mr. Bullock's" –

'Mr. Morgan and I had got into a short cool way of speaking to each other ever since we had differed so much about the treatment of Brouncker's arm; and I had heard once or twice of his shakes of the head over John's case. He would not have spoken against my method for the world, and fancied that he concealed his fears.

'"Miss Horsman is very ill-natured, I think," sighed forth Mrs. Rose.

'I saw that something had been said of which I had not heard; for the mere fact of collecting money for the widow was good-natured, whoever did it. So I asked quietly what she had said.

'"Oh, I don't know if I should tell you. I only know she made me cry; for I'm not well, and I can't bear to hear any one I live with abused."

'Come! this was pretty plain.

'"What did Miss Horsman say of me?" asked I, half laughing, for I knew there was no love lost between us.

'"Oh, she only said she wondered you could go to sales, and spend your money there, when your ignorance had made Jane Brouncker a widow, and her children fatherless."

'"Pooh! pooh! John's alive, and likely to live as long as you or me, thanks to you, Mrs. Rose."

'When my work-table came home, Mrs. Rose was so struck with its beauty and completeness, and I was so much obliged to her for her identification of my interests with hers, and the kindness of her whole conduct about John, that I begged her to accept of it. She seemed very much pleased; and, after a few apologies, she consented to take it, and placed it in the most conspicuous part of the front parlour, where she usually sat. There was a good deal of morning calling in Duncombe after the sale; and, during this time, the fact of John's being alive was established to the conviction of all except Miss Horsman, who, I believe, still doubted. I myself told Mr. Morgan, who immediately went to reclaim his money; saying to me, that he was thankful of the information; he was truly glad to hear it; and he shook me warmly by the hand for the first time for a month.

CHAPTER XVII.

'A FEW days after the sale, I was in the consulting room. The servant must have left the folding-doors a little ajar I think. Mrs. Munton came to call on Mrs. Rose; and the former being deaf, I heard all the speeches of the latter lady, as she was obliged to speak very loud in order to be heard. She began: –

'"This is a great pleasure, Mrs. Munton; so seldom as you are well enough to go out."

'Mumble, mumble, mumble, through the door.

'"Oh, very well, thank you. Take this seat, and then you can admire my new work-table, ma'am; a present from Mr. Harrison."

'Mumble, mumble.

'"Who could have told you, ma'am? Miss Horsman. Oh yes, I showed it Miss Horsman."

'Mumble, mumble.

'"I don't quite understand you, ma'am."

'Mumble, mumble.

'"I'm not blushing, I believe. I really am quite in the dark as to what you mean."

'Mumble, mumble.

'"Oh yes, Mr. Harrison and I are most comfortable together. He reminds me so of my dear Mr. Rose; – just as fidgetty and anxious in his profession."

'Mumble, mumble.

'"I'm sure you are joking now, ma'am." Then I heard a pretty loud –

'"Oh no;' mumble, mumble, mumble, for a long time.

'"Did he really? Well, I'm sure I don't know. I should be sorry to think he was doomed to be unfortunate in so serious an affair; but you know my undying regard for the late Mr. Rose."

'Another long mumble.

'"You're very kind, I'm sure. Mr. Rose always thought more of my happiness than his own" – a little crying – "but the turtle dove has always been my ideal, ma'am."

'Mumble, mumble.

'"No one could have been happier than I. As you say, it is a compliment to matrimony."

'Mumble.

'"Oh, but you must not repeat such a thing. Mr. Harrison would not like it. He can't bear to have his affairs spoken about."

'Then there was a change of subject; an inquiry after some poor person, I imagine; I heard Mrs. Rose say –

'"She has got a mucous membrane I'm afraid, ma'am."

'A commiserating mumble.

'"Not always fatal. I believe Mr. Rose knew some cases that lived for years after it was discovered that they had a mucous membrane.' – a pause. Then Mrs. Rose spoke in a different tone.

'"Are you sure, ma'am, there is no mistake about what he said?"

'Mumble.

'"Pray don't be so observant, Mrs. Munton; you find out too much. One can have no little secrets."

'The call broke up; and I heard Mrs. Munton say in the passage, "I wish you joy, ma'am, with all my heart. There's no use denying it; for I've seen all along what would happen."

'When I went in to dinner, I said to Mrs. Rose –

'"You've had Mrs. Munton here, I think. Did she bring any news?" To my surprise, she bridled and simpered, and replied, "Oh, you must not ask, Mr. Harrison: such foolish reports."

'I did not ask, as she seemed to wish me not, and I knew there were silly reports always about. Then I think she was vexed that I did not ask. Altogether she went on so strangely that I could not help looking at her; and then she took up a hand-screen, and held it between me and her. I really felt rather anxiously.

'"Are you not feeling well?" said I, innocently.

'"Oh, thank you, I believe I'm quite well; only the room is rather warm, is it not?"

'"Let me put the blinds down for you; the sun begins to have a good deal of power." I drew down the blinds.

'"You are so attentive, Mr. Harrison. Mr. Rose himself never did more for my little wishes than you do."

'"I wish I could do more, – I wish I could show you how much I feel –" her kindness to John Brouncker, I was going on to say; but I was just then called out to a patient. Before I went I turned back, and said –

'"Take care of yourself, my dear Mrs. Rose; you had better rest a little."

'"For your sake, I will," said she tenderly.

'I did not care for whose sake she did it. Only I really thought she was not quite well, and required rest. I thought she was more affected than usual at tea-time; and could have been angry with her nonsensical ways once or twice; but that I knew the real goodness of her heart. She said she wished she had the power to sweeten my life as she could my tea. I told her what a comfort she had been all during my late time of anxiety; and then I stole out to try if I could hear the evening singing at the Vicarage, by standing close to the garden wall.

CHAPTER XVIII.

'THE next morning I met Mr. Bullock by appointment, to talk a little about the legacy which was paid into his hands. As I was leaving his office, feeling full of my riches, I met Miss Horsman. She smiled rather grimly, and said:

'"Oh! Mr. Harrison, I must congratulate, I believe. I don't know whether I ought to have known, but as I do, I must wish you joy. A very nice little sum, too. I always said you would have money."

'So she had found out my legacy, had she? Well, it was no secret, and one likes the reputation of being a person of property. Accordingly I smiled, and said I was much obliged to her, and if I could alter the figures to my liking, she might congratulate me still more.

'She said, "Oh, Mr. Harrison, you can't have every thing, It would be better the other way, certainly. Money is the great thing, as you've found out. The relation died most opportunely, I must say."

'"He was no relative," said I; "only an intimate friend."

'"Dear-ah-me! I thought it had been a brother! Well, at any rate, the legacy is safe."

'I wished her good morning, and passed on. Before long I was sent for to Miss Tomkinson's.

'Miss Tomkinson sat in severe state to receive me. I went in with an air of ease, because I always felt so uncomfortable.

'"Is this true that I hear?" asked she, in an inquisitorial manner.

'I thought she alluded to my five hundred pounds. So I smiled, and said that I believed it was.

'"Can money be so great an object with you, Mr. Harrison?" she asked again.

'I said I had never cared much for money, except as an assistance to any plan of settling in life; and then, as I did not like her severe way of treating the subject, I said that I hoped every one was well; though of course I expected some one was ill, or I should not have been sent for.

'Miss Tomkinson looked very grave and sad. Then she answered, "Caroline is very poorly – the old palpitations at the heart; but of course that is nothing to you."

'I said I was very sorry. She had a weakness there, I knew. Could I see her? I might be able to order something for her.

'I thought I heard Miss Tomkinson say something in a low voice about my being a heartless deceiver. Then she spoke up. "I was always distrustful of you, Mr. Harrison. I never liked your looks. I begged Caroline again and again not to confide in you. I foresaw how it would end. And now I fear her precious life will be a sacrifice."

'I begged her not to distress herself, for in all probability there was very little the matter with her sister. Might I see her?

'"No!" she said, shortly, standing up as if to dismiss me. "There has been too much of this seeing and calling. By my consent, you shall never see her again."

'I bowed. I was annoyed, of course. Such a dismissal might injure my practice just when I was most anxious to increase it.

'"Have you no apology, no excuse, to offer?"

'I said I had done my best; I did not feel that there was any reason to offer an apology. I wished her good morning. Suddenly she came forwards.

'"Oh, Mr. Harrison," said she, "if you have really loved Caroline, do not let a little paltry money make you desert her for another."

'I was struck dumb. Loved Miss Caroline! I loved Miss Tomkinson a great deal better, and yet I disliked her. She went on.

'"I have saved nearly three thousand pounds. If you think you are too poor to marry without money, I will give it all to Caroline. I am strong, and can go on working; but she is weak, and this disappointment will kill her."

She sat down suddenly, and covered her face with her hands. Then she looked up.

'"You are unwilling, I see. Don't suppose I would have urged you if it had been for myself; but she has had so much sorrow." And now she fairly cried aloud. I tried to explain; but she would not listen, but kept saying, "Leave the house, sir! leave the house!" But I would be heard.

'"I have never had any feeling warmer than respect for Miss Caroline, and I have never shown any different feeling. I never for an instant thought of making her my wife, and she has had no cause in my behaviour to imagine I entertained any such intention.

'"This is adding insult to injury," said she. "Leave the house, sir, this instant!"

<hr>

CHAPTER XIX.

'I WENT, and sadly enough. In a small town such an occurrence is sure to be talked about, and to make a great deal of mischief. When I went home to dinner I was so full of it, and foresaw so clearly that I should need some advocate soon to set the case in its right light, that I determined on making a confidante of good Mrs. Rose. I could not eat. She watched me tenderly, and sighed when she saw my want of appetite.

'"I am sure you have something on your mind, Mr. Harrison. Would it be – would it not be – a relief to impart it to some sympathising friend?"

'It was just what I wanted to do.

'"My dear kind Mrs. Rose," said I, "I must tell you, if you will listen."

'She took up the fire-screen, and held it, as yesterday, between me and her.

'"The most unfortunate misunderstanding has taken place. Miss Tomkin-son thinks that I have been paying attentions to Miss Caroline; when, in fact – may I tell you, Mrs. Rose? – my affections are placed elsewhere. Perhaps you have found it out already?" for indeed I thought I had been too much in love to conceal my attachment to Sophy from any one who knew my movements as well as Mrs. Rose.

'She hung down her head, and said she believed she had found out my secret.

'"Then only think how miserably I am situated. If I have any hope – oh, Mrs. Rose, do you think I have any hope?" –

'She put the hand-screen still more before her face, and after some hesitation she said she thought "if I persevered – in time – I might have hope." And then she suddenly got up, and left the room.

CHAPTER XX.

'THAT afternoon I met Mr. Bullock in the street. My mind was so full of the affair with Miss Tomkinson, that I should have passed him without notice, if he had not stopped me short, and said that he must speak to me; about my wonderful five hundred pounds, I supposed. But I did not care for that now.

'"What is this I hear," said he, severely, "about your engagement with Mrs. Rose?"

'"With Mrs. Rose!" said I, almost laughing, although my heart was heavy enough.

'"Yes! with Mrs. Rose!" said he, sternly.

'"I'm not engaged to Mrs. Rose," I replied. "There is some mistake."

'"I'm glad to hear it, sir," he answered; "very glad. It requires some explanation, however. Mrs. Rose has been congratulated, and has acknowledged the truth of the report. It is confirmed by many facts. The work-table you bought, confessing your intention of giving it to your future wife, is given to her. How do you account for these things, sir?"

'I said I did not pretend to account for them. At present, a good deal was inexplicable; and when I could give an explanation, I did not think that I should feel myself called upon to give it to him.

'"Very well, sir; very well," replied he, growing very red. "I shall take care, and let Mr. Morgan know the opinion I entertain of you. What do you think that man deserves to be called, who enters a family under the plea of friendship, and takes advantage of his intimacy to win the affections of the daughter, and then engages himself to another woman?"

'I thought he referred to Miss Caroline. I simply said I could only say that I was not engaged; and that Miss Tomkinson had been quite mistaken in supposing I had been paying any attentions to her sister beyond those dictated by mere civility.

'"Miss Tomkinson! Miss Caroline! I don't understand to what you refer. Is there another victim to your perfidy? What I allude to are the attentions you have paid to my daughter, Miss Bullock."

'Another! I could but disclaim, as I had done in the case of Miss Caroline; but I began to be in despair. Would Miss Horsman, too, come forward as a victim to my tender affections? It was all Mr. Morgan's doing, who had lectured me into this tenderly deferential manner. But on the score of Miss Bullock, I was brave in my innocence. I had positively disliked her; and so I told her father, though in more civil and measured terms, adding that I was sure the feeling was reciprocal.

'He looked as if he would like to horse-whip me. I longed to call him out.

'"I hope my daughter has had sense enough to despise you; I hope she has, that's all. I trust my wife may be mistaken as to her feelings."

'So, he had heard all through the medium of his wife. That explained something, and rather calmed me. I begged he would ask Miss Bullock if she had ever thought I had any ulterior object in my intercourse with her, beyond mere friendliness (and not so much of that, I might have added). I would refer it to her.

'"Girls," said Mr. Bullock, a little more quietly, "do not like to acknowledge that they have been deceived and disappointed. I consider my wife's testimony as likely to be nearer the truth than my daughter's, for that reason. And she tells me she never doubted but that, if not absolutely engaged, you understood each other perfectly. She is sure Jemima is deeply wounded by your engagement to Mrs. Rose."

'"Once for all, I am not engaged to anybody. Till you have seen your daughter, and learnt the truth from her, I will wish you farewell."

'I bowed in a stiff, haughty manner, and walked off homewards. But when I got to my own door, I remembered Mrs. Rose, and all that Mr. Bullock had said about her acknowledging the truth of the report of my engagement to her. Where could I go to be safe? Mrs. Rose, Miss Bullock, Miss Caroline – they lived as it were at the three points of an equilateral triangle; here was I in the centre. I would go to Mr. Morgan's, and drink tea with him. There, at any rate, I was secure from any one wanting to marry me; and I might be as professionally bland as I liked, without being misunderstood. But there, too, a *contretemps* awaited me.

<hr>

CHAPTER XXI.

'MR. MORGAN was looking grave. After a minute, or two of humming and hawing, he said,

'"I have been sent for to Miss Caroline Tomkinson, Mr. Harrison. I am sorry to hear of this – I am grieved to find that there seems to have been some trifling with the affections of a very worthy lady. Miss Tomkinson, who is in sad distress, tells me that they had every reason to believe that you were attached to her sister. May I ask if you do not intend to marry her?"

'I said nothing was farther from my thoughts.

'"My dear sir," said Mr. Morgan, rather agitated, "do not express yourself so strongly and vehemently. It is derogatory to the sex to speak so. It is more respectful to say, in these cases, that you do not venture to entertain a hope; such a manner is generally understood, and does not sound like such positive objection."

'"I cannot help it, sir; I must talk in my own natural manner. I would not speak disrespectfully of any woman; but nothing should induce me to marry Miss Caroline Tomkinson; not if she were Venus herself, and Queen of

England into the bargain. I cannot understand what has given rise to the idea."

"'Indeed, sir; I think that is very plain. You have a trifling case to attend to in the house, and you invariably make it a pretext for seeing and conversing with the lady."

"'That was her doing, not mine!" said I, vehemently.

"'Allow me to go on. You are discovered on your knees before her, – a positive injury to the establishment, as Miss Tomkinson observes; a most passionate valentine is sent, and when questioned, you acknowledge the sincerity of meaning which you affix to such things," – he stopped, for in his earnestness he had been talking more quickly than usual, and was out of breath. I burst in with my explanations –

"'The valentine I knew nothing about."

"'It is in your handwriting," said he, coldly. "I should be most deeply grieved to – in fact, I will not think it possible of your father's son. But I must say, it is in your handwriting."

'I tried again, and at last succeeded, in convincing him that I had been only unfortunate, not intentionally guilty of winning Miss Caroline's affections. I said that I had been endeavouring, it was true, to practise the manner he had recommended, of universal sympathy, and recalled to his mind some of the advice he had given me. He was a good deal hurried.

"'But, my dear sir, I had no idea you would carry it out to such consequences. 'Philandering' Miss Tomkinson called it. That is a hard word, sir. My manner has been always tender and sympathetic; but I am not aware that I ever excited any hopes; there never was any report about me. I believe no lady was ever attached to me. You must strive after this happy medium, sir."

'I was still distressed. Mr. Morgan had only heard of one, but there were three ladies (including Miss Bullock), hoping to marry me. He saw my annoyance.

"Don't be too much distressed about it, my dear sir; I was sure you were too honourable a man, from the first. With a conscience like yours, I would defy the world.'

'He became anxious to console me, and I was hesitating whether I would not tell him all my three dilemmas, when a note was brought in to him. It was from Mrs. Munton. He threw it to me with a face of dismay.

"My dear Mr. Morgan. – I most sincerely congratulate you on the happy matrimonial engagement I hear you have formed with Miss Tomkinson. All previous circumstances, as I have just been remarking to Miss Horsman, combine to promise you felicity. And I wish that every blessing may attend your married life.

"Most sincerely yours,
"JANE MUNTON.'

'I could not help laughing, he had been so lately congratulating himself that no report of the kind had ever been circulated about himself. He said: –

'"Sir! this is no laughing matter; I assure you it is not." I could not resist asking, if I was to conclude that there was no truth in the report.

'"Truth, sir! it's a lie from beginning to end. I don't like to speak too decidedly about any lady; and I've a great respect for Miss Tomkinson; but I do assure you, sir, I'd as soon marry one of Her Majesty's Life-guards. I would rather; – it would be more suitable. Miss Tomkinson is a very worthy lady; but she's a perfect grenadier.'

'He grew very nervous. He was evidently insecure. He thought it not impossible that Miss Tomkinson might come and marry him, *vi et armis*.[43] I am sure he had some dim idea of abduction in his mind. Still, he was better off than I was; for he was in his own house, and report had only engaged him to one lady; while I stood like Paris[44] among three contending beauties. Truly, an apple of discord had been thrown into our little town. I suspected at the time, what I know now, that it was Miss Horsman's doing; not intentionally, I will do her the justice to say. But she had shouted out the story of my behaviour to Miss Caroline up Mrs. Munton's trumpet; and that lady, possessed with the idea that I was engaged to Mrs. Rose, had imagined the masculine pronoun to relate to Mr. Morgan, whom she had seen only that afternoon *tête-a-tête* with Miss Tomkinson, condoling with her in some tender deferential manner, I'll be bound.

CHAPTER XXII.

'I WAS very cowardly. I positively dared not go home; but at length I was obliged to go. I had done all I could to console Mr. Morgan, but he refused to be comforted. I went at last. I rang at the bell. I don't know who opened the door, but I think it was Mrs. Rose. I kept a handkerchief to my face, and, muttering something about having a dreadful toothache, I flew up to my room, and bolted the door. I had no candle; but what did that signify. I was safe. I could not sleep; and when I did fall into a sort of doze, it was ten times worse wakening up. I could not remember whether I was engaged or not. If I was engaged, who was the lady? I had always considered myself as rather plain than otherwise; but surely I had made a mistake. Fascinating I certainly must be; but perhaps I was handsome. As soon as day dawned, I got up to ascertain the fact at the looking-glass. Even with the best dispositon to be convinced, I could not see any striking beauty in my round face, with an unshaven beard and a night-cap, like a fool's-cap, at the top. I took off my night-cap. No! I must be content to be plain, but agreeable. All this I tell you in confidence. I would not have my little bit of vanity known for the world. I fell asleep towards morning. I was awakened by a tap at my door. It was Peggy: she put in a hand with a note. I took it.

'"It is not from Miss Horsman?" said I, half in joke, – half in very earnest fright.

'"No, sir; Mr. Morgan's man brought it."

'I opened it. It ran thus:

"My dear Sir, – It is now nearly twenty years since I have had a little relaxation, and I find that my health requires it. I have also the utmost confidence in you, and I am sure this feeling is shared by our patients. I have, therefore, no scruple in putting in execution a hastily formed plan, and going to Chesterton to catch the early train on my way to Paris. If your accounts are good, I shall remain away probably a fortnight. Direct to Meurice's.[45]

"Yours, most truly,

"J. MORGAN.

"P.S. Perhaps it may be as well not to name where I am gone, especially to Miss Tomkinson.'

'He had deserted me. He, – with only one report, – had left me to stand my ground with three.

'"Mrs. Rose's kind regards, sir, and it's nearly nine o'clock. Breakfast has been ready this hour, sir."

'"Tell Mrs. Rose I don't want any breakfast. Or stay (for I was very hungry), I will take a cup of tea and some toast up here."

'Peggy brought the tray to the door.

'"I hope you're not ill, sir?" said she, kindly.

'"Not very. I shall be better when I get into the air."

'"Mrs. Rose seems sadly put about,' said she, 'she seems so grieved like."

'I watched my opportunity, and went out by the side door in the garden.

CHAPTER XXIII.

'I HAD intended to ask Mr. Morgan to call at the Vicarage, and give his parting explanation before they could hear the report. Now, I thought that if I could see Sophy, I would speak to her myself; but I did not wish to encounter the Vicar. I went along the lane at the back of the Vicarage, and came suddenly upon Miss Bullock. She coloured, and asked me if I would allow her to speak to me. I could only be resigned; but I thought I could probably set one report at rest by this conversation.

'She was almost crying.

'"I must tell you, Mr. Harrison, I have watched you here in order to speak to you. I heard with the greatest regret of papa's conversation with you yesterday." She was fairly crying. "I believe Mrs. Bullock finds me in her way, and wants to have me married. It is the only way in which I can account for such a complete misrepresentation as she had told papa. I don't care for you, in the least, sir. You never paid me any attentions. You've been almost rude to me; and I have liked you the better. That's to say, I never have liked you."

"'I am truly glad to hear what you say," answered I. "Don't distress yourself. I was sure there was some mistake."

'But she cried bitterly.

"'It is so hard to feel that my marriage – my absence – is desired so earnestly at home. I dread every new acquaintance we form with any gentleman. It is sure to be the beginning of a series of attacks on him, of which everybody must be aware, and to which they may think I am a willing party. But I should not much mind if it were not for the conviction that she wishes me so earnestly away. Oh, my own dear mama, you would never – "

'She cried more than ever. I was truly sorry for her, and had just taken her hand, and began – "My dear Miss Bullock –" when the door in the wall of the Vicarage garden opened. It was the Vicar letting out Miss Tomkinson, whose face was all swelled with crying. He saw me; but he did not bow, or make any sign. On the contrary, he looked down as from a severe eminence, and shut the door hastily. I turned to Miss Bullock.

"'I am afraid the Vicar has been hearing something to my disadvantage from Miss Tomkinson, and it is very awkward –" She finished my sentence, "To have found us here together. Yes, but as long as we understand that we do not care for each other, it does not signify what people say."

"'Oh, but to me it does," said I; "I may, perhaps, tell you – but do not mention it to a creature – I am attached to Miss Hutton."

"'To Sophy! Oh, Mr. Harrison, I am so glad; she is such a sweet creature. Oh, I wish you joy!"

"'Not yet; I have never spoken about it."

"'Oh, but it is certain to happen." She jumped with a woman's rapidity to a conclusion. And then she began to praise Sophy. Never was a man yet who did not like to hear the praises of his mistress. I walked by her side; we came past the front of the Vicarage together. I looked up, and saw Sophy there, and she saw me.

'That afternoon she was sent away; sent to visit her aunt ostensibly; in reality, because of the reports of my conduct, which were showered down upon the Vicar, and one of which he saw confirmed by his own eyes.

CHAPTER XXIV.

'I HEARD of Sophy's departure as one heard of everything, soon after it had taken place. I did not care for the awkwardness of my situation, which had so perplexed and amused me in the morning. I felt that something was wrong; that Sophy was taken away from me. I sank into despair. If any body liked to marry me they might. I was willing to be sacrificed. I did not speak to Mrs. Rose. She wondered at me, and grieved over my coldness, I saw; but I had left off feeling anything. Miss Tomkinson cut me in the street; and it did not break my heart. Sophy was gone away; that was all I cared for. Where had they sent her to? Who was her aunt, that she should go and visit her? One day I met Lizzie, who looked as though she had been told not to speak to me, but could not help doing so.

'"Have you heard from your sister?" said I.

'"Yes."

'"Where is she? I hope she is well."

'"She is at the Leoms (I was not much wiser). Oh yes, she is very well. Fanny says she was at the Assembly last Wednesday, and danced all night with the officers."

'I thought I would enter myself a member of the Peace Society[46] at once. She was a little flirt, and a hard-hearted creature. I don't think I wished Lizzie good-bye.

<hr>

CHAPTER XXV.

'WHAT most people would have considered a more serious evil than Sophy's absence, befell me. I found that my practice was falling off. The prejudice of the town ran strongly against me. Mrs. Munton told me all that was said. She heard it through Miss Horsman. It was said, – cruel little town, – that my negligence or ignorance had been the cause of Walter's death; that Miss Tyrrell had become worse under my treatment; and that John Brouncker was all but dead, if he was not quite, from my mismanagement. All Jack Marshland's jokes and revelations, which had, I thought, gone to oblivion, were raked up to my discredit. He himself, formerly, to my astonishment, rather a favourite with the good people of Duncombe, was spoken of as one of my disreputable friends.

'In short, so prejudiced were the good people of Duncombe that I believe a very little would have made them suspect me of a brutal highway robbery, which took place in the neighbourhood about this time. Mrs. Munton told me, *àpropos* of the robbery – that she had never yet understood the cause of my year's imprisonment in Newgate; she had no doubt, from what Mr. Morgan had told her, there was some good reason for it; but if I would tell her the particulars, she should like to know them.

'Miss Tomkinson sent for Mr. White, from Chesterton, to see Miss Caroline; and, as he was coming over, all our old patients seemed to take advantage of it, and send for him too.

'But the worst of all was the Vicar's manner to me. If he had cut me, I could have asked him why he did so. But the freezing change in his behaviour was indescribable, though bitterly felt. I heard of Sophy's gaiety from Lizzie. I thought of writing to her. Just then Mr. Morgan's fortnight of absence expired. I was wearied out by Mrs. Rose's tender vagaries, and took no comfort from her sympathy, which indeed I rather avoided. Her tears irritated, instead of grieving me. I wished I could tell her at once that I had no intention of marrying her.

CHAPTER XXVI.

'MR. MORGAN had not been at home above two hours before he was sent for to the Vicarage. Sophy had come back, and I had never heard of it. She had come home ill and weary, and longing for rest; and the *rest* seemed approaching with awful strides. Mr. Morgan forgot all his Parisian adventures, and all his terror of Miss Tomkinson, when he was sent for to see her. She was ill of a fever, which made fearful progress. When he told me, I wished to force the Vicarage door, if I might but see her. But I controlled myself; and only cursed my weak indecision, which had prevented my writing to her. It was well I had no patients; they would have had but a poor chance of attention. I hung about Mr. Morgan, who might see her, and did see her. But from what he told me, I perceived that the measures he was adopting were powerless to check so sudden and violent an illness. Oh! if they would but let me see her! But that was out of the question. It was not merely that the Vicar had heard of my character as a gay Lothario,[47] but that doubts had been thrown out of my medical skill. The accounts grew worse. Suddenly, my resolution was taken. Mr. Morgan's very regard for Sophy made him more than usually timid in his practice. I had my horse saddled, and galloped to Chesterton. I took the express train to town. I went to Dr.— .I told him every particular of the case. He listened; but shook his head. He wrote down a prescription; and recommended a new preparation, not yet in full use: a preparation of a poison, in fact.

'"It may save her," said he. "It is a chance, in such a state of things as you describe. It must be given on the fifth day, if the pulse will bear it. Crabbe makes up the preparation most skilfully. Let me hear from you, I beg."

'I went to Crabbe's. I begged to make it up myself; but my hands trembled, so that I could not weigh the quantities. I asked the young man to do it for me. I went, without touching food, to the station, with my medicine and my prescription in my pocket. Back we flew through the country. I sprang on Bay Maldon,[48] which my groom had in waiting, and galloped across the country to Duncombe.

'But I drew bridle when I came to the top of the hill – the hill above the old hall, from which we catch the first glimpse of the town, for I thought within myself that she might be dead; and I dreaded to come near certainty. The hawthorns were out in the woods, the young lambs were in the meadows, the song of the thrushes filled the air; but it only made the thought the more terrible.

'"What, if in this world of hope and life she lies dead!" I heard the church bells soft and clear. I sickened to listen. Was it the passing-bell? No! – it was ringing eight o'clock. I put spurs to my horse, down hill as it was. We dashed into the town. I turned him, saddle and bridle, into the stable-yard, and went off to Mr. Morgan's.

'"Is she –?" said I. "How is she?"

'"Very ill. My poor fellow, I see how it is with you. She may live – but I fear. My dear sir, I am very much afraid."

'I told him of my journey, and consultation with Dr.—,and showed him the prescription. His hands trembled as he put on his spectacles to read it.

'"This is a very dangerous medicine, sir," said he, with his finger under the name of the poison.

'"It is a new preparation," said I. "Dr.— relies much upon it."

'"I dare not administer it," he replied. "I have never tried it. It must be very powerful. I dare not play tricks in this case."

'I believe I stamped with impatience; but it was all of no use. My journey had been in vain. The more I urged the imminent danger of the case requiring some powerful remedy, the more nervous he became.

'I told him I would throw up the partnership. I threatened him with that, though, in fact, it was only what I felt I ought to do, and had resolved upon before Sophy's illness, as I had lost the confidence of his patients. He only said –

'"I cannot help it, sir. I shall regret it for your father's sake; but I must do my duty. I dare not run the risk of giving Miss Sophy this violent medicine, – a preparation of a deadly poison."

'I left him without a word. He was quite right in adhering to his own views, as I can see now; but, at the time, I thought him brutal and obstinate.

<hr>

CHAPTER XXVII.

'I WENT home. I spoke rudely to Mrs. Rose, who awaited my return at the door. I rushed past, and locked myself in my room. I could not go to bed.

'The morning sun came pouring in, and enraged me, as everything did since Mr. Morgan refused. I pulled the blind down so violently that the string broke. What did it signify? The light might come in. What was the sun to me? And then I remembered that that sun might be shining on her, – dead.

'I sat down and covered my face. Mrs.Rose knocked at the door. I opened it. She had never been in bed, and had been crying too.

'"Mr. Morgan wants to speak to you, sir!"

'I rushed back for my medicine, and went to him. He stood at the door, pale and anxious.

'"She's alive, sir," said he; "but that's all. We have sent for Dr. Hamilton. I'm afraid he will not come in time. Do you know, sir, I think we should venture, – with Dr.—'s sanction, – to give her that medicine. It is but a chance; but it is the only one, I'm afraid." He fairly cried before he had ended.

'"I've got it here," said I, setting off to walk; but he could not go so fast.

'I beg your pardon, sir,' said he, 'for my abrupt refusal last night.'

'"Indeed, sir," said I; "I ought much rather to beg your pardon. I was very violent."

'"Oh! never mind! never mind! Will you repeat what Dr.— said?"

'I did so; and then I asked, with a meekness that astonished myself, if I might not go in and administer it.

'"No, sir," said he, "I'm afraid not. I am sure your good heart would not wish to give pain. Besides, it might agitate her, if she has any consciousness before death. In her delirium she has often mentioned your name; and, sir, I'm sure you won't name it again, as it may, in fact, be considered a professional secret; but I did hear our good Vicar speak a little strongly about you; in fact, sir, I did hear him curse you. You see the mischief it might make in the parish, I'm sure, if this were known."

'I gave him the medicine, and watched him in, and saw the door shut. I hung about the place all day. Poor and rich, all came to inquire. The county people drove up in their carriages, – the halt and the lame came on their crutches. Their anxiety did my heart good. Mr. Morgan told me that she slept, and I watched Dr. Hamilton into the house. The night came on. She slept. I watched round the house. I saw the light high up, burning still and steady. Then I saw it moved. It was the crisis, in one way or other.

———

CHAPTER XXVIII.

'MR. MORGAN came out. Good old man! The tears were running down his cheeks: he could not speak; but kept shaking my hands. I did not want words. I understood that she was better.

'"Dr. Hamilton says, it was the only medicine that could have saved her. I was an old fool, sir. I beg your pardon. The Vicar shall know all. I beg your pardon, sir, if I was abrupt."

'Every thing went on brilliantly from this time.

'Mr. Bullock called to apologise for his mistake, and consequent upbraiding. John Brouncker came home, brave and well.

'There was still Miss Tomkinson in the ranks of the enemy; and Mrs. Rose, too much, I feared, in the ranks of the friends.

<hr>

CHAPTER XXIX.

'ONE night she had gone to bed, and I was thinking of going. I had been studying in the back room, where I went for refuge from her in the present position of affairs; (I read a good number of surgical books about this time, and also "Vanity Fair;") when I heard a loud, long-continued knocking at the door, enough to waken the whole street. Before I could get to open it, I heard that well-known bass of Jack Marshland's, once heard never to be forgotten, pipe up the negro song,[49]

'"Who's dat knocking at de door?"

'Though it was raining hard at the time, and I stood waiting to let him in, he would finish his melody in the open air; loud and clear along the street it sounded. I saw Miss Tomkinson's nightcapped head emerge from a window. She called out "Police! police!"

'Now there were no police, only a rheumatic constable, in the town; but it was the custom of the ladies, when alarmed at night, to call an imaginary police, which had, they thought, an intimidating effect; but as every one knew the real state of the unwatched town, we did not much mind it in general. Just now, however, I wanted to regain my character. So I pulled Jack in, quavering as he entered.

'"You've spoilt a good shake," said he, "that's what you have. I'm nearly up to Jenny Lind;[50] and you see I'm a nightingale, like her."

'We sat up late; and I don't know how it was, but I told him all my matrimonial misadventures.

'"I thought I could imitate your hand pretty well," said he. "My word! it was a flaming valentine! No wonder she thought you loved her!"

'"So that was your doing, was it? Now I'll tell you what you shall do to make up for it? You shall write me a letter confessing your hoax – a letter that I can show."

'"Give me pen and paper, my boy; you shall dictate. 'With a deeply penitent heart –' will that do for a beginning?"

'I told him what to write; a simple, straightforward confession, of his practical joke. I enclosed it in a few lines of regret that, unknown to me, any of my friends should have so acted.

CHAPTER XXX.

'ALL this time I knew that Sophy was slowly recovering. One day I met Miss Bullock, who had seen her.

'"We have been talking about you," said she, with a bright smile; for since she knew I disliked her, she felt quite at her ease, and could smile very pleasantly. I understood that she had been explaining the misunderstanding about herself to Sophy; so that when Jack Marshaland's note had been sent to Miss Tomkinson's, I thought myself in a fair way to have my character established in two quarters. But the third was my dilemma. Mrs.Rose had really so much of my true regard for her good qualities, that I disliked the idea of a formal explanation, in which a good deal must be said on my side to wound her. We had become very much estranged ever since I had heard of this report of my engagement to her. I saw that she grieved over it. While Jack Marshland stayed with us, I felt at my ease in the presence of a third person. But he told me confidentially he durst not stay long, for fear some of the ladies should snap him up, and marry him. Indeed I myself did not think it unlikely that he would snap one of them up if he could. For when we met Miss Bullock one day, and heard her hopeful, joyous account, of Sophy's progress (to whom she was a daily visitor), he asked me who that bright-looking girl was? And when I told him she was the Miss Bullock of whom I had spoken to him, he was pleased to observe that he thought I had been a great fool, and asked me if Sophy had anything like such splendid eyes. He made me repeat about Miss Bullock's unhappy circumstances at home, and then became very thoughtful – a most unusual and morbid symptom in his case.

'Soon after he went, by Mr. Morgan's kind offices and explanations, I was permitted to see Sophy. I might not speak much; it was prohibited for fear of agitating her. We talked of the weather and the flowers; and we were silent. But her little white thin hand lay in mine; and we understood each other without words. I had a long interview with the Vicar afterwards; and came away glad and satisfied.

'Mr. Morgan called in the afternoon, evidently anxious, though he made no direct inquiries (he was too polite for that), to hear the result of my visit at the Vicarage. I told him to give me joy. He shook me warmly by the hand; and then rubbed his own together. I thought I would consult him about my dilemma with Mrs. Rose, who, I was afraid, would be deeply affected by my engagement.

'"There is only one awkward circumstance," said I; – "about Mrs.Rose." I hesitated how to word the fact of her having received congratulations on her supposed engagement with me, and her manifest attachment; but, before I could speak, he broke in.

'"My dear sir, you need not trouble yourself about that; she will have a home. In fact, sir," said he, reddening a little, "I thought it would, perhaps, put a stop to those reports connecting my name with Miss Tomkinson's, if I married some one else. I hoped it might prove an efficacious contradiction. And I was struck with admiration for Mrs.Rose's undying memory of her late husband. Not to be prolix, I have this morning obtained Mrs.Rose's consent to – to marry her, in fact, sir!" said he, jerking out the climax.

'Here was an event! Then Mr. Morgan had never heard the report about Mrs. Rose and me. (To this day, I think she would have taken me, if I had proposed.) So much the better.

'Marriages were in the fashion that year. Mr. Bullock met me one morning, as I was going to ride with Sophy. He and I had quite got over our misunderstanding, thanks to Jemima, and were as friendly as ever. This morning he was chuckling aloud as he walked.

'"Stop, Mr. Harrison!" he said, as I went quickly past. "Have you heard the news? Miss Horsman has just told me Miss Caroline has eloped with young Hoggins! She is ten years older than he is! How can her gentility like being married to a tallow-chandler?[51] It is a very good thing for her, though," he added, in a more serious manner; "Old Hoggins is very rich; and though he's angry just now, he will soon be reconciled."

'Any vanity I might have entertained on the score of the three ladies who were, at one time, said to be captivated by my charms, was being rapidly dispersed. Soon after Mr. Hoggins' marriage, I met Miss Tomkinson face to face, for the first time since our memorable conversation. She stopped me, and said,

'"Don't refuse to receive my congratulations, Mr. Harrison, on your most happy engagement to Miss Hutton. I owe you an apology, too, for my behaviour when I last saw you at our house. I really did think Caroline was attached to you then; and it irritated me, I confess, in a very wrong and unjustifiable way. But I heard her telling Mr. Hoggins only yesterday that she had been attached to him for years; ever since he was in pinafores, she dated it from; and when I asked her afterwards how she could say so, after her distress on hearing that false report about you and Mrs.Rose, she cried, and said I never had understood her; and that the hysteries which alarmed me so much, were simply caused by eating pickled cucumber. I am very sorry for my stupidity and improper way of speaking; but I hope we are friends now, Mr. Harrison, for I should wish to be liked by Sophy's husband."

'Good Miss Tomkinson! to believe the substitution of indigestion for disappointed affection. I shook her warmly by the hand; and we have been all right ever since. I think I told you she is baby's godmother.

CHAPTER XXXI.

'I HAD some difficulty in persuading Jack Marshland to be groomsman; but
when he heard all the arrangements, he came. Miss Bullock was bridesmaid.
He liked us all so well, that he came again at Christmas, and was far better
behaved than he had been the year before. He won golden opinions indeed.
Miss Tomkinson said he was a reformed young man. We dined altogether at
Mr. Morgan's (the Vicar wanted us to go there; but, from what Sophy told
me, Helen was not confident of the mince-meat, and rather dreaded so large
a party). We had a jolly day of it. Mrs. Morgan was as kind and motherly as
ever. Miss Horsman certainly did set out a story that the Vicar was thinking
of Miss Tomkinson for his second; or else, I think, we had no other report
circulated in consequence of our happy, merry Christmas-day; and it is a
wonder, considering how Jack Marshland went on with Jemima.'

Here Sophy came back from putting baby to bed; and Charles wakened
up.

CRANFORD

Cranford was first published in *Household Words* in irregularly spaced instalments from 13 December 1851 to 21 May 1853. Each instalment was separately titled, but the work was not regularly divided into chapters. It was then published in one volume by Chapman and Hall on 18 June 1853 with consistent chapter divisions. A table indicating the relationship of the instalment divisions to the one-volume text is given in Appendix B. A 'Second Edition' of 1853 that has been recorded is in fact a second impression of the first edition. A 'Cheap Edition' was published by Chapman and Hall in 1855, and an 'Illustrated Edition', with four illustrations by George Du Maurier, by Smith, Elder and Co., in 1864. These illustrations are reproduced in Appendix C.

It seems unlikely that EG made any attempt to revise her text for the editions of 1855 and 1864, although there were negotiations relating to copyright when she transferred the work from Chapman and Hall to Smith, Elder for the 1864 edition, and given her good relationship with George Smith it would seem possible that she may have been consulted about any remaining textual uncertainties. No other editions were published in England in EG's lifetime; although an edition of 1858 has been recorded no copies have been traced, and Collin argues that it is a 'ghost' (*Collin*, p. 72). An undated reprint of the 1855 'Cheap Edition', with advertisements suggesting its appearance in c. 1864 is to be found in the holdings of Manchester Central Library. Citing the evidence of advertisements, Smith suggests that 'Chapman and Hall evidently published other undated impressions between 1855 and 1864' (*Smith*, p. 75). The Manchester copy has clearly been reprinted from the plates of 1855, although there is some evidence of minor alterations. All four distinct editions, identified as *HW, 1853, 1855* and *1864* have been collated for this edition and the first edition of 1853 has been used as copy-text.

Except for the amendment of three specific typographical errors, all of which I have identified, I have reprinted the text of *1853* as it stands. It is clear that EG took the opportunity to make alterations to the *HW* text for the 1853 first edition, introducing chapter divisions and titles, and altering the names of some of her characters, notably changing 'Miss Matey' to 'Miss Matty' throughout. I have not recorded individual instances of this change, but have recorded all changes in the case of other characters. For *1853*

Gaskell restored her several references to Dickens and to his works, Dickens himself having altered them to references to Thomas Hood for *HW*. In addition she took the opportunity to adjust inconsistencies of chronology. Elsewhere there are frequent alterations to paragraphing and to punctuation, and while these can be accidental there are occasions when they clearly achieve differences of emphasis, and are thus perhaps authorial. The manuscript for *HW* would have passed through at least three hands: those of EG herself, her editor at *HW* and the printer. Furthermore evidence from surviving EG manuscripts of other works indicates that her husband, William, often oversaw her work in manuscript and he may have been involved in authorial corrections and changes at proof stage and beyond. The absence of the manuscript is thus more than usually frustrating for the textual editor since it is all the more difficult to estimate precisely to what extent changes between different versions of her text can be regarded as truly authorial.

In the Textual Notes I have listed all substantive variants between *1853* and *HW*. I have exercised my own discretion over the inclusion of apparently accidental variants; where these impact upon the reading of the text itself I have included them. I have identified all alterations of paragraphing, but only such other matters of punctuation as can be said to affect the reading of the text. I have retained EG's use of 'sate' for 'sat'. Some changes are clearly a matter of house style: thus *HW* has 'rector' throughout, whereas editions from *1853* normally capitalise the first letter. Where *HW*, *1853* and *1855*, all published by Chapman and Hall, have 'Captain' throughout, Smith, Elder's *1864* has lower case 'c' except when the term is specifically applied, e.g., 'Captain Brown'. In all of these instances I have retained the *1853* reading, and identified anomalies in the notes. Variants from *1855* and *1864* have only been listed where they have a significant bearing upon the copy-text. *1864* italicises the titles of literary works; the previous texts use roman and single inverted commas to identify them.

Publication details of first and early editions of *Cranford* in England and America are given in Walter E. Smith, *Elizabeth Gaskell: A Bibliographical Guide* (Los Angeles: Heritage Bookshop Inc., 1998), and in Dorothy Collin's article, 'The Composition and Publication of Elizabeth Gaskell's *Cranford*', *BJRL*, 69:1 (Autumn 1986), pp. 59–95. A concise analysis of the nature of the revisions to *Cranford*, with examples, is given in *Watson* (pp. 179–83).

In my Explanatory Notes I am inevitably heavily indebted to my predecessors in the field, and most notably to Elizabeth Porges Watson and to Charlotte Mitchell whose editions (see Abbreviations) have been at my right hand throughout the editing process. I have only acknowledged this debt in individual notes where I have drawn exclusively on their work, but it extends far more fully throughout my annotations.

CRANFORD.

BY THE AUTHOR OF

'MARY BARTON,' 'RUTH,' &c.

LONDON:
CHAPMAN & HALL, 193, PICCADILLY.
1853.

REPUBLISHED FROM 'HOUSEHOLD WORDS.'

CONTENTS.

CRANFORD.

CHAPTER I.[a]

OUR SOCIETY.[b]

IN the first place, Cranford is in possession of the Amazons; all the holders of houses, above a certain rent, are women. If a married couple come to settle in the town, somehow the gentleman disappears; he is either fairly frightened to death by being the only man in the Cranford evening parties, or he is accounted for by being with his regiment, his ship, or closely engaged in business all the week in the great neighbouring commercial town of Drumble, distant only twenty miles on a railroad. In short, whatever does become of the gentlemen, they are not at Cranford. What could they do if they were there? The surgeon has his round of thirty miles, and sleeps at Cranford; but every man cannot be a surgeon. For keeping the trim gardens full of choice flowers without a weed to speck them; for frightening away little boys who look wistfully at the said flowers through the railings; for rushing out at the geese that occasionally venture into the gardens if the gates are left open; for deciding all questions of literature and politics without troubling themselves with unnecessary reasons or arguments; for obtaining clear and correct knowledge of everybody's affairs in the parish; for keeping their neat maid-servants in admirable order; for kindness (somewhat dictatorial) to the poor, and real tender good offices to each other whenever they are in distress, the ladies of Cranford are quite sufficient. 'A man,' as one of them observed to me once; 'is *so* in the way in the house!' Although the ladies of Cranford know all each other's proceedings, they are exceedingly indifferent to each other's opinions. Indeed, as each has her own individuality, not to say eccentricity, pretty strongly developed, nothing is so easy as verbal retaliation; but somehow good-will reigns among them to a considerable degree.

The Cranford ladies have only an occasional little quarrel, spirted out in a few peppery words and angry jerks of the head; just enough to prevent the even tenor of their lives[1] from becoming too flat. Their dress is very independent of fashion; as they observe, 'What does it signify how we dress here at Cranford, where everybody knows us?' And if they go from home, their reason is equally cogent: 'What does it signify how we dress here, where nobody knows us?' The materials of their clothes are, in general, good and plain, and most of them are nearly as scrupulous as Miss Tyler, of cleanly memory;[2] but I will answer for it, the last gigot,[3] the last tight and scanty petticoat in wear in England, was seen in Cranford – and seen without a smile.

I can testify to a magnificent family red silk umbrella, under which a gentle little spinster, left alone of many brothers and sisters, used to patter to church on rainy days. Have you any red silk umbrellas in London? We had a tradition of the first that had ever been seen in Cranford; and the little boys mobbed it, and called it 'a stick in petticoats.' It might have been the very red silk one I have described, held by a strong father over a troop of little ones; the poor little lady – the survivor of all – could scarcely carry it.

Then there were rules and regulations for visiting and calls; and they were announced to any young people, who might be staying in the town, with all the solemnity with which the old Manx laws were read once a year on the Tinwald Mount.[4a]

'Our friends have sent to inquire how you are after your journey to-night, my dear, (fifteen miles, in a gentleman's carriage); they[b] will give you some rest to-morrow, but the next day, I have no doubt, they will call; so be at liberty after twelve; – from twelve to three are our calling-hours.'

Then, after they had called,

'It is the third day; I dare say your mamma has told you, my dear, never to let more than three days elapse between receiving a call and returning it; and also, that you are never to stay longer than a quarter of an hour.'

'But am I to look at my watch? How am I to find out when a quarter of an hour has passed?'

'You must keep thinking about the time, my dear, and not allow yourself to forget it in conversation.'

As everybody had this rule in their minds, whether they received or paid a call, of course no absorbing subject was ever spoken about. We kept ourselves to short sentences of small talk, and were punctual to our time.

I imagine that a few of the gentlefolks of Cranford were poor, and had some difficulty in making both ends meet; but they were like the Spartans, and concealed their smart under a smiling face. We none of us spoke of money, because that subject savoured of commerce and trade, and though some might be poor, we were all aristocratic. The Cranfordians had that kindly *esprit de corps* which made them overlook all deficiencies in success when some among them tried to conceal their poverty. When Mrs. Forrester, for instance, gave a party in her baby-house of a dwelling, and the little maiden disturbed the ladies on the sofa by a request that she might get the tea-tray out from underneath, every one took this novel proceeding as the most natural thing in the world; and talked on about household forms and ceremonies; as if we all believed that our hostess had a regular servants' hall, second table, with house-keeper and steward; instead of the one little charity-school maiden, whose short ruddy arms could never have been strong enough to carry the tray up-stairs, if she had not been assisted in private by her mistress, who now sate in state, pretending not to know what cakes were sent up; though she knew, and we knew, and she knew that we knew, and we knew that she knew that we knew, she had been busy all the morning making tea-bread and sponge-cakes.

There were one or two consequences arising from this general but unacknowledged poverty, and this very much acknowledged gentility, which were not amiss, and which might be introduced into many circles of society to their great improvement. For instance, the inhabitants of Cranford kept early hours, and clattered home in their pattens, under the guidance of a lantern-bearer, about nine o'clock at night; and the whole town was abed and asleep by half-past ten. Moreover, it was considered 'vulgar' (a tremendous word in Cranford) to give anything expensive, in the way of eatable or drinkable, at the evening entertainments. Wafer bread-and-butter and sponge-biscuits were all that the Honourable Mrs. Jamieson gave; and she was sister-in-law to the late Earl of Glenmire,[a] although she did practise such 'elegant economy.'

'Elegant economy!' How naturally one falls back into the phraseology of Cranford! There, economy was always 'elegant,' and money-spending always 'vulgar and ostentatious;' a sort of sour-grapeism, which made us very peaceful and satisfied. I never shall forget the dismay felt when a certain Captain Brown came to live at Cranford, and openly spoke about his being poor – not in a whisper to an intimate friend, the doors and windows being previously closed; but, in the public street! in a loud military voice! alleging his poverty as a reason for not taking a particular house. The ladies of Cranford were already rather moaning over the invasion of their territories by a man and a gentleman. He was a half-pay Captain,[5] and had obtained some situation on a neighbouring railroad, which had been vehemently petitioned against by the little town; and if, in addition to his masculine gender,[6b] and his connexion with the obnoxious railroad, he was so brazen as to talk of being poor – why! then, indeed, he must be sent to Coventry. Death was as true and as common as poverty; yet people never spoke about that, loud out in the streets. It was a word not to be mentioned to ears polite.[7] We had tacitly agreed to ignore that any with whom we associated on terms of visiting equality could ever be prevented by poverty from doing anything that they wished. If we walked[c] to or from a party, it was because the night was *so* fine, or the air *so* refreshing; not because sedan-chairs were expensive. If we wore prints, instead of summer silks, it was because we preferred a washing material; and so on, till we blinded ourselves to the vulgar fact, that we were, all of us, people of very moderate means. Of course, then, we did not know what to make of a man who could speak of poverty as if it was not a disgrace. Yet, somehow Captain Brown made himself respected in Cranford, and was called upon, in spite of all resolutions to the contrary. I was surprised to hear his opinions quoted as authority, at a visit which I paid to Cranford, about a year after he had settled in the town. My own friends had been among the bitterest opponents of any proposal to visit the Captain and his daughters, only twelve months before; and now he was even admitted in the tabooed hours before twelve. True, it was to discover the cause of a smoking chimney, before the fire was lighted; but still Captain Brown walked up-stairs, nothing daunted, spoke in a voice too large for the room, and joked quite in the way of a tame man, about the house. He had been blind to all the small slights and omissions of trivial ceremonies with which he had been received. He had been friendly, though the Cranford ladies had been cool; he had answered small sarcastic compliments in good faith; and with his manly frankness had overpowered all the shrinking which met him as a man who was not ashamed to be poor. And, at last, his excellent masculine common sense, and his facility in devising expedients to overcome domestic dilemmas, had gained him an extraordinary place as authority among the Cranford ladies. He, himself, went on in his course, as unaware of his popularity, as he had been of the reverse; and I am sure he was startled one day, when he found his advice so highly esteemed, as to make some counsel which he had given in jest, be taken in sober, serious earnest.

It was on this subject; – an old lady had an Alderney cow, which she looked upon as a daughter. You could not pay the short quarter-of-an-hour call, without being told of the wonderful milk or wonderful intelligence of this animal. The whole town knew and kindly regarded Miss Betsy Barker's Alderney; therefore great was the sympathy and regret when, in an unguarded moment, the poor cow tumbled into a lime-pit. She moaned so loudly that she was soon heard, and rescued; but meanwhile the poor beast had lost most of her hair, and came out looking naked, cold, and miserable, in a bare skin. Everybody pitied the animal, though a few could not restrain their smiles at her droll appearance. Miss Betsy Barker absolutely cried with sorrow and dismay; and it was said she thought of trying a bath of oil. This remedy, perhaps, was recommended by some one of the number whose advice she asked; but the proposal, if ever it was made, was knocked on the head by Captain Brown's decided 'Get her a flannel waistcoat and flannel drawers, Ma'am, if you wish to keep her alive. But my advice is, kill the poor creature at once.'

Miss Betsy Barker dried her eyes, and thanked the Captain heartily; she set to work, and by-and-by all the town turned out to see the Alderney meekly going to her pasture, clad in dark grey flannel. I have watched her myself many a time. Do you ever see cows dressed in grey flannel in London?

Captain Brown had taken a small house on the outskirts of the town, where he lived with his two daughters. He must have been upwards of sixty at the time of the first visit I paid to Cranford, after I had left it as a residence. But he had a wiry, well-trained, elastic figure; a stiff military throwback of his head, and a springing step, which made him appear much younger than he was. His eldest daughter looked almost as old as himself, and betrayed the fact that his real, was more than his apparent, age. Miss Brown must have been forty; she had a sickly, pained, careworn expression on her face, and looked as if the gaiety of youth had long faded out of sight. Even when young she must have been plain and hard-featured. Miss Jessie Brown was ten years younger than her sister, and twenty shades prettier. Her face was round and dimpled. Miss Jenkyns once said, in a passion against Captain Brown (the cause of which I will tell you presently), 'that she thought it was time for Miss Jessie to leave off her dimples, and not always to be trying to look like a child.' It was true there was something child-like in her face; and there will be, I think, till she dies, though she should live to a hundred. Her eyes were large blue wondering[a] eyes, looking straight at you; her nose was unformed and snub, and her lips were red and dewy; she wore her hair, too, in little rows of curls, which heightened this appearance. I do not know if she was pretty or not; but I liked her face, and so did everybody, and I do not think she could help her dimples. She had something of her father's jauntiness of gait and manner; and any female observer might detect a slight difference in the attire of the two sisters – that of Miss Jessie being about two pounds per annum more expensive than Miss Brown's. Two pounds was a large sum in Captain Brown's annual disbursements.

Such was the impression made upon me by the Brown family, when I first saw them altogether[b] in Cranford church. The Captain I had met before – on the occasion of the smoky chimney, which he had cured by some simple alteration in the flue. In church, he held his double eye-glass to his eyes during the Morning Hymn,[8] and then lifted up his head erect, and sang out loud and joyfully. He made the responses louder than the clerk – an old man with a piping feeble voice, who, I think, felt aggrieved at the Captain's sonorous bass, and quavered higher and higher in consequence.

On coming out of church, the brisk Captain paid the most gallant attention to his two daughters. He nodded and smiled to his two daughters. He nodded and smiled to his acquaintances; but he shook hands with none until he had helped Miss Brown to unfurl her umbrella, had relieved her of her prayer-book, and had waited patiently till she, with trembling nervous hands, had taken up her gown to walk through the wet roads.

I wondered what the Cranford ladies did with Captain Brown at their parties. We had often rejoiced, in former days, that there was no gentleman to be attended to, and to find conversation for, at the card-parties. We had congratulated ourselves upon the snugness of the evenings; and, in our love for gentility, and distaste of mankind, we had almost persuaded ourselves that to be a man was to be 'vulgar;' so that when I found my friend and hostess, Miss Jenkyns, was going to have a party in my honour, and that Captain and the Miss Browns were invited, I wondered much what would be the course of the evening. Card-tables, with green-baize tops, were set out by day-light, just as usual; it was the third week in November, so the evenings closed in about four. Candles, and clean packs of cards were arranged on each table. The fire was made up, the neat maid-servant had received her last directions; and, there we stood dressed in our best, each with a candle-lighter in our hands, ready to dart at the candles as soon as the first knock came. Parties in Cranford were solemn festivities, making the ladies feel gravely elated, as they sat together in their best dresses. As soon as three had arrived, we sat down to 'Preference,'[9] I being the unlucky fourth. The next four comers were put down immediately to another table; and presently the tea-trays, which I had seen set out in the store-room as I passed in the morning, were placed each on the middle of a card-table. The china was delicate egg-shell; the old-fashioned silver glittered with polishing; but the eatables were of the slightest description. While the trays were yet on the tables, Captain and the Miss Browns came in; and I could see, that somehow or other the Captain was a favourite with all the ladies present. Ruffled brows were smoothed, sharp voices lowered at his approach. Miss Brown looked ill, and depressed almost to gloom. Miss Jessie smiled as usual, and seemed nearly as popular as her father. He immediately and quietly assumed the man's place in the room; attended to every one's wants, lessened the pretty maid-servant's labour by waiting on empty cups, and bread-and-butterless ladies; and yet did it all in so easy and dignified a manner, and so much as if it were a matter of course for the strong to attend to the weak, that he was a true man throughout. He played for three-penny points with as grave an interest as if they had been pounds; and yet, in all his attention to strangers he had an eye on his suffering daughter; for suffering I was sure she was, though to many eyes she might only appear to be irritable. Miss Jessie could not play cards; but she talked to the sitters-out, who, before her coming, had been rather inclined to be cross. She sang, too, to an old cracked piano, which I think had been a spinnet in its youth. Miss Jessie sang 'Jock of Hazeldean'[10] a little out of tune; but we were none of us musical, though Miss Jenkyns beat time, out of time, by way of appearing to be so.

It was very good of Miss Jenkyns to do this; for I had seen that, a little before, she had been a good deal annoyed by Miss Jessie Brown's unguarded admission (*à propos* of Shetland wool) that she had an uncle, her mother's brother, who was a shopkeeper in Edinburgh. Miss Jenkyns tried to drown this confession by a terrible cough – for the Honourable Mrs. Jamieson was sitting at the card-table nearest Miss Jessie, and what would she say or think, if she found out she was in the same room with a shopkeeper's niece! But Miss Jessie Brown (who had no tact, as we all agreed, the next morning) *would* repeat the information, and assure Miss Pole she could easily get her the identical Shetland wool required, 'through my uncle, who has the best assortment of Shetland goods of any one in Edinbro'.' It was to take the taste of this out of our mouths, and the sound of this out of our ears, that Miss Jenkyns proposed music; so I say again, it was very good of her to beat time to the song.

When the trays re-appeared with biscuits and wine, punctually at a quarter to nine, there was conversation; comparing of cards, and talking over tricks; but, by-and-by, Captain Brown sported a bit of literature.

'Have you seen any numbers of "The Pickwick Papers?"'[11a] said he. (They[b] were then publishing in parts.) 'Capital thing!'

Now, Miss Jenkyns was daughter of a deceased rector of Cranford; and, on the strength of a number of manuscript sermons, and a pretty good library of divinity, considered herself literary, and looked upon any conversation about books as a challenge to her. So she answered and said, 'Yes, she had seen them;[c] indeed, she might say she had read them.'[d]

'And what do you think of them?'[e] exclaimed Captain Brown. 'Aren't they[f] famously good?'

So urged, Miss Jenkyns could not but speak.

'I must say I don't think they are[g] by any means equal to Dr. Johnson. Still, perhaps, the author is young. Let him persevere, and who knows what he may become if he will take the great Doctor for his model.' This was evidently too much for Captain Brown to take placidly; and I saw the words on the tip of his tongue before Miss Jenkyns had finished her sentence.

'It is quite a different sort of thing, my dear madam,' he began.

'I am quite aware of that,' returned she. 'And I make allowances, Captain Brown.'

'Just allow me to read you a scene out of this month's number,' pleaded he. 'I had it only this morning, and I don't think the company can have read it yet.'

'As you please,' said she, settling herself with an air of resignation. He read the account of the 'swarry' which Sam. Weller gave at Bath.[12h] Some of us laughed heartily. *I* did not dare, because I was staying in the house. Miss Jenkyns sat in patient gravity. When it was ended, she turned to me, and said with mild dignity,

'Fetch me "Rasselas,"[13] my dear, out of the book-room.'

When I brought it to her, she turned to Captain Brown:

'Now allow *me* to read you a scene, and then the present company can judge between your favourite, Mr. Boz[i] and Dr. Johnson.'

She read one of the conversations between Rasselas and Imlac, in a high-pitched majestic voice; and when she had ended, she said, 'I imagine I am now justified in my preference of Dr. Johnson, as a writer of fiction.' The Captain screwed his lips up, and drummed on the table, but he did not speak. She thought she would give a finishing blow or two.

'I consider it vulgar, and below the dignity of literature, to publish in numbers.'

'How was the "Rambler"[14] published, Ma'am?' asked Captain Brown, in a low voice; which I think Miss Jenkyns could not have heard.

'Dr. Johnson's style is a model for young beginners. My father recommended it to me when I began to write letters. – I have formed my own style upon it; I recommend it to your favourite.'

'I should be very sorry for him to exchange his style for any such pompous writing,' said Captain Brown.

Miss Jenkyns felt this as a personal affront, in a way of which the Captain had not dreamed. Epistolary writing, she and her friends considered as her *forte*. Many a copy of many a letter have I seen written and corrected on the slate, before she 'seized the half-hour just previous to post-time to assure' her friends of this or of that; and Dr. Johnson was, as she said, her model in these compositions. She drew herself up with dignity, and only replied to Captain Brown's last remark by saying with marked emphasis on every syllable, 'I prefer Dr. Johnson to Mr. Boz.'[a]

It is said – I won't vouch for the fact – that Captain Brown was heard to say, *sotto voce*, 'D—n Dr. Johnson!' If he did, he was penitent afterwards, as he showed by going to stand near Miss Jenkyns's arm-chair, and endeavouring to beguile her into conversation on some more pleasing subject. But she was inexorable. The next day, she made the remark I have mentioned, about Miss Jessie's dimples.

CHAPTER II.

THE CAPTAIN.[a]

IT was impossible to live a month at Cranford, and not know the daily habits of each resident; and long before my visit was ended, I knew much concerning the whole Brown trio. There was nothing new to be discovered respecting their poverty; for they had spoken simply and openly about that from the very first. They made no mystery of the necessity for their being economical. All that remained to be discovered was the Captain's infinite kindness of heart, and the various modes in which, unconsciously to himself, he manifested it. Some little anecdotes were talked about for some time after they occurred. As we did not read much, and as all the ladies were pretty well suited with servants, there was a dearth of subjects for conversation. We therefore discussed the circumstance of the Captain taking a poor old woman's dinner out of her hands, one very slippery Sunday. He had met her returning from the bakehouse as he came from church, and noticed her precarious footing; and, with the grave dignity with which he did everything, he relieved her of her burden, and steered along the street by her side, carrying her baked mutton and potatoes safely home. This was thought very eccentric; and it was rather expected that he would pay a round of calls, on the Monday morning, to explain and apologise to the Cranford sense of propriety: but he did no such thing; and then it was decided that he was ashamed, and was keeping out of sight. In a kindly pity for him, we began to say – 'After all, the Sunday morning's occurrence showed great goodness of heart;' and it was resolved that he should be comforted on his next appearance amongst us; but, lo! he came down upon us, untouched by any sense of shame, speaking loud and bass as ever, his head thrown back, his wig as jaunty and well-curled as usual, and we were obliged to conclude he had forgotten all about Sunday.

Miss Pole and Miss Jessie Brown had set up a kind of intimacy, on the strength of the Shetland wool and the new knitting stitches; so it happened that when I went to visit Miss Pole, I saw more of the Browns than I had done while staying with Miss Jenkyns; who had never got over what she called Captain Brown's disparaging remarks upon Dr. Johnson, as a writer of light and agreeable fiction. I found that Miss Brown was seriously ill of some lingering, incurable complaint, the pain occasioned by which gave the uneasy expression to her face that I had taken for unmitigated crossness.

Cross, too, she was at times, when the nervous irritability occasioned by her disease became past endurance. Miss Jessie bore with her at these times even more patiently than she did with the bitter self-upbraidings by which they were invariably succeeded. Miss Brown used to accuse herself, not merely of hasty and irritable temper; but also of being the cause why her father and sister were obliged to pinch, in order to allow her the small luxuries which were necessaries in her condition. She would so fain have made sacrifices for them and have lightened their cares, that the original generosity of her disposition added acerbity to her temper. All this was borne by Miss Jessie and her father with more than placidity – with absolute tenderness. I forgave Miss Jessie her singing out of tune, and her juvenility of dress, when I saw her at home. I came to perceive that Captain Brown's dark Brutus wig[15] and padded coat (alas! too often threadbare) were remnants of the military smartness of his youth, which he now wore unconsciously. He was a man of infinite resources, gained in his barrack experience. As he confessed, no one could black his boots to please him, except himself; but, indeed, he was not above saving the little maid-servant's labours in every way, – knowing, most likely,[a] that his daughter's illness made the place a hard one.

He endeavoured to make peace with Miss Jenkyns soon after the memorable dispute I have named, by a present of a wooden fire-shovel (his own making), having heard her say how much the grating of an iron one annoyed her. She received the present with cool gratitude, and thanked him formally. When he was gone, she bade me put it away in the lumber-room; feeling, probably, that no present from a man who preferred Mr. Boz[b] to Dr. Johnson could be less jarring than an iron fire-shovel.

Such was the state of things when I left Cranford and went to Drumble. I had, however, several correspondents who kept me *au fait* to[c] the proceedings of the dear little town. There was Miss Pole, who was becoming as much absorbed in crochet as she had been once in knitting; and the burden of whose letter was something like, 'But don't you forget the white worsted at Flint's,' of the old song;[16] for, at the end of every sentence of news, came a fresh direction as to some crochet commission which I was to execute for her. Miss Matilda Jenkyns (who did not mind being called Miss Matty,[d] when Miss Jenkyns was not by) wrote nice, kind, rambling letters; now and then venturing into an opinion of her own; but suddenly pulling herself up, and either begging me not to name what she had said, as Deborah thought differently, and *she* knew; or else, putting in a postscript to the effect that, since writing the above, she had been talking over the subject with Deborah, and was quite convinced that, &c.; – (here, probably, followed a recantation of every opinion she had given in the letter.) Then came Miss Jenkyns – Debōrah, as she liked Miss Matty to call her; her father having once said that the Hebrew name ought to be so pronounced. I secretly think she took the Hebrew prophetess[17] for a model in character; and, indeed, she was not unlike the stern prophetess in some ways; making allowance, of course, for modern customs and difference in dress. Miss Jenkyns wore a cravat, and a little bonnet like a jockey-cap, and altogether had the appearance of a strong-minded woman; although she would have despised the modern idea of women being equal to men. Equal, indeed! she knew they were superior. – But to return to her letters. Everything in them was stately and grand, like herself. I have been looking them over (dear Miss Jenkyns, how I honoured[a] her!) and I will give an extract, more especially because it relates to our friend Captain Brown: –

'The Honourable Mrs. Jamieson has only just quitted me; and, in the course of conversation, she communicated to me the intelligence, that she had yesterday received a call from her revered husband's quondam friend, Lord Mauleverer. You will not easily conjecture what brought his lordship within the precincts of our little town. It was to see Captain Brown, with whom, it appears, his lordship was acquainted in the "plumed wars,"[18] and who had the privilege of averting destruction from his lordship's head, when some great peril was impending over it, off the misnomered Cape of Good Hope. You know our friend the Honourable Mrs. Jamieson's deficiency in the spirit of innocent curiosity; and you will therefore not be so much surprised when I tell you she was quite unable to disclose to me the exact nature of the peril in question. I was anxious, I confess, to ascertain in what manner Captain Brown, with his limited establishment, could receive so distinguished a guest; and I discovered that his lordship retired to rest, and, let us hope, to refreshing slumbers, at the Angel Hotel; but shared the Brunonian meals during the two days that he honoured Cranford with his august presence. Mrs. Johnson, our civil butcher's wife, informs me that Miss Jessie purchased a leg of lamb; but, besides this, I can hear of no preparation whatever to give a suitable reception to so distinguished a visitor. Perhaps they entertained him with "the feast of reason and the flow of soul;"[19] and to us, who are acquainted with Captain Brown's sad want of relish for "the pure wells of English undefiled,"[20] it may be matter for congratulation, that he has had the opportunity of improving his taste by holding converse with an elegant and refined member of the British aristocracy. But from some mundane feelings who is free?'[b]

Miss Pole and Miss Matty wrote to me by the same post. Such a piece of news as Lord Mauleverer's visit was not to be lost on the Cranford letter-writers: they made the most of it. Miss Matty humbly apologised for writing at the same time as her sister, who was so much more capable than she to describe the honour done to Cranford; but, in spite of a little bad spelling, Miss Matty's account gave me the best idea of the commotion occasioned by his lordship's visit, after it had occurred; for, except the people at the Angel, the Browns, Mrs. Jamieson, and a little lad his lordship had sworn at for driving a dirty hoop against the aristocratic legs, I could not hear of any one with whom his lordship had held conversation.

My next visit to Cranford was in the summer. There had been neither births, deaths, nor marriages since I was there last. Everybody lived in the same house, and wore pretty nearly the same well-preserved, old-fashioned clothes. The greatest event was, that Miss Jenkynses had purchased a new carpet for the drawing-room. Oh the busy work Miss Matty and I had in chasing the sunbeams, as they fell in an afternoon right down on this carpet through the blindless window! We spread newspapers over the places, and sat down to our book or our work; and, lo! in a quarter of an hour the sun had moved, and was blazing away on a fresh spot; and down again we went on our knees to alter the position of the newspapers. We were very busy, too, one whole morning before Miss Jenkyns gave her party, in following her directions, and in cutting out and stitching together pieces of newspaper, so as to form little paths to every chair, set for the expected visitors, lest their shoes might dirty or defile the purity of the carpet. Do you make paper paths for every guest to walk upon in London?

Captain Brown and Miss Jenkyns were not very cordial to each other. The literary dispute, of which I had seen the beginning, was a 'raw,' the slightest touch on which made them wince. It was the only difference of opinion they had ever had; but that difference was enough. Miss Jenkyns could not refrain from talking *at* Captain Brown; and though he did not reply, he drummed with his fingers; which action she felt and resented as very disparaging to Dr. Johnson. He was rather ostentatious in his preference of the writings of Mr. Boz;[a] would walk through the street so absorbed in them, that he all but ran against Miss Jenkyns; and though his apologies were earnest and sincere, and though he did not, in fact, do more than startle her and himself, she owned to me she had rather he had knocked her down, if he had only been reading a higher style of literature. The poor, brave Captain! he looked older, and more worn, and his clothes were very threadbare. But he seemed as bright and cheerful as ever, unless he was asked about his daughter's health.

'She suffers a great deal, and she must suffer more; we do what we can to alleviate her pain – God's will be done!' He took off his hat at these last words. I found, from Miss Matty,[b] that everything had been done, in fact. A medical man, of high repute in that country neighbourhood, had been sent for, and every injunction he had given was attended to, regardless of expense. Miss Matty[c] was sure they denied themselves many things in order to make the invalid comfortable; but they never spoke about it; and as for Miss Jessie! 'I really think she's an angel,' said poor Miss Matty,[d] quite overcome. 'To see her way of bearing with Miss Brown's crossness, and the bright face she puts on after she's been sitting up a whole night and scolded above half of it, is quite beautiful. Yet she looks as neat and as ready to welcome the Captain at breakfast-time, as if she had been asleep in the Queen's bed all night. My dear! you could never laugh at her prim little curls or her pink bows again, if you saw her as I have done.' I could only feel very penitent, and greet Miss Jessie with double respect when I met her next. She looked faded and pinched; and her lips began to quiver, as if she was very weak, when she spoke of her sister. But she brightened, and sent back the tears that were glittering in her pretty eyes, as she said: –

'But, to be sure, what a town Cranford is for kindness! I don't suppose any one has a better dinner than usual cooked, but the best part of all comes in a little covered basin for my sister. The poor people will leave their earliest vegetables at our door for her. They speak short and gruff, as if they were ashamed of it; but I am sure it often goes to my heart to see their thoughtfulness.' The tears now came back and overflowed; but after a minute or two, she began to scold herself, and ended by going away, the same cheerful Miss Jessie as ever.

'But why does not this Lord Mauleverer do something for the man who saved his life?' said I.

'Why, you see, unless Captain Brown has some reason for it, he never speaks about being poor; and he walked along by his lordship, looking as happy and cheerful as a prince; and as they never called attention to their dinner by apologies, and as Miss Brown was better that day, and all seemed bright, I dare say his lordship never knew how much care there was in the background. He did send game in the winter pretty often, but now he is gone abroad.'

I had often occasion to notice the use that was made of fragments and small opportunities in Cranford; the rose-leaves that were gathered ere they fell, to make into a pot-pourri for some one who had no garden; the little bundles of lavender-flowers sent to strew the drawers of some town-dweller, or to burn in the chamber of some invalid. Things that many would despise, and actions which it seemed scarcely worth while to perform, were all attended to in Cranford. Miss Jenkyns stuck an apple full of cloves, to be heated and smell pleasantly in Miss Brown's room; and as she put in each clove, she uttered a Johnsonian sentence. Indeed, she never could think of the Browns without talking Johnson; and, as they were seldom absent from her thoughts just then, I heard many a rolling three-piled sentence.

Captain Brown called one day to thank Miss Jenkyns for many little kindnesses, which I did not know until then that she had rendered. He had suddenly become like an old man; his deep bass voice had a quavering in it; his eyes looked dim, and the lines on his face were deep. He did not – could not – speak cheerfully of his daughter's state, but he talked with manly pious resignation, and not much. Twice over he said, 'What Jessie has been to us, God only knows!' and after the second time, he got up hastily, shook hands all round without speaking, and left the room.

That afternoon we perceived little groups in the street, all listening with faces aghast to some tale or other. Miss Jenkyns wondered what could be the matter, for some time before she took the undignified step of sending Jenny out to inquire.

Jenny came back with a white face of terror. 'Oh, Ma'am! oh, Miss Jenkyns, Ma'am! Captain Brown is killed by them nasty cruel railroads!'[21] and she burst into tears. She, along with many others, had experienced the poor Captain's kindness.

'How? – where – where? Good God! Jenny, don't waste time in crying, but tell us something.' Miss Matty rushed out into the street at once, and collared the man who was telling the tale.

'Come in – come to my sister at once, – Miss Jenkyns, the rector's daughter. Oh, man, man! say it is not true,' – she cried, as she brought the affrighted carter, sleeking down his hair, into the drawing-room, where he stood with his wet boots on the new carpet, and no one regarded it.

'Please mum, it is true. I seed it myself,' and he shuddered at the recollection. 'The Captain was a-reading some new book as he was deep in, a-waiting for the down train; and there was a little lass as wanted to come to it's mammy, and gave it's[22a] sister the slip, and came toddling across the line. And he looked up sudden at the sound of the train coming, and seed the child, and he darted on the line and cotched it up, and his foot slipped, and the train came over him in no time. Oh Lord, Lord! Mum, it's quite true – and they've come over to tell his daughters. The child's safe, though, with only a bang on its shoulder, as he threw it to its mammy. Poor Captain would be glad of that, mum, would not he? God bless him!' The great rough carter puckered up his manly face, and turned away to hide his tears. I turned to Miss Jenkyns. She looked very ill, as if she were going to faint, and signed to me to open the window.

'Matilda, bring me my bonnet. I must go to those girls. God pardon me if ever I have spoken contemptuously to the Captain!'

Miss Jenkyns arrayed herself to go out, telling Miss Matilda to give the man a glass of wine. While she was away, Miss Matty and I huddled over the fire, talking in a low and awestruck voice. I know we cried quietly all the time.

Miss Jenkyns came home in a silent mood, and we durst not ask her many questions. She told us that Miss Jessie had fainted, and that she and Miss Pole had had some difficulty in bringing her round:[b] but that, as soon as she recovered, she begged one of them to go and sit with her sister.

'Mr. Hoggins[c] says she cannot live many days, and she shall be spared this shock,' said Miss Jessie, shivering with feelings to which she dared not give way.

'But how can you manage, my dear?' asked Miss Jenkyns; 'you cannot bear up, she must see your tears.'

'God will help me – I will not give way – she was asleep when the news came; she may be asleep yet. She would be so utterly miserable, not merely at my father's death, but to think of what would become of me; she is so good to me.' She looked up earnestly in their faces with her soft true eyes, and Miss Pole told Miss Jenkyns afterwards she could hardly bear it, knowing, as she did, how Miss Brown treated her sister.

However, it was settled according to Miss Jessie's wish. Miss Brown was to be told her father had been summoned to take a short journey on railway business. They had managed it in some way – Miss Jenkyns could not exactly say how. Miss Pole was to stop with Miss Jessie. Mrs. Jamieson had sent to inquire. And this was all we heard that night; and a sorrowful night it was. The next day a full account of the fatal accident was in the country paper, which Miss Jenkyns took in. Her eyes were very weak, she said, and she asked me to read it. When I came to the 'gallant gentleman was deeply engaged in the perusal of a number of "Pickwick,"[a] which he had just received,' Miss Jenkyns shook her head long and solemnly, and then sighed out, 'Poor, dear, infatuated man!'

The corpse was to be taken from the station to the parish church, there to be interred. Miss Jessie had set her heart on following it to the grave; and no dissuasives could alter her resolve. Her restraint upon herself made her almost obstinate; she resisted all Miss Pole's entreaties, and Miss Jenkyns's advice. At last Miss Jenkyns gave up the point; and after a silence, which I feared portended some deep displeasure against Miss Jessie, Miss Jenkyns said she should accompany the latter to the funeral.

'It is not fit for you to go alone. It would be against both propriety and humanity were I to allow it.'

Miss Jessie seemed as if she did not half like this arrangement; but her obstinacy, if she had any, had been exhausted in her determination to go to the interment. She longed, poor thing! I have no doubt, to cry alone over the grave of the dear father to whom she had been all in all; and to give way, for one little half-hour, uninterrupted by sympathy, and unobserved by friendship. But it was not to be. That afternoon Miss Jenkyns sent out for a yard of black crape, and employed herself busily in trimming the little black silk bonnet I have spoken about. When it was finished she put it on, and looked at us for approbation – admiration she despised. I was full of sorrow, but, by one of those whimsical thoughts which come unbidden into our heads, in times of deepest grief, I no sooner saw the bonnet than I was reminded of a helmet; and in that hybrid bonnet, half-helmet, half-jockey cap, did Miss Jenkyns attend Captain Brown's funeral; and I believe supported Miss Jessie with a tender indulgent firmness which was invaluable, allowing her to weep her passionate fill before they left.

Miss Pole, Miss Matty, and I, meanwhile, attended to Miss Brown: and hard work we found it to relieve her querulous and never-ending complaints. But if we were so weary and dispirited, what must Miss Jessie have been! Yet she came back almost calm, as if she had gained a new strength. She put off her mourning dress, and came in, looking pale and gentle; thanking us each with a soft long pressure of the hand. She could even smile – a faint, sweet, wintry smile, as if to reassure us of her power to endure; but her look made our eyes fill suddenly with tears, more than if she had cried outright.

It was settled that Miss Pole was to remain with her all the watching live-long night; and that Miss Matty and I were to return in the morning to relieve them, and give Miss Jessie the opportunity for a few hours of sleep. But when the morning came, Miss Jenkyns appeared at the breakfast table, equipped in her helmet bonnet, and ordered Miss Matty to stay at home, as she meant to go and help to nurse. She was evidently in a state of great friendly excitement, which she showed by eating her breakfast standing, and scolding the household all round.

No nursing – no energetic strong-minded woman could help Miss Brown now. There was that in the room as we entered, which was stronger than us all, and made us shrink into solemn awestruck helplessness. Miss Brown was dying. We hardly knew her voice, it was so devoid of the com-plaining tone we had always associated with it. Miss Jessie told me afterwards that it, and her face too, were just what they had been formerly, when her mother's death left her the young anxious head of the family, of whom only Miss Jessie survived.

She was conscious of her sister's presence, though not, I think, of ours. We stood a little behind the curtain: Miss Jessie knelt with her face near her sister's, in order to catch the last soft awful whispers.

'Oh, Jessie! Jessie! How selfish I have been! God forgive me for letting you sacrifice yourself for me as you did. I have so loved you – and yet I have thought only of myself. God forgive me!'

'Hush, love! hush!' said Miss Jessie, sobbing.

'And my father! my dear, dear father! I will not complain now, if God will give me strength to be patient. But, oh, Jessie! tell my father how I longed and yearned to see him at last, and to ask his forgiveness. He can never know now how I loved him – oh! if I might but tell him, before I die; what[a] a life of sorrow his has been, and I have done so little to cheer him!'

A light came into Miss Jessie's face. 'Would it comfort you, dearest, to think that he does know – would it comfort you, love, to know that his cares, his sorrows –' Her voice quivered, but she steadied it into calmness, – 'Mary! he has gone before you to the place where the weary are at rest.[23] He knows now how you loved him.'

A strange look, which was not distress, came over Miss Brown's face. She did not speak for some time, but then we saw her lips form the words, rather than heard the sound – 'Father, mother, Harry, Archy!' – then, as if it was a new idea throwing a filmy shadow over her darkening mind – 'But you will be alone – Jessie!'

Miss Jessie had been feeling this all during the silence, I think; for the tears rolled down her cheeks like rain, at these words; and she could not answer at first. Then she put her hands together tight, and lifted them up, and said, – but not to us –

'Though He slay me, yet will I trust in Him.'[24]

In a few moments more, Miss Brown lay calm and still; never to sorrow or murmur more.

After this second funeral, Miss Jenkyns insisted that Miss Jessie should come to stay with her, rather than go back to the desolate house; which, in fact, we learned from Miss Jessie, must now be given up, as she had not wherewithal to maintain it. She had something about[a] twenty pounds a-year,[b] besides the interest of the money for which the furniture would sell; but she could not live upon that: and so we talked over her qualifications for earning money.

'I can sew neatly,' said she, 'and I like nursing. I think, too, I could manage a house, if any one would try me as housekeeper; or I would go into a shop, as saleswoman, if they would have patience with me at first.'

Miss Jenkyns declared, in an angry voice, that she should do no such thing; and talked to herself about 'some people having no idea of their rank as a Captain's daughter,' nearly an hour afterwards, when she brought Miss Jessie up a basin of delicately-made arrow-root, and stood over her like a dragoon until the last spoonful was finished: then she disappeared. Miss Jessie began to tell me some more of the plans which had suggested themselves to her, and insensibly fell into talking of the days that were past and gone, and interested me so much, I neither knew nor heeded how time passed. We were both startled when Miss Jenkyns reappeared, and caught us crying. I was afraid lest she would be displeased, as she often said that crying hindered digestion, and I knew she wanted Miss Jessie to get strong; but, instead, she looked queer and excited, and fidgeted round us without saying anything. At last she spoke. 'I[c] have been so much startled – no, I've not been at all startled – don't mind me, my dear Miss Jessie – I've been very much surprised – in fact, I've had a caller, whom you knew once, my dear Miss Jessie –'

Miss Jessie went very white, then flushed scarlet, and looked eagerly at Miss Jenkyns –

'A gentleman, my dear, who wants to know if you would see him.'

'Is it? – it is not –' stammered out Miss Jessie – and got no farther.

'This is his card,' said Miss Jenkyns, giving it to Miss Jessie; and while her head was bent over it, Miss Jenkyns went through a series of winks and odd faces to me, and formed her lips into a long sentence, of which, of course, I could not understand a word.

'May he come up?' asked Miss Jenkyns at last.

'Oh, yes! certainly!' said Miss Jessie, as much as to say, this is your house, you may show any visitor where you like. She took up some knitting of Miss Matty's and began to be very busy, though I could see how she trembled all over.

Miss Jenkyns rang the bell, and told the servant who answered it to show Major Gordon[a] up-stairs; and, presently, in walked a tall, fine, frank-looking man of forty, or upwards. He shook hands with Miss Jessie; but he could not see her eyes, she kept them so fixed on the ground. Miss Jenkyns asked me if I would come and help her to tie up the preserves in the store-room; and, though Miss Jessie plucked at my gown, and even looked up at me with begging eye, I durst not refuse to go where Miss Jenkyns asked. Instead of tying up preserves in the store-room, however, we went to talk in the dining-room; and there Miss Jenkyns told me what Major Gordon[b] had told her; – how he had served in the same regiment with Captain Brown, and had become acquainted with Miss Jessie, then a sweet-looking, blooming girl of eighteen; how the acquaintance had grown into love, on his part, though it had been some years before he had spoken; how, on becoming possessed, through the will of an uncle, of a good estate in Scotland, he had offered, and been refused, though with so much agitation, and evident distress, that he was sure she was not indifferent to him; and how he had discovered that the obstacle was the fell disease which was, even then, too surely threatening her sister. She had mentioned that the surgeons foretold intense suffering; and there was no one but herself to nurse her poor Mary, or cheer and comfort her father during the time of illness. They had had long discussions; and, on her refusal to pledge herself to him as his wife, when all should be over, he had grown angry, and broken off entirely, and gone abroad, believing that she was a cold-hearted person, whom he would do well to forget. He had been travelling in the East, and was on his return home when, at Rome, he saw the account of Captain Brown's death in 'Galignani.'[25]

Just then Miss Matty, who had been out all the morning, and had only lately returned to the house, burst in with a face of dismay and outraged propriety: –

'Oh, goodness me!' she said. 'Deborah,[c] there's a gentleman sitting in the drawing-room, with his arm round Miss Jessie's waist!' Miss Matty's eyes looked large with terror.

Miss Jenkyns snubbed her down in an instant: –

'The most proper place in the world for his arm to be in. Go away, Matilda, and mind your own business.' This from her sister, who had hitherto been a model of feminine decorum, was a blow for poor Miss Matty, and with a double shock she left the room.

The last time I ever saw poor Miss Jenkyns was many years after this. Mrs. Gordon[d] had kept up a warm and affectionate intercourse with all at Cranford. Miss Jenkyns, Miss Matty, and Miss Pole had all been to visit her, and returned with wonderful accounts of her house, her husband, her dress, and her looks. For, with happiness, something of her early bloom returned; she had been a year or two younger than we had taken her for. Her eyes were always lovely, and, as Mrs. Gordon,[a] her dimples were not out of place. At the time to which I have referred, when I last saw Miss Jenkyns, that lady was old and feeble, and had lost something of her strong mind. Little Flora Gordon[b] was staying with the Misses Jenkyns, and when I came in she was reading aloud to Miss Jenkyns, who lay feeble and changed on the sofa. Flora put down the 'Rambler' when I came in.

'Ah!' said Miss Jenkyns, 'you find me changed, my dear. I can't see as I used to do. If Flora were not here to read to me, I hardly know how I should get through the day. Did you ever read the "Rambler?" It's a wonderful book – wonderful! and the most improving reading for Flora' – (which I dare say it would have been, if she could have read half the words without spelling, and could have understood the meaning of a third) – 'better than that strange old book, with the queer name, poor Captain Brown was killed for reading – that book by Mr. Boz, you know – "Old Poz;" when I was a girl, but that's a long time ago, – I acted Lucy in "Old Poz"' –[26] she babbled on long enough for Flora to get a good long spell at the 'Christmas Carol,'[27] which Miss Matty had left on the table.[c]

CHAPTER III.[a]

A LOVE AFFAIR OF LONG AGO.[b]

I THOUGHT that probably my connection with Cranford would cease after Miss Jenkyns's death;[c] at least, that it would have to be kept up by correspondence, which bears much the same relation to personal intercourse that the books of dried plants I sometimes see ('Hortus Siccus,'[28] I think they call the thing,) do to the living and fresh flowers in the lanes and meadows. I was pleasantly surprised, therefore, by receiving a letter from Miss Pole (who had always come in for a supplementary week after my annual visit to Miss Jenkyns) proposing that I should go and stay with her; and then, in a couple of days after my acceptance, came a note from Miss Matty, in which, in a rather circuitous and very humble manner, she told me how much pleasure I should confer, if I could spend a week or two with her, either before or after I had been at Miss Pole's; 'for,' she said, 'since my dear sister's death, I am well aware I have no attractions to offer; it is only to the kindness of my friends that I can owe their company.'

Of course, I promised to come to dear Miss Matty, as soon as I had ended my visit to Miss Pole; and the day after my arrival at Cranford, I went to see her, much wondering what the house would be like without Miss Jenkyns, and rather dreading the changed aspect of things. Miss Matty began to cry as soon as she saw me. She was evidently nervous from having anticipated my call. I comforted her as well as I could; and I found the best consolation I could give was the honest praise that came from my heart as I spoke of the deceased. Miss Matty slowly shook her head over each virtue as it was named and attributed to her sister; at last she could not restrain the tears which had long been silently flowing, but hid her face behind her handkerchief, and sobbed aloud.

'Dear Miss Matty!' said I, taking her hand – for indeed I did not know in what way to tell her how sorry I was for her, left deserted in the world. She put down her handkerchief, and said –

'My dear, I'd rather you did not call me Matty. *She* did not like it; but I did many a thing she did not like, I'm afraid – and now she's gone! If you please, my love, will you call me Matilda?'

I promised faithfully, and began to practise the new name with Miss Pole that very day; and, by degrees, Miss Matilda's feeling on the subject was known through Cranford, and we all tried to drop the more familiar name, but with so little success that by and by we gave up the attempt.[a]

My visit to Miss Pole was very quiet. Miss Jenkyns had so long taken the lead in Cranford, that, now she was gone, they hardly knew how to give a party. The Honourable Mrs. Jamieson, to whom Miss Jenkyns herself had always yielded the post of honour, was fat and inert, and very much at the mercy of her old servants. If they chose that she should give a party,[b] they reminded her of the necessity for so doing; if not, she let it alone. There was all the more time for me to hear old-world stories from Miss Pole, while she sat knitting, and I making my father's shirts. I always took a quantity of plain sewing to Cranford; for, as we did not read much, or walk much, I found it a capital time to get through my work. One of Miss Pole's stories related to a shadow of a love affair that was dimly perceived or suspected long years before.[c]

Presently, the time arrived when I was to remove to Miss Matilda's house. I found her timid and anxious about the arrangements for my comfort. Many a time, while I was unpacking, did she come backwards and forwards to stir the fire, which burned all the worse for being so frequently poked.

'Have you drawers enough, dear?' asked she. 'I don't know exactly how my sister used to arrange them. She had capital methods. I am sure she would have trained a servant in a week to make a better fire than this, and Fanny has been with me four months.'

This subject of servants was a standing grievance, and I could not wonder much at it; for if gentlemen were scarce, and almost unheard of in the 'genteel society' of Cranford, they or their counterparts – handsome young men – abounded in the lower classes. The pretty neat servant-maids had their choice of desirable 'followers;' and their mistresses, without having the sort of mysterious dread of men and matrimony that Miss Matilda had, might well feel a little anxious, lest the heads of their comely maids should be turned by the joiner, or the butcher, or the gardener; who were obliged, by their callings, to come to the house; and who, as ill-luck would have it, were generally handsome and unmarried. Fanny's lovers, if she had any – and Miss Matilda suspected her of so many flirtations, that, if she had not been very pretty, I should have doubted her having one – were a constant anxiety to her mistress. She was forbidden, by the articles of her engagement, to have 'followers;' and though she had answered innocently enough, doubling up the hem of her apron as she spoke, 'Please, ma'am, I never had more than one at a time,' Miss Matty prohibited that one. But a vision of a man seemed to haunt the kitchen. Fanny assured me that it was all fancy; or else I should have said myself that I had seen a man's coat-tails whisk into the scullery once, when I went on an errand into the store-room at night; and another evening, when, our watches having stopped, I went to look at the clock, there was a very odd appearance, singularly like a young man squeezed up between the clock and the back of the open kitchen-door: and I thought Fanny snatched up the candle very hastily, so as to throw the shadow on the clock-face, while she very positively told me the time half-an-hour too early, as we found out afterwards by the church-clock. But I did not add to Miss Matty's anxieties by naming my suspicions, especially as Fanny said to me, the next day, that it was such a queer kitchen for having odd shadows about it, she really was almost afraid to stay; 'for you know Miss,' she added, 'I don't see a creature from six o'clock tea, till Missus rings the bell for prayers at ten.'

However, it so fell out that Fanny had to leave; and Miss Matilda begged me to stay and 'settle her' with the new maid; to which I consented, after I had heard from my father that he did not want me at home. The new servant was a rough, honest-looking country-girl, who had only lived in a farm place before; but I liked her looks when she came to be hired; and I promised Miss Matilda to put her in the ways of the house. The[a] said ways were religiously such as Miss Matilda thought her sister would approve. Many a domestic rule and regulation had been a subject of plaintive whispered murmur to me, during Miss Jenkyns's life; but now that she was gone, I do not think that even I, who was a favourite, durst have suggested an alteration. To give an instance: we constantly adhered to the forms which were observed, at meal times, in 'my father, the Rector's house.' Accordingly, we had always wine and dessert; but the decanters were only filled when there was a party; and what remained was seldom touched, though we had two wine glasses apiece every day after dinner, until the next festive occasion arrived; when the state of the remainder wine was examined into, in a family council. The dregs were often given to the poor; but occasionally, when a good deal had been left at the last party (five months ago, it might be,) it was added to some of a fresh bottle, brought up from the cellar. I fancy poor Captain Brown did not much like wine; for I noticed he never finished his first glass, and most military men take several. Then, as to our dessert, Miss Jenkyns used to gather currants and gooseberries for it herself, which I sometimes thought would have tasted better fresh from the trees; but then, as Miss Jenkyns observed, there would have been nothing for dessert in summer-time. As it was, we felt very genteel with our two glasses apiece, and a dish of gooseberries at the top, of currants and biscuits at the sides, and two decanters at the bottom. When oranges came in, a curious proceeding was gone through. Miss Jenkyns did not like to cut the fruit; for, as she observed, the juice all ran out nobody knew where; sucking (only I think she used some more recondite word) was in fact the only way of enjoying oranges; but then there was the unpleasant association with a ceremony frequently gone through by little babies; and so, after dessert, in orange season, Miss Jenkyns and Miss Matty used to rise up, possess themselves each of an orange in silence, and withdraw to the privacy of their own rooms, to indulge in sucking oranges.

I had once or twice tried, on such occasions, to prevail on Miss Matty to stay; and had succeeded in her sister's life-time. I held up a screen, and did not look, and, as she said, she tried not to make the noise very offensive; but now that she was left alone, she seemed quite horrified when I begged her to remain with me in the warm dining-parlour, and enjoy her orange as she liked best. And so it was in everything. Miss Jenkyns's rules were made more stringent than ever, because the framer of them was gone where there could be no appeal. In all things else Miss Matilda was meek and undecided to a fault. I have heard Fanny turn her round twenty times in a morning about dinner, just as the little hussy chose; and I sometimes fancied she worked on Miss Matilda's weakness in order to bewilder her, and to make her feel more in the power of her clever servant. I determined that I would not leave her till I had seen what sort of a person Martha was; and, if I found her trustworthy, I would tell her not to trouble her mistress with every little decision.

Martha was blunt and plain-spoken to a fault; otherwise she was a brisk, well-meaning, but very ignorant girl. She had not been with us a week before Miss Matilda and I were astounded one morning by the receipt of a letter from a cousin of hers, who had been twenty or thirty years in India, and who had lately, as we had seen by the 'Army List,' returned to England, bringing with him an invalid wife, who had never been introduced to her English relations. Major Jenkyns wrote to propose that he and his wife should spend a night at Cranford, on his way to Scotland – at the inn, if it did not suit Miss Matilda to receive them into her house; in which case they should hope to be with her as much as possible during the day. Of course, it *must*[a] suit her, as she said; for all Cranford knew that she had her sister's bedroom at liberty; but I am sure she wished the Major had stopped in India and forgotten his cousins out and out.

'Oh! how must I manage?' asked she, helplessly. 'If Deborah had been alive, she would have known what to do with a gentleman-visitor. Must I put razors in his dressing-room? Dear! dear! and I've got none. Deborah would have had them. And slippers, and coat-brushes?' I suggested that probably he would bring all these things with him. 'And after dinner, how am I to know when to get up, and leave him to his wine? Deborah would have done it so well; she would have been quite in her element. Will he want coffee, do you think?' I undertook the management of the coffee, and told her I would instruct Martha in the art of waiting, in which it must be owned she was terribly deficient; and that I had no doubt Major and Mrs. Jenkyns would understand the quiet mode in which a lady lived by herself in a country town. But she was sadly fluttered. I made her empty her decanters, and bring up two fresh bottles of wine. I wished I could have prevented her from being present at my instructions to Martha; for she frequently cut in with some fresh direction, muddling the poor girl's mind, as she stood open-mouthed, listening to us both.

'Hand the vegetables round,' said I (foolishly, I see now – for it was aiming at more than we could accomplish with quietness and simplicity): and then, seeing her look bewildered, I added, 'Take the vegetables round to people, and let them help themselves.'

'And mind you go first to the ladies,' put in Miss Matilda. 'Always go to the ladies before gentlemen, when you are waiting.'

'I'll do it as you tell me, ma'am,' said Martha; 'but I like lads best.'

We felt very uncomfortable and shocked at this speech of Martha's; yet I don't think she meant any harm; and, on the whole, she attended very well to our directions, except that she 'nudged' the Major, when he did not help himself as soon as she expected, to the potatoes, while she was handing them round.

The Major and his wife were quiet, unpretending people enough when they did come; languid, as all East Indians are, I suppose. We were rather dismayed at their bringing two servants with them, a Hindoo body-servant for the Major, and a steady elderly maid for his wife; but they slept at the inn, and took off a good deal of the responsibility by attending carefully to their master's and mistress's comfort. Martha, to be sure, had never ended her staring at the East Indian's white turban, and brown complexion, and I saw that Miss Matilda shrunk away from him a little as he waited at dinner. Indeed, she asked me, when they were gone, if he did not remind me of Blue Beard?[29] On the whole, the visit was most satisfactory, and is a subject of conversation even now with Miss Matilda; at the time, it greatly excited Cranford, and even stirred up the apathetic and Honourable Mrs. Jamieson to some expression of interest, when I went to call and thank her for the kind answers she had vouchsafed to Miss Matilda's inquiries as to the arrangement of a gentleman's dressing-room – answers which I must confess she had given in the wearied manner of the Scandinavian prophetess, –

'Leave me, leave me to repose.'[30]

And *now* I come to the love affair.

It seems that Miss Pole had a cousin, once or twice removed, who had offered to Miss Matty long ago. Now, this cousin lived four or five miles from Cranford on his own estate; but his property was not large enough to entitle him to rank higher than a yeoman; or rather, with something of the 'pride which apes humility,'[31] he had refused to push himself on, as so many of his class had done, into the ranks of the squires. He would not allow himself to be called Thomas Holbrook, *Esq.*;[a] he even sent back letters with this address, telling the postmistress at Cranford that his name was *Mr.*[b] Thomas Holbrook, yeoman. He rejected all domestic innovations; he would have the house door stand open in summer, and shut in winter, without knocker or bell to summon a servant. The closed fist or the knob of the stick did this office for him, if he found the door locked. He despised every refinement which had not its root deep down in humanity. If people were not ill, he saw no necessity for moderating his voice. He spoke the dialect of the country in perfection, and constantly used it in conversation; although Miss Pole (who gave me these particulars) added, that he read aloud more beautifully and with more feeling than any one she had ever heard, except the late Rector.

'And how came Miss Matilda not to marry him?' asked I.

'Oh, I don't know. She was willing enough, I think; but you know Cousin Thomas would not have been enough of a gentleman for the Rector, and Miss[32a] Jenkyns.'

'Well! but they were not to marry him,' said I, impatiently.

'No; but they did not like Miss Matty to marry below her rank. You know she was the Rector's daughter, and somehow they are related to Sir Peter Arley: Miss Jenkyns thought a deal of that.'

'Poor Miss Matty!' said I.

'Nay, now, I don't know anything more than that he offered and was refused. Miss Matty might not like him – and Miss Jenkyns might never have said a word – it is only a guess of mine.'

'Has she never seen him since?' I inquired.

'No, I think not. You see, Woodley, Cousin Thomas's house, lies half-way between Cranford and Misselton; and I know he made Misselton his market-town very soon after he had offered to Miss Matty; and I don't think he has been into Cranford above once or twice since – once, when I was walking with Miss Matty, in High Street; and suddenly she darted from me, and went up Shire Lane. A few minutes after, I was startled by meeting Cousin Thomas.'

'How old is he?' I asked, after a pause of castle-building.

'He must be about seventy, I think, my dear,' said Miss Pole, blowing up my castle, as if by gunpowder, into small fragments.

Very soon after – at least during my long visit to Miss Matilda – I had the opportunity of seeing Mr. Holbrook; seeing, too, his first encounter with his former love, after thirty or forty years' separation. I was helping to decide whether any of the new assortment of coloured silks which they had just received at the shop, would do to match a grey and black mousseline-de-laine[33] that wanted a new breadth, when a tall, thin, Don Quixote-looking old man came into the shop for some woollen gloves. I had never seen the person, (who was rather striking) before, and I watched him rather attentively, while Miss Matty listened to the shopman. The stranger wore a blue coat with brass buttons, drab breeches, and gaiters, and drummed with his fingers on the counter until he was attended to. When he answered the shop-boy's question, 'What can I have the pleasure of showing you to-day, Sir?' I saw Miss Matilda start, and then suddenly sit down; and instantly I guessed who it was. She had made some inquiry which had to be carried round to the other shopman.

'Miss Jenkyns wants the black sarsenet[34a] two-and-twopence the yard;' and Mr. Holbrook had caught the name, and was across the shop in two strides.

'Matty – Miss Matilda – Miss Jenkyns! God bless my soul! I should not have known you. How are you? how are you?' He kept shaking her hand in a way which proved the warmth of his friendship; but he repeated so often, as if to himself, 'I should not have known you!' that any sentimental romance which I might be inclined to build, was quite done away with by his manner.

However, he kept talking to us all the time we were in the shop; and then waving the shopman with the unpurchased gloves on one side, with 'Another time, sir! another time!' he walked home with us. I am happy to say my client, Miss Matilda, also left the shop in an equally bewildered state, not having purchased either green or red silk. Mr. Holbrook was evidently full with honest, loud-spoken joy at meeting his old love again; he touched on the changes that had taken place; he even spoke of Miss Jenkyns as 'Your poor sister! Well, well! we have all our faults;' and bade us good-bye with many a hope that he should soon see Miss Matty again. She went straight to her room; and never came back till our early tea-time, when I thought she looked as if she had been crying.

CHAPTER IV.

A VISIT TO AN OLD BACHELOR.[a]

A FEW days after, a note came from Mr. Holbrook, asking us – impartially asking both of us – in a formal, old-fashioned style, to spend a day at his house – a long June day – for it was June now. He named that he had also invited his cousin, Miss Pole; so that we might join in a fly, which could be put up at his house.

I expected Miss Matty to jump at this invitation; but, no! Miss Pole and I had the greatest difficulty in persuading her to go. She thought it was improper; and was even half annoyed when we utterly ignored the idea of any impropriety in her going with two other ladies to see her old lover. Then came a more serious difficulty. She did not think Deborah would have liked her to go. This took us half a day's good hard talking to get over; but, at the first sentence of relenting, I seized the opportunity, and wrote and despatched an acceptance in her name – fixing day and hour, that all might be decided and done with.

The next morning she asked me if I would go down to the shop with her; and there, after much hesitation, we chose out three caps to be sent home and tried on, that the most becoming might be selected to take with us on Thursday.

She was in a state of silent agitation all the way to Woodley. She had evidently never been there before; and, although she little dreamt I knew anything of her early story, I could perceive she was in a tremor at the thought of seeing the place which might have been her home, and round which it is probable that many of her innocent girlish imaginations had clustered. It was a long drive there, through paved jolting lanes. Miss Matilda sate bolt upright, and looked wistfully out of the windows, as we drew near the end of our journey. The aspect of the country was quiet and pastoral. Woodley stood among fields; and there was an old-fashioned garden, where roses and currant-bushes touched each other, and where the feathery asparagus formed a pretty back-ground to the pinks and gilly-flowers; there was no drive up to the door: we got out at a little gate, and walked up a straight box-edged path.

'My cousin might make a drive, I think,' said Miss Pole, who was afraid of ear-ache, and had only her cap on.

'I think it is very pretty,' said Miss Matty, with a soft plaintiveness in her voice, and almost in a whisper; for just then Mr. Holbrook appeared at the door, rubbing his hands in very effervescence of hospitality. He looked more like my idea of Don Quixote than ever, and yet the likeness was only external. His respectable housekeeper stood modestly at the door to bid us welcome; and, while she led the elder ladies upstairs to a bed-room, I begged to look about the garden. My request evidently pleased the old gentleman; who took me all round the place, and showed me his six-and-twenty cows, named after the different letters of the alphabet. As we went along, he surprised me occasionally by repeating apt and beautiful quotations from the poets, ranging easily from Shakspeare and George Herbert to those of our own day. He did this as naturally as if he were thinking aloud, that their true and beautiful words were the best expression he could find for what he was thinking or feeling. To be sure, he called Byron 'my lord Bÿrron,'[a] and pronounced the name of Goethe strictly in accordance with the English sound of the letters – 'As Goëthe says, "Ye ever-verdant palaces,"'[35] &c. Altogether, I never met with a man, before or since, who had spent so long a life in a secluded and not impressive country, with ever-increasing delight in the daily and yearly change of season and beauty.

When he and I went in, we found that dinner was nearly ready in the kitchen, – for so I suppose the room ought to be called, as there were oak dressers and cupboards all round, all over by the side of the fire-place, and only a small Turkey carpet in the middle of the flag-floor. The room might have been easily made into a handsome dark-oak dining-parlour, by removing the oven, and a few other appurtenances of a kitchen, which were evidently never used; the real cooking place being at some distance. The room in which we were expected to sit was a stiffly furnished, ugly apartment; but that in which we did sit was what Mr. Holbrook called the counting-house, when he paid his labourers their weekly wages, at a great desk near the door. The rest of the pretty sitting-room – looking into the orchard, and all covered over with dancing tree-shadows – was filled with books. They lay on the ground, they covered the walls, they strewed the table. He was evidently half ashamed and half proud of his extravagance in this respect. They were of all kinds, – poetry, and wild weird tales prevailing. He evidently chose his books in accordance with his own tastes, not because such and such were classical, or established favourites.

'Ah!' he said, 'we farmers ought not to have much time for reading; yet somehow one can't help it.'

'What a pretty room!' said Miss Matty, *sotto voce*.

'What a pleasant place!' said I, aloud, almost simultaneously.

'Nay! if you like it,' – replied he; 'but can you sit on these great black leather three-cornered chairs? I like it better than the best parlour; but I thought ladies would take that for the smarter place.'

It was the smarter place; but, like most smart things,[a] not at all pretty, or pleasant, or home-like; so, while we were at dinner, the servant-girl dusted and scrubbed the counting-house chairs, and we sate there all the rest of the day.

We had pudding before meat; and I thought Mr. Holbrook was going to make some apology for his old-fashioned ways, for he began, –

'I don't know whether you like new-fangled ways.'

'Oh! not at all!' said Miss Matty.

'No more do I,' said he. 'My housekeeper *will* have these[b] in her new fashion; or else I tell her, that when I was a young man, we used to keep strictly to my father's rule, "No broth, no ball; no ball, no beef;" and always began dinner with broth. Then we had suet puddings, boiled in the broth with the beef; and then the meat itself. If we did not sup our broth, we had no ball, which we liked a deal better; and the beef came last of all, and only those had it who had done justice to the broth and the ball. Now folks begin with sweet things, and turn their dinners topsy-turvy.'

When the ducks and green peas[c] came, we looked at each other in dismay; we had only two-pronged, black-handled forks. It is true, the steel was as bright as silver; but what were we to do? Miss Matty picked up her peas, one by one, on the point of the prongs, much as Aminé ate her grains of rice after her previous feast with the Ghoul.[36] Miss Pole sighed over her delicate young peas as she left them on one side of her plate untasted; for they *would* drop between the prongs. I looked at my host: the peas were going wholesale into his capacious mouth, shovelled up by his large round-ended knife. I saw, I imitated, I survived! My friends, in spite of my precedent, could not muster up courage enough to do an ungenteel thing; and, if Mr. Holbrook had not been so heartily hungry, he would probably have seen that the good peas went away almost untouched.

After dinner, a clay pipe was brought in, and a spittoon; and, asking us to retire to another room, where he would soon join us if we disliked tobacco-smoke, he presented his pipe to Miss Matty, and requested her to fill the bowl. This was a compliment to a lady in his youth; but it was rather inappropriate to propose it as an honour to Miss Matty, who had been trained by her sister to hold smoking of every kind in utter abhorrence. But if it was a shock to her refinement, it was also a gratification to her feelings to be thus selected; so she daintily stuffed the strong tobacco into the pipe; and then we withdrew.

'It is very pleasant dining with a bachelor,' said Miss Matty, softly, as we settled ourselves in the counting-house.' 'I only hope it is not improper; so many pleasant things are!'

'What a number of books he has!' said Miss Pole, looking round the room. 'And how dusty they are!'

'I think it must be like one of the great Dr. Johnson's rooms,' said Miss Matty. 'What a superior man your cousin must be!'

'Yes!' said Miss Pole; 'he's a great reader; but I am afraid he has got into very uncouth habits with living alone.

'Oh! uncouth is too hard a word. I should call him eccentric; very clever people always are!' replied Miss Matty.

When Mr. Holbrook returned, he proposed a walk in the fields; but the two elder ladies were afraid of damp, and dirt; and had only very unbecoming calashes to put on over their caps; so they declined; and I was again his companion in a turn which he said he was obliged to take, to see after his men.[a] He strode along, either wholly forgetting my existence, or soothed into silence by his pipe – and yet it was not silence exactly. He walked before me, with a stooping gait, his hands clasped behind him; and, as some tree or cloud, or glimpse of distant upland pastures, struck him, he quoted poetry to himself; saying it out loud in a grand sonorous voice, with just the emphasis that true feeling and appreciation give. We came upon an old cedar-tree, which stood at one end of the house;

'The cedar spreads his dark-green layers of shade.'[37b]

'Capital term – "layers!" Wonderful man!' I did not know whether he was speaking to me or not; but I put in an assenting 'wonderful,' although I knew nothing about it; just because I was tired of being forgotten, and of being consequently silent.

He turned sharp round. 'Aye! you may say "wonderful." Why, when I saw the review of his poems in "Blackwood,"[38] I set off within an hour, and walked seven miles to Misselton (for the horses were not in the way) and ordered them. Now, what colour are ash-buds in March?'

Is the man going mad? thought I. He is very like Don Quixote.

'What colour are they, I say?' repeated he vehemently.

'I am sure I don't know, sir,' said I, with the meekness of ignorance.

'I knew you didn't. No more did I – an old fool that I am! till this young man comes and tells me. Black as ash-buds in March.[39] And I've lived all my life in the country; more shame for me not to know. Black: they are jet-black, madam.' And he went off again, swinging along to the music of some rhyme he had got hold of.

When we came back, nothing would serve him but[c] he must read us the poems he had been speaking of; and Miss Pole encouraged him in his proposal, I thought, because she wished me to hear his beautiful reading, of which she had boasted; but she afterwards said it was because she had got to a difficult part of her crochet, and wanted to count her stitches without having to talk. Whatever he had proposed would have been right to Miss Matty; although she did fall sound asleep within five minutes after he had begun a long poem, called 'Locksley Hall,'[40] and had a comfortable nap, unobserved, till he ended; when the cessation of his voice wakened her up, and she said, feeling that something was expected, and that Miss Pole was counting: –

'What a pretty book!'

'Pretty! madam! it's beautiful! Pretty, indeed!'

'Oh yes! I meant beautiful!' said she, fluttered at his disapproval of her word. 'It is so like that beautiful poem of Dr. Johnson's my sister used to read – I forget the name of it, what was it, my dear?' turning to me.

'Which do you mean, ma'am? What was it about?'

'I don't remember what it was about, and I've quite forgotten what the name of it was; but it was written by Dr. Johnson, and was very beautiful, and very like what Mr. Holbrook has just been reading.'

'I don't remember it,' said he, reflectively. 'But I don't know Dr. Johnson's poems well. I must read them.'

As we were getting into the fly to return, I heard Mr. Holbrook say he should call on the ladies soon, and inquire how they got home; and this evidently pleased and fluttered Miss Matty at the time he said it; but after we had lost sight of the old house among the trees, her sentiments towards the master of it were gradually absorbed into a distressing wonder as to whether Martha had broken her word, and seized on the opportunity of her mistress's absence to have a 'follower.' Martha looked good, and steady, and composed enough, as she came to help us out; she was always careful of Miss Matty, and to-night she made use of this unlucky speech: –

'Eh! dear ma'am, to think of your going out in an evening in such a thin shawl! It is no better than muslin. At your age, ma'am, you should be careful.'

'My age!' said Miss Matty, almost speaking crossly, for her; for she was usually gentle. 'My age! Why, how old do you think I am, that you talk about my age?'

'Well, ma'am! I should say you were not far short of sixty; but folks' looks is often against them – and I'm sure I meant no harm.'

'Martha, I'm not yet fifty-two!' said Miss Matty, with grave emphasis; for probably the remembrance of her youth had come very vividly before her this day, and she was annoyed at finding that golden time so far away in the past.

But she never spoke of any former and more intimate acquaintance with Mr. Holbrook. She had probably met with so little sympathy in her early love, that she had shut it up close in her heart; and it was only by a sort of watching, which I could hardly avoid, since Miss Pole's confidence, that I saw how faithful her poor heart had been in its sorrow and its silence.

She gave me some good reason for wearing her best cap every day, and sate near the window, in spite of her rheumatism, in order to see, without being seen, down into the street.

He came. He put his open palms upon his knees, which were far apart, as he sate with his head bent down, whistling, after we had replied to his inquiries about our safe return. Suddenly, he jumped up.

'Well, madam! have you any commands for Paris? I am going there in a week or two.'

'To Paris!' we both exclaimed.

'Yes, madam! I've never been there, and always had a wish to go; and I think if I don't go soon, I mayn't go at all; so as soon as the hay is got in I shall go, before harvest-time.'

We were so much astonished, that we had no commissions.

Just as he was going out of the room, he turned back, with his favourite exclamation:

'God bless my soul, madam! but I nearly forgot half my errand. Here are the poems for you, you admired so much the other evening at my house.' He tugged away at a parcel in his coat-pocket. 'Good-bye, miss,' said he; 'good-bye, Matty! take care of yourself.' And he was gone. But he had given her a book, and he had called her Matty, just as he used to do thirty years ago.

'I wish he would not go to Paris,' said Miss Matilda, anxiously. 'I don't believe frogs will agree with him; he used to have to be very careful what he ate, which was curious in so strong-looking a young man.'

Soon after this I took my leave, giving many an injunction to Martha to look after her mistress, and to let me know if she thought that Miss Matilda was not so well; in which case I would volunteer a visit to my old friend, without noticing Martha's intelligence to her.

Accordingly I received a line or two from Martha every now and then; and, about November, I had a note to say her mistress was 'very low and sadly off her food;' and the account made me so uneasy, that, although Martha did not decidedly summon me, I packed up my things and went.

I received a warm welcome, in spite of the little flurry produced by my impromptu visit, for I had only been able to give a day's notice. Miss Matilda looked miserably ill; and I prepared to comfort and cosset her.

I went down to have a private talk with Martha.

'How long has your mistress been so poorly?' I asked, as I stood by the kitchen fire.

'Well! I think it's better than a fortnight; it is, I know: it was one Tuesday, after Miss Pole had been, that she went into this moping way. I thought she was tired, and it would go off with a night's rest; but, no! she has gone on and on ever since, till I thought it my duty to write to you, ma'am.'

'You did quite right, Martha. It is a comfort to think she has so faithful a servant about her. And I hope you find your place comfortable?'

'Well, ma'am, missus is very kind, and there's plenty to eat and drink, and no more work but what I can do easily, – but' – Martha hesitated.

'But what, Martha?'

'Why, it seems so hard of missus not to let me have any followers; there's such lots of young fellows in the town; and many a one has as much as offered to keep company with me; and I may never be in such a likely place again, and it's like wasting an opportunity. Many a girl as I know would have 'em unbeknownst to missus; but I've given my word, and I'll stick to it; or else this is just the house for missus never to be the wiser if they did come: and it's such a capable kitchen – there's such good dark corners in it – I'd be bound to hide any one. I counted up last Sunday night – for I'll not deny I was crying because I had to shut the door in Jem Hearn's face; and he's a steady young man, fit for any girl; only I had given missus my word.' Martha was all but crying again; and I had little comfort to give her, for I knew, from old experience, of the horror with which both the Miss Jenkynses looked upon 'followers;' and in Miss Matty's present nervous state this dread was not likely to be lessened.

I went to see Miss Pole the next day, and took her completely by surprise; for she had not been to see Miss Matilda for two days.

'And now I must go back with you, my dear, for I promised to let her know how Thomas Holbrook went on; and I'm sorry to say his housekeeper has sent me word to-day that he has'nt long to live. Poor Thomas! That journey to Paris was quite too much for him. His housekeeper says he has hardly ever been round his fields since; but just sits with his hands on his knees in the counting-house, not reading or anything, but only saying, what a wonderful city Paris was! Paris has much to answer for, if it's killed my cousin Thomas, for a better man never lived.'

'Does Miss Matilda know of his illness?' asked I; – a new light as to the cause of her indisposition dawning upon me.

'Dear!^a to be sure, yes! Has not she told you? I let her know a fortnight ago, or more, when first I heard of it. How odd, she shouldn't have told you!'

Not at all, I thought; but I did not say anything. I felt almost guilty of having spied too curiously into that tender heart, and I was not going to speak of its secrets, – hidden, Miss Matty believed, from all the world. I ushered Miss Pole into Miss Matilda's little drawing-room; and then left them alone. But I was not surprised when Martha came to my bed-room door, to ask me to go down to dinner alone, for that missus had one of her bad headaches. She came into the drawing-room at tea-time; but it was evidently an effort to her; and, as if to make up for some reproachful feeling against her late sister, Miss Jenkyns, which had been troubling her all the afternoon,^b and for which she now felt penitent, she kept telling me how good and how clever Deborah was in her youth; how she used to settle what gowns they were to wear at all the parties (faint, ghostly ideas of dim^c parties far away in the distance, when Miss Matty and Miss Pole were young!); and how Deborah and her mother had started the benefit society for the poor,[41] and taught girls cooking and plain sewing; and how Deborah had once danced with a lord; and how she used to visit at Sir Peter Arley's, and try to remodel the quiet rectory establishment on the plans of Arley Hall, where they kept thirty servants; and how she had nursed Miss Matty through a long, long illness, of which I had never heard before, but which I now dated in my own mind as following the dismissal of the suit of Mr. Holbrook. So we talked softly and quietly of old times, through the long November evening.

The next day Miss Pole brought us word that Mr. Holbrook was dead. Miss Matty heard the news in silence; in fact, from the account of the previous day, it was only what we had to expect. Miss Pole kept calling upon us for some expression of regret, by asking if it was not sad that he was gone: and saying,

'To think of that pleasant day last June, when he seemed so well! And he might have lived this dozen years if he had not gone to that wicked Paris, where they are always having Revolutions.'

She paused for some demonstration on our part. I saw Miss Matty could not speak, she was trembling so nervously; so I said what I really felt: and after a call of some duration – all the time of which I have no doubt Miss Pole thought Miss Matty received the news very calmly – our visitor took her leave. But the effort at self-control Miss Matty had made to conceal her feelings – a concealment she practised even with me, for she has never alluded to Mr. Holbrook again, although the book he gave her lies with her Bible on the little table by her bedside; she did not think I heard her when she asked the little milliner of Cranford to make her caps something like the Honourable Mrs. Jamieson's, or that I noticed the reply –

'But she wears widows' caps, ma'am?'

'Oh! I only meant something in that style; not widows', of course, but rather like Mrs. Jamieson's.'

This effort at concealment was the beginning of the tremulous motion of head and hands which I have seen ever since in Miss Matty.

The evening of the day on which we heard of Mr. Holbrook's death, Miss Matilda was very silent and thoughtful; after prayers she called Martha back, and then she stood uncertain what to say.

'Martha!' she said at last; 'you are young,' – and then she made so long a pause that Martha, to remind her of her half-finished sentence, dropped a courtesy, and said –

'Yes, please, ma'am; two-and-twenty last third of October, please, ma'am.'

'And perhaps, Martha, you may some time meet with a young man you like, and who likes you. I did say you were not to have followers; but if you meet with such a young man, and tell me, and I find he is respectable, I have no objection to his coming to see you once a week. God forbid!' said she, in a low voice, 'that I should grieve any young hearts.' She spoke as if she were providing for some distant contingency, and was rather startled when Martha made her ready eager answer: –

'Please, ma'am, there's Jem Hearn,[42] and he's a joiner, making three-and-sixpence a-day, and six foot one in his stocking-feet, please, ma'am; and if you'll ask about him to-morrow morning, every one will give him a character for steadiness; and he'll be glad enough to come to-morrow night, I'll be bound.'

Though Miss Matty was startled, she submitted to Fate and Love.

CHAPTER V.^a

OLD LETTERS.^b

I HAVE often noticed that almost every one has his own individual small economies – careful habits of saving fractions of pennies in some one peculiar direction – any disturbance of which annoys him more than spending shillings or pounds on some real extravagance. An old gentleman of my acquaintance, who took the intelligence of the failure of a Joint-Stock Bank,[43] in which some of his money was invested, with stoical mildness, worried his family all through a long summer's day, because one of them had torn (instead of cutting) out the written leaves of his now useless bank-book; of course, the corresponding pages at the other end came out as well; and this little unnecessary waste of paper (his private economy) chafed him more than all the loss of his money. Envelopes fretted his soul terribly when they first came in; the only way in which he could reconcile himself to such waste of his cherished article was by patiently turning inside out all that were sent to him, and so making them serve again. Even now, though tamed by age, I see him casting wistful glances at his daughters when they send a whole instead of a half sheet of note-paper, with the three lines of acceptance to an invitation, written on only one of the sides. I am not above owning that I have this human weakness myself. String is my foible. My pockets get full of little hanks of it, picked up and twisted together, ready for uses that never come. I am seriously annoyed if any one cuts the string of a parcel, instead of patiently and faithfully undoing it fold by fold. How people can bring themselves to use Indian-rubber rings, which are a sort of deification of string, as lightly as they do, I cannot imagine. To me an Indian-rubber ring is a precious treasure. I have one which is not new; one that I picked up off the floor, nearly six years ago. I have really tried to use it; but my heart failed me, and I could not commit the extravagance.

Small pieces of butter grieve others. They cannot attend to conversation, because of the annoyance occasioned by the habit which some people have of invariably taking more butter than they want. Have you not seen the anxious look (almost mesmeric) which such persons fix on the article? They would feel it a relief if they might bury it out of their sight, by popping it into their own mouths, and swallowing it down; and they are really made happy if the person on whose plate it lies unused, suddenly breaks off a piece of toast (which he does not want at all) and eats up his butter. They think that this is not waste.

Now Miss Matty Jenkyns was chary of candles. We had many devices to use as few as possible. In the winter afternoons she would sit knitting for two or three hours; she could do this in the dark, or by fire-light; and when I asked if I might not ring for candles to finish stitching my wristbands, she told me to 'keep blind man's holiday.'[44] They were usually brought in with tea; but we only burnt one at a time. As we lived in constant preparation for a friend who might come in, any evening (but who never did), it required some contrivance to keep our two candles of the same length, ready to be lighted, and to look as if we burnt two always. The candles took it in turns; and, whatever we might be talking about or doing, Miss Matty's eyes were habitually fixed upon the candle, ready to jump up and extinguish it, and to light the other before they had become too uneven in length to be restored to equality in the course of the evening.

One night, I remember that this candle economy particularly annoyed me. I had been very much tired of my compulsory 'blind-man's holiday,' – especially as Miss Matty had fallen asleep, and I did not like to stir the fire, and run the risk of awakening her; so I could not even sit on the rug, and scorch myself with sewing by firelight, according to my usual custom. I fancied Miss Matty must be dreaming of her early life; for she spoke one or two words, in her uneasy sleep, bearing reference to persons who were dead long before. When Martha brought in the lighted candle and tea, Miss Matty started into wakefulness, with a strange bewildered look around, as if we were not the people she expected to see about her. There was a little sad expression that shadowed her face as she recognised me; but immediately afterwards she tried to give me her usual smile. All through tea-time, her talk ran upon the days of her childhood and youth. Perhaps this reminded her of the desirableness of looking over all the old family letters, and destroying such as ought not to be allowed to fall into the hands of strangers; for she had often spoken of the necessity of this task, but had always shrunk from it, with a timid dread of something painful. To-night, however, she rose up after tea, and went for them – in the dark; for she piqued herself on the precise neatness of all her chamber arrangements, and used to look uneasily at me, when I lighted a bed-candle to go to another room for anything. When she returned, there was a faint pleasant smell of Tonquin beans[45] in the room. I had always noticed this scent about any of the things which had belonged to her mother; and many of the letters were addressed to her – yellow bundles of love-letters, sixty or seventy years old.

Miss Matty undid the packet with a sigh; but she stifled it directly, as if it were hardly right to regret the flight of time, or of life either. We agreed to look them over separately, each taking a different letter out of the same bundle, and describing its contents to the other, before destroying it. I never knew what sad work the reading of old letters was before that evening, though I could hardly tell why. The letters were as happy as letters could be – at least those early letters were. There was in them a vivid and intense sense of the present time, which seemed so strong and full, as if it could never pass away, and as if the warm, living hearts that so expressed themselves could never die, and be as nothing to the sunny earth. I should have felt less melancholy, I believe, if the letters had been more so. I saw the tears quietly stealing down the well-worn furrows of Miss Matty's cheeks, and her spectacles often wanted wiping. I trusted at last that she would light the other candle, for my own eyes were rather dim, and I wanted more light to see the pale, faded ink; but no – even through her tears, she saw and remembered her little economical ways.

The earliest set of letters were two bundles tied together, and ticketed (in Miss Jenkyns's handwriting), 'Letters interchanged between my ever-honoured father and my dearly-beloved mother, prior to their marriage, in July, 1774.'[a] I should guess that the Rector of Cranford was about twenty-seven years of age when he wrote those letters; and Miss Matty told me that her mother was just eighteen at the time of her wedding. With my idea of the Rector, derived from a picture in the dining parlour, stiff and stately, in a huge full-bottomed wig, with gown, cassock, and bands, and his hand upon a copy of the only sermon he ever published, – it was strange to read these letters. They were full of eager, passionate ardour; short homely sentences, right fresh from the heart; (very different from the grand Latinised, Johnsonian style of the printed sermon, preached before some judge at assize time.) His letters were a curious contrast to those of his girl-bride. She was evidently rather annoyed at his demands upon her for expressions of love, and could not quite understand what he meant by repeating the same thing over in so many different ways; but what she was quite clear about was her longing for a white 'Paduasoy,' –[46b] whatever that might be; and six or seven letters were principally occupied in asking her lover to use his influence with her parents (who evidently kept her in good order) to obtain this or that article of dress, more especially the white 'Paduasoy.'[c] He cared nothing how she was dressed; she was always lovely enough for him, as he took pains to assure her, when she begged him to express in his answers a predilection for particular pieces of finery, in order that she might show what he said to her parents. But at length he seemed to find out that she would not be married till she had a 'trousseau' to her mind; and then he sent her a letter, which had evidently accompanied a whole box full of finery, and in which he requested that she might be dressed in everything her heart desired. This was the first letter, ticketed in a frail, delicate hand, 'From my dearest John.' Shortly afterwards they were married, – I suppose, from the intermission in their correspondence.

'We must burn them, I think,' said Miss Matty, looking doubtfully at me. 'No one will care for them when I am gone.' And one by one she dropped them into the middle of the fire; watching each blaze up, die out, and rise away, in faint, white, ghostly semblance, up the chimney, before she gave up another to the same fate. The room was light enough now; but I, like her, was fascinated into watching the destruction of those letters, into which the honest warmth of a manly heart had been poured forth.

The next letter, likewise docketed by Miss Jenkyns, was endorsed, 'Letter of pious congratulation and exhortation from my venerable grandfather to my mother, on occasion of my own birth. Also some practical remarks on the desirability of keeping warm the extremities of infants, from my excellent grandmother.'

The first part was, indeed, a severe and forcible picture of the responsibilities of mothers, and a warning against the evils that were in the world, and lying in ghastly wait for the little baby of two days old. His wife did not write, said the old gentleman, because he had forbidden it, she being indisposed with a sprained ankle, which (he said) quite incapacitated her from holding a pen. However, at the foot of the page was a small 'T.O.,' and on turning it over, sure enough, there was a letter to 'my dear, dearest Molly,' begging her, when she left her room, whatever she did, to go *up* stairs before going *down*: and telling her to wrap her baby's feet up in flannel, and keep it warm by the fire, although it was summer, for babies were so tender.

It was pretty to see from the letters, which were evidently exchanged with some frequency, between the young mother and the grandmother, how the girlish vanity was being weeded out of her heart by love for her baby. The white 'Paduasoy'[a] figured again in the letters, with almost as much vigour as before. In one, it was being made into a christening cloak for the baby. It decked it when it went with its parents to spend a day or two at Arley Hall. It added to its charms when it was 'the prettiest little baby that ever was seen. Dear mother, I wish you could see her! Without any parshality, I do think she will grow up a regular bewty!' I thought of Miss Jenkyns, grey, withered, and wrinkled; and I wondered if her mother had known her in the courts of heaven; and then I knew that she had, and that they stood there in angelic guise.

There was a great gap before any of the Rector's letters appeared. And then his wife had changed her mode of endorsement. It was no longer from 'My dearest John;' it was from 'My honoured Husband.' The letters were written on occasion of the publication of the same Sermon which was represented in the picture. The preaching before 'My Lord Judge,' and the 'publishing by request,' was evidently the culminating point – the event of his life. It had been necessary for him to go up to London to superintend it through the press. Many friends had to be called upon, and consulted, before he could decide on any printer fit for so onerous a task; and at length it was arranged that J. and J. Rivingtons[47] were to have the honourable responsibility. The worthy Rector seemed to be strung up by the occasion to a high literary pitch, for he could hardly write a letter to his wife without cropping out into Latin. I remember the end of one of his letters ran thus: – 'I shall ever hold the virtuous qualities of my Molly in remembrance, *dum memor ipse mei, dum spiritus regit artus*,'[48] which, considering that the English of his correspondent was sometimes at fault in grammar, and often in spelling, might be taken as a proof of how much he 'idealised' his Molly; and, as Miss Jenkyns used to say, 'People talk a great deal about idealising now-a-days, whatever that may mean.' But this was nothing to a fit of writing classical poetry, which soon seized him; in which his Molly figured away as 'Maria.' The letter containing the *carmen*[49] was endorsed by her, 'Hebrew verses sent me by my honoured husband. I thowt to have had a letter about killing the pig, but must wait. Mem., to send the poetry to Sir Peter Arley, as my husband desires.' And in a post-scriptum note in his handwriting, it was stated that the Ode had appeared in the 'Gentleman's Magazine,'[50] December, 1782.

Her letters[a] back to her husband (treasured as fondly by him as if they had been M. T. Ciceronis Epistolæ)[51] were more satisfactory to an absent husband and father, than his could ever have been to her. She told him how Deborah sewed her seam very neatly every day, and read to her in the books he had set her; how she was a very 'forrard,' good child, but *would* ask questions her mother could not answer; but how she did not let herself down by saying she did not know, but took to stirring the fire, or sending the 'forrard' child on an errand. Matty was now the mother's darling, and promised (like her sister at her age) to be a great beauty. I was reading this aloud to Miss Matty, who smiled and sighed a little at the hope, so fondly expressed, that 'little Matty might not be vain, even if she were a beauty.'

'I had very pretty hair, my dear,' said Miss Matilda; 'and not a bad mouth.' And I saw her soon afterwards adjust her cap and draw herself up.

But to return to Mrs. Jenkyns's letters. She told her husband about the poor in the parish; what homely domestic medicines she had administered; what kitchen physic she had sent. She had evidently held his displeasure as a rod in pickle over the heads of all the ne'er-do-wells. She asked for his directions about the cows and pigs; and did not always obtain them, as I have shown before.

The kind old grandmother[b] was dead, when a little boy was born, soon after the publication of the Sermon; but there was another letter of exhortation from the grandfather, more stringent and admonitory than ever, now that there was a boy to be guarded from the snares of the world. He described all the various sins into which men might fall, until I wondered how any man ever came to a natural death. The gallows seemed as if it must have been the termination of the lives of most of the grandfather's friends and acquaintance; and I was not surprised at the way in which he spoke of this life being 'a vale of tears.'

It seemed curious that I should never have heard of this brother before; but I concluded that he had died young; or else surely his name would have been alluded to by his sisters.

By-and-by[a] we came to packets of Miss Jenkyns's letters. These, Miss Matty did regret to burn. She said all the others had been only interesting to those who loved the writers; and that it seemed as if it would have hurt her to allow them to fall into the hands of strangers, who had not known her dear mother, and how good she was, although she did not always spell quite in the modern fashion; but Deborah's letters were so very superior! Any one might profit by reading them. It was a long time since she had read Mrs. Chapone,[52] but she knew she used to think that Deborah could have said the same things quite as well; and as for Mrs. Carter! people thought a deal of her letters, just because she had written Epictetus,[53] but she was quite sure Deborah would never have made use of such a common expression as 'I canna be fashed!'[54]

Miss Matty did grudge burning these letters, it was evident. She would not let them be carelessly passed over with any quiet reading, and skipping, to myself. She took them from me, and even lighted the second candle in order to read them aloud with a proper emphasis, and without stumbling over the big words. Oh dear! how I wanted facts instead of reflections, before those letters were concluded! They lasted us two nights; and I won't deny that I made use of the time to think of many other things, and yet I was always at my post at the end of each sentence.

The Rector's[b] letters, and those of his wife and mother-in-law, had all been tolerably short and pithy, written in a straight hand, with the lines very close together. Sometimes the whole letter was contained on a mere scrap of paper. The paper was very yellow, and the ink very brown; some of the sheets were (as Miss Matty made me observe) the old original Post, with the stamp in the corner, representing a post-boy riding for life and twanging his horn.[55] The letters of Mrs. Jenkyns and her mother were fastened with a great round, red wafer; for it was before Miss Edgeworth's 'Patronage' had banished wafers from polite society.[56] It was evident, from the tenor of what was said, that franks were in great request, and were even used as a means of paying debts by needy Members of Parliament.[57] The Rector sealed his epis-tles with an immense coat of arms, and showed by the care with which he had performed this ceremony, that he expected they should be cut open, not broken by any thoughtless or impatient hand. Now, Miss Jenkyns's letters were of a later date in form and writing. She wrote on the square sheet, which we have learned to call old-fashioned. Her hand was admirably calcu-lated, together with her use of many-syllabled words, to fill up a sheet, and then came the pride and delight of crossing.[58] Poor Miss Matty got sadly puzzled with this, for the words gathered size like snow-balls, and towards the end of her letter, Miss Jenkyns used to become quite sesquipedalian. In one to her father, slightly theological and controversial in its tone, she had spoken of Herod, Tetrarch of Idumea. Miss Matty read it 'Herod Petrach of Etruriæ,'[59] and was just as well pleased as if she had been right.

I can't[a] quite remember the date, but I think it was in 1805 that Miss Jenkyns wrote the longest series of letters; on occasion of her absence on a visit to some friends near Newcastle-upon-Tyne.[60] These friends were intimate with the commandant of the garrison there, and heard from him of all the preparations that were being made to repel the invasion of Buonaparte, which some people imagined might take place at the mouth of the Tyne. Miss Jenkyns was evidently very much alarmed; and the first part of her letters was often written in pretty intelligible English, conveying particulars of the preparations which were made in the family with whom she was residing against the dreaded event; the bundles of clothes that were packed up ready for a flight to Alston Moor (a wild hilly piece of ground between Northumberland and Cumberland); the signal that was to be given for this flight, and for the simultaneous turning out of the volunteers under arms; which said signal was to consist (if I remember rightly) in ringing the church bells in a particular and ominous manner. One day, when Miss Jenkyns and her hosts were at a dinner-party in Newcastle, this warning-summons was actually given[b] (not a very wise proceeding, if there be any truth in the moral attached to the fable of the Boy and the Wolf; but so it was,) and Miss Jenkyns, hardly recovered from her fright, wrote the next day to describe the sound, the breathless shock, the hurry and alarm; and then, taking breath, she added, 'How trivial, my dear father, do all our apprehensions of the last evening appear, at the present moment, to calm and inquiring minds!' And here Miss Matty broke in with – 'But, indeed, my dear, they were not at all trivial or trifling at the time. I know I used to wake up in the night many a time, and think I heard the tramp of the French entering Cranford. Many people talked[c] of hiding themselves in the salt-mines; –[61] and meat would have kept capitally down there, only perhaps we should have been thirsty. And my father preached a whole set of sermons on the occasion; one set in the mornings, all about David and Goliath, to spirit up the people to fighting with spades or bricks, if need were; and the other set in the afternoons, proving that Napoleon (that was another name for Bony, as we used to call him) was all the same as an Apollyon[d] and Abaddon.[62] I remember, my father rather thought he should be asked to print this last set; but the parish had, perhaps, had enough of them with hearing.'

Peter Marmaduke Arley Jenkyns, ('poor Peter!' as Miss Matty began to call him) was at school at Shrewsbury[63] by this time. The Rector took up his pen, and rubbed up his Latin, once more, to correspond with his boy. It was very clear that the lad's were what are called show-letters. They were of a highly mental description, giving an account of his studies, and his intellectual hopes of various kinds, with an occasional quotation from the classics; but, now and then, the animal nature broke out in such a little sentence as this, evidently written in a trembling hurry, after the letter had been inspected: 'Mother, dear, do send me a cake, and put plenty of citron in.' The 'mother, dear,' probably answered her boy in the form of cakes and 'goody,' for there were none of her letters among this set; but a whole collection of the Rector's, to whom the Latin in his boy's letters was like a trumpet to the old war-horse. I do not know much about Latin, certainly, and it is, perhaps, an ornamental language; but not very useful, I think – at least to judge from the bits I remember out of the Rector's letters. One was: 'You have not got that town in your map of Ireland; but *Bonus Bernardus non videt omnia*, as the Proverbia say.'[64] Presently it became very evident that 'poor Peter' got himself into many scrapes. There were letters of stilted penitence to his father, for some wrong-doing; and, among them all, was a badly written, baldly-sealed, badly-directed, blotted note – 'My dear, dear, dear, dearest mother, I will be a better boy – I will, indeed; but don't, please, be ill for me; I am not worth it; but I will be good, darling mother.'

Miss Matty could not speak for crying, after she had read this note. She gave it to me in silence, and then got up and took it to her sacred recesses in her own room, for fear, by any chance, it might get burnt. 'Poor Peter!' she said; 'he was always in scrapes; he was too easy. They led him wrong, and then left him in the lurch. But he was too fond of mischief. He could never resist a joke. Poor Peter!'

CHAPTER VI.

POOR PETER.[a]

POOR Peter's career lay before him rather pleasantly mapped out by kind friends, but *Bonus Bernardus non videt omnia*, in this map too. He was to win honours at Shrewsbury School, and carry them thick to Cambridge,[65] and after that, a living awaited him, the gift of his godfather, Sir Peter Arley. Poor Peter! his lot in life was very different to what his friends had hoped and planned. Miss Matty told me all about it, and I think it was a relief to her when she had done so.

He was the darling of his mother, who seemed to dote on all her children, though she was, perhaps, a little afraid of Deborah's superior acquirements. Deborah was the favourite of her father, and when Peter disappointed him, she became his pride. The sole honour Peter brought away from Shrewsbury, was the reputation of being the best good fellow that ever was, and of being the captain of the school in the art of practical joking. His father was disappointed, but set about remedying the matter in a manly way. He could not afford to send Peter to read with any tutor, but he could read with him himself; and Miss Matty told me much of the awful preparations in the way of dictionaries and lexicons that were made in her father's study the morning Peter began.

'My poor mother!' said she. 'I remember how she used to stand in the hall, just near enough to the study-door to catch the tone of my father's voice. I could tell in a moment if all was going right, by her face. And it did go right for a long time.'

'What went wrong at last?' said I. 'That tiresome Latin, I dare say.'

'No! it was not the Latin. Peter was in high favour with my father, for he worked up well for him. But he seemed to think that the Cranford people might be joked about, and made fun of, and they did not like it; nobody does. He was always hoaxing them; "hoaxing" is not a pretty word, my dear, and I hope you won't tell your father I used it, for I should not like him to think that I was not choice in my language, after living with such a woman as Deborah. And be sure you never use it yourself. I don't know how it slipped out of my mouth, except it was that I was thinking of poor Peter, and it was always his expression. But he was a very gentlemanly boy in many things. He was like dear Captain Brown in always being ready to help any old person or a child. Still, he did like joking and making fun; and he seemed to think the old ladies in Cranford would believe anything. There were many old ladies living here then; we are principally ladies now, I know; but we are not so old as the ladies used to be when I was a girl. I could laugh to think of some of Peter's jokes. No! my dear, I won't tell you of them, because they might not shock you as they ought to do; and they were very shocking. He even took in my father once, by dressing himself up as a lady that[a] was passing through the town and wished to see the Rector of Cranford, "who had published that admirable Assize Sermon." Peter said, he was awfully frightened himself when he saw how my father took it all in, and even offered to copy out all his Napoleon Buonaparte sermons for her – him, I mean – no, her, for Peter was a lady then. He told me he was more terrified than he ever was before, all the time my father was speaking. He did not think my father would have believed him; and yet if he had not, it would have been a sad thing for Peter. As it was, he was none so glad of it, for my father kept him hard at work copying out all those twelve Buonaparte sermons for the lady – that was for Peter himself, you know. He was the lady. And once when he wanted to go fishing, Peter said, "Confound the woman!" – very bad language, my dear; but Peter was not always so guarded as he should have been; my father[b] was so angry with him, it nearly frightened me out of my wits: and yet I could hardly keep from laughing at the little curtsies Peter kept making, quite slyly, whenever my father spoke of the lady's excellent taste and sound discrimination.'

'Did Miss Jenkyns know of these tricks?' said I.

'Oh no! Deborah would have been too much shocked. No! no one knew but me. I wish I had always known of Peter's plans; but sometimes he did not tell me. He used to say, the old ladies in the town wanted something to talk about; but I don't think they did. They had the St. James's Chronicle[66] three times a-week, just as we have now, and we have plenty to say;[c] and I remember the clacking noise there always was when some of the ladies got together. But, probably, school-boys talk more than ladies. At last there was a terrible sad thing happened.' Miss Matty got up, went to the door, and opened it; no one was there. She rang the bell for Martha; and when Martha came, her mistress told her to go for eggs to a farm at the other end of the town.

'I will lock the door after you, Martha. You are not afraid to go, are you?'

'No, Ma'am, not at all; Jem Hearn will be only too proud to go with me.'

Miss Matty drew herself up, and, as soon as we were alone, she wished that Martha had more maidenly reserve.

'We'll put out the candle, my dear. We can talk just as well by fire-light, you know. There! well! you see, Deborah had gone from home for a fortnight or so; it was a very still, quiet day, I remember, overhead; and the lilacs were all in flower, so I suppose it was spring. My father had gone out to see some sick people in the parish; I recollect seeing him leave the house, with his wig and shovel-hat, and cane. What possessed our poor Peter I don't know; he had the sweetest temper, and yet he always seemed to like to plague Deborah. She never laughed at his jokes, and thought him ungenteel, and not careful enough about improving his mind; and that vexed him.

'Well! he went to her room, it seems, and dressed himself in her old gown, and shawl, and bonnet; just the things she used to wear in Cranford, and was known by everywhere; and he made the pillow into a little – you are sure you locked the door, my dear, for I should not like any one to hear – into – into – a little baby, with white long clothes. It was only, as he told me afterwards, to make something to talk about in the town; he never thought of it as affecting Deborah. And he went and walked up and down in the Filbert walk – just half hidden by the rails, and half seen; and he cuddled his pillow, just like a baby; and talked to it all the nonsense people do. Oh dear! and my father came stepping stately up the street, as he always did; and what should he see but a little black crowd of people – I dare say as many as twenty – all peeping through his garden rails. So he thought, at first, they were only looking at a new rhododendron that was in full bloom, and that he was very proud of; and he walked slower, that they might have more time to admire. And he wondered if he could make out a sermon from the occasion, and thought, perhaps, there was some relation between the rhododendrons and the lilies of the field. My poor father! When he came nearer, he began to wonder that they did not see him; but their heads were all so close together, peeping and peeping! My father was amongst them, meaning, he said, to ask them to walk into the garden with him, and admire the beautiful vegetable production, when – oh, my dear! I tremble to think of it – he looked through the rails himself, and saw – I don't know what he thought he saw, but old Clare told me his face went quite grey-white with anger, and his eyes blazed out under his frowning black brows; and he spoke out – oh, so terribly! – and[a] bade them all stop where they were – not one of them to go, not one to stir a step; and, swift as light, he was in at the garden door, and down the Filbert walk, and seized hold of poor Peter, and tore his clothes off his back – bonnet, shawl, gown, and all – and threw the pillow among the people over the railings: and then he was very, very angry indeed; and before all the people he lifted up his cane, and flogged Peter!

'My dear!'[b] that boy's trick, on that sunny day, when all seemed going straight and well, broke my mother's heart, and changed my father for life. It did, indeed. Old Clare said, Peter looked as white as my father; and stood as still as a statue to be flogged; and my father struck hard! When my father stopped to take breath, Peter said, "Have you done enough, Sir?" quite hoarsely, and still standing quite quiet. I don't know what my father said – or if he said anything. But old Clare said, Peter turned to where the people outside the railing were, and made them a low bow, as grand and as grave as any gentleman; and then walked slowly into the house. I was in the store-room helping my mother to make cowslip-wine. I cannot abide the wine now, nor the scent of the flowers; they turn me sick and faint, as they did that day, when Peter came in, looking as haughty as any man – indeed, looking like a man, not like a boy. "Mother!" he said, "I am come to say, God bless you for ever." I saw his lips quiver as he spoke; and I think he durst not say anything more loving, for the purpose that was in his heart. She looked at him rather frightened, and wondering, and asked him what was to do? He did not smile or speak, but put his arms round her, and kissed her as if he did not know how to leave off; and before she could speak again, he was gone. We talked it over, and could not understand it, and she bade me go and seek my father, and ask what it was all about. I found him walking up and down, looking very highly displeased.

'"Tell your mother I have flogged Peter, and that he richly deserved it."

'I durst not ask any more questions. When I told my mother, she sat down, quite faint, for a minute. I remember, a few days after, I saw the poor, withered cowslip-flowers thrown out to the leaf-heap, to decay and die there. There was no making of cowslip-wine that year at the Rectory – nor, indeed, ever after.

'Presently,[a] my mother went to my father. I know I thought of Queen Esther and King Ahasuerus;[67] for my mother was very pretty and delicate-looking, and my father looked as terrible as King Ahasuerus. Some time after, they came out together; and then my mother told me what had happened, and that she was going up to Peter's room, at my father's desire – though she was not to tell Peter this – to talk the matter over with him. But no Peter was there. We looked over the house; no Peter was there! Even my father, who had not liked to join in the search at first, helped us before long. The Rectory was a very old house: steps up into a room, steps down into a room, all through. At first, my mother went calling low and soft – as if to reassure the poor boy – "Peter! Peter, dear! it's only me;" but, by-and-by, as the servants came back from the errands my father had sent them, in different directions, to find where Peter was – as we found he was not in the garden, nor the hayloft, nor anywhere about – my mother's cry grew louder and wilder – "Peter! Peter, my darling! where are you?" for then she felt and understood that that long kiss meant some sad kind of "good-bye." The afternoon went on – my mother never resting, but seeking again and again in every possible place that had been looked into twenty times before; nay, that she had looked into over and over again herself. My father sat with his head in his hands, not speaking, except when his messengers came in, bringing no tidings; then he lifted up his face so strong and sad, and told them to go again in some new direction. My mother kept passing from room to room, in and out of the house, moving noiselessly, but never ceasing. Neither she nor my father durst leave the house, which was the meeting-place for all the messengers. At last (and it was nearly dark), my father rose up. He took hold of my mother's arm, as she came with wild, sad pace, through one door, and quickly towards another. She started at the touch of his hand, for she had forgotten all in the world but Peter.

'"Molly!" said he, "I did not think all this would happen." He looked into her face for comfort – her poor face, all wild and white; for neither she nor my father had dared to acknowledge – much less act upon – the terror that was in their hearts, lest Peter should have made away with himself. My father saw no conscious look in his wife's hot, dreary eyes, and he missed the sympathy that she had always been ready to give him – strong man as he was; and at the dumb despair in her face, his tears began to flow. But when she saw this, a gentle sorrow came over her countenance, and she said, "Dearest John! don't cry; come with me, and we'll find him," almost as cheerfully as if she knew where he was. And she took my father's great hand in her little soft one, and led him along, the tears dropping, as he walked on that same unceasing, weary walk, from room to room, through house and garden.

'Oh! how I wished for Deborah! I had no time for crying, for now all seemed to depend on me. I wrote for Deborah to come home. I sent a message privately to that same Mr. Holbrook's house – poor Mr. Holbrook! – you know who I mean. I don't mean I sent a message to him, but I sent one that I could trust, to know if Peter was at his house. For at one time Mr. Holbrook was an occasional visitor at the Rectory – you know he was Miss Pole's cousin – and he had been very kind to Peter, and taught him how to fish – he was very kind to everybody, and I thought Peter might have gone off there. But Mr. Holbrook was from home, and Peter had never been seen. It was night now; but the doors were all wide open, and my father and mother walked on and on; it was more than an hour since he had joined her, and I don't believe they had ever spoken all that time. I was getting the parlour fire lighted, and one of the servants was preparing tea, for I wanted them to have something to eat and drink and warm them, when old Clare asked to speak to me.

'"I have borrowed the nets from the weir, Miss Matty. Shall we drag the ponds to-night, or wait for the morning?"

'I remember staring in his face to gather his meaning; and when I did, I laughed out loud. The horror of that new thought – our bright, darling Peter, cold, and stark, and dead! I remember the ring of my own laugh now.

'The next day Deborah was at home before I was myself again. She would not have been so weak to give way as I had done; but my screams (my horrible laughter had ended in crying) had roused my sweet dear mother, whose poor wandering wits were called back and collected, as soon as a child needed her care. She and Deborah sat by my bedside; I knew by the looks of each that there had been no news of Peter – no awful, ghastly news, which was what I most had dreaded in my dull state between sleeping and waking.

'The same[a] result of all the searching had brought something of the same relief to my mother, to whom I am sure, the thought that Peter might even then be hanging dead in some of the familiar home places, had caused that never-ending walk of yesterday. Her soft eyes never were the same again after that; they had always a restless craving look, as if seeking for what they could not find. Oh! it was an awful time; coming down like a thunderbolt on the still sunny day, when the lilacs were all in bloom.'

'Where was Mr. Peter?' said I.

'He had made his way to Liverpool; and there was war then;[68] and some of the king's ships lay off the mouth of the Mersey; and they were only too glad to have a fine likely boy such as him (five foot nine he was) come to offer himself. The captain wrote to my father, and Peter wrote to my mother. Stay! those letters will be somewhere here.'

We lighted the candle, and found the captain's letter, and Peter's too. And we also found a little simple begging letter from Mrs. Jenkyns to Peter, addressed to him at the house of an old school-fellow, whither she fancied he might have gone. They had returned it unopened; and unopened it had remained ever since, having been inadvertently put by among the other letters of that time. This is it: –

> 'My dearest Peter,
>
> 'You did not think we should be so sorry as we are, I know, or you would never have gone away. You are too good. Your father sits and sighs till my heart aches to hear him. He cannot hold up his head for grief; and yet he only did what he thought was right. Perhaps he has been too severe, and perhaps I have not been kind enough; but God knows how we love you, my dear only boy. Dor[69] looks so sorry you are gone. Come back, and make us happy, who love you so much. I *know* you will come back.'

But Peter did not come[b] back. That spring day was the last time he ever saw his mother's face.[c] The writer of the letter – the last – the only person who had ever seen what was written in it, was dead long ago – and I, a stranger, not born at the time when this occurance took place, was the only one to open it.

The captain's letter summoned the father and mother to Liverpool instantly, if they wished to see their boy; and by some of the wild chances of life, the captain's letter had been detained somewhere, somehow.

Miss Matty went on: – 'And it was race-time, and all the post-horses at Cranford were gone to the races; but my father and mother set off in our own gig, – and, oh! my dear, they were too late – the ship was gone! And now, read Peter's letter to my mother!'

It was full of love, and sorrow, and pride in his new profession, and a sore sense of his disgrace in the eyes of the people at Cranford; but ending with a passionate entreaty that she would come and see him before he left the Mersey: – 'Mother! we may go into battle. I hope we shall, and lick those French; but I must see you again before that time.'

'And she was too late,' said Miss Matty; 'too late!'

We sat in silence, pondering on the full meaning of those sad, sad words. At length I asked Miss Matty to tell me how her mother bore it.

'Oh!' she said, 'she was patience itself. She had never been strong, and this weakened her terribly. My father used to sit looking at her: far more sad than she was. He seemed as if he could look at nothing else when she was by; and he was so humble, – so very gentle now. He would, perhaps, speak in his old way – laying down the law, as it were – and then, in a minute or two, he would come round and put his hand on our shoulders, and ask us in a low voice if he had said anything to hurt us? I did not wonder at his speaking so to Deborah, for she was so clever; but I could not bear to hear him talking so to me.

'But, you see, he saw what we did not – that it was killing my mother. Yes! killing her – (put out the candle, my dear; I can talk better in the dark) – for she was but a frail woman, and ill fitted to stand the fright and shock she had gone through; and she would smile at him and comfort him, not in words but in her looks and tones, which were always cheerful when he was there. And she would speak of how she thought Peter stood a good chance of being admiral very soon – he was so brave and clever; and how she thought of seeing him in his navy uniform, and what sort of hats admirals wore; and how much more fit he was to be a sailor than a clergyman; and all in that way, just to make my father think she was quite glad of what came of that unlucky morning's work, and the flogging which was always in his mind, as we all knew. But, oh, my dear! the bitter, bitter crying she had when she was alone; – and at last, as she grew weaker, she could not keep her tears in, when Deborah or me was by, and would give us message after message for Peter, – (his ship had gone to the Mediterranean, or somewhere down there, and then he was ordered off to India, and there was no overland route then); – but she still said that no one knew where their death lay in wait, and that we were not to think hers was near. We did not think it, but we knew it, as we saw her fading away.

'Well, my dear, it's very foolish of me, I know, when in all likelihood I am so near seeing her again.[a]

'And only think, love! the very day after her death – for she did not live quite a twelvemonth after Peter went away – the very day after – came a parcel for her from India – from her poor boy. It was a large, soft, white India shawl, with just a little narrow border all round; just what my mother would have liked.

'We thought[b] it might rouse my father, for he had sat with her hand in his all night long; so Deborah took it in to him, and Peter's letter to her, and all.

'At first, he took no notice; and we tried to make a kind of light careless talk about the shawl, opening it out and admiring it. Then, suddenly, he got up, and spoke: – "She shall be buried in it," he said; "Peter shall have that comfort; and she would have liked it."

'Well!ᵃ perhaps it was not reasonable, but what could we do or say? One gives people in grief their own way. He took it up and felt it – "It is just such a shawl as she wished for when she was married, and her mother did not give it her. I did not know of it till after, or she should have had it – she should; but she shall have it now."

'My mother looked so lovely in her death! She was always pretty, and now she looked fair, and waxen, and young – younger than Deborah, as she stood trembling and shivering by her. We decked her in the long soft folds; she lay, smiling, as if pleased; and people came – all Cranford came – to beg to see her, for they had loved her dearly – as well they might; and the country-women brought posies; old Clare's wife brought some white violets, and begged they might lie on her breast.

'Deborah said to me, the day of my mother's funeral, that if she had a hundred offers, she never would marry and leave my father. It was not very likely she would have so many – I don't know that she had one; but it was not less to her credit to say so. She was such a daughter to my father, as I think there never was before, or since. His eyes failed him, and she read book after book, and wrote, and copied, and was always at his service in any parish business. She could do many more things than my poor mother could; she even once wrote a letter to the bishop for my father. But he missed my mother sorely; the whole parish noticed it. Not that he was less active; I think he was more so, and more patient in helping every one. I did all I could to set Deborah at liberty to be with him; for I knew I was good for little, and that my best work in the world was to do odd jobs quietly, and set others at liberty. But my father was a changed man.'

'Did Mr. Peter ever come home?'

'Yes, once. He came home a Lieutenant; he did not get to be Admiral. And he and my father were such friends! My father took him into every house in the parish, he was so proud of him. He never walked out without Peter's arm to lean upon. Deborah used to smile (I don't think we ever laughed again after my mother's death), and say she was quite put in a cor-ner. Not but what my father always wanted her when there was letter-writing, or reading to be done, or anything to be settled.'

'And then?' said I, after a pause.

'Then Peter went to sea again; and, by-and-by, my father died, blessing us both, and thanking Deborah for all she had been to him; and, of course, our circumstances were changed; and, instead of living at the Rectory, and keep-ing three maids and a man, we had to come to this small house, and be content with a servant-of-all-work; but, as Deborah used to say, we have

always lived genteelly, even if circumstances have compelled us to simplicity.
– Poor Deborah!'

'And, Mr. Peter?' asked I.

'Oh, there was some great war in India –[70] I forget what they call it – and
we have never heard of Peter since then. I believe he is dead myself; and it
sometimes fidgets me that we have never put on mourning for him. And
then, again, when I sit by myself, and all the house is still, I think I hear his
step coming up the street, and my heart begins to flutter and beat; but the
sound always goes past – and Peter never comes.

'That's[a] Martha back? No! *I'*ll go, my dear; I can always find my way in
the dark, you know. And a blow of fresh air at the door will do my head
good, and it's rather got a trick of aching.'

So she[b] pattered off. I had lighted the candle, to give the room a cheerful
appearance against her return.

'Was it Martha?' asked I.

'Yes. And I am rather uncomfortable, for I heard such a strange noise just
as I was opening the door.'

'When?' I asked, for her eyes were round with affright.

'In the street – just outside – it sounded like –

'Talking?' I put in, as she hesitated a little.

'No! kissing – '

CHAPTER VII.^a

VISITING.^b

ONE morning, as Miss Matty and I sat at our work – it was before twelve
o'clock, and Miss Matty had not yet changed the cap with yellow ribbons,
that had been Miss Jenkyns's^c best, and which Miss Matty was now wearing
out in private, putting on the one made in imitation of Mrs. Jamieson's at all
times when she expected to be seen – Martha came up, and asked if Miss
Betty Barker might speak to her mistress. Miss Matty assented, and quickly
disappeared to change the yellow ribbons, while Miss Barker came up stairs;
but, as she had forgotten her spectacles, and was rather flurried by the unu-
sual time of the visit, I was not surprised to see her return with one cap on
the top of the other. She was quite unconscious of it herself, and looked at us
with bland satisfaction. Nor do I think Miss Barker perceived it; for, putting
aside the little circumstance that she was not so young as she had been, she
was very much absorbed in her errand; which she delivered herself of, with
an oppressive modesty that found vent in endless apologies.

Miss Betty Barker was the daughter of the old clerk at Cranford, who had
officiated in Mr. Jenkyns's^d time. She and her sister had had pretty good sit-
uations as ladies' maids, and had saved up money enough to set up a
milliner's shop, which had been patronised by the ladies in the neighbour-
hood. Lady Arley, for instance, would occasionally give Miss Barkers the
pattern of an old cap of hers, which they immediately copied and circulated
among the *élite* of Cranford. I say the *élite*, for Miss Barkers had caught the
trick of the place, and piqued themselves upon their 'aristocratic connec-
tion.' They would not sell their caps and ribbons to any one without a
pedigree. Many a farmer's wife or daughter turned away huffed from Miss
Barkers' select millinery, and went rather to the universal shop, where the
profits of brown soap and moist sugar enabled the proprietor to go straight
to (Paris, he said, until he found his customers too patriotic and John Bullish
to wear what the Mounseers wore) London; where, as he often told his cus-
tomers, Queen Adelaide had appeared, only the very week before, in a cap
exactly like the one he showed them, trimmed with yellow and blue rib-
bons, and had been complimented by King William[71] on the becoming
nature of her head-dress.

Miss Barkers, who confined themselves to truth, and did not approve of
miscellaneous customers, throve notwithstanding. They were self-denying,

good people. Many a time have I seen the eldest of them (she that had been maid to Mrs. Jamieson) carrying out some delicate mess to a poor person. They only aped their betters in having 'nothing to do' with the class immediately below theirs. And when Miss Barker died, their profits and income were found to be such that Miss Betty was justified in shutting up shop, and retiring from business. She also (as I think I have before said) set up her cow; a mark of respectability in Cranford, almost as decided as setting up a gig is among some people. She dressed finer than any lady in Cranford; and we did not wonder at it; for it was understood that she was wearing out all the bonnets and caps, and outrageous ribbons, which had once formed her stock in trade. It was five or six years since they had given up shop: so in any other place than Cranford her dress might have been considered *passée*.

And now, Miss Betty Barker had called to invite Miss Matty to tea at her house on the following Tuesday. She gave me also an impromptu invitation, as I happened to be a visitor; though I could see she had a little fear lest, since my father had gone to live in Drumble, he might have engaged in that 'horrid cotton trade,' and so dragged his family down out of 'aristocratic society.' She prefaced this invitation with so many apologies, that she quite excited my curiosity. 'Her presumption' was to be excused. What had she been doing? She seemed so overpowered by it, I could only think that she had been writing to Queen Adelaide, to ask for a receipt for washing lace; but the act which she so characterised was only an invitation she had carried to her sister's former mistress, Mrs. Jamieson. 'Her former occupation considered, could Miss Matty excuse the liberty?' Ah! thought I, she has found out that double cap, and is going to rectify Miss Matty's head-dress. No! it was simply to extend her invitation to Miss Matty and to me. Miss Matty bowed acceptance; and I wondered that, in the graceful action, she did not feel the unusual weight and extraordinary height of her head-dress. But I do not think she did; for she recovered her balance, and went on talking to Miss Betty in a kind, condescending manner, very different from the fidgety way she would have had, if she had suspected how singular her appearance was.

'Mrs. Jamieson is coming, I think you said?' asked Miss Matty.

'Yes. Mrs. Jamieson most kindly and condescendingly said she would be happy to come. One little stipulation she made, that she should bring Carlo. I told her that if I had a weakness, it was for dogs.'

'And Miss Pole?' questioned Miss Matty, who was thinking of her pool at Preference, in which Carlo would not be available as a partner.

'I am going to ask Miss Pole. Of course, I could not think of asking her until I had asked you, Madam – the rector's daughter, Madam. Believe me, I do not forget the situation my father held under yours.'

'And Mrs. Forrester, of course?'

'And Mrs. Forrester. I thought, in fact, of going to her before I went to Miss Pole. Although her circumstances are changed, Madam, she was born a Tyrrell, and[a] we can never forget her alliance to the Bigges, of Bigelow Hall.

Miss Matty cared much more for the little circumstance of her being a very good card-player.

'Mrs. Fitz-Adam – I suppose' –

'No, Madam. I must draw a line somewhere. Mrs. Jamieson would not, I think, like to meet Mrs. Fitz-Adam. I have the greatest respect for Mrs. Fitz-Adam – but I cannot think her fit society for such ladies as Mrs. Jamieson and Miss Matilda Jenkyns.'

Miss Betty Barker bowed low to Miss Matty, and pursed up her mouth. She looked at me with sidelong dignity, as much as to say, although a retired milliner, she was no democrat, and understood the difference of ranks.

'May I beg you to come as near half-past six, to my little dwelling, as possible, Miss Matilda? Mrs. Jamieson dines at five, but has kindly promised not to delay her visit beyond that time – half-past six.' And with a swimming curtesy Miss Betty Barker took her leave.

My prophetic soul foretold a visit that afternoon from Miss Pole, who usually came to call on Miss Matilda after any event – or indeed in sight of any event – to talk it over with her.

'Miss Betty told me it was to be a choice and select few,' said Miss Pole, as she and Miss Matty compared notes.

'Yes, so she said. Not even Mrs. Fitz-Adam.'

Now Mrs. Fitz-Adam was the widowed sister of the Cranford surgeon, whom I have named before. Their parents were respectable farmers, content with their station. The name of these good people was Hoggins. Mr. Hoggins was the Cranford doctor now; we disliked the name, and considered it coarse; but, as Miss Jenkyns said, if he changed it to Piggins it would not be much better. We had hoped to discover a relationship between him and that Marchioness of Exeter whose name was Molly Hoggins;[72] but the man, careless of his own interests, utterly ignored and denied any such relationship; although, as dear Miss Jenkyns had said, he had a sister called Mary, and the same Christian names were very apt to run in families.

Soon after[b] Miss Mary Hoggins married Mr. Fitz-Adam, she disappeared from the neighbourhood for many years. She did not move in a sphere in Cranford society sufficiently high to make any of us care to know what Mr. Fitz-Adam was. He died and was gathered to his fathers, without our ever having thought about him at all. And then Mrs. Fitz-Adam reappeared in Cranford, 'as bold as a lion,' Miss Pole said, a well-to-do widow, dressed in rustling black silk, so soon after her husband's death, that poor Miss Jenkyns was justified in the remark she made, that 'bombazine'[73] would have shown a deeper sense of her loss.'

I remember the convocation of ladies, who assembled to decide whether or not Mrs. Fitz-Adam should be called upon by the old blue-blooded inhabitants of Cranford. She had taken a large rambling house, which had been usually considered to confer a patent of gentility upon its tenant; because, once upon a time, seventy or eighty years before, the spinster daughter of an earl had resided in it. I am not sure if the inhabiting this house was not also believed to convey some unusual power of intellect; for the earl's daughter, Lady Jane, had a sister, Lady Anne, who had married a general officer, in the time of the American war;[74] and this general officer had written one or two comedies, which were still acted on the London boards; and which, when we saw them advertised, made us all draw up, and feel that Drury Lane was paying a very pretty compliment to Cranford. Still, it was not at all a settled thing that Mrs. Fitz-Adam was to be visited, when dear Miss Jenkyns died; and, with her, something of the clear knowledge of the strict code of gentility went out too. As Miss Pole observed, 'As most of the ladies of good family in Cranford were elderly spinsters, or widows without children, if we did not relax a little, and become less exclusive, by-and-by we should have no society at all.'

Mrs. Forrester continued on the same side.

'She had always understood that Fitz meant something aristocratic; there was Fitz-Roy – she thought that some of the King's children had been called Fitz-Roy: and there was Fitz-Clarence now – they were the children of dear good King William the Fourth. Fitz-Adam! – it was a pretty name; and she thought it very probably meant 'Child of Adam.' No one, who had not some good blood in their veins, would dare to be called Fitz; there was a deal in a name – she had had a cousin who spelt his name with two little ffs – ffoulkes, – and he always looked down upon capital letters, and said they belonged to lately invented families. She had been afraid he would die a bachelor, he was so very choice. When he met with a Mrs. ffaringdon, at a watering-place, he took to her immediately; and a very pretty genteel woman she was – a widow with a very good fortune; and 'my cousin,' Mr. ffoulkes, married her; and it was all owing to her two little ffs.'

Mrs. Fitz-Adam did not stand a chance of meeting with a Mr. Fitz-anything in Cranford, so that could not have been her motive for settling there. Miss Matty thought it might have been the hope of being admitted in the society of the place, which would certainly be a very agreeable rise for *ci-devant* Miss Hoggins; and if this had been her hope, it would be cruel to disappoint her.

So[a] everybody called upon Mrs. Fitz-Adam – everybody but Mrs. Jamieson, who used to show how honourable she was by never seeing Mrs. Fitz-Adam, when they met at the Cranford parties. There would be only eight or ten ladies in the room, and Mrs. Fitz-Adam was the largest of all, and she invariably used to stand up when Mrs. Jamieson came in, and curtsey very low to her whenever she turned in her direction – so low, in fact, that I think Mrs. Jamieson must have looked at the wall above her, for she never moved a muscle of her face, no more than if she had not seen her. Still Mrs. Fitz-Adam persevered.

The spring evenings were getting bright and long, when three or four ladies in calashes met at Miss Barker's door. Do you know what a calash is? It is a covering worn over caps, not unlike the heads fastened on old-fashioned gigs; but sometimes it is not quite so large. This kind of head-gear always made an awful impression on the children in Cranford; and now two or three left off their play in the quiet sunny little street, and gathered, in wondering silence, round Miss Pole, Miss Matty, and myself. We were silent, too, so that we could hear loud, suppressed whispers, inside Miss Barker's house: 'Wait, Peggy! wait till I've run upstairs, and washed my hands. When I cough, open the door; I'll not be a minute.'

And, true enough, it was not a minute before we heard a noise, between a sneeze and a crow; on which the door flew open. Behind it stood a round-eyed maiden, all aghast at the honourable company of calashes, who marched in without a word. She recovered presence of mind enough to usher us into a small room, which had been the shop, but was now converted into a temporary dressing-room. There we unpinned and shook ourselves, and arranged our features before the glass into a sweet and gracious company-face; and then, bowing backwards with 'After you, ma'am,' we allowed Mrs. Forrester to take precedence up the narrow staircase that led to Miss Barker's drawing-room. There she sat, as stately and composed as though we had never heard that odd-sounding cough, from which her throat must have been even then sore and rough. Kind, gentle, shabbily dressed Mrs. Forrester was immediately conducted to the second place of honour – a seat arranged something like Prince Albert's near the Queen's – good, but not so good. The place of pre-eminence was, of course, reserved for the Honourable Mrs. Jamieson, who presently came panting up the stairs – Carlo rushing round her on her progress, as if he meant to trip her up.

And now, Miss Betty Barker was a proud and happy woman! She stirred the fire, and shut the door, and sat as near to it as she could, quite on the edge of her chair. When Peggy came in, tottering under the weight of the tea-tray, I noticed that Miss Barker was sadly afraid lest Peggy should not keep her distance sufficiently. She and her mistress were on very familiar terms in their every-day intercourse, and Peggy wanted now to make several little confidences to her, which Miss Barker was on thorns to hear; but which she thought it her duty, as a lady, to repress. So she turned away from all Peggy's asides and signs; but she made one or two very mal-apropos answers to what was said; and at last, seized with a bright idea, she exclaimed, 'Poor sweet Carlo! I'm forgetting him. Come down stairs with me, poor ittie doggie, and it shall have its tea, it shall!'

In[a] a few minutes she returned, bland and benignant as before; but I thought she had forgotten to give the 'poor ittie doggie' anything to eat; judging by the avidity with which he swallowed down chance pieces of cake. The tea-tray was abundantly loaded. I was pleased to see it, I was so hungry; but I was afraid the ladies present might think it vulgarly heaped up. I know they would have done at their own houses; but somehow the heaps disappeared here. I saw Mrs. Jamieson eating seed-cake, slowly and considerately, as she did everything; and I was rather surprised, for I knew she had told us, on the occasion of her last party, that she never had it in her house, it reminded her so much of scented soap. She always gave us Savoy biscuits. However, Mrs. Jamieson was kindly indulgent to Miss Barker's want of knowledge of the customs of high life; and, to spare her feelings, ate three large pieces of seed-cake, with a placid, ruminating expression of countenance, not unlike a cow's.

After tea there was some little demur and difficulty. We were six in number; four could play at Preference, and for the other two there was Cribbage. But all, except myself – (I was rather afraid of the Cranford ladies at cards, for it was the most earnest and serious business they ever engaged in) – were anxious to be of the 'pool.' Even Miss Barker, while declaring she did not know Spadille from Manille,[75] was evidently hankering to take a hand. The dilemma was soon put an end to by a singular kind of noise. If a Baron's daughter-in-law could ever be supposed to snore, I should have said Mrs. Jamieson did so then; for, overcome by the heat of the room, and inclined to doze by nature, the temptation of that very comfortable arm-chair had been too much for her, and Mrs. Jamieson was nodding. Once or twice she opened her eyes with an effort, and calmly but unconsciously smiled upon us; but, by-and-by, even her benevolence was not equal to this exertion, and she was sound asleep.

'It is very gratifying to me,' whispered Miss Barker at the card-table to her three opponents, whom, notwithstanding her ignorance of the game, she was 'basting'[76] most unmercifully – 'very gratifying indeed, to see how completely Mrs. Jamieson feels at home in my poor little dwelling; she could not have paid me a greater compliment.'

Miss[b] Barker provided me with some literature, in the shape of three or four handsomely bound fashion-books ten or twelve years old, observing, as she put a little table and a candle for my especial benefit, that she knew young people liked to look at pictures. Carlo lay, and snorted, and started at his mistress's feet. He, too, was quite at home.

The card-table[c] was an animated scene to watch; four ladies' heads, with niddle-noddling caps, all nearly meeting over the middle of the table, in their eargerness to whisper quick enough and loud enough: and every now and then came Miss Barker's 'Hush, ladies! if you please, hush! Mrs. Jamieson is asleep.'

It was very difficult to steer clear between Mrs. Forrester's deafness and Mrs. Jamieson's sleepiness. But Miss Barker managed her arduous task well. She repeated the whisper to Mrs. Forrester, distorting her face considerably, in order to show, by the motions of her lips, what was said; and then she smiled kindly all round at us, and murmured to herself, 'Very gratifying, indeed; I wish my poor sister had been alive to see this day.'

Presently the door was thrown wide open; Carlo started to his feet, with a loud snapping bark, and Mrs. Jamieson awoke: or, perhaps, she had not been asleep – as she said almost directly, the room had been so light she had been glad to keep her eyes shut, but had been listening with great interest to all our amusing and agreeable conversation. Peggy came in once more, red with importance. Another tray! 'Oh, gentility!' thought I, 'can you endure this last shock?' For Miss Barker had ordered (nay, I doubt not prepared, although she did say, 'Why! Peggy, what have you brought us?' and looking[a] pleasantly surprised at the unexpected pleasure) all sorts[b] of good things for supper – scalloped oysters, potted lobsters, jelly, a dish called 'little Cupids,'[77] (which was in great favour with the Cranford ladies; although too expensive to be given, except on solemn and state occasions – maccaroons sopped in brandy, I should have called it, if I had not known its more refined and classical name). In short, we were evidently to be feasted with all that was sweetest and best; and we thought it better to submit graciously, even at the cost of our gentility – which never ate suppers in general – but which, like most non-supper-eaters, was particularly hungry on all special occasions.

Miss Barker, in her former sphere, had, I dare say, been made acquainted with the beverage they call cherry-brandy. We none of us had ever seen such a thing, and rather shrunk back when she proffered it us – 'just a little, leetle glass, ladies; after the oysters and lobsters, you know. Shellfish are sometimes thought not very wholesome.' We all shook our heads like female mandarins; but, at last, Mrs. Jamieson suffered herself to be persuaded, and we followed her lead. It was not exactly unpalatable, though so hot and so strong that we thought ourselves bound to give evidence that we were not accustomed to such things, by coughing terribly – almost as strangely as Miss Barker had done, before we were admitted by Peggy.

'It's very strong,' said Miss Pole, as she put down her empty glass; 'I do believe there's spirit in it.'

'Only a little drop – just necessary to make it keep!' said Miss Barker. 'You know we put brandy-paper over preserves to make them keep. I often feel tipsy myself from eating damson tart.'

I question whether damson tart would have opened Mrs. Jamieson's heart as the cherry-brandy did; but she told us of a coming event, respecting which she had been quite silent till that moment.

'My sister-in-law, Lady Glenmire, is coming to stay with me.'

There was a chorus of 'Indeed!' and then a pause. Each one rapidly reviewed her wardrobe, as to its fitness to appear in the presence of a Baron's widow; for, of course, a series of small festivals were always held in Cranford on the arrival of a visitor at any of our friends' houses. We felt very pleasantly excited on the present occasion.

Not long after this, the maids and the lanterns were announced. Mrs. Jamieson had the sedan chair, which had squeezed itself into Miss Barker's narrow lobby with some difficulty; and most literally, stopped the way. It required some skilful manœuvring on the part of the old chairmen (shoe-makers by day; but, when summoned to carry the sedan, dressed up in a strange old livery – long great-coats, with small capes, coeval with the sedan, and similar to the dress of the class in Hogarth's pictures) to edge, and back, and try at it again, and finally to succeed in carrying their burden out of Miss Barker's front-door. Then we heard their quick pit-a-pat along the quiet lit-tle street, as we put on our calashes, and pinned up our gowns; Miss Barker hovering about us with offers of help; which, if she had not remembered her former occupation, and wished us to forget it, would have been much more pressing.

CHAPTER VIII.

'YOUR LADYSHIP.'[a]

EARLY the next morning – directly after twelve – Miss Pole made her appearance at Miss Matty's. Some very trifling piece of business was alleged as a reason for the call; but there was evidently something behind. At last out it came.

'By the way, you'll think I'm strangely ignorant; but, do you really know, I am puzzled how we ought to address Lady Glenmire. Do you say, "Your Ladyship," where you would say "you" to a common person? I have been puzzling all morning; and are we to say "My lady," instead of "Ma'am?" Now, you knew Lady Arley – will you kindly tell me the most correct way of speaking to the Peerage?'

Poor Miss Matty! she took off her spectacles, and she put them on again – but how Lady Arley was addressed, she could not remember.

'It is so long ago!' she said. 'Dear! dear! how stupid I am! I don't think I ever saw her more than twice. I know we used to call Sir Peter, "Sir Peter," – but he came much oftener to see us than Lady Arley did. Deborah would have known in a minute. My lady – your ladyship. It sounds very strange, and as if it was not natural. I never thought of it before; but, now you have named it, I am all in a puzzle.'

It was very certain Miss Pole would obtain no wise decision from Miss Matty, who got more bewildered every moment, and more perplexed as to etiquettes of address.

'Well, I really think,' said Miss Pole, 'I had better just go and tell Mrs. Forrester about our little difficulty. One sometimes grows nervous; and yet one would not have Lady Glenmire think we were quite ignorant of the etiquettes of high life in Cranford.'

'And will you just step in here, dear Miss Pole, as you come back, please; and tell me what you decide upon. Whatever you and Mrs. Forrester fix upon, will be quite right, I'm sure. "Lady Arley," "Sir Peter,"' said Miss Matty, to herself, trying to recall the old forms of words.

'Who is Lady Glenmire?' asked I.

'Oh! she's the widow of Mr. Jamieson – that's Mrs. Jamieson's late husband, you know – widow of his eldest brother. Mrs. Jamieson was a Miss Walker, daughter of Governor Walker. Your ladyship. My dear, if they fix on that way of speaking, you must just let me practise a little on you first, for I shall feel so foolish and hot, saying it the first time to Lady Glenmire.'

It was really a relief to Miss Matty when Mrs. Jamieson came on a very unpolite errand. I notice that apathetic people have more quiet impertinence than any others; and Mrs. Jamieson came now to insinuate pretty plainly, that she did not particularly wish that the Cranford ladies should call upon her sister-in-law. I can hardly say how she made this clear; for I grew very indignant and warm, while with slow deliberation she was explaining her wishes to Miss Matty, who, a true lady herself, could hardly understand the feeling which made Mrs. Jamieson wish to appear to her noble sister-in-law as if she only visited 'county' families. Miss Matty remained puzzled and perplexed long after I had found out the object of Mrs. Jamieson's visit.

When she did understand the drift of the honourable lady's call, it was pretty to see with what quiet dignity she received the intimation thus uncourteously given. She was not in the least hurt – she was of too gentle a spirit for that; nor was she exactly conscious of disapproving of Mrs. Jamieson's conduct; but there was something of this feeling in her mind, I am sure, which made her pass from the subject to others, in a less flurried and more composed manner than usual. Mrs. Jamieson was, indeed, the more flurried of the two, and I could see she was glad to take her leave.

A little while afterwards, Miss Pole returned, red and indignant. 'Well! to be sure! You've had Mrs. Jamieson here, I find from Martha; and we are not to call on Lady Glenmire. Yes! I met Mrs. Jamieson, half-way between here and Mrs. Forrester's, and she told me; she took me so by surprise, I had nothing to say. I wish I had thought of something very sharp and sarcastic; I dare say I shall to-night. And Lady Glenmire is but the widow of a Scotch baron after all! I went on to look at Mrs. Forrester's Peerage, to see who this lady was, that is to be kept under a glass case: widow of a Scotch peer – never sat in the House of Lords – and as poor as Job I dare say; and she – fifth daughter of some Mr. Campbell or other. You are the daughter of a rector, at any rate, and related to the Arleys; and Sir Peter might have been Viscount Arley, every one says.'

Miss Matty tried to soothe Miss Pole, but in vain. That lady, usually so kind and good-humoured, was now in a full flow of anger.

'And I went and ordered a cap this morning, to be quite ready,' said she, at last, – letting out the secret which gave sting to Mrs. Jamieson's intimation. 'Mrs. Jamieson shall see if it's so easy to get me to make fourth at a pool, when she has none of her fine Scotch relations with her!'

In coming out of church, the first Sunday on which Lady Glenmire appeared in Cranford, we sedulously talked together, and turned our backs on Mrs. Jamieson and her guest. If we might not call on her, we would not even look at her, though we were dying with curiosity to know what she was like. We had the comfort of questioning Martha in the afternoon. Martha did not belong to a sphere of society whose observation could be an implied compliment to Lady Glenmire, and Martha had made good use of her eyes.

'Well, ma'am! is it the little lady with Mrs. Jamieson, you mean? I thought you would like more to know how young Mrs. Smith was dressed, her being a bride.' (Mrs. Smith was the butcher's wife.)

Miss Pole said, 'Good gracious me! as if we cared about a Mrs. Smith;' but was silent, as Martha resumed her speech.

'The little lady in Mrs. Jamieson's pew had on, ma'am, rather an old black silk, and a shepherd's plaid cloak, ma'am, and very bright black eyes she had, ma'am, and a pleasant, sharp face; not over young, ma'am, but yet, I should guess, younger than Mrs. Jamieson herself. She looked up and down the church, like a bird, and nipped up her petticoats, when she came out, as quick and sharp as ever I see. I'll tell you what, ma'am, she's more like Mrs. Deacon, at the "Coach and Horses," nor any one.'

'Hush, Martha!' said Miss Matty, 'that's not respectful.'

'Isn't it, ma'am? I beg pardon, I'm sure; but Jem Hearn said so as well. He said, she was just such a sharp, stirring sort of a body' –

'Lady,' said Miss Pole.

'Lady – as Mrs. Deacon.'

Another Sunday passed away, and we still averted our eyes from Mrs. Jamieson and her guest, and made remarks to ourselves that we thought were very severe – almost too much so. Miss Matty was evidently uneasy at our sarcastic manner of speaking.

Perhaps by this time Lady Glenmire had found out that Mrs. Jamieson's was not the gayest, liveliest house in the world; perhaps Mrs. Jamieson had found out that most of the county families were in London, and that those who remained in the country[a] were not so alive as they might have been to the circumstance of Lady Glenmire being in their neighbourhood. Great events spring out of small causes; so I will not pretend to say what induced Mrs. Jamieson to alter her determination of excluding the Cranford ladies, and send notes of invitation all round for a small party, on the following Tuesday. Mr. Mulliner himself brought them round. He *would* always ignore the fact of there being a back-door to any house, and gave a louder rat-tat than his mistress, Mrs. Jamieson. He had three little notes, which he carried in a large basket, in order to impress his mistress with an idea of their great weight, though they might easily have gone into his waistcoat pocket.

Miss Matty and I quietly decided we would have a previous engagement at home: – it was the evening on which Miss Matty usually made candle-lighters of all the notes and letters of the week; for on Mondays her accounts were always made straight – not a penny owing from the week before; so, by a natural arrangement, making candle-lighters fell upon a Tuesday evening, and gave us a legitimate excuse for declining Mrs. Jamieson's invitation. But before our answer was written, in came Miss Pole, with an open note in her hand.

'So!' she said. 'Ah! I see you have got your note, too. Better late than never. I could have told my Lady Glenmire she would be glad enough of our society before a fortnight was over.'

'Yes,' said Miss Matty, 'we're asked for Tuesday evening. And perhaps you would just kindly bring your work across and drink tea with us that night. It is my usual regular time for looking over the last week's bills, and notes, and letters, and making candle-lighters of them; but that does not seem quite reason enough for saying I have a previous engagement at home, though I meant to make it do. Now, if you would come, my conscience would be quite at ease, and luckily the note is not written yet.'

I saw Miss Pole's countenance change while Miss Matty was speaking.

'Don't you mean to go then?' asked she.

'Oh no!' said Miss Matty quietly. 'You don't either, I suppose?'

'I don't know,' replied Miss Pole. 'Yes, I think I do,' said she rather briskly; and on seeing Miss Matty look surprised, she added, 'You see one would not like Mrs. Jamieson to think that anything she could do, or say, was of consequence enough to give offence; it would be a kind of letting down of ourselves, that I, for one, should not like. It would be too flattering to Mrs. Jamieson, if we allowed her to suppose that what she had said affected us a week, nay ten days afterwards.'

'Well! I suppose it is wrong to be hurt and annoyed so long about any-thing; and, perhaps, after all, she did not mean to vex us. But I must say, I could not have brought myself to say the things Mrs. Jamieson did about our not calling. I really don't think I shall go.'

'Oh, come! Miss Matty, you must go; you know our friend Mrs. Jamie-son is much more phlegmatic than most people, and does not enter into the little delicacies of feeling which you possess in so remarkable a degree.'

'I thought you possessed them, too, that day Mrs. Jamieson called to tell us not to go,' said Miss Matty innocently.

But Miss Pole, in addition to her delicacies of feeling, possessed a very smart cap, which she was anxious to show to an admiring world; and so she seemed to forget all her angry words uttered not a fortnight before, and to be ready to act on what she called the great Christian principle of 'Forgive and forget;' and she lectured dear Miss Matty so long on this head, that she abso-lutely ended by assuring her it was her duty, as a deceased rector's daughter, to buy a new cap, and go to the party at Mrs. Jamieson's. So 'we were most happy to accept,' instead of 'regretting that we were obliged to decline.'

The expenditure in dress in Cranford was principally in that one article referred to. If the heads were buried in smart new caps, the ladies were like ostriches, and cared not what became of their bodies. Old gowns, white and venerable collars, any number of brooches, up and down and everywhere (some with dogs' eyes painted in them; some that were like small picture-frames with mausoleums and weeping-willows neatly executed in hair inside; some, again, with miniatures of ladies and gentlemen sweetly smiling out of a nest of stiff muslin) – old brooches for a permanent ornament, and new caps to suit the fashion of the day; the ladies of Cranford always dressed with chaste elegance and propriety, as Miss Barker once prettily expressed it.

And with[a] three new caps, and a greater array of brooches than had ever been seen together at one time, since Cranford was a town, did Mrs. Forrester, and Miss Matty, and Miss Pole appear on that memorable Tuesday evening. I counted seven brooches myself on Miss Pole's dress. Two were fixed negligently in her cap (one was a butterfly made of Scotch pebbles, which a vivid imagination might believe to be the real insect); one fastened her net neck-kerchief; one her collar; one ornamented the front of her gown, midway between her throat and waist; and another adorned the point of her stomacher. Where the seventh was I have forgotten, but it was somewhere about her, I am sure.

But I am getting on too fast in describing the dresses of the company. I should first relate the gathering, on the way to Mrs. Jamieson's. That lady lived in a large house just outside the town. A road, which had known what it was to be a street, ran right before the house, which opened out upon it, without any intervening garden or court. Whatever the sun was about, he never shone on the front of that house. To be sure, the living-rooms were at the back, looking on to a pleasant garden; the front windows only belonged to kitchens and housekeepers' rooms, and pantries; and in one of them Mr. Mulliner was reported to sit. Indeed, looking askance, we often saw the back of a head, covered with hair-powder, which also extended itself over his coat-collar down to his very waist; and this imposing back was always engaged in reading the 'St. James's Chronicle,' opened wide, which, in some degree, accounted for the length of time the said newspaper was in reaching us – equal subscribers with Mrs. Jamieson, though, in right of her honourableness, she always had the reading of it first. This very Tuesday, the delay in forwarding the last number had been particularly aggravating; just when both Miss Pole and Miss Matty, the former more especially, had been wanting to see it, in order to coach up the court-news, ready for the evening's interview with aristocracy. Miss Pole told us she had absolutely taken time by the fore-lock, and been dressed by five o'clock, in order to be ready, if the 'St. James's Chronicle' should come in at the last moment – the very 'St. James's Chronicle' which the powdered-head was tranquilly and composedly reading as we passed the accustomed window this evening.

'The impudence of the man!' said Miss Pole, in a low indignant whisper. 'I should like to ask him, whether his mistress pays her quarter-share for his exclusive use.'

We looked at her in admiration of the courage of her thought; for Mr. Mulliner was an object of great awe to all of us. He seemed never to have forgotten his condescension in coming to live at Cranford. Miss Jenkyns, at times, had stood forth as the undaunted champion of her sex, and spoken to him on terms of equality; but even Miss Jenkyns could get no higher. In his pleasantest and most gracious moods, he looked like a sulky cockatoo. He did not speak except in gruff monosyllables. He would wait in the hall when we begged him not to wait, and then looked deeply offended because we had kept him there, while, with trembling, hasty hands, we prepared ourselves for appearing in company.

Miss Pole[a] ventured on a small joke as we went up-stairs, intended, though addressed to us, to afford Mr. Mulliner some slight amusement. We all smiled, in order to seem as if we felt at our ease, and timidly looked for Mr. Mulliner's sympathy. Not a muscle of that wooden face had relaxed; and we were grave in an instant.

Mrs. Jamieson's drawing-room was cheerful; the evening sun came streaming into it, and the large square window was clustered round with flowers. The furniture was white and gold; not the later style, Louis Quatorze I think they call it, all shells and twirls; no, Mrs. Jamieson's chairs and tables had not a curve or bend about them. The chair and table legs diminished as they neared the ground, and were straight and square in all their corners. The chairs were all a-row against the walls, with the exception of four or five which stood in a circle round the fire. They were railed with white bars across the back, and knobbed with gold; neither the railings nor the knobs invited to ease. There was a japanned table devoted to literature, on which lay a Bible, a Peerage, and a Prayer-Book. There was another square Pembroke table dedicated to the Fine Arts, on which there was a kaleidoscope, conversation-cards, puzzle-cards[78] (tied together to an interminable length with faded pink satin ribbon), and a box painted in fond imitation of the drawings which decorate tea-chests. Carlo lay on the worsted-worked rug, and ungraciously barked at us as we entered. Mrs. Jamieson stood up, giving us each a torpid smile of welcome, and looking helplessly beyond us at Mr. Mulliner, as if she hoped he would place us in chairs, for if he did not, she never could. I suppose he thought we could find our way to the circle round the fire, which reminded me of Stonehenge, I don't know why. Lady Glenmire came to the rescue of our hostess; and somehow or other we found ourselves for the first time placed agreeably, and not formally, in Mrs. Jamieson's house. Lady Glenmire, now we had time to look at her, proved to be a bright little woman of middle age, who had been very pretty in the days of her youth, and who was even yet very pleasant-looking. I saw Miss Pole appraising her dress in the first five minutes; and I take her word, when she said the next day,

'My dear! ten pounds would have purchased every stitch she had on – lace and all.'

It was pleasant to suspect that a peeress could be poor, and partly reconciled us to the fact that her husband had never sat in the House of Lords; which, when we first heard of it seemed a kind of swindling us out of our respect on false pretences; a sort of 'A Lord and No Lord'[79] business.

We were all very silent at first. We were thinking what we could talk about, that should be high enough to interest My Lady. There had been a rise in the price of sugar, which, as preserving-time was near, was a piece of intelligence to all our housekeeping hearts, and would have been the natural topic if Lady Glenmire had not been by. But we were not sure if the Peerage ate preserves – much less knew how they were made. At last, Miss Pole, who had always a great deal of courage and *savoir faire*, spoke to Lady Glenmire, who on her part had seemed just as much puzzled to know how to break the silence as we were.

'Has your ladyship been to Court, lately?' asked she; and then gave a little glance round at us, half timid, and half triumphant, as much as to say, 'See how judiciously I have chosen a subject befitting the rank of the stranger!'

'I never was there in my life,' said Lady Glenmire, with a broad Scotch accent, but in a very sweet voice. And then, as if she had been too abrupt, she added, 'We very seldom went to London; only twice, in fact, during all my married life; and before I was married, my father had far too large a family' – (fifth daughter of Mr. Campbell, was in all our minds, I am sure) – 'to take us often from our home, even to Edinburgh. Ye'll have been in Edinburgh, may be?' said she, suddenly brightening up with the hope of a common interest. We had none of us been there; but Miss Pole had an uncle who once had passed a night there, which was very pleasant.

Mrs. Jamieson, meanwhile, was absorbed in wonder why Mr. Mulliner did not bring the tea; and, at length, the wonder oozed out of her mouth.

'I had better ring the bell, my dear, had not I?' said Lady Glenmire, briskly.

'No – I think not – Mulliner does not like to be hurried.'

We[a] should have liked our tea, for we dined at an earlier hour than Mrs. Jamieson. I suspect Mr. Mulliner had to finish the 'St. James's Chronicle'[b] before he chose to trouble himself about tea. His mistress fidgetted and fidgetted, and kept saying, 'I can't think why Mulliner does not bring tea. I can't think what he can be about.' And Lady Glenmire at last grew quite impatient, but it was a pretty kind of impatience after all; and she rung the bell rather sharply, on receiving a half permission from her sister-in-law to do so. Mr. Mulliner appeared in dignified surprise. 'Oh!' said Mrs. Jamieson, 'Lady Glenmire rang the bell; I believe it was for tea.'

In a few minutes tea was brought. Very delicate was the china, very old the plate, very thin the bread and butter, and very small the lumps of sugar.

Sugar was evidently Mrs. Jamieson's favourite economy. I question if the little filigree sugar-tongs, made something like scissors, could have opened themselves wide enough to take up an honest, vulgar, good-sized piece; and when I tried to take two little minnikin[a] pieces at once, so as not to be detected in too many returns to the sugar-basin, they absolutely dropped one, with a little sharp clatter, quite in a malicious and unnatural manner. But before this happened, we had had a slight disappointment. In the little silver jug was cream, in the larger one was milk. As soon as Mr. Mulliner came in, Carlo began to beg, which was a thing our manners forbade us to do, though I am sure we were just as hungry; and Mrs. Jamieson said she was certain we would excuse her if she gave her poor dumb Carlo his tea first. She accordingly mixed a saucer-full for him, and put it down for him to lap; and then she told us how intelligent and sensible the dear little fellow was; he knew cream quite well, and constantly refused tea with only milk in it: so the milk was left for us, but we silently thought we were quite as intelligent and sensible as Carlo, and felt as if insult were added to injury, when we were called upon to admire the gratitude evinced by his wagging his tail for the cream, which should have been ours.

After tea we thawed down into common-life subjects. We were thankful to Lady Glenmire for having proposed some more bread and butter, and this mutual want made us better acquainted with her than we should ever have been with talking about the Court, though Miss Pole did say, she had hoped to know how the dear Queen was from some one who had seen her.

The friendship,[b] begun over bread and butter, extended on to cards. Lady Glenmire played Preference to admiration, and was a complete authority as to Ombre and Quadrille. Even Miss Pole quite forgot to say 'my lady,' and 'your ladyship,' and said 'Basto![80] ma'am;' 'you have Spadille, I believe,' just as quietly as if we had never held the great Cranford parliament on the subject of the proper mode of addressing a peeress.

As a proof of how thoroughly we had forgotten that we were in the presence of one who might have sat down to tea with a coronet, instead of a cap, on her head, Mrs. Forrester related a curious little fact to Lady Glenmire – an anecdote known to the circle of her intimate friends, but of which even Mrs. Jamieson was not aware. It related to some fine old lace, the sole relic of better days, which Lady Glenmire was admiring on Mrs. Forrester's collar.

'Yes,' said that lady, 'such lace cannot be got now for either love or money; made by the nuns abroad they tell me. They say that they can't make it now, even there. But perhaps they can now they've passed the Catholic Emancipation Bill.[81] I should not wonder. But, in the meantime, I treasure up my lace very much. I daren't even trust the washing of it to my maid' (the little charity school-girl I have named before, but who sounded well as 'my maid.') 'I always wash it myself. And once it had a narrow escape. Of course, your ladyship knows that such lace must never be starched or ironed. Some people wash it in sugar and water; and some in coffee, to make it the right yellow colour; but I myself have a very good receipt for washing it in milk, which stiffens it enough, and gives it a very good creamy colour. Well, ma'am, I had tacked it together (and the beauty of this fine lace is, that when it is wet, it goes into a very little space), and put it to soak in milk, when, unfortunately, I left the room; on my return, I found pussy on the table, looking very like a thief, but gulping very uncomfortably, as if she was half-choked with something she wanted to swallow, and could not. And, would you believe it? At first, I pitied her, and said, "Poor pussy! poor pussy!" till, all at once, I looked and saw the cup of milk empty – cleaned out! "You naughty cat!" said I; and I believe I was provoked enough to give her a slap, which did no good, but only helped the lace down – just as one slaps a choking child on the back. I could have cried, I was so vexed; but I determined I would not give the lace up without a struggle for it. I hoped the lace might disagree with her, at any rate; but it would have been too much for Job, if he had seen, as I did, that cat come in, quite placid and purring, not a quarter of an hour after, and almost expecting to be stroked. "No, pussy!" said I; "if you have any conscience, you ought not to expect that!" And then a thought struck me; and I rang the bell for my maid, and sent her to Mr. Hoggins, with my compliments, and would he be kind enough to lend me one of his top-boots for an hour? I did not think there was anything odd in the message; but Jenny said, the young men in the surgery laughed as if they would be ill, at my wanting a top-boot. When it came, Jenny and I put pussy in, with her fore-feet straight down, so that they were fastened, and could not scratch, and we gave her a tea-spoonful of currant-jelly, in which (your lady-ship must excuse me) I had mixed some tartar emetic. I shall never forget how anxious I was for the next half-hour.[a] I took pussy to my own room, and spread a clean towel on the floor. I could have kissed her when she returned the lace to sight, very much as it had gone down. Jenny had boiling water ready, and we soaked it and soaked it, and spread it on a lavender-bush in the sun, before I could touch it again, even to put it in milk. But now, your ladyship would never guess that it had been in pussy's inside.'

We found out, in the course of the evening, that Lady Glenmire was going to pay Mrs. Jamieson a long visit, as she had given up her apartments in Edinburgh, and had no ties to take her back there in a hurry. On the whole, we were rather glad to hear this, for she had made a pleasant impression upon us; and it was also very comfortable to find, from things which dropped out in the course of conversation, that, in addition to many other genteel qualities, she was far removed from the vulgarity of wealth.

'Don't you find it very unpleasant, walking?' asked Mrs. Jamieson, as our respective servants were announced. It was a pretty regular question from Mrs. Jamieson, who had her own carriage in the coach-house, and always went out in a sedan-chair to the very shortest distances. The answers were nearly as much a matter of course.

'Oh dear, no! it is so pleasant and still at night!' 'Such a refreshment after the excitement of a party!' 'The stars are so beautiful!' This last was from Miss Matty.

'Are you fond of astronomy?' Lady Glenmire asked.

'Not very' – replied Miss Matty, rather confused at the moment to remember which was astronomy, and which was astrology – but the answer was true under either circumstance, for she read, and was slightly alarmed at, Francis Moore's astrological predictions;[82] and, as to astronomy, in a private and confidential conversation, she had told me, she never could believe that the earth was moving constantly, and that she would not believe it if she could, it made her feel so tired and dizzy whenever she thought about it.

In our pattens, we picked our way home with extra care that night; so refined and delicate were our perceptions after drinking tea with 'my lady.'

CHAPTER IX.

SIGNOR BRUNONI.[a]

SOON after the events of which I gave an account in my last paper, I was summoned home by my father's illness; and for a time I forgot, in anxiety about him, to wonder how my dear friends at Cranford were getting on, or how Lady Glenmire could reconcile herself to the dulness of the long visit which she was still paying to her sister-in-law, Mrs. Jamieson. When my father grew a little stronger I accompanied him to the sea-side, so that altogether I seemed banished from Cranford, and was deprived of the opportunity of hearing any chance intelligence of the dear little town for the greater part of that year.[83]

Late in[b] November – when we had returned home again, and my father was once more in good health – I received a letter from Miss Matty; and a very mysterious letter it was. She began many sentences without ending them, running them one into another, in much the same confused sort of way in which written words run together on blotting-paper. All I could make out was, that if my father was better (which she hoped he was), and would take warning and wear a great coat from Michaelmas to Lady-day,[84] if turbans were in fashion, could I tell her? such a piece of gaiety was going to happen as had not been seen or known of since Wombwell's lions[85] came, when one of them ate a little child's arm; and she was, perhaps, too old to care about dress, but a new cap she must have; and, having heard that turbans were worn, and some of the county families likely to come, she would like to look tidy, if I would bring her a cap from the milliner I employed; and oh, dear! how careless of her to forget that she wrote to beg I would come and pay her a visit next Tuesday; when she hoped to have something to offer me in the way of amusement, which she would not now more particularly describe, only sea-green was her favourite colour. So she ended her letter; but in a P.S. she added, she thought she might as well tell me what was the peculiar attraction to Cranford just now; Signor Brunoni was going to exhibit his wonderful magic in the Cranford Assembly Rooms, on Wednesday and Friday evening in the following week.

I was very glad to accept the invitation from my dear Miss Matty, independently of the conjuror; and most particularly anxious to prevent her from disfiguring her small gentle mousey face with a great Saracen's-head turban; and, accordingly I bought her a pretty, neat, middle-aged cap, which, however, was rather a disappointment to her when, on my arrival, she followed me into my bed-room, ostensibly to poke the fire, but in reality, I do believe, to see if the sea-green turban was not inside the cap-box with which I had travelled. It was in vain that I twirled the cap round on my hand to exhibit back and side fronts: her heart had been set upon a turban, and all she could do was to say, with resignation in her look and voice:

'I am sure you did your best, my dear. It is just like the caps all the ladies in Cranford are wearing, and they have had theirs for a year, I dare say. I should have liked something newer, I confess – something more like the turbans Miss Betty Barker tells me Queen Adelaide wears; but it is very pretty, my dear. And I dare say lavender will wear better than sea-green. Well, after all, what is dress that we should care about it! You'll tell me if you want anything, my dear. Here is the bell. I suppose turbans have not got down to Drumble yet?'

So saying, the dear old lady gently bemoaned herself out of the room, leaving me to dress for the evening, when, as she informed me, she expected Miss Pole and Mrs. Forrester, and she hoped I should not feel myself too much tired to join the party. Of course I should not; and I made some haste to unpack and arrange my dress; but, with all my speed, I heard the arrivals and the buzz of conversation in the next room before I was ready. Just as I opened the door, I caught the words – 'I was foolish to expect anything very genteel out of the Drumble shops – poor girl! she did her best, I've no doubt.' But for all that, I had rather that she blamed Drumble and me than disfigured herself with a turban.

Miss Pole[a] was always the person, in the trio of Cranford ladies now assembled, to have had adventures. She was in the habit of spending the morning in rambling from shop to shop; not to purchase anything (except an occasional reel of cotton, or a piece of tape), but to see the new articles and report upon them, and to collect all the stray pieces of intelligence in the town. She had a way, too, of demurely popping hither and thither into all sorts of places to gratify her curiosity on any point; a way which, if she had not looked so very genteel and prim, might have been considered impertinent. And now, by the expressive way in which she cleared her throat, and waited for all minor subjects (such as caps and turbans) to be cleared off the course, we knew she had something very particular to relate, when the due pause came – and I defy any people, possessed of common modesty, to keep up a conversation long, where one among them sits up aloft in silence, looking down upon all the things they chance to say as trivial and contemptible compared to what they could disclose, if properly entreated. Miss Pole began:

'As I was stepping out of Gordon's shop, to-day, I chanced to go into the George (my Betty has a second-cousin who is chamber-maid there, and I thought Betty would like to hear how she was), and, not seeing any one about, I strolled up the staircase, and found myself in the passage leading to the Assembly Room (you and I remember the Assembly Room, I am sure, Miss Matty! and the *minuets de la cour!*)[86] so I went on, not thinking of what I was about, when, all at once, I perceived that I was in the middle of the preparations for to-morrow night – the room being divided with great clothes-maids,[87] over which Crosby's men were tacking red flannel; very dark and odd it seemed; it quite bewildered me, and I was going on behind the screens, in my absence of mind, when a gentleman (quite the gentleman, I can assure you,) stepped forwards and asked if I had any business he could arrange for me. He spoke such pretty broken English, I could not help thinking of Thaddeus of Warsaw and the Hungarian Brothers, and Santo Sebastiani;[88] and while I was busy picturing his past life to myself, he had bowed me out of the room. But wait a minute! You have not heard half my story yet! I was going down-stairs, when who should I meet but Betty's second cousin. So, of course, I stopped to speak to her for Betty's sake; and she told me that I had really seen the conjuror; the gentleman who spoke broken English was Signor Brunoni himself. Just at this moment he passed us on the stairs, making such a graceful bow, in reply to which I dropped a curtsey – all foreigners have such polite manners, one catches something of it. But when he had gone downstairs, I bethought me that I had dropped my glove in the Assembly Room (it was safe in my muff all the time, but I never found it till afterwards); so I went back, and, just as I was creeping up the passage left on one side of the great screen that goes nearly across the room, who should I see but the very same gentleman that had met me before, and passed me on the stairs, coming now forwards from the inner part of the room, to which there is no entrance – you remember Miss Matty! – and just repeating in his pretty broken English, the inquiry if I had any business there – I don't mean that he put it quite so bluntly, but he seemed very determined that I should not pass the screen – so, of course, I explained about my glove, which, curiously enough, I found at that very moment.'

Miss Pole then had seen the conjuror – the real live conjuror! and numerous were the questions we all asked her: 'Had he a beard?' 'Was he young or old?' 'Fair or dark?' 'Did he look' –[a] (unable to shape my question prudently, I put it in another form) – 'How did he look?' In short, Miss Pole was the heroine of the evening, owing to her morning's encounter. If she was not the rose (that is to say the conjuror), she had been near it.

Conjuration, sleight of hand, magic, witchcraft were the subjects of the evening. Miss Pole was slightly sceptical, and inclined to think there might be a scientific solution found for even the proceedings of the Witch of Endor.[89] Mrs. Forrester believed everything from ghosts to death-watches.[90] Miss Matty ranged between the two – always convinced by the last speaker. I think she was naturally more inclined to Mrs. Forrester's side, but a desire of proving herself a worthy sister to Miss Jenkyns kept her equally balanced –

Miss Jenkyns, who would never allow a servant to call the little rolls of tallow that formed themselves round candles, 'winding-sheets,' but insisted on their being spoken of as 'roly-poleys!'[91] A sister of hers to be superstitious! It would never do.

After tea, I was dispatched[a] downstairs into the dining-parlour for that volume of the old encyclopædia[b] which contained the nouns beginning with C, in order that Miss Pole might prime herself with scientific explanations for the tricks of the following evening. It spoilt the pool at Preference which Miss Matty and Mrs. Forrester had been looking forward to, for Miss Pole became so much absorbed in her subject, and the plates by which it was illustrated, that we felt it would be cruel to disturb her, otherwise than by one or two well-timed yawns, which I threw in now and then, for I was really touched by the meek way in which the two ladies were bearing their disappointment. But Miss Pole only read the more zealously, imparting to us no more interesting information than this:

'Ah! I see; I comprehend perfectly. A represents the ball. Put A between B and D – no! between C and F, and turn the second joint of the third finger of your left hand over the wrist of your right H. Very clear indeed! My dear Mrs. Forrester, conjuring and witchcraft is a mere affair of the alphabet. Do let me read you this one passage?'

Mrs. Forrester implored Miss Pole to spare her, saying, from a child upwards, she never could understand being read aloud to; and I dropped the pack of cards, which I had been shuffling very audibly; and by this discreet movement, I obliged Miss Pole to perceive that Preference was to have been the order of the evening, and to propose, rather unwillingly, that the pool should commence. The pleasant brightness that stole over the other two ladies' faces on this! Miss Matty had one or two twinges of self-reproach for having interrupted Miss Pole in her studies: and did not remember her cards well, or give her full attention to the game, until she had soothed her conscience by offering to lend the volume of the Encyclopædia to Miss Pole, who accepted it thankfully, and said Betty should take it home when she came with the lantern.

The next evening we were all in a little gentle flutter at the idea of the gaiety before us. Miss Matty went up to dress betimes, and hurried me until I was ready, when we found we had an hour and a half to wait before the 'doors opened at seven precisely.' And we had only twenty yards to go! However, as Miss Matty said, it would not do to get too much absorbed in anything, and forget the time; so, she thought we had better sit quietly, without lighting the candles, till five minutes to seven. So Miss Matty dozed, and I knitted.

At length we set off; and at the door, under the carriage-way at the George, we met Mrs. Forrester and Miss Pole: the latter was discussing the subject of the evening with more vehemence than ever, and throwing A's and B's at our heads like hail-stones. She had even copied one or two of the 'receipts' – as she called them – for the different tricks, on backs of letters, ready to explain and to detect Signor Brunoni's arts.

We went[a] into the cloak-room adjoining the Assembly Room; Miss Matty gave a sigh or two to her departed youth, and the remembrance of the last time she had been there, as she adjusted her pretty new cap before the strange, quaint old mirror in the cloak-room. The Assembly Room had been added to the inn about a hundred years before, by the different county families, who met together there once a month during the winter, to dance and play at cards. Many a county beauty had first swam through the minuet that she afterwards danced before Queen Charlotte, in this very room. It was said that one of the Gunnings[92] had graced the apartment with her beauty; it was certain that a rich and beautiful widow, Lady Williams, had here been smitten with the noble figure of a young artist, who was staying with some family in the neighbourhood for professional purposes, and accompanied his patrons to the Cranford Assembly. And a pretty bargain poor Lady Williams had of her handsome husband, if all tales were true! Now, no beauty blushed and dimpled along the sides of the Cranford Assembly Room; no handsome artist won hearts by his bow, *chapeau bras*[93] in hand: the old room was dingy; the salmon-coloured paint had faded into a drab; great pieces of plaster had chipped off from the white wreaths and festoons on its walls; but still a mouldy odour of aristocracy lingered about the place, and a dusty recollection of the days that were gone made Miss Matty and Mrs. Forrester bridle up as they entered, and walk mincingly up the room, as if there were a number of genteel observers, instead of two little boys, with a stick of toffy between them with which to beguile the time.

We stopped short at the second front row; I could hardly understand why, until I heard Miss Pole ask a stray waiter if any of the County families were expected; and when he shook his head, and believed not, Mrs. Forester and Miss Matty moved forwards, and our party represented a conversational square. The front row was soon augmented and enriched by Lady Glenmire and Mrs. Jamieson. We six occupied the two front rows, and our aristocratic seclusion was respected by the groups of shopkeepers who strayed in from time to time, and huddled together on the back benches. At least I conjectured so, from the noise they made, and the sonorous bumps they gave in sitting down; but when, in weariness of the obstinate green curtain, that would not draw up, but would stare at me with two odd eyes, seen through holes, as in the old tapestry story, I would fain have looked round at the merry chattering people behind me, Miss Pole clutched my arm, and begged me not to turn, for 'it was not the thing.' What 'the thing' was, I never could find out, but it must have been something eminently dull and tiresome. However, we all sat eyes right, square front, gazing at the tantalising curtain, and hardly speaking intelligibly, we were so afraid of being caught in the vulgarity of making any noise in a place of public amusement. Mrs. Jamieson was the most fortunate, for she fell asleep.

At length[a] the eyes disappeared – the curtain quivered – one side went up before the other, which stuck fast; it was dropped again, and, with a fresh effort, and a vigorous pull from some unseen hand, it flew up, revealing to our sight a magnificent gentleman in the Turkish costume, seated before a little table, gazing at us (I should have said with the same eyes that I had last seen through the hole in the curtain) with calm and condescending dignity, 'like a being of another sphere,' as I heard a sentimental voice ejaculate behind me.

'That's not Signor Brunoni!' said Miss Pole decidedly, and so audibly that I am sure he heard, for he glanced down over his flowing beard at our party with an air of mute reproach. 'Signor Brunoni had no beard – but perhaps he'll come soon.' So she lulled herself into patience. Meanwhile, Miss Matty had reconnoitered through her eye-glass; wiped it, and looked again. Then she turned round, and said to me, in a kind, mild, sorrowful tone: –

'You see, my dear, turbans *are* worn.'

But we had no time for more conversation. The Grand Turk, as Miss Pole chose to call him, arose and announced himself as Signor Brunoni.

'I don't believe him!' exclaimed Miss Pole, in a defiant manner. He looked at her again, with the same dignified upbraiding in his countenance. 'I don't!' she repeated, more positively than ever. 'Signor Brunoni had not got that muffy sort of thing about his chin, but looked like a close-shaved Christian gentleman.'

Miss Pole's energetic speeches had the good effect of wakening up Mrs. Jamieson, who opened her eyes wide, in sign of the deepest attention – a proceeding which silenced Miss Pole, and encouraged the Grand Turk to proceed, which he did in very broken English – so broken that there was no cohesion between the parts of his sentences; a fact which he himself perceived at last, and so left off speaking and proceeded to action.

Now we *were* astonished. How he did his tricks I could not imagine; no, not even when Miss Pole pulled out her pieces of paper and began reading aloud – or at least in a very audible whisper – the separate 'receipts' for the most common of his tricks. If ever I saw a man frown, and look enraged, I saw the Grand Turk frown at Miss Pole; but, as she said, what could be expected but unchristian looks from a Mussulman? If Miss Pole was sceptical, and more engrossed with her receipts and diagrams than with his tricks, Miss Matty and Mrs. Forrester were mystified and perplexed to the highest degree. Mrs. Jamieson kept taking her spectacles off and wiping them, as if she thought it was something defective in them which made the legerdemain; and Lady Glenmire, who had seen many curious sights in Edinburgh, was very much struck with the tricks, and would not at all agree with Miss Pole, who declared that anybody could do them with a little practice – and that she would, herself, undertake to do all he did, with two hours given to study the Encyclopædia, and made her third finger flexible.

At last, Miss Matty and Mrs. Forrester became perfectly awe-struck. They whispered together. I sat just behind them, so I could not help hearing what they were saying. Miss Matty asked Mrs. Forrester, 'if she thought it was quite right to have come to see such things? She could not help fearing they were lending encouragement to something that was not quite –' a little shake of the head filled up the blank. Mrs. Forrester replied, that the same thought had crossed her mind; she, too, was feeling very uncomfortable; it was so very strange. She was quite certain that it was her pocket-handkerchief which was in that loaf just now; and it had been in her own hand not five minutes before. She wondered who had furnished the bread? She was sure it could not be Dakin,[a] because he was the churchwarden. Suddenly, Miss Matty half turned towards me: –

'Will you look, my dear – you are a stranger in the town, and it won't give rise to unpleasant reports – will you just look round and see if the rector is here? If he is, I think we may conclude that this wonderful man is sanctioned by the Church, and that will be a great relief to my mind.'

I looked, and I saw the tall, thin, dry, dusty rector, sitting surrounded by National School boys,[94] guarded by troops of his own sex from any approach of the many Cranford spinsters. His kind face was all agape with broad smiles, and the boys around him were in chinks[95] of laughing. I told Miss Matty that the Church was smiling approval, which set her mind at ease.

I have[b] never named Mr. Hayter, the rector, because I, as a well-to-do and happy young woman, never came in contact with him. He was an old bachelor, but as afraid of matrimonial reports getting abroad about him as any girl of eighteen: and he would rush into a shop, or dive down an entry, sooner than encounter any of the Cranford ladies in the street; and, as for the Preference parties, I did not wonder at his not accepting invitations to them. To tell the truth, I always suspected Miss Pole of having given very vigorous chace to Mr. Hayter when he first came to Cranford; and not the less, because now she appeared to share so vividly in his dread lest her name should ever be coupled with his. He found all his interests among the poor and helpless; he had treated the National School boys this very night to the performance; and virtue was for once its own reward, for they guarded him right and left, and clung round him as if he had been the queen bee, and they the swarm. He felt so safe in their environment, that he could even afford to give our party a bow as we filed out. Miss Pole ignored his presence, and pretended to be absorbed in convincing us that we had been cheated, and had not seen Signor Brunoni after all.

CHAPTER X.

THE PANIC.[a]

I THINK a series of circumstances dated from Signor Brunoni's visit to Cranford, which seemed at the time connected in our minds with him, though I don't know that he had anything really to do with them. All at once all sorts of uncomfortable rumours got afloat in the town. There were one or two robberies – real *bonâ fide* robberies; men had up before the magistrates and committed for trial; and that seemed to make us all afraid of being robbed; and for a long time at Miss Matty's, I know, we used to make a regular expedition all round the kitchens and cellars every night, Miss Matty leading the way, armed with the poker, I following with the hearth-brush, and Martha carrying the shovel and fire-irons with which to sound the alarm; and by the accidental hitting together of them she often frightened us so much that we bolted ourselves up, all three together, in the back kitchen, or store-room, or wherever we happened to be, till, when our affright was over, we recollected ourselves, and set out afresh with double valiance. By day we heard strange stories from the shopkeepers and cottagers, of carts that went about in the dead of night, drawn by horses shod with felt, and guarded by men in dark clothes, going round the town, no doubt, in search of some unwatched house or some unfastened door.

Miss Pole,[b] who affected great bravery herself, was the principal person to collect and arrange these reports, so as to make them assume their most fearful aspect. But we discovered that she had begged one of Mr. Hoggins's[c] worn-out hats to hang up in her lobby, and we (at least I) had my doubts as to whether she really would enjoy the little adventure of having her house broken into, as she protested she should. Miss Matty made no secret of being an arrant coward; but she went regularly through her housekeeper's duty of inspection – only the hour for this became earlier and earlier, till at last we went the rounds at half-past six, and Miss Matty adjourned to bed soon after seven, 'in order to get the night over the sooner.'

Cranford had so long piqued itself on being an honest and moral town, that it had grown to fancy itself too genteel and well-bred to be otherwise, and felt the stain upon its character at this time doubly. But we comforted ourselves with the assurance which we gave to each other, that the robberies could never have been committed by any Cranford person; it must have been a stranger or strangers, who brought this disgrace upon the town, and occasioned as many precautions as if we were living among the Red Indians or the French.

This last[a] comparison of our nightly state of defence and fortification, was made by Mrs. Forrester, whose father had served under General Burgoyne in the American war,[96] and whose husband had fought the French in Spain. She indeed inclined to the idea that, in some way, the French were connected with the small thefts, which were ascertained facts, and the burglaries and highway robberies, which were rumours. She had been deeply impressed with the idea of French spies, at some time in her life; and the notion could never be fairly eradicated, but sprung up again from time to time. And now her theory was this: the Cranford people respected themselves too much, and were too grateful to the aristocracy who were so kind as to live near the town, ever to disgrace their bringing up by being dishonest or immoral; therefore, we must believe that the robbers were strangers – if strangers, why not foreigners? – if foreigners, who so likely as the French? Signor Brunoni spoke broken English like a Frenchman, and, though he wore a turban like a Turk, Mrs. Forrester had seen a print of Madame de Staël with a turban on, and another of Mr. Denon[97] in just such a dress as that in which the conjuror had made his appearance; showing clearly that the French, as well as the Turks, wore turbans: there could be no doubt Signor Brunoni was a Frenchman – a French spy, come to discover the weak and undefended places of England; and, doubtless, he had his accomplices; for her part, she, Mrs. Forrester, had always had her own opinion of Miss Pole's adventure at the George Inn – seeing two men where only one was believed to be: French people had ways and means, which she was thankful to say the English knew nothing about; and she had never felt quite easy in her mind about going to see that conjuror; it was rather too much like a forbidden thing, though the Rector was there. In short, Mrs. Forrester grew more excited than we had ever known her before; and, being an officer's daughter and widow, we looked up to her opinion, of course.

Really I[b] do not know how much was true or false in the reports which flew about like wildfire just at this time; but it seemed to me then that there was every reason to believe that at Mardon (a small town about eight miles from Cranford) houses and shops were entered by holes made in the walls, the bricks being silently carried away in the dead of the night, and all done so quietly that no sound was heard either in or out of the house. Miss Matty gave it up in despair when she heard of this. 'What was the use,' said she, 'of locks and bolts, and bells to[c] the windows, and going round the house every night? That last trick was fit for a conjuror. Now she did believe that Signor Brunoni was at the bottom of it.'

One afternoon, about five o'clock, we were startled by a hasty knock at the door. Miss Matty bade me run and tell Martha on no account to open the door till she (Miss Matty) had reconnoitred through the window; and she armed herself with a footstool to drop down on the head of the visitor, in case he should show a face covered with black crape, as he looked up in answer to her inquiry of who was there. But it was nobody but Miss Pole and Betty. The former came upstairs, carrying a little hand-basket, and she was evidently in a state of great agitation.

'Take care of that!' said she to me, as I offered to relieve her of her basket. 'It's my plate. I am sure there is a plan to rob my house to-night. I am come to throw myself on your hospitality, Miss Matty. Betty is going to sleep with her cousin at the George. I can sit up here all night, if you will allow me; but my house is so far from any neighbours; and I don't believe we could be heard if we screamed ever so!'

'But,' said Miss Matty, 'what has alarmed you so much? Have you seen any men lurking about the house?'

'Oh yes!' answered Miss Pole. 'Two very bad-looking men have gone three times past the house, very slowly; and an Irish beggar-woman came not half an hour ago, and all but forced herself in past Betty, saying her children were starving, and she must speak to the mistress. You see, she said "mistress," though there was a hat hanging up in the hall, and it would have been more natural to have said "master." But Betty shut the door in her face, and came up to me, and we got the spoons together, and sat in the parlour-window watching, till we saw Thomas Jones going from his work, when we called to him and asked him to take care of us into the town.'

We might have triumphed over Miss Pole, who had professed such bravery until she was frightened; but we were too glad to perceive that she shared in the weaknesses of humanity to exult over her; and I gave up my room to her very willingly, and shared Miss Matty's bed for the night. But before we retired, the two ladies rummaged up, out of the recesses of their memory, such horrid stories of robbery and murder, that I quite quaked in my shoes. Miss Pole was evidently anxious to prove that such terrible events had occurred within her experience that she was justified in her sudden panic; and Miss Matty did not like to be outdone, and capped every story with one yet more horrible, till it reminded me, oddly enough, of an old story I had read somewhere, of a nightingale and a musician, who strove one against the other which could produce the most admirable music, till poor Philomel dropped down dead.[98]

One of the stories that haunted me for a long time afterwards, was of a girl, who was left in charge of a great house in Cumberland, on some particular fair-day, when the other servants all went off to the gaieties. The family were away in London, and a pedlar came by, and asked to leave his large and heavy pack in the kitchen, saying, he would call for it again at night; and the girl (a gamekeeper's daughter) roaming about in search of amusement, chanced to hit upon a gun hanging up in the hall, and took it down to look at the chasing; and it went off through the open kitchen door, hit the pack, and a slow dark thread of blood came oozing out.[99] (How Miss Pole enjoyed this part of the story, dwelling on each word as if she loved it!) She rather hurried over the further account of the girl's bravery, and I have but a confused idea that, somehow, she baffled the robbers with Italian irons,[100] heated red hot, and then restored to blackness by being dipped in grease.

We parted[a] for the night with an awe-struck wonder as to what we should hear of in the morning – and, on my part, with a vehement desire for the night to be over and gone: I was so afraid lest the robbers should have seen, from some dark lurking-place, that Miss Pole had carried off her plate, and thus have a double motive for attacking our house.

But, until Lady Glenmire came to call next day, we heard of nothing unusual. The kitchen fire-irons were in exactly the same position against the back door, as when Martha and I had skilfully piled them up like spillikins,[101] ready to fall with an awful clatter, if only a cat had touched the outside panels. I had wondered what we should all do if thus awakened and alarmed, and had proposed to Miss Matty that we should cover up our faces under the bed-clothes, so that there should be no danger of the robbers thinking that we could identify them; but Miss Matty who was trembling very much, scouted this idea, and said we owed it to society to apprehend them, and that she should certainly do her best to lay hold of them, and lock them up in the garret till morning.

When Lady Glenmire came, we almost felt jealous of her. Mrs. Jamieson's house had really been attacked; at least there were men's footsteps to be seen on the flower-borders, underneath the kitchen windows, 'where nae men should be;'[102] and Carlo had barked all through the night as if strangers were abroad. Mrs. Jamieson had been awakened by Lady Glenmire, and they had rung the bell which communicated with Mr. Mulliner's room, in the third story, and when his night-capped head had appeared over the bannisters, in answer to the summons, they had told him of their alarm, and the reasons for it; whereupon he retreated into his bed-room, and locked the door (for fear of draughts, as he informed them in the morning), and opened the window, and called out valiantly to say, if the supposed robbers would come to him he would fight them; but, as Lady Glenmire observed, that was but poor comfort, since they would have to pass by Mrs. Jamieson's room and her own, before they could reach him, and must be of a very pugnacious disposition indeed, if they neglected the opportunities of robbery presented by the unguarded lower stories to go up to a garret, and there force a door in order to get at the champion of the house. Lady Glenmire, after waiting and listening for some time in the drawing-room, had proposed to Mrs. Jamieson that they should go to bed; but that lady said she should not feel comfortable unless she sat up and watched; and, accordingly, she packed herself warmly up on the sofa, where she was found by the housemaid, when she came into the room at six o'clock, fast asleep; but Lady Glenmire went to bed, and kept awake all night.

When Miss Pole heard of this, she nodded her head in great satisfaction. She had been sure we should hear of something happening in Cranford that night; and we had heard. It was clear enough they had first proposed to attack her house; but when they saw that she and Betty were on their guard, and had carried off the plate, they had changed their tactics and gone to Mrs. Jamieson's, and no one knew what might have happened if Carlo had not barked, like a good dog as he was!

Poor Carlo![a] his barking days were nearly over. Whether the gang who infested the neighbourhood were afraid of him; or whether they were revengeful enough for the way in which he had baffled them on the night in question to poison him; or whether, as some among the more uneducated people thought, he died of apoplexy, brought on by too much feeding and too little exercise; at any rate, it is certain that, two days after this eventful night, Carlo was found dead, with his poor little legs stretched out stiff in the attitude of running, as if by such unusual exertion he could escape the sure pursuer, Death.

We[b] were all sorry for Carlo, the old familiar friend who had snapped at us for so many years; and the mysterious mode of his death made us very uncomfortable. Could Signor Brunoni be at the bottom of this? He had apparently killed a canary with only a word of command; his will seemed of deadly force; who knew but what he might yet be lingering in the neighbourhood willing all sorts of awful things!

We[c] whispered these fancies among ourselves in the evenings; but in the mornings our courage came back with the daylight, and in a week's time we had got over the shock of Carlo's death; all but Mrs. Jamieson. She, poor thing, felt it as she had felt no event since her husband's death; indeed Miss Pole said, that as the Honourable Mr. Jamieson drank a good deal, and occasioned her much uneasiness, it was possible that Carlo's death might be the greater affliction. But there was always a tinge of cynicism in Miss Pole's remarks. However, one thing was clear and certain; it was necessary for Mrs. Jamieson to have some change of scene; and Mr. Mulliner was very impressive on this point, shaking his head whenever we inquired after his mistress, and speaking of her loss of appetite and bad nights very ominously; and with justice too, for if she had two characteristics in her natural state of health, they were a facility of eating and sleeping. If she could neither eat nor sleep, she must be indeed out of spirits and out of health.

Lady Glenmire[d] (who had evidently taken very kindly to Cranford), did not like the idea of Mrs. Jamieson's going to Cheltenham, and more than once insinuated pretty plainly that it was Mr. Mulliner's doing, who had been much alarmed on the occasion of the house being attacked, and since had said, more than once, that he felt it a very responsible charge to have to defend so many women. Be that as it might,[a] Mrs. Jamieson went to Cheltenham, escorted by Mr. Mulliner; and Lady Glenmire remained in possession of the house, her ostensible office being to take care that the maid-servants did not pick up followers. She made a very pleasant-looking dragon: and, as soon as it was arranged for her stay[b] in Cranford, she found out that Mrs. Jamieson's visit to Cheltenham was just the best thing in the world. She had let her house in Edinburgh, and was for the time houseless, so the charge of her sister-in-law's comfortable abode was very convenient and acceptable.[c]

Miss Pole was very much inclined to install herself as a heroine, because of the decided steps she had taken in flying from the two men and one woman, whom she entitled 'that murderous gang.' She described their appearance in glowing colours, and I noticed that every time she went over the story some fresh trait of villany was added to their appearance. One was tall – he grew to be gigantic in height before we had done with him; he of course had black hair – and by and by, it hung in elf-locks over his forehead and down his back. The other was short and broad – and a hump sprouted out on his shoulder before we heard the last of him; he had red hair – which deepened into carrotty; and she was almost sure he had a cast in his eye – a decided squint. As for the woman, her eyes glared, and she was masculine-looking – a perfect virago; most probably a man dressed in woman's clothes: afterwards, we heard of a beard on her chin, and a manly voice and a stride.

If Miss[d] Pole was delighted to recount the events of that afternoon to all inquirers, others were not so proud of their adventures in the robbery line. Mr. Hoggins, the surgeon, had been attacked at his own door by two ruffians, who were concealed in the shadow of the porch, and so effectually silenced him, that he was robbed in the interval between ringing his bell and the servant's answering it. Miss Pole was sure it would turn out that this robbery had been committed by 'her men,' and went the very day she heard of the report to have her teeth examined, and to question Mr. Hoggins. She came to us afterwards; so we heard what she had heard, straight and direct from the source, while we were yet in the excitement and flutter of the agitation caused by the first intelligence; for the event had only occurred the night before.

'Well!' said Miss Pole, sitting down with the decision of a person who has made up her mind as to the nature of life and the world, (and such people never tread lightly, or seat themselves without a bump) – 'Well, Miss Matty! men will be men. Every mother's son of them wishes to be considered Samson and Solomon rolled into one – too strong ever to be beaten or discomfited – too wise ever to be outwitted. If you will notice, they have always foreseen events, though they never tell one for one's warning before the events happen; my father was a man, and I know the sex pretty well.'

She had talked herself out of breath, and we should have been very glad to fill up the necessary pause as chorus, but we did not exactly know what to say, or which man had suggested this diatribe against the sex; so we only joined in generally, with a grave shake of the head, and a soft murmur of 'They are very incomprehensible, certainly!'

'Now only think,' said she. 'There I have undergone the risk of having one of my remaining teeth drawn (for one is terribly at the mercy of any surgeon-dentist; and I, for one, always speak them fair till I have got my mouth out of their clutches), and after all, Mr. Hoggins is too much of a man to own that he was robbed last night.'

'Not robbed!' exclaimed the chorus.

'Don't tell me!' Miss Pole exclaimed, angry that we could be for a moment imposed upon. 'I believe he was robbed, just as Betty told me, and he is ashamed to own it: and, to be sure it was very silly of him to be robbed just at his own door; I dare say, he feels that such a thing won't raise him in the eyes of Cranford society, and is anxious to conceal it – but he need not have tried to impose upon me, by saying I must have heard an exaggerated account of some petty theft of a neck of mutton, which, it seems, was stolen out of the safe in his yard last week; he had the impertinence to add, he believed that that was taken by the cat. I have no doubt, if I could get at the bottom of it, it was that Irishman dressed up in woman's clothes, who came spying about my house, with the story about the starving children.'

After we had duly condemned the want of candour which Mr. Hoggins had evinced, and abused men in general, taking him for the representative and type, we got round to the subject about which we had been talking when Miss Pole came in – namely, how far, in the present disturbed state of the country, we could venture to accept an invitation which Miss Matty had just received from Mrs. Forrester, to come as usual and keep the anniversary of her wedding-day, by drinking tea with her at five o'clock, and playing a quiet pool afterwards. Mrs. Forrester had said, that she asked us with some diffidence, because the roads were, she feared, very unsafe. But she suggested that perhaps one of us would not object to take the sedan; and that the others, by walking briskly, might keep up with the long trot of the chairmen, and so we might all arrive safely at Over Place, a suburb of the town. (No. That is too large an expression: a small cluster of houses separated from Cranford by about two hundred yards of a dark and lonely lane.) There was no doubt but that a similar note was awaiting Miss Pole at home; so her call was a very fortunate affair, as it enabled us to consult together. We would all much rather have declined this invitation; but we felt that it would not be quite kind to Mrs. Forrester, who would otherwise be left to a solitary retrospect of her not very happy or fortunate life. Miss Matty and Miss Pole had been visitors on this occasion for many years; and now they gallantly determined to nail their colours to the mast, and to go through Darkness Lane rather than fail in loyalty to their friend.

But when the evening came, Miss Matty (for it was she who was voted into the chair, as she had a cold), before being shut down in the sedan, like jack-in-a-box, implored the chairmen, whatever might befall, not to run away and leave her fastened up there, to be murdered; and even after they had promised, I saw her tighten her features into the stern determination of a martyr, and she gave me a melancholy and ominous shake of the head through the glass. However, we got there safely, only rather out of breath, for it was who could trot hardest through Darkness Lane, and I am afraid poor Miss Matty was sadly jolted.

Mrs. Forrester had made extra preparations in acknowledgment of our exertion in coming to see her through such dangers. The usual forms of genteel ignorance as to what her servants might send up were all gone through; and harmony and Preference seemed likely to be the order of the evening, but for an interesting conversation that began I don't know how, but which had relation, of course, to the robbers who infested the neighbourhood of Cranford.

Having[a] braved the dangers of Darkness Lane, and thus having a little stock of reputation for courage to fall back upon; and also, I dare say, desirous of proving ourselves superior to men (*videlicet* Mr. Hoggins), in the article of candour, we began to relate our individual fears, and the private precautions we each of us took. I owned that my pet apprehension was eyes – eyes looking at me, and watching me, glittering out from some dull flat wooden surface; and that if I dared to go up to my looking-glass when I was panic-stricken, I should certainly turn it round, with its back towards me, for fear of seeing eyes behind me looking out of the darkness. I saw Miss Matty nerving herself up for a confession; and at last out it came. She owned that, ever since she had been a girl, she had dreaded being caught by her last leg, just as she was getting into bed, by some one concealed under the bed. She said, when she was younger and more active, she used to take a flying leap from a distance, and so bring both her legs up safely into bed at once; but that this had always annoyed Deborah, who piqued herself upon getting into bed gracefully, and she had given it up in consequence. But now the old terror would often come over her, especially since Miss Pole's house had been attacked (we had got quite to believe in the fact of the attack having taken place), and yet it was very unpleasant to think of looking under a bed, and seeing a man concealed, with a great fierce face staring out at you; so she had bethought herself of something – perhaps I had noticed that she had told Martha to buy her a penny ball, such as children play with – and now she rolled this ball under the bed every night; if it came out on the other side, well and good; if not, she always took care to have her hand on the bell-rope, and meant to call out John and Harry, just as if she expected men-servants to answer her ring.

We all applauded this ingenious contrivance, and Miss Matty sank back into satisfied silence, with a look at Mrs. Forrester as if to ask for *her* private weakness.

Mrs. Forrester looked askance at Miss Pole, and tried to change the subject a little, by telling us that she had borrowed a boy from one of the neighbouring cottages, and promised his parents a hundredweight of coals at Christmas, and his supper every evening, for the loan of him at nights. She had instructed him in his possible duties when he first came; and, finding him sensible, she had given him the major's sword (the major was her late husband), and desired him to put it very carefully behind his pillow at night, turning the edge towards the head of the pillow. He was a sharp lad, she was sure; for, spying out the major's cocked hat, he had said, if he might have that to wear he was sure he could frighten two Englishmen, or four French-men, any day. But she had impressed upon him anew that he was to lose no time in putting on hats or anything else; but, if he heard any noise, he was to run at it with his drawn sword. On my suggesting that some accident might occur from such slaughterous and indiscriminate directions, and that he might rush on Jenny getting up to wash, and have spitted her before he had discovered that she was not a Frenchman, Mrs. Forrester said she did not think that that was likely, for he was a very sound sleeper, and generally had to be well shaken, or cold-pigged[103] in a morning before they could rouse him. She sometimes thought such dead sleep must be owing to the hearty suppers the poor lad ate, for he was half-starved at home, and she told Jenny to see that he got a good meal at night.

Still this was no confession of Mrs. Forrester's peculiar timidity, and we urged her to tell us what she thought would frighten her more than anything. She paused, and stirred the fire, and snuffed the candles, and then she said, in a sounding whisper, –

'Ghosts!'

She looked at Miss Pole, as much as to say she had declared it, and would stand by it. Such a look was a challenge in itself. Miss Pole came down upon her with indigestion, spectral illusions, optical delusions, and a great deal out of Dr. Ferrier and Dr. Hibbert[104] besides. Miss Matty had rather a leaning to ghosts, as I have said before, and what little she did say, was all on Mrs. Forrester's side, who, emboldened by sympathy, protested that ghosts were a part of her religion; that surely she, the widow of a major in the army, knew what to be frightened at, and what not; in short, I never saw Mrs. Forrester so warm either before or since, for she was a gentle, meek, enduring old lady in most things. Not all the elder-wine that ever was mulled, could this night wash out the remembrance of this difference between Miss Pole and her hostess. Indeed, when the elder-wine was brought in, it gave rise to a new burst of discussion: for Jenny, the little maiden who staggered under the tray, had to give evidence of having seen a ghost with her own eyes, not so many nights ago, in Darkness Lane – the very lane we were to go through on our way home.

In spite[a] of the uncomfortable feeling which this last consideration gave me, I could not help being amused at Jenny's position, which was exceedingly like that of a witness being examined and cross-examined by two counsel who are not at all scrupulous about asking leading questions. The conclusion I arrived at was, that Jenny had certainly seen something beyond what a fit of indigestion would have caused. A lady all in white, and without her head, was what she deposed and adhered to, supported by a consciousness of the secret sympathy of her mistress under the withering scorn with which Miss Pole regarded her. And not only she, but many others, had seen this headless lady, who sat by the roadside wringing her hands as in deep grief. Mrs. Forrester looked at us from time to time, with an air of conscious triumph; but then she had not to pass through Darkness Lane before she could bury herself beneath her own familiar bed-clothes.

We preserved a discreet silence as to the headless lady while we were putting on our things to go home, for there was no knowing how near the ghostly head and ears might be, or what spiritual connection they might be keeping up with the unhappy body in Darkness Lane; and therefore, even Miss Pole felt that it was as well not to speak lightly on such subjects, for fear of vexing or insulting that woe-begone trunk. At least, so I conjecture; for, instead of the busy clatter usual in the operation, we tied on our cloaks as sadly as mutes at a funeral. Miss Matty drew the curtains round the windows of the chair to shut out disagreeable sights; and the men (either because they were in spirits that their labours were so nearly ended, or because they were going down hill) set off at such a round and merry pace, that it was all Miss Pole and I could do to keep up with them. She had breath for nothing beyond an imploring 'Don't leave me!' uttered as she clutched my arm so tightly that I could not have quitted her, ghost or no ghost. What a relief it was when the men, weary of their burden and their quick trot, stopped just where Headingley-cause-way branches off from Darkness Lane! Miss Pole unloosed me and caught at one of the men.

'Could not you – could not you take Miss Matty round by Headingley-causeway, – the pavement in Darkness Lane jolts so, and she is not very strong?'

A smothered voice was heard from the inside of the chair –

'Oh! pray go on! what is the matter? What is the matter? I will give you sixpence more to go on very fast; pray don't stop here.'

'And[b] I'll give you a shilling,' said Miss Pole, with tremulous dignity, 'if you'll go by Headingley-causeway.'

The two men grunted acquiescence and took up the chair and went along the causeway, which certainly answered Miss Pole's kind purpose of saving Miss Matty's bones; for it was covered with soft thick mud, and even a fall there would have been easy, till the getting up came, when there might have been some difficulty in extrication.

CHAPTER XI.

SAMUEL BROWN.[a]

THE next morning I met Lady Glenmire and Miss Pole, setting out on a long walk to find some old woman who was famous in the neighbourhood for her skill in knitting woollen stockings. Miss Pole said to me, with a smile half kindly and half contemptuous upon her countenance, 'I have been just telling Lady Glenmire of our poor friend Mrs. Forrester, and her terror of ghosts. It comes from living so much alone, and listening to the bug-a-boo stories of that Jenny of hers.' She was so calm and so much above superstitious fears herself, that I was almost ashamed to say how glad I had been of her Headingley-causeway proposition the night before, and turned off the conversation to something else.

In the afternoon Miss Pole called on Miss Matty to tell her of the adventure – the real adventure they had met with on their morning's walk. They had been perplexed about the exact path which they were to take across the fields, in order to find the knitting old woman, and had stopped to inquire at a little way-side public-house, standing on the high road to London, about three miles from Cranford. The good woman had asked them to sit down and rest themselves, while she fetched her husband, who could direct them better than she could; and, while they were sitting in the sanded parlour, a little girl came in. They thought that she belonged to the landlady, and began some trifling conversation with her; but, on Mrs. Roberts's return, she told them that the little thing was the only child of a couple who were staying in the house. And then she began a long story, out of which Lady Glenmire and Miss Pole could only gather one or two decided facts; which were that, about six weeks ago, a light spring-cart had broken down just before their door, in which there were two men, one woman, and this child. One of the men was seriously hurt – no bones broken, only 'shaken,' the landlady called it; but he had probably sustained some severe internal injury, for he had languished in their house ever since, attended by his wife, the mother of this little girl. Miss Pole had asked what he was, what he looked like. And Mrs. Roberts had made answer that he was not like a gentleman, nor yet like a common person; if it had not been that he and his wife were such decent, quiet people, she could almost have thought he was a mountebank, or something of that kind, for they had a great box in the cart, full of she did not know what. She had helped to unpack it, and take out their linen and clothes, when the other man – his twin brother, she believed he was – had gone off with the horse and cart.

Miss Pole had begun to have her suspicions at this point, and expressed her idea that it was rather strange that the box and cart and horse and all should have disappeared; but good Mrs. Roberts seemed to have become quite indignant at Miss Pole's implied suggestion; in fact, Miss Pole said, she was as angry as if Miss Pole had told her that she herself was a swindler. As the best way of convincing the ladies, she bethought her of begging them to see the wife; and, as Miss Pole said, there was no doubting the honest, worn, bronze face of the woman, who, at the first tender word from Lady Glenmire, burst into tears, which she was too weak to check, until some word from the landlady made her swallow down her sobs, in order that she might testify to the Christian kindness shown by Mr. and Mrs. Roberts. Miss Pole came round with a swing to as vehement a belief in the sorrowful tale as she had been sceptical before; and, as a proof of this, her energy in the poor sufferer's behalf was nothing daunted when she found out that he, and no other, was our Signor Brunoni, to whom all Cranford had been attributing all manner of evil this six weeks past! Yes! his wife said his proper name was Samuel Brown – 'Sam,' she called him – but to the last we preferred calling him 'the Signor;' it sounded so much better.

The end of their conversation with the Signora Brunoni was, that it was agreed that he should be placed under medical advice, and for any expense incurred in procuring this Lady Glenmire promised to hold herself responsible; and had accordingly gone to Mr. Hoggins to beg him to ride over to the Rising Sun that very afternoon, and examine into the Signor's real state; and as Miss Pole said, if it was desirable to remove him to Cranford to be more immediately under Mr. Hoggins's eye, she would undertake to see for lodgings, and arrange about the rent. Mrs. Roberts had been as kind as could be all throughout; but it was evident that their long residence there had been a slight inconvenience.

Before[a] Miss Pole left us, Miss Matty and I were as full of the morning's adventure as she was. We talked about it all the evening, turning it in every possible light, and we went to bed anxious for the morning, when we should surely hear from some one what Mr. Hoggins thought and recommended. For, as Miss Matty observed, though Mr. Hoggins did say 'Jack's up,' 'a fig for his heels,' and call Preference 'Pref,'[105] she believed he was a very worthy man, and a very clever surgeon. Indeed, we were rather proud of our doctor at Cranford, as a doctor. We often[b] wished, when we heard of Queen Adelaide or the Duke of Wellington being ill, that they would send for Mr. Hoggins; but, on consideration, we were rather glad they did not, for if we were ailing, what should we do if Mr. Hoggins had been appointed physician-in-ordinary to the Royal Family? As a surgeon we were proud of him; but as a man – or rather, I should say, as a gentleman – we could only shake our heads over his name and himself, and wished that he had read Lord Chesterfield's Letters[106] in the days when his manners were susceptible of improvement. Nevertheless, we all regarded his dictum in the Signor's case as infallible; and when he said, that with care and attention he might rally, we had no more fear for him.

But although we had no more fear, everybody did as much as if there was great cause for anxiety – as indeed there was, until Mr. Hoggins took charge of him. Miss Pole looked out clean and comfortable, if homely, lodgings; Miss Matty sent the sedan-chair for him; and Martha and I aired it well before it left Cranford, by holding a warming-pan full of red-hot coals in it, and then shutting it up close, smoke and all, until the time when he should get into it at the Rising Sun. Lady Glenmire undertook the medical department under Mr. Hoggins's directions; and rummaged up all Mrs. Jamieson's medicine glasses, and spoons, and bed-tables, in a free and easy way, that made Miss Matty feel a little anxious as to what that lady and Mr. Mulliner might say, if they knew. Mrs. Forrester made some of the bread-jelly, for which she was so famous, to have ready as a refreshment in the lodgings when he should arrive. A present of this bread-jelly was the highest mark of favour dear Mrs. Forrester could confer. Miss Pole had once asked her for the receipt, but she had met with a very decided rebuff; that lady told her that she could not part with it to any one during her life, and that after her death it was bequeathed, as her executors would find, to Miss Matty. What Miss Matty – or, as Mrs. Forrester called her (remembering the clause in her will, and the dignity of the occasion) Miss Matilda Jenkyns – might choose to do with the receipt when it came into her possession – whether to make it public, or to hand it down as an heir-loom – she did not know, nor would she dictate. And a mould of this admirable, digestible, unique bread-jelly was sent by Mrs. Forrester to our poor sick conjuror. Who says that the aristocracy are proud? Here was a lady, by birth a Tyrrell, and descended from the great Sir Walter that shot King Rufus, and in whose veins ran the blood of him who murdered the little Princes in the Tower,[107] going every day to see what dainty dishes she could prepare for Samuel Brown, a mountebank! But, indeed, it was wonderful to see what kind feelings were called out by this poor man's coming amongst us. And also wonderful to see how the great Cranford panic, which had been occasioned by his first coming in his Turkish dress, melted away into thin air on his second coming – pale and feeble, and with his heavy filmy eyes, that only brightened a very little when they fell upon the countenance of his faithful wife, or their pale and sorrowful little girl.

Somehow, we all forgot to be afraid. I dare say it was, that finding out that he, who had first excited our love of the marvellous by his unprecedented arts, had not sufficient every-day gifts to manage a shying horse, made us feel as if we were ourselves again. Miss Pole came with her little basket at all hours of the evening, as if her lonely house, and the unfrequented road to it, had never been infested by that 'murderous gang;' Mrs. Forrester said, she thought that neither Jenny nor she need mind the headless lady who wept and wailed in Darkness Lane, for surely the power was never given to such beings to harm those who went about to try to do what little good was in their power; to which Jenny, trembling, assented; but the[a] mistress's theory had little effect on the maid's practice, until she had sewed two pieces of red flannel, in the shape of a cross, on her inner garment.[108]

I found Miss Matty covering her penny ball – the ball that she used to roll under her bed – with gay-coloured worsted in rainbow stripes.

'My dear,' said she, 'my heart is sad for that little care-worn child. Although her father is a conjuror, she looks as if she had never had a good game of play in her life. I used to make very pretty balls in this way when I was a girl, and I thought I would try if I could not make this one smart and take it to Phœbe this afternoon. I think "the gang" must have left the neighbourhood, for one does not hear any more of their violence and robbery now.'

We were all of us far too full of the Signor's precarious state to talk about either robbers or ghosts. Indeed, Lady Glenmire said, she never had heard of any actual robberies; except that two little boys had stolen some apples from Farmer Benson's orchard, and that some eggs had been missed on a market-day off Widow Hayward's stall. But that was expecting too much of us; we could not acknowledge that we had only had this small foundation for all our panic. Miss Pole drew herself up at this remark of Lady Glenmire's; and said 'that she wished she could agree with her as to the very small reason we had had for alarm; but, with the recollection of a man disguised as a woman, who had endeavoured to force herself into her house, while his confederates waited outside; with the knowledge gained from Lady Glenmire herself, of the foot-prints seen on Mrs. Jamieson's flower-borders; with the fact before her of the audacious robbery committed on Mr. Hoggins at his own door –' But here Lady Glenmire broke in with a very strong expression of doubt as to whether this last story was not an entire fabrication, founded upon the theft of a cat; she grew so red while she was saying all this, that I was not surprised at Miss Pole's manner of bridling up, and I am certain if Lady Glenmire had not been 'her ladyship,' we should have had a more emphatic contradiction than the 'Well, to be sure!' and similar fragmentary ejaculations, which were all that she ventured upon in my lady's presence. But when she was gone, Miss Pole began a long congratulation to Miss Matty that, so far they had escaped marriage, which she noticed always made people credulous to the last degree; indeed, she thought it argued great natural credulity in a woman if she could not keep herself from being married; and in what Lady Glenmire had said about Mr. Hoggins's robbery, we had a specimen of what people came to, if they gave way to such a weakness; evidently, Lady Glenmire would swallow anything, if she could believe the poor vamped-up story about a neck of mutton and a pussy, with which he had tried to impose on Miss Pole, only she had always been on her guard against believing too much of what men said.

We were thankful, as Miss Pole desired us to be, that we had never been married; but I think, of the two, we were even more thankful that the robbers had left Cranford; at least I judge so from a speech of Miss Matty's that evening, as we sat over the fire, in which she evidently looked upon a husband as a great protector against thieves, burglars, and ghosts; and said, that she did not think that she should dare to be always warning young people of matrimony, as Miss Pole did continually; – to be sure, marriage was a risk, as she saw now she had had some experience; but she remembered the time when she had looked forward to being married as much as any one.

'Not to any particular person, my dear,' said she, hastily checking herself up as if she were afraid of having admitted too much; 'only the old story, you know, of ladies always saying "*When*[a] I marry," and gentlemen, "*If*[b] I marry."' It was a joke spoken in rather a sad tone, and I doubt if either of us smiled; but I could not see Miss Matty's face by the flickering fire-light. In a little while she continued:

'But after all I have not told you the truth. It is so long ago, and no one ever knew how much I thought of it at the time, unless, indeed, my dear mother guessed; but I may say that there was a time when I did not think I should have been only Miss Matty Jenkyns all my life; for even if I did meet with any one who wished to marry me now (and as Miss Pole says, one is never too safe), I could not take him – I hope he would not take it too much to heart, but I could *not* take him – or any one but the person I once thought I should be married to, and he is dead and gone, and he never knew how it all came about that I said "no," when I had thought many and many a time – Well, it's no matter what I thought. God ordains it all, and I am very happy, my dear. No one has such kind friends as I,' continued she, taking my hand and holding it in hers.

If I[c] had never known of Mr. Holbrook, I could have said something in this pause, but as I had, I could not think of anything that would come in naturally, and so we both kept silence for a little time.

'My father once made us,' she began, 'keep a diary in two columns; on one side we were to put down in the morning what we thought would be the course and events of the coming day, and at night we were to put down on the other side what really had happened. It would be to some people rather a sad way of telling their lives' – (a tear dropped upon my hand at these words) – 'I don't mean that mine has been sad, only so very different to what I expected. I remember, one winter's evening, sitting over our bed-room fire with Deborah – I remember it as if it were yesterday – and we were planning our future lives – both of us were planning, though only she talked about it. She said she should like to marry an archdeacon, and write his charges;[109] and you know, my dear, she never was married, and, for aught I know, she never spoke to an unmarried archdeacon in her life. I never was ambitious, nor could I have written charges, but I thought I could manage a house (my mother used to call me her right hand), and I was always so fond of little children – the shyest babies would stretch out their little arms to come to me; when I was a girl, I was half my leisure time nursing in the neighbouring cottages – but I don't know how it was, when I grew sad and grave – which I did a year or two after this time – the little things drew back from me, and I am afraid I lost the knack, though I am just as fond of children as ever, and have a strange yearning at my heart whenever I see a mother with her baby in her arms. Nay, my dear,' – (and by a sudden blaze which sprang up from a fall of the unstirred coals, I saw that her eyes were full of tears – gazing intently on some vision of what might have been) – 'do you know, I dream sometimes that I have a little child – always the same – a little girl of about two years old; she never grows older, though I have dreamt about her for many years. I don't think I ever dream of any words or sound she makes; she is very noiseless and still, but she comes to me when she is very sorry or very glad, and I have wakened with the clasp of her dear little arms round my neck. Only last night – perhaps because I had gone to sleep thinking of this ball for Phœbe – my little darling came in my dream, and put up her mouth to be kissed, just as I have seen real babies do to real mothers before going to bed. But all this is nonsense, dear! only don't be frightened by Miss Pole from being married. I can fancy it may be a very happy state, and a little credulity helps one on through life very smoothly, – better than always doubting and doubting, and seeing difficulties and disagreeable in everything.'

If I had been inclined to be daunted from matrimony, it would not have been Miss Pole to do it; it would have been the lot of poor Signor Brunoni and his wife. And yet again, it was an encouragement to see how, through all their cares and sorrows, they thought of each other and not of themselves; and how keen were their joys, if they only passed through each other, or through the little Phœbe.

The Signora[a] told me, one day, a good deal about their lives up to this period. It began by my asking her whether Miss Pole's story of the twin brothers was true; it sounded so wonderful a likeness, that I should have had my doubts, if Miss Pole had not been unmarried. But the Signora, or (as we found out she preferred to be called) Mrs. Brown, said it was quite true; that her brother-in-law was by many taken for her husband, which was of great assistance to them in their profession; 'though,' she continued, 'how people can mistake Thomas for the real Signor Brunoni, I can't conceive; but he says they do; so I suppose I must believe him. Not but what he is a very good man; I am sure I don't know how we should have paid our bill at the

Rising Sun, but for the money he sends; but people must know very little about art, if they can take him for my husband. Why, Miss, in the ball trick, where my husband spreads his fingers wide, and throws out his little finger with quite an air and a grace, Thomas just clumps up his hand like a fist, and might have ever so many balls hidden in it. Besides, he has never been in India, and knows nothing of the proper sit of a turban.'

'Have you been in India?' said I, rather astonished.

'Oh yes! many a year, ma'am. Sam was a serjeant in the 31st; and when the regiment was ordered to India, I drew a lot to go,[110] and I was more thankful than I can tell; for it seemed as if it would only be a slow death to me to part from my husband. But, indeed, ma'am, if I had known all, I don't know whether I would not rather have died there and then, than gone through what I have done since. To be sure, I've been able to comfort Sam, and to be with him; but, ma'am, I've lost six children,' said she, looking up at me with those strange eyes, that I have never noticed but in mothers of dead children – with a kind of wild look in them, as if seeking for what they never more might find. 'Yes! Six children died off, like little buds nipped untimely, in that cruel India. I thought, as each died, I never could – I never would – love a child again; and when the next came, it had not only its own love, but the deeper love that came from the thoughts of its little dead brothers and sisters. And when Phœbe was coming, I said to my husband, "Sam, when the child is born, and I am strong, I shall leave you; it will cut my heart cruel; but if this baby dies too, I shall go mad; the madness is in me now; but if you let me go down to Calcutta, carrying my baby step by step, it will may-be work itself off; and I will save, and I will hoard, and I will beg, – and I will die, to get a passage home to England, where our baby may live!" God bless him! he said I might go; and he saved up his pay, and I saved every pice[111] I could get for washing or any way; and when Phœbe came, and I grew strong again, I set off. It was very lonely; through the thick forests, dark again with their heavy trees – along by the rivers' side – (but I had been brought up near the Avon in Warwickshire, so that flowing noise sounded like home), from station to station, from Indian village to village, I went along, carrying my child. I had seen one of the officer's ladies with a little picture, ma'am – done by a Catholic foreigner, ma'am – of the Virgin and the little Saviour,[112] ma'am. She had him on her arm, and her form was softly curled round him, and their cheeks touched. Well, when I went to bid good-bye to this lady, for whom I had washed, she cried sadly; for she, too, had lost her children, but she had not another to save, like me; and I was bold enough to ask her, would she give me that print? And she cried the more, and said *her* children were with that little blessed Jesus; and gave it me, and told me she had heard it had been painted on the bottom of a cask, which made it have that round shape. And when my body was very weary, and my heart was sick – (for there were times when I misdoubted if I could ever reach my home, and there were times when I thought of my husband; and one time when I thought my baby was dying) –

I took out that picture and looked at it, till I could have thought the mother spoke to me, and comforted me. And the natives were very kind. We could not understand one another; but they saw my baby on my breast, and they came out to me, and brought me rice and milk, and sometimes flowers – I have got some of the flowers dried. Then, the next morning, I was so tired![a] and they wanted me to stay with them – I could tell that – and tried to frighten me from going into the deep woods, which, indeed, looked very strange and dark; but it seemed to me as if Death was following me to take my baby away from me; and as if I must go on, and on – and I thought how God had cared for mothers ever since the world was made, and would care for me; so I bade them good-bye, and set off afresh. And once when my baby was ill, and both she and I needed rest, He led me to a place where I found a kind Englishman lived, right in the midst of the natives.'

'And you reached Calcutta safely at last?'

'Yes! safely. Oh! when I knew I had only two days' journey more before me, I could not help it, ma'am – it might be idolatry, I cannot tell – but I was near one of the native temples, and I went in it with my baby to thank God for his great mercy; for it seemed to me that where others had prayed before to their God, in their joy or in their agony, was of itself a sacred place. And I got as servant to an invalid lady, who grew quite fond of my baby aboard-ship; and, in two years' time, Sam earned his discharge, and came home to me, and to our child. Then he had to fix on a trade; but he knew of none; and, once, once upon a time, he had learnt some tricks from an Indian jug-gler; so he set up conjuring, and it answered so well that he took Thomas to help him – as his man, you know, not as another conjuror, though Thomas has set it up now on his own hook. But it has been a great help to us that likeness between the twins, and made a good many tricks go off well that they made up together. And Thomas is a good brother, only he has not the fine carriage of my husband, so that I can't think how he can be taken for Signor Brunoni himself, as he says he is.'

'Poor little Phœbe!' said I, my thoughts going back to the baby she carried all those hundred miles.

'Ah! you may say so! I never thought I should have reared her, though, when she fell ill at Chunderabaddad;[113] but that good, kind Aga[114] Jenkyns took us in, which I believe was the very saving of her.'

'Jenkyns!' said I.

'Yes! Jenkyns. I shall think all people of that name are kind; for here is that nice old lady who comes every day to take Phœbe a walk!'

But an idea had flashed through my head: could[b] the Aga Jenkyns be the lost Peter? True, he was reported by many to be dead. But, equally true, some had said that he had arrived at the dignity of great Lama of Thibet. Miss Matty thought he was alive. I would make further inquiry.

CHAPTER XII.[a]

—————•—————

ENGAGED TO BE MARRIED![b]

WAS the 'poor Peter' of Cranford the Aga Jenkyns of Chunderabaddad, or was he not? As somebody says, that was the question.[115]

In my own home, whenever people had nothing else to do, they blamed me for want of discretion. Indiscretion was my bugbear fault. Everybody has a bugbear fault; a sort of standing characteristic – a *pièce de résistance* for their friends to cut at; and in general they cut and come again. I was tired of being called indiscreet and incautious; and I determined for once to prove myself a model of prudence and wisdom. I would not even hint my suspicions respecting the Aga. I would collect evidence and carry it home to lay before my father, as the family friend of the two Miss Jenkynses.

In my[c] search after facts, I was often reminded of a description my father had once given of a Ladies' Committee that he had had to preside over. He said he could not help thinking of a passage in Dickens,[d] which spoke of a chorus in which every man took the tune he knew best, and sang it to his own satisfaction.[116] So, at[e] this charitable committee, every lady took the subject uppermost in her mind, and talked about it to her own great contentment, but not much to the advancement of the subject they had met to discuss. But even that committee could have been nothing to the Cranford ladies when I attempted to gain some clear and definite information as to poor Peter's height, appearance, and when and where he was seen and heard of last. For instance, I remember asking Miss Pole (and I thought the question was very opportune, for I put it when I met her at a call at Mrs. Forrester's, and both the ladies had known Peter, and I imagined that they might refresh each other's memories); I asked Miss Pole what was the very last thing they had ever heard about him; and then she named the absurd report to which I have alluded, about his having been elected great Lama of Thibet; and this was a signal for each lady to go off on her separate idea. Mrs. Forrester's start was made on the Veiled Prophet in Lalla Rookh –[117f] whether I thought he was meant for the Great Lama, though Peter was not so ugly, indeed rather handsome if he had not been freckled. I was thankful to see her double upon Peter; but, in a moment, the delusive lady was off upon Rowland's Kalydor,[118] and the merits of cosmetics and hair oils in general, and holding forth so fluently that I turned to listen to Miss Pole, who (through the llamas, the beasts of burden) had got to Peruvian bonds,[119] and the Share Market, and her poor opinion of joint-stock banks in general, and of that one in particular in which Miss Matty's money was invested. In vain I put in, 'When was it – in what year was it, that you heard that Mr. Peter was the Great Lama?' They only joined issue to dispute whether llamas were carnivorous animals or not; in which dispute they were not quite on fair grounds, as Mrs. Forrester (after they had grown warm and cool again) acknowledged that she always confused carnivorous and graminivorous together, just as she did horizontal and perpendicular; but then she apologised for it very prettily, by saying that in her day the only use people made of four-syllabled words was to teach how they should be spelt.

The only[a] fact I gained from this conversation was that certainly Peter had last been heard of in India, 'or that neighbourhood;' and that this scanty intelligence of his whereabouts had reached Cranford in the year when Miss Pole had bought her India muslin gown, long since worn out (we washed it and mended it, and traced its decline and fall into a window-blind, before we could go on); and in a year when Wombwell[120] came to Cranford, because Miss Matty had wanted to see an elephant in order that she might the better imagine Peter riding on one; and had seen a boa-constrictor too, which was more than she wished to imagine in her fancy pictures of Peter's locality; – and in a year when Miss Jenkyns had learnt some piece of poetry off by heart, and used to say, at all the Cranford parties, how Peter was 'surveying mankind from China to Peru,'[121b] which everybody had thought very grand, and rather appropriate, because India was between China and Peru, if you took care to turn the globe to the left instead of the right.

I suppose all these inquiries of mine, and the consequent curiosity excited in the minds of my friends, made us blind and deaf to what was going on around us. It seemed to me as if the sun rose and shone, and as if the rain rained on Cranford just as usual, and I did not notice any sign of the times that could be considered as a prognostic of any uncommon event; and, to the best of my belief, not only Miss Matty and Mrs. Forrester, but even Miss Pole herself, whom we looked upon as a kind of prophetess from the knack she had of foreseeing things before they came to pass – although she did not like to disturb her friends by telling them her fore-knowledge – even Miss Pole herself was breathless with astonishment, when she came to tell us of the astounding piece of news. But I must recover myself; the contemplation of it, even at this distance of time, has taken away my breath and my grammar, and unless I subdue my emotion, my spelling will go too.

We were sitting – Miss Matty and I much as usual; she in the blue chintz easy chair, with her back to the light, and her knitting in her hand – I reading aloud the St. James's Chronicle.[122] A few[c] minutes more, and we should have gone to make the little alterations in dress usual before calling time (twelve o'clock) in Cranford. I remember the scene and the date well. We had been talking of the Signor's rapid recovery since the warmer weather had set in, and praising Mr. Hoggins's skill, and lamenting his want of refinement and manner – (it seems a curious coincidence that this should have been our subject, but so it was) – when a knock was heard; a caller's knock – three distinct taps – and we were flying (that is to say, Miss Matty could not walk very fast, having had a touch of rheumatism) to our rooms, to change cap and collars, when Miss Pole arrested us by calling out as she came up the stairs, 'Don't go – I can't wait – it is not twelve, I know – but never mind your dress – I must speak to you.' We did our best to look as if it was not we who had made the hurried movement, the sound of which she had heard; for, of course, we did not like to have it supposed that we had any old clothes that it was convenient to wear out in the 'sanctuary of home,' as Miss Jenkyns once prettily called the back parlour, where she was tying up preserves. So we threw our gentility with double force into our manners, and very genteel we were for two minutes while Miss Pole recovered breath, and excited our curiosity strongly by lifting up her hands in amazement, and bringing them down in silence, as if what she had to say was too big for words, and could only be expressed by pantomime.

'What do you think, Miss Matty? What *do* you think? Lady Glenmire is to marry – is to be married, I mean – Lady Glenmire – Mr. Hoggins – Mr. Hoggins is going to marry Lady Glenmire!'[a]

'Marry!' said we. 'Marry! Madness!'

'Marry!' said Miss Pole, with the decision that belonged to her character. 'I said Marry! as you do; and I also said, 'What a fool my lady is going to make of herself!' I could have said 'Madness!' but I controlled myself, for it was in a public shop that I heard of it. Where feminine delicacy is gone to, I don't know! You and I, Miss Matty, would have been ashamed to have known that our marriage was spoken of in a grocer's shop, in the hearing of shopmen!'

'But,' said Miss Matty, sighing as one recovering from a blow, 'perhaps it is not true. Perhaps we are doing her injustice.'

'No!' said Miss Pole. 'I have taken care to ascertain that. I went straight to Mrs. Fitz Adam, to borrow a cookery book which I knew she had; and I introduced my congratulations *apropos* of the difficulty gentlemen must have in house-keeping; and Mrs. Fitz Adam bridled up, and said, that she believed it was true, though how and where I could have heard it she did not know. She said her brother and Lady Glenmire had come to an understanding at last. 'Understanding!' such a coarse word! But my lady will have to come down to many a want of refinement. I have reason to believe Mr. Hoggins sups on bread-and-cheese and beer every night.'

'Marry!' said Miss Matty once again. 'Well! I never thought of it. Two people that we know going to be married. It's coming very near!'

'So near that my heart stopped beating, when I heard of it, while you might have counted twelve,' said Miss Pole.

'One does not know whose turn may come next. Here, in Cranford, poor Lady Glenmire might have thought herself safe,' said Miss Matty, with a gentle pity in her tones.

'Bah!' said Miss Pole, with a toss of her head. 'Don't you remember poor dear Captain Brown's song "Tibbie Fowler,"[123a] and the line –

> "Set her on the Tintock[b] Tap,
> The wind will blaw a man 'till her."'

'That was because "Tibbie Fowler"[c] was rich I think.'

'Well! there is a kind of attraction about Lady Glenmire that I, for one, should be ashamed to have.'

I put in my wonder. 'But how can she have fancied Mr. Hoggins? I am not surprised that Mr. Hoggins has liked her.'

'Oh! I don't know. Mr. Hoggins is rich, and very pleasant-looking,'[d] said Miss Matty, 'and very good-tempered and kind-hearted.'

'She has married for an establishment, that's it. I suppose she takes the surgery with it,' said Miss Pole, with a little dry laugh at her own joke. But, like many people who think they have made a severe and sarcastic speech, which yet is clever of its kind, she began to relax in her grimness from the moment when she made this allusion to the surgery; and we turned to speculate on the way in which Mrs. Jamieson would receive the news. The person whom she had left in charge of her house to keep off followers from her maids, to set up a follower of her own! And that follower a man whom Mrs. Jamieson had tabooed as vulgar, and inadmissible to Cranford society; not merely on account of his name, but because of his voice, his complexion, his boots, smelling of the stable, and himself, smelling of drugs. Had he ever been to see Lady Glenmire at Mrs. Jamieson's? Chloride of lime would not purify the house in its owner's estimation if he had. Or had their interviews been confined to the occasional meetings in the chamber of the poor sick conjuror, to whom, with all our sense of the *mésalliance* we could not help allowing that they had both been exceedingly kind? And now it turned out that a servant of Mrs. Jamieson's had been ill, and Mr. Hoggins had been attending her for some weeks. So the wolf had got into the fold, and now he was carrying off the shepherdess. What would Mrs. Jamieson say? We looked into the darkness of futurity as a child gazes after a rocket up in the cloudy sky, full of wondering expectation of the rattle, the discharge, and the brilliant shower of sparks and light. Then we brought ourselves down to earth and the present time, by questioning each other (being all equally ignorant, and all equally without the slightest data to build any conclusions upon) as to when IT would take place? Where? How much a year Mr. Hoggins had? Whether she would drop her title? And how Martha and the other correct servants in Cranford would ever be brought to announce a married couple as Lady Glenmire and Mr. Hoggins? But would they be visited?

Would Mrs. Jamieson let us? Or must we choose between the Honourable Mrs. Jamieson and the degraded Lady Glenmire. We all liked Lady Glenmire the best. She was bright, and kind, and sociable, and agreeable; and Mrs. Jamieson was dull, and inert, and pompous, and tiresome. But we had acknowledged the sway of the latter so long, that it seemed like a kind of disloyalty now even to meditate disobedience to the prohibition we anticipated.

Mrs. Forrester surprised us in our darned caps and patched collars; and we forgot all about them in our eagerness to see how she would bear the information, which we honourably left to Miss Pole to impart, although, if we had been inclined to take unfair advantage, we might have rushed in ourselves, for she had a most out-of-place fit of coughing for five minutes after Mrs. Forrester entered the room. I shall never forget the imploring expression of her eyes, as she looked at us over her pocket-handkerchief. They said, as plain as words could speak, 'Don't let Nature deprive me of the treasure which is mine, although for a time I can make no use of it.' And we did not.

Mrs. Forrester's[a] surprise was equal to ours; and her sense of injury rather greater, because she had to feel for her Order, and saw more fully than we could do how such conduct brought stains on the aristocracy.

When she[b] and Miss Pole left us, we endeavoured to subside into calmness; but Miss Matty was really upset by the intelligence she had heard. She reckoned it up, and it was more than fifteen years since she had heard of any of her acquaintance going to be married, with the one exception of Miss Jessie Brown; and, as she said, it gave her quite a shock, and made her feel as if she could not think what would happen next.

I don't[c] know if it is a fancy of mine, or a real fact, but I have noticed that, just after the announcement of an engagement in any set, the unmarried ladies in that set flutter out in an unusual gaiety and newness of dress, as much as to say, in a tacit and unconscious manner, 'We also are spinsters.' Miss Matty and Miss Pole talked and thought more about bonnets, gowns, caps, and shawls, during the fortnight that succeeded this call, than I had known them do for years before. But it might be the spring weather, for it was a warm and pleasant March; and merinoes and beavers, and woollen materials of all sorts, were but ungracious receptacles of the bright sun's glancing rays. It had not been Lady Glenmire's dress that had won Mr. Hoggins's heart, for she went about on her errands of kindness more shabby than ever. Although in the hurried glimpses I caught of her at church or elsewhere, she appeared rather to shun meeting any of her friends, her face seemed to have almost something of the flush of youth in it; her lips looked redder, and more trembling full than in their old compressed state, and her eyes dwelt on all things with a lingering light, as if she was learning to love Cranford and its belongings. Mr. Hoggins looked broad and radiant, and creaked up the middle aisle at church in a bran-new pair of top-boots – an audible, as well as visible, sign of his purposed change of state; for the tradition went, that the boots he had worn till now were the identical pair in which he first set out on his rounds in Cranford twenty-five years ago; only they had been new-pieced,[124] high and low, top and bottom, heel and sole, black leather and brown leather, more times than any one could tell.

None of the ladies in Cranford chose to sanction the marriage by congratulating either of the parties. We wished to ignore the whole affair until our liege lady, Mrs. Jamieson, returned. Till[a] she came back to give us our cue, we felt that it would be better to consider the engagement in the same light as the Queen of Spain's legs –[125] facts which certainly existed, but the less said about the better. This restraint upon our tongues – for you see if we did not speak about it to any of the parties concerned, how could we get answers to the questions that we longed to ask? – was beginning to be irksome, and our idea of the dignity of silence was paling before our curiosity, when another direction was given to our thoughts, by an announcement on the part of the principal shopkeeper of Cranford, who ranged the trades from grocer and cheesemonger to man-milliner, as occasion required, that the Spring Fashions were arrived, and would be exhibited on the following Tuesday, at his rooms in High Street. Now Miss Matty had been only waiting for this before buying herself a new silk gown. I had offered, it is true, to send to Drumble for patterns, but she had rejected my proposal, gently implying that she had not forgotten her disappointment about the seagreen turban. I was thankful that I was on the spot now, to counteract the dazzling fascination of any yellow or scarlet silk.

I must[b] say a word or two here[c] about myself. I have spoken of my father's old friendship for the Jenkyns[d] family; indeed, I am not sure if there was not some distant relationship. He had willingly allowed me to remain all the winter at Cranford, in consideration of a letter which Miss Matty had written to him, about the time of the panic, in which I suspect she had exaggerated my powers and my bravery as a defender of the house. But now that the days were longer and more cheerful, he was beginning to urge the necessity of my return; and I only delayed in a sort of odd forlorn hope that if I could obtain any clear information, I might make the account given by the Signora of the Aga Jenkyns tally with that of 'poor Peter,'[e] his appearance and disappearance, which I had winnowed out of the conversation of Miss Pole and Mrs. Forrester.

CHAPTER XIII.

STOPPED PAYMENT.[a]

THE very Tuesday morning on which Mr. Johnson was going to show fashions, the post-woman brought two letters to the house. I say the post-woman, but I should say the postman's wife. He was a lame shoemaker, a very clean, honest man, much respected in the town; but he never brought the letters round except on unusual occasions, such as Christmas Day, or Good Friday; and on those days the letters, which should have been delivered at eight in the morning, did not make their appearance until two or three in the afternoon; for every one liked poor Thomas, and gave him a welcome on these festive occasions. He used to say, 'he was welly stawed[126] wi' eating, for there were three or four houses where nowt would serve 'em but he must share in their breakfast;' and by the time he had done his last breakfast, he came to some other friend who was beginning dinner; but come what might in the way of temptation, Tom was always sober, civil, and smiling; and, as Miss Jenkyns used to say, it was a lesson in patience, that she doubted not would call out that precious quality in some minds, where, but for Thomas, it might have lain dormant and undiscovered. Patience was certainly very dormant in Miss Jenkyns's mind. She was always expecting letters, and always drumming on the table till the post-woman had called or gone past. On Christmas Day and Good Friday, she drummed from breakfast till church, from church-time till two o'clock – unless when the fire wanted stirring, when she invariably knocked down the fire-irons, and scolded Miss Matty for it. But equally certain was the hearty welcome and the good dinner for Thomas; Miss Jenkyns standing over him like a bold dragoon, questioning him as to his children – what they were doing – what school they went to; upbraiding him if another was likely to make its appearance, but sending even the little babies the shilling and the mince-pie which was her gift to all the children, with half-a-crown in addition for both father and mother. The Post was not half of so much consequence to dear Miss Matty; but not for the world would she have diminished Thomas's welcome, and his dole, though I could see that she felt rather shy over the ceremony, which had been regarded by Miss Jenkyns as a glorious opportunity for giving advice and benefiting her fellow-creatures. Miss Matty would steal the money all in a lump into his hand, as if she were ashamed of herself. Miss Jenkyns gave him each individual coin separate, with a 'There! that's for yourself; that's for Jenny,' &c. Miss Matty would even beckon Martha out of the kitchen while he ate his food: and once, to my knowledge, winked at its rapid disappearance into a blue cotton pocket-handkerchief. Miss Jenkyns almost scolded him if he did not leave a clean plate, however heaped it might have been, and gave an injunction with every mouthful.

I have wandered a long way from the two letters that awaited us on the breakfast-table that Tuesday morning. Mine was from my father. Miss Matty's was printed. My father's was just a man's letter; I mean it was very dull, and gave no information beyond that he was well, that they had had a good deal of rain, that trade was very stagnant, and there were many disagreeable rumours afloat. He then asked me, if I knew whether Miss Matty still retained her shares in the Town and County Bank, as there were very unpleasant reports about it; though nothing more than he had always foreseen, and had prophesied to Miss Jenkyns years ago, when she would invest their little property in it – the only unwise step that clever woman had ever taken, to his knowledge – (the only time she ever acted against his advice, I knew). However, if anything had gone wrong, of course I was not to think of leaving Miss Matty while I could be of any use, &c.

'Who is your letter from, my dear? Mine is a very civil invitation, signed Edwin Wilson, asking me to attend an important meeting of the shareholders of the Town and County Bank, to be held in Drumble, on Thursday the twenty-first. I am sure, it is very attentive of them to remember me.'

I did not like to hear of this 'important meeting,' for though I did not know much about business, I feared it confirmed what my father said: however, I thought, ill news always came fast enough, so I resolved to say nothing about my alarm, and merely told her that my father was well, and sent his kind regards to her. She kept turning over, and admiring her letter. At last she spoke:[a]

'I remember their sending one to Deborah just like this; but that I did not wonder at, for everybody knew she was so clear-headed. I am afraid I could not help them much; indeed, if they came to accounts, I should be quite in the way, for I never could do sums in my head. Deborah, I know, rather wished to go, and went so far as to order a new bonnet for the occasion; but when the time came, she had a bad cold; so they sent her a very polite account of what they had done. Chosen a Director, I think it was. Do you think they want me to help them to choose a Director? I am sure, I should choose your father at once.

'My father has no shares in the Bank,' said I.

'Oh, no! I remember! He objected very much to Deborah's buying any, I believe. But she was quite the woman of business, and always judged for herself; and here, you see, they have paid eight per cent all these years.'

It was a very uncomfortable subject to me, with my half knowledge; so I thought I would change the conversation, and I asked at what time she thought we had better go and see the Fashions. 'Well, my dear,' she said, 'the thing is this; it is not etiquette to go till after twelve, but then, you see, all Cranford will be there, and one does not like to be too curious about dress and trimmings and caps, with all the world looking on. It is never genteel to be over-curious on these occasions. Deborah had the knack of always looking as if the latest fashion was nothing new to her; a manner she had caught from Lady Arley who did see all the new modes in London, you know. So I thought we would just slip down this morning, soon after breakfast; for I do want half a pound of tea; and then we could go up and examine the things at our leisure, and see exactly how my new silk gown must be made; and then, after twelve, we could go with our minds disengaged, and free from thoughts of dress.'

We began to talk of Miss Matty's new silk gown. I discovered that it would be really the first time in her life that she had had to choose anything of consequence for herself; for Miss Jenkyns had always been the more decided character, whatever her taste might have been; and it is astonishing how such people carry the world before them by the mere force of will. Miss Matty anticipated the sight of the glossy folds with as much delight as if the five sovereigns, set apart for the purchase, could buy all the silks in the shop; and (remembering my own loss of two hours in a toy-shop before I could tell on what wonder to spend a silver threepence) I was very glad that we were going early, that dear Miss Matty might have leisure for the delights of perplexity.

If a happy sea-green could be met with, the gown was to be sea-green: if not, she inclined to maize, and I to silver grey; and we discussed the requisite number of breadths until we arrived at the shop-door. We were to buy the tea, select the silk, and then clamber up the iron corkscrew stairs that led into what was once a loft, though now a Fashion show-room.

The young men at Mr. Johnson's had on their best looks, and their best cravats, and pivotted themselves over the counter with surprising activity. They wanted to show us upstairs at once; but on the principle of business first and pleasure afterwards, we stayed to purchase the tea. Here Miss Matty's absence of mind betrayed itself. If she was made aware that she had been drinking green tea[127] at any time, she always thought it her duty to lie awake half through the night afterward – (I have known her take it in ignorance many a time without such effects) – and consequently green tea was prohibited the house; yet to-day she herself asked for the obnoxious article, under the impression that she was talking about the silk. However, the mistake was soon rectified; and then the silks were unrolled in good truth. By this time the shop was pretty well filled, for it was Cranford market-day, and many of the farmers and country people from the neighbourhood round came in, sleeking down their hair, and glancing shyly about from under their eyelids, as anxious to take back some notion of the unusual gaiety to the mistress or the lasses at home, and yet feeling that they were out of place among the smart shopmen and gay shawls, and summer prints. One honest-looking man, however, made his way up to the counter at which we stood, and boldly asked to look at a shawl or two. The other country folk confined themselves to the grocery side; but our neighbour was evidently too full of some kind intention towards mistress, wife, or daughter, to be shy; and it soon became a question with me, whether he or Miss Matty would keep their shopman the longest time. He thought each shawl more beautiful than the last; and, as for Miss Matty, she smiled and sighed over each fresh bale that was brought out; one colour set off another, and the heap together would, as she said, make even the rainbow look poor.

'I am afraid,' said she, hesitating, 'whichever[a] I choose I shall wish I had taken another. Look at this lovely crimson! it would be so warm in winter. But spring is coming on, you know, I wish I could have a gown for every season,' said she, dropping her voice – as we all did in Cranford whenever we talked of anything we wished for but could not afford. 'However,' she continued in a louder and more cheerful tone, 'it would give me a great deal of trouble to take care of them if I had them; so, I think, I'll only take one. But which must it be, my dear?'

And[b] now she hovered over a lilac with yellow spots, while I pulled out a quiet sage-green, that had faded into insignificance under the more brilliant colours, but which was nevertheless a good silk in its humble way. Our attention was called off to our neighbour. He had chosen a shawl of about thirty shillings' value; and his face looked broadly happy, under the anticipation, no doubt, of the pleasant surprise he should give to some Molly or Jenny at home; he had tugged a leathern purse out of his breeches pocket, and had offered a five-pound note in payment for the shawl, and for some parcels which had been brought round to him from the grocery counter; and it was just at this point that he attracted our notice. The shopman was examining the note with a puzzled, doubtful air:

'Town and County Bank! I am not sure, sir, but I believe we have received a warning against notes issued by this bank only this morning. I will just step and ask Mr. Johnson, sir; but I'm afraid, I must trouble you for payment in cash, or in a note of a different bank.'

I never saw a man's countenance fall so suddenly into dismay and bewilderment. It was almost piteous to see the rapid change.

'Dang it!' said he, striking his fist down on the table, as if to try which was the harder; 'the chap talks as if notes and gold were to be had for the picking up.'

Miss Matty had forgotten her silk gown in her interest for the man. I don't think she had caught the name of the bank, and in my nervous cowardice, I was anxious that she should not; and so I began admiring the yellow-spotted lilac gown that I had been utterly condemning only a minute before. But it was of no use.

'What bank was it? I mean what bank did your note belong to?'

'Town and County Bank.'

'Let me see it,' said she quietly to the shopman, gently taking it out of his hand, as he brought it back to return it to the farmer.

Mr. Johnson was very sorry, but, from information he had received, the notes issued by that bank were little better than waste paper.

'I don't understand it,' said Miss Matty to me. in a low voice. 'That is our bank, is it not? – the Town and County Bank?'

'Yes,' said I. 'This lilac silk will just match the ribbons in your new cap, I believe,' I continued – holding up the folds so as to catch the light, and wishing that the man would make haste and be gone – and yet having a new wonder, that had only just sprung up, how far it was wise or right in me to allow Miss Matty to make this expensive purchase, if the affairs of the bank were really so bad as the refusal of the note implied.

But Miss Matty put on the soft dignified manner peculiar to her, rarely used, and yet which became her so well, and laying her hand gently on mine, she said,

'Never mind the silks for a few minutes, dear. I don't understand you, sir,' turning now to the shopman, who had been attending to the farmer. 'Is this a forged note?'

'Oh, no, ma'am. It is a true note of its kind; but you see, ma'am, it is a Joint Stock Bank,[128] and there are reports out that it is likely to break. Mr. Johnson is only doing his duty, ma'am, as I am sure Mr. Dobson knows.'

But Mr. Dobson could not respond to the appealing bow by any answering smile. He was turning the note absently over in his fingers, looking gloomily enough at the parcel containing the lately chosen shawl.

'It's hard upon a poor man,' said he, 'as earns every farthing with the sweat of his brow. However, there's no help for it. You must take back your shawl, my man; Lizzie must do on[129] with her cloak for a while. And yon figs for the little ones – I promised them to 'em – I'll take them; but the 'bacco, and the other things –'

'I will give you five sovereigns for your note, my good man' said Miss Matty. 'I think there is some great mistake about it, for I am one of the shareholders, and I'm sure they would have told me if things had not been going on right.'

The shopman whispered a word or two across the table to Miss Matty. She looked at him with a dubious air.

'Perhaps so,' said she. 'But I don't pretend to understand business; I only know, that if it is going to fail, and if honest people are to lose their money because they have taken our notes – I can't explain myself,' said she, suddenly becoming aware that she had got into a long sentence with four people for audience – 'only I would rather exchange my gold for the note, if you please,' turning to the farmer, 'and then you can take your wife the shawl. It is only going without my gown a few days longer,' she continued, speaking to me. 'Then, I have no doubt, everything will be cleared up.'

'But if it is cleared up the wrong way?' said I.

'Why! then it will only have been common honesty in me, as a shareholder, to have given this good man the money. I am quite clear about it in my own mind; but, you know, I can never speak quite as comprehensibly as others can; – only you must give me your note, Mr. Dobson, if you please, and go on with your purchases with these sovereigns.'

The man looked at her with silent gratitude – too awkward to put his thanks into words; but he hung back for a minute or two, fumbling with his note.

'I'm loth to make another one lose instead of me, if it is a loss; but, you see, five pounds is a deal of money to a man with a family; and, as you say, ten to one in a day or two, the note will be as good as gold again.'

'No hope of that, my friend,' said the shopman.

'The more reason why I should take it,' said Miss Matty quietly. She pushed her sovereigns towards the man, who slowly laid his note down in exchange. 'Thank you. I will wait a day or two before I purchase any of these silks; perhaps you will then have a greater choice. My dear! will you come upstairs?'

We inspected the Fashions with as minute and curious an interest as if the gown to be made after them had been bought. I could not see that the little event in the shop below had in the least damped Miss Matty's curiosity as to the make of sleeves, or the sit of skirts. She once or twice exchanged congratulations with me on our private and leisurely view of the bonnets and shawls; but I was, all the time, not so sure that our examination was so utterly private, for I caught glimpses of a figure dodging behind the cloaks and mantles; and, by a dextrous move, I came face to face with Miss Pole, also in morning costume (the principal feature of which was her being without teeth,[130] and wearing a veil to conceal the deficiency), come on the same errand as ourselves. But she quickly took her departure, because, as she said, she had[a] a bad headache and did not feel herself up to conversation.

As we came down through the shop, the civil Mr. Johnson was awaiting us; he had been informed of the exchange of the note for gold, and with much good feeling and real kindness, but with a little want of tact, he wished to condole with Miss Matty, and impress upon her the true state of the case. I could only hope that he had heard an exaggerated rumour, for he said that her shares were worse than nothing, and that the bank could not pay a shilling in the pound. I was glad that Miss Matty seemed still a little incredulous; but I could not tell how much of this was real or assumed, with that self-control which seemed habitual to ladies of Miss Matty's standing in Cranford, who would have thought their dignity compromised by the slightest expression of surprise, dismay, or any similar feeling to an inferior in station, or in a public shop. However, we walked home very silently. I am ashamed to say, I believe I was rather vexed and annoyed at Miss Matty's conduct, in taking the note to herself so decidedly. I had so set my heart upon her having a new silk gown, which she wanted sadly; in general she was so undecided anybody might turn her round; in this case I had felt that it was no use attempting it, but I was not the less put out at the result.

Somehow, after twelve o'clock, we both acknowledged to a sated curiosity about the Fashions; and to a certain fatigue of body (which was, in fact, depression of mind) that indisposed us to go out again. But still we never spoke of the note; till, all at once, something possessed me to ask Miss Matty, if she would think it her duty to offer sovereigns for all the notes of the Town and County Bank she met with? I could have bitten my tongue out the minute I had said it. She looked up rather sadly, and as if I had thrown a new perplexity into her already distressed mind; and for a minute or two, she did not speak. Then she said – my own dear Miss Matty – without a shade of reproach in her voice:

'My dear! I never feel as if my mind was what people call very strong; and it's often hard enough work for me to settle what I ought to do with the case right before me. I was very thankful to – I was very thankful, that I saw my duty this morning, with the poor man standing by me; but it's rather a strain upon me to keep thinking and thinking what I should do if such and such a thing happened; and, I believe, I had rather wait and see what really does come; and I don't doubt I shall be helped then, if I don't fidget myself, and get too anxious beforehand. You know, love, I'm not like Deborah. If Deborah had lived, I've no doubt she would have seen after them, before they had got themselves into this state.'

We had neither of us much appetite for dinner, though we tried to talk cheerfully about indifferent things. When we returned into the drawing-room, Miss Matty unlocked her desk and began to look over her account-books. I was so penitent for what I had said in the morning, that I did not choose to take upon myself the presumption to suppose that I could assist her; I rather left her alone, as, with puzzled brow, her eye followed her pen up and down the ruled page. By-and-by she shut the book, locked her desk, and came and drew a chair to mine, where I sat in moody sorrow over the fire. I stole my hand into hers; she clasped it, but did not speak a word. At last she said, with forced composure in her voice, 'If that bank goes wrong, I shall lose one hundred and forty-nine pounds thirteen shillings and four-pence a year; I shall only have thirteen pounds a year left.' I squeezed her hand hard and tight. I did not know what to say. Presently (it was too dark to see her face) I felt her fingers work convulsively in my grasp; and I knew she was going to speak again. I heard the sobs in her voice as she said, 'I hope it's not wrong – not wicked – but oh! I am so glad poor Deborah is spared this.

She could not have borne to come down in the world, – she had such a noble, lofty spirit.'

This was all she said about the sister who had insisted upon investing their little property in that unlucky bank. We were later in lighting the candle than usual that night, and until that light shamed us into speaking, we sat together very silently and sadly.

However, we took to our work after tea with a kind of forced cheerfulness (which soon became real as far as it went), talking of that never-ending wonder, Lady Glenmire's engagement. Miss Matty was almost coming round to think it a good thing.

'I don't mean to deny that men are trouble-some in a house. I don't judge from my own experience, for my father was neatness itself, and wiped his shoes on coming in as carefully as any woman; but still a man has a sort of knowledge of what should be done in difficulties, that it is very pleasant to have one at hand ready to lean upon. Now, Lady Glenmire, instead of being tossed about, and wondering where she is to settle, will be certain of a home among pleasant and kind people, such as our good Miss Pole and Mrs. Forrester. And Mr. Hoggins is really a very personable man; and as for his manners – why, if they are not very polished, I have known people with very good hearts and very clever minds too, who were not what some people reckoned refined, but who were both true and tender.'

She fell off into a soft reverie about Mr. Holbrook, and I did not interrupt her, I was so busy maturing a plan I had had in my mind for some days, but which this threatened failure of the bank had brought to a crisis. That night, after Miss Matty went to bed, I treacherously lighted the candle again, and sat down in the drawing-room to compose a letter to the Aga Jenkyns – a letter which should affect him, if he were Peter, and yet seem a mere statement of dry facts if he were a stranger. The church clock pealed out two before I had done.

The next morning news came, both official and otherwise, that the Town and County Bank had stopped payment. Miss Matty was ruined.

She tried to speak quietly to me; but when she came to the actual fact, that she would have but about five shillings a week to live upon, she could not restrain a few tears.

'I am not crying for myself, dear,' said she, wiping them away; 'I believe I am crying for the very silly thought, of how my mother would grieve if she could know – she always cared for us so much more than for herself. But many a poor person has less; and I am not very extravagant, and, thank God, when the neck of mutton, and Martha's wages, and the rent, are paid, I have not a farthing owing. Poor Martha! I think she'll be sorry to leave me.'

Miss Matty[a] smiled at me through her tears, and she would fain have had me see only the smile, not the tears.

CHAPTER XIV.[a]

FRIENDS IN NEED.[b]

IT was an example to me, and I fancy it might be to many others, to see how immediately Miss Matty set about the retrenchment which she knew to be right under her altered circumstances. While she went down to speak to Martha, and break the intelligence to her, I stole out with my letter to the Aga Jenkyns, and went to the Signor's lodgings to obtain the exact address. I bound the Signora to secresy; and indeed, her military manners had a degree of shortness and reserve in them, which made her always say as little as possible, except when under the pressure of strong excitement. Moreover – (which made my secret doubly sure) – the Signor was now so far recovered as to be looking forward to travelling and conjuring again, in the space of a few days, when he, his wife, and little Phœbe, would leave Cranford. Indeed I found him looking over a great black and red placard, in which the Signor Brunoni's accomplishments were set forth, and to which only the name of the town where he would next display them was wanting. He and his wife were so much absorbed in deciding where the red letters would come in with most effect (it might have been the Rubric[131] for that matter), that it was some time before I could get my question asked privately, and not before I had given several decisions, the wisdom of which I questioned afterwards with equal sincerity as soon as the Signor threw in his doubts and reasons on the important subject. At last I got the address, spelt by sound; and very queer it looked! I dropped it in the post on my way home; and then for a minute I stood looking at the wooden pane, with a gaping slit, which divided me from the letter, but a moment ago in my hand. It was gone from me like life – never to be recalled. It would get tossed about on the sea, and stained with sea-waves perhaps; and be carried among palm-trees, and scented with all tropical fragrance; – the little piece of paper, but an hour ago so familiar and commonplace, had set out on its race to the strange wild countries beyond the Ganges! But I could not afford to lose much time on this speculation. I hastened home, that Miss Matty might not miss me. Martha opened the door to me, her face swollen with crying. As soon as she saw me, she burst out afresh, and taking hold of my arm she pulled me in, and banged the door to, in order to ask me if indeed it was all true that Miss Matty had been saying.

'I'll never leave her! No! I won't. I telled her so, and said I could not think how she could find in her heart to give me warning. I could not have had the face to do it, if I'd been her. I might ha' been just as good-for-nothing as Mrs. Fitz-Adam's Rosy,[a] who struck for wages after living seven years and a half in one place. I said I was not one to go and serve Mammon at that rate; that I knew when I'd got a good Missus, if she didn't know when she'd got a good servant –'

'But Martha;' said I, cutting in while she wiped her eyes.

'Don't "but Martha" me,' she replied to my deprecatory tone.

'Listen to reason –'

'I'll not listen to reason,' she said – now in full possession of her voice, which had been rather choked with sobbing. 'Reason always means what some one else has got to say. Now I think what I've got to say is good enough reason. But, reason or not, I'll say it, and I'll stick to it. I've money in the Savings' Bank,[132] and I've a good stock of clothes, and I'm not going to leave Miss Matty. No! not if she gives me warning every hour in the day!'

She put her arms akimbo, as much as to say she defied me; and, indeed, I could hardly tell how to begin to remonstrate with her, so much did I feel that Miss Matty in her increasing infirmity needed the attendance of this kind and faithful woman.

'Well!' said I at last –

'I'm thankful you begin with "well!" If you'd ha' begun with "but," as you did afore, I'd not ha' listened to you. Now you may go on.'

'I know you would be a great loss to Miss Matty, Martha –'

'I telled her so. A loss she'd never cease to be sorry for,' broke in Martha, triumphantly.

'Still she will have so little – so very little – to live upon, that I don't see just now how she could find you food – she will even be pressed for her own. I tell you this, Martha, because I feel you are like a friend to dear Miss Matty – but you know she might not like to have it spoken about.'

Apparently this was even a blacker view of the subject than Miss Matty had presented to her; for Martha just sat down on the first chair that came to hand, and cried out loud – (we had been standing in the kitchen).

At last she put her apron down, and looking me earnestly in the face, asked, 'Was that the reason Miss Matty wouldn't order a pudding to-day? She said she had no great fancy for sweet things, and you and she would just have a mutton chop. But I'll be up to her. Never you tell, but I'll make her a pudding, and a pudding she'll like, too, and I'll pay for it myself; so mind you see she eats it. Many a one has been comforted in their sorrow by seeing a good dish come upon the table.'[b]

I was rather glad that Martha's energy had taken the immediate and practical direction of pudding-making, for it staved off the quarrelsome discussion as to whether she should or should not leave Miss Matty's service. She began to tie on a clean apron, and otherwise prepare herself for going to the shop for the butter, eggs, and what else she might require; she would not use a scrap of the articles already in the house for her cookery, but went to an old tea-pot in which her private store of money was deposited, and took out what she wanted.

I found Miss Matty very quiet, and not a little sad; but by-and-by she tried to smile for my sake. It was settled that I was to write to my father, and ask him to come over and hold a consultation; and as soon as this letter was despatched, we began to talk over future plans. Miss Matty's idea was to take a single room, and retain as much of her furniture as would be necessary to fit up this, and sell the rest; and there to quietly exist upon what would remain after paying the rent. For my part, I was more ambitious and less contented. I thought of all the things by which a woman, past middle age, and with the education common to ladies fifty years ago, could earn or add to a living, without materially losing caste; but at length I put even this last clause on one side, and wondered what in the world Miss Matty could do.

Teaching was, of course, the first thing that suggested itself. If Miss Matty could teach children anything, it would throw her among the little elves in whom her soul delighted. I ran over her accomplishments. Once upon a time I had heard her say she could play, 'Ah! vous dirai-je, maman?'[133] on the piano; but that was long, long ago; that faint shadow of musical acquirement had died out years before. She had also once been able to trace out patterns very nicely for muslin embroidery, by dint of placing a piece of silver-paper over the design to be copied, and holding both against the window-pane, while she marked the scollop and eyelet-holes. But that was her nearest approach to the accomplishment of drawing, and I did not think it would go very far. Then again as to the branches of a solid English education[134] – fancy-work and the use of the globes – such as the mistress of the Ladies' Seminary, to which all the tradespeople in Cranford sent their daughters, professed to teach; Miss Matty's eyes were failing her, and I doubted if she could discover the number of threads in a worsted-work pattern, or rightly appreciate the different shades required for Queen Adelaide's face, in the loyal wool-work[135] now fashionable in Cranford. As for the use of the globes, I had never been able to find it out myself, so perhaps I was not a good judge of Miss Matty's capability of instructing in this branch of education; but it struck me that equators and tropics, and such mystical circles, were very imaginary lines indeed to her, and that she looked upon the signs of the Zodiac as so many remnants of the Black Art.[136]

What she piqued herself upon, as arts, in which she excelled, was making candle-lighters, or 'spills' (as she preferred calling them), of coloured paper, cut so as to resemble feathers, and knitting garters in a variety of dainty stitches. I had once said, on receiving a present of an elaborate pair, that I should feel quite tempted to drop one of them in the street, in order to have it admired; but I found this little joke (and it was a very little one) was such a distress to her sense of propriety, and was taken with such anxious, earnest alarm, lest the temptation might some day prove too strong for me, that I quite regretted having ventured upon it. A present of these delicately-wrought garters, a bunch of gay 'spills,' or a set of cards on which sewing-silk was wound in a mystical manner, were the well-known tokens of Miss Matty's favour. But would any one pay to have their children taught these arts? or indeed would Miss Matty sell, for filthy lucre, the knack and the skill with which she made trifles of value to those who loved her?

I had[a] to come down to reading, writing, and arithmetic; and, in reading the chapter[137] every morning, she always coughed before coming to long words. I doubted her power of getting through a genealogical chapter, with any number of coughs. Writing she did well and delicately; but spelling! She seemed to think that the more out-of-the-way this was, and the more trouble it cost her, the greater the compliment she paid to her correspondent; and words that she would spell quite correctly in her letters to me, became perfect enigmas when she wrote to my father.

No![b] there was nothing she could teach to the rising generation of Cranford; unless they had been quick learners and ready imitators of her patience, her humility, her sweetness, her quiet contentment with all that she could not do. I pondered and pondered until dinner was announced by Martha, with a face all blubbered and swollen with crying.

Miss Matty had a few little peculiarities, which Martha was apt to regard as whims below her attention, and appeared to consider as childish fancies, of which an old lady of fifty-eight should try and cure herself. But to-day everything was attended to with the most careful regard. The bread was cut to the imaginary pattern of excellence that existed in Miss Matty's mind, as being the way which her mother had preferred; the curtain was drawn so as to exclude the dead-brick wall of a neighbour's stables, and yet left so as to show every tender leaf of the poplar which was bursting into spring beauty. Martha's tone to Miss Matty was just such as that good, rough-spoken servant usually kept sacred for little children, and which I had never heard her use to any grown-up person.

I had[c] forgotten to tell Miss Matty about the pudding, and I was afraid she might not do justice to it; for she had evidently very little appetite this day; so I seized the opportunity of letting her into the secret while Martha took away the meat. Miss Matty's eyes filled with tears, and she could not speak, either to express surprise or delight, when Martha returned, bearing it aloft, made in the most wonderful representation of a lion *couchant*[138] that ever was moulded. Martha's face gleamed with triumph, as she set it down before Miss Matty with an exultant 'There!' Miss Matty wanted to speak her thanks, but could not; so she took Martha's hand and shook it warmly, which set Martha off crying, and I myself could hardly keep up the necessary composure. Martha burst out of the room; and Miss Matty had to clear her voice once or twice before she could speak. At last she said, 'I should like to keep this pudding under a glass shade, my dear!' and the notion of the lion *couchant* with his currant eyes, being hoisted up to the place of honour on a mantel-piece, tickled my hysterical fancy, and I began to laugh, which rather surprised Miss Matty.

'I am sure, dear, I have seen uglier things under a glass shade before now,' said she.

So had I, many a time and oft; and I accordingly composed my countenance (and now I could hardly keep from crying), and we both fell to upon the pudding, which was indeed excellent – only every morsel seemed to choke us, our hearts were so full.

We had too much to think about to talk much that afternoon. It passed over very tranquilly. But when the tea-urn was brought in, a new thought came into my head. Why should not Miss Matty sell tea – be an agent to the East India Tea Company which then existed?[139] I could see no objections to this plan, while the advantages were many – always supposing that Miss Matty could get over the degradation of condescending to anything like trade. Tea was neither greasy, nor sticky – grease and stickiness being two of the qualities which Miss Matty could not endure. No shop-window would be required. A small genteel notification of her being licensed to sell tea, would, it is true, be necessary; but I hoped that it could be placed where no one could see it. Neither was tea a heavy article, so as to tax Miss Matty's fragile strength. The only thing against my plan was the buying and selling involved.

While I[a] was giving but absent answers to the questions Miss Matty was putting – almost as absently – we heard a clumping sound on the stairs, and a whispering outside the door: which indeed once opened and shut as if by some invisible agency. After a little while, Martha came in, dragging after her a great tall young man, all crimson with shyness, and finding his only relief in perpetually sleeking down his hair.

'Please, ma'am, he's only Jem Hearn,' said Martha, by way of an introduction; and so out of breath was she, that I imagine she had had some bodily struggle before she could overcome his reluctance to be presented on the courtly scene of Miss Matilda Jenkyns's[b] drawing-room.

'And please, ma'am, he wants to marry me off-hand. And please, ma'am, we want to take a lodger – just one quiet lodger, to make our two ends meet; and we'd take any house conformable; and, oh dear Miss Matty, if I may be so bold, would you have any objections to lodging with us? Jem wants it as much I do.' [To Jem:] – 'You great oaf! why can't you back me? – But he does want it, all the same, very bad – don't you, Jem? – only, you see, he's dazed at being called on to speak before quality.'

'It's not that,' broke in Jem. 'It's that you've taken me all on a sudden, and I didn't think for to get married so soon – and such quick work does flabbergast a man. It's not that I'm against it, ma'am,' (addressing Miss Matty), 'only Martha has such quick ways with her, when once she takes a thing into her head; and marriage, ma'am, – marriage nails a man, as one may say. I dare say I shan't mind it after it's once over.'

'Please, ma'am,' said Martha – who had plucked at his sleeve, and nudged him with her elbow, and otherwise tried to interrupt him all the time he had been speaking – 'dont mind him, he'll come to; 'twas only last night he was an-axing me, and an-axing me, and all the more because I said I could not think of it for years to come, and now he's only taken aback with the suddenness of the joy; but you know, Jem, you are just as full as me about wanting a lodger.' (Another great nudge.)

'Ay! if Miss Matty would lodge with us – otherwise I've no mind to be cumbered with strange folk in the house,' said Jem, with a want of tact which I could see enraged Martha, who was trying to represent a lodger as the great object they wished to obtain, and that, in fact, Miss Matty would be smoothing their path, and conferring a favour, if she would only come and live with them.

Miss Matty herself was bewildered by the pair: their, or rather Martha's sudden resolution in favour of matrimony staggered her, and stood between her and the contemplation of the plan which Martha had at heart. Miss Matty began, –

'Marriage is a very solemn thing, Martha.'

'It is indeed, ma'am,' quoth Jem. 'Not that I've no objections to Martha.'

'You've never let me a-be for asking me for to fix when I would be married,' said Martha – her face all a-fire, and ready to cry with vexation – 'and now you're shaming me before my missus and all.'

'Nay, now! Martha, don't ee! don't ee! only a man likes to have breathing-time,' said Jem, trying to possess himself of her hand, but in vain. Then seeing that she was more seriously hurt than he had imagined, he seemed to try to rally his scattered faculties, and with more straight-forward dignity than, ten minutes before, I should have thought it possible for him to assume, he turned to Miss Matty, and said, 'I hope, ma'am, you know that I am bound to respect every one who has been kind to Martha. I always looked on her as to be my wife – some time; and she has often and often spoken of you as the kindest lady that ever was; and though the plain truth is I would not like to be troubled with lodgers of the common run; yet if, ma'am, you'd honour us by living with us, I am sure Martha would do her best to make you comfortable; and I'd keep out of your way as much as I could, which I reckon would be the best kindness such an awkward chap as me could do.'

Miss Matty had been very busy with taking off her spectacles, wiping them, and replacing them; but all she could say was, 'Don't let any thought of me hurry you into marriage: pray don't! Marriage is such a very solemn thing!'

'But Miss Matilda will think of your plan, Martha,' said I – struck with the advantages that it offered, and unwilling to lose the opportunity of considering about it. 'And I'm sure neither she nor I can ever forget your kindness; nor yours either, Jem.'

'Why, yes, ma'am! I'm sure I mean kindly, though I'm a bit fluttered by being pushed straight a-head into matrimony, as it were, and mayn't express myself conformable. But I'm sure I'm willing enough, and give me time to get accustomed; so, Martha, wench, what's the use of crying so, and slapping me if I come near?'

This last was *sotto voce*, and had the effect of making Martha bounce out of the room, to be followed and soothed by her lover. Whereupon Miss Matty sat down and cried very heartily, and accounted for it by saying that the thought of Martha being married so soon gave her quite a shock, and that she should never forgive herself if she thought she was hurrying the poor creature. I think my pity was more for Jem, of the two: but both Miss Matty and I appreciated to the full the kindness of the honest couple, although we said little about this, and a good deal about the chances and dangers of matrimony.

The next morning, very early, I received a note from Miss Pole, so mysteriously wrapped up, and with so many seals on it to secure secresy, that I had to tear the paper before I could unfold it. And when I came to the writing I could hardly understand the meaning, it was so involved and oracular. I made out, however, that I was to go to Miss Pole's at eleven o'clock; the number *eleven*[a] being written in full length as well as in numerals, and *A.M.* twice dashed under, as if I were very likely to come at eleven at night, when all Cranford was usually a-bed, and asleep by ten. There was no signature except Miss Pole's initials, reversed, P.E., but as Martha had given me the note, 'with Miss Pole's kind regards,' it needed no wizard to find out who sent it; and if the writer's name was to be kept secret, it was very well that I was alone when Martha delivered it.

I went, as requested, to Miss Pole's. The door was opened to me by her little maid Lizzy, in Sunday trim, as if some grand event was impending over this work-day. And the drawing-room upstairs was arranged in accordance with this idea. The table was set out, with the best green card-cloth, and writing-materials upon it. On the little chiffonier was a tray with a newly-decanted bottle of cowslip wine, and some ladies'-finger biscuits. Miss Pole herself was in solemn array, as if to receive visitors, although it was only eleven o'clock. Mrs. Forrester was there, crying quietly and sadly, and my arrival seemed only to call forth fresh tears. Before we had finished our greetings, performed with lugubrious mystery of demeanour, there was another rat-tat-tat, and Mrs. Fitz-Adam appeared, crimson with walking and excitement. It seemed as if this was all the company expected; for now Miss Pole made several demonstrations of being about to open the business of the meeting, by stirring the fire, opening and shutting the door, and coughing and blowing her nose. Then she arranged us all round the table, taking care to place me opposite to her; and last of all, she inquired of me, if the sad report was true, as she feared it was, that Miss Matty had lost all her fortune?

Of course, I had but one answer to make; and I never saw more unaffected sorrow depicted on any countenances, than I did there on the three before me.

'I wish Mrs. Jamieson was here!' said Mrs. Forrester at last; but to judge from Mrs. Fitz-Adam's face, she could not second the wish.

'But without Mrs. Jamieson,' said Miss Pole, with just a sound of offended merit in her voice, 'we, the ladies of Cranford, in my drawing-room assembled, can resolve upon something. I imagine we are none of us what may be called rich, though we all possess a genteel competency, sufficient for tastes that are elegant and refined, and would not, if they could, be vulgarly ostentatious.' (Here I observed Miss Pole refer to a small card concealed in her hand, on which I imagine she had put down a few notes.)

'Miss Smith,' she continued, addressing me, (familiarly known as 'Mary' to all the company assembled, but this was a state occasion,) 'I have conversed in private – I made it my business to do so yesterday afternoon – with these ladies on the misfortune which has happened to our friend, – and one and all of us have agreed that, while we have a superfluity, it is not only a duty but a pleasure, – a true pleasure, Mary!' – her voice was rather choked just here, and she had to wipe her spectacles before she could go on – 'to give what we can to assist her – Miss Matilda Jenkyns. Only, in consideration of the feelings of delicate independence existing in the mind of every refined female,' – I was sure she had got back to the card now – 'we wish to contribute our mites in a secret and concealed manner, so as not to hurt the feelings I have referred to. And our object in requesting you to meet us this morning, is, that believing you are the daughter – that your father is, in fact, her confidential adviser in all pecuniary matters, we imagined that, by consulting with him, you might devise some mode in which our contribution could be made to appear the legal due which Miss Matilda Jenkyns ought to receive from ——. Probably, your father, knowing her investments, can fill up the blank.'

Miss Pole concluded her address, and looked round for approval and agreement.

'I have expressed your meaning, ladies, have I not? And while Miss Smith considers what reply to make, allow me to offer you some little refreshment.'

I had no great reply to make; I had more thankfulness at my heart for their kind thoughts than I cared to put into words; and so I only mumbled out something to the effect 'that I would name what Miss Pole had said to my father, and that if anything could be arranged for dear Miss Matty,' – and here I broke down utterly, and had to be refreshed with a glass of cowslip wine before I could check the crying which had been repressed for the last two or three days. The worst was, all the ladies cried in concert. Even Miss Pole cried, who had said a hundred times that to betray emotion before any one was a sign of weakness and want of self-control. She recovered herself into a slight degree of impatient anger, directed against me, as having set them all off; and, moreover, I think she was vexed that I could not make a speech back in return for hers; and if I had known beforehand what was to be said, and had had a card on which to express the probable feelings that would rise in my heart, I would have tried to gratify her. As it was, Mrs. Forrester was the person to speak when we had recovered our composure.

'I don't[a] mind, among friends, stating that I – no! I'm not poor exactly, but I don't think I'm what you may call rich; I wish I were, for dear Miss Matty's sake, – but, if you please, I'll write down, in a sealed paper, what I can give. I only wish it was more: my dear Mary, I do indeed.'

Now I saw why paper, pens, and ink, were provided. Every lady wrote down the sum she could give annually, signed the paper, and sealed it mysteriously. If their proposal was acceded to, my father was to be allowed to open the papers, under pledge of secresy. If not, they were to be returned to their writers.

When[b] this ceremony had been gone through, I rose to depart; but each lady seemed to wish to have a private conference with me. Miss Pole kept me in the drawing-room to explain why, in Mrs. Jamieson's absence, she had taken the lead in this 'movement,' as she was pleased to call it, and also to inform me that she had heard from good sources that Mrs. Jamieson was coming home directly, in a state of high displeasure against her sister-in-law, who was forthwith to leave her house; and was, she believed, to return to Edinburgh that very afternoon. Of course this piece of intelligence could not be communicated before Mrs. Fitz-Adam, more especially as Miss Pole was inclined to think that Lady Glenmire's engagement to Mr. Hoggins could not possibly hold against the blaze of Mrs. Jamieson's displeasure. A few hearty inquiries after Miss Matty's health concluded my interview with Miss Pole.

On[c] coming downstairs, I found Mrs. Forrester waiting for me at the entrance to the dining parlour; she drew me in, and when the door was shut, she tried two or three times to begin on some subject, which was so unapproachable apparently, that I began to despair of our ever getting to a clear understanding. At last out it came; the poor old lady trembling all the time as if it were a great crime which she was exposing to daylight, in telling me how very, very little she had to live upon; a confession which she was brought to make from a dread lest we should think that the small contribution named in her paper bore any proportion to her love and regard for Miss Matty. And yet that sum which she so eagerly relinquished was, in truth, more than a twentieth part of what she had to live upon, and keep house, and a little serving-maid, all as became one born a Tyrrell. And when the whole income does not nearly amount to a hundred pounds, to give up a twentieth of it will necessitate many careful economies, and many pieces of self-denial – small and insignificant in the world's account, but bearing a different value in another account-book that I have heard of. She did so wish she was rich, she said; and this wish she kept repeating, with no thought of herself in it, only with a longing, yearning desire to be able to heap up Miss Matty's measure of comforts.

It was[a] some time before I could console her enough to leave her; and then, on quitting the house, I was waylaid by Mrs. Fitz-Adam, who had also her confidence to make of pretty nearly the opposite description. She had not liked to put down all that she could afford, and was ready to give. She told me she thought she never could look Miss Matty in the face again if she presumed to be giving her so much as she should like to do. 'Miss Matty!' continued she, 'that I thought was such a fine young lady, when I was nothing but a country girl, coming to market with eggs and butter and such like things. For my father, though well to do, would always make me go on as my mother had done before me; and I had to come in to Cranford every Saturday and see after sales and prices, and what not. And one day, I remember, I met Miss Matty in the lane that leads to Combehurst; she was walking on the footpath which, you know, is raised a good way above the road, and a gentleman rode beside her, and was talking to her, and she was looking down at some primroses she had gathered, and pulling them all to pieces, and I do believe she was crying. But after she had passed,[b] she turned round and ran after me to ask – oh so kindly – after my poor mother, who lay on her death-bed; and when I cried, she took hold of my hand to comfort me; and the gentleman waiting for her all the time; and her poor heart very full of something, I am sure; and I thought it such an honour to be spoken to in that pretty way by the rector's daughter, who visited at Arley Hall. I have loved her ever since, though perhaps I'd no right to do it; but if you can think of any way in which I might be allowed to give a little more without any one knowing it, I should be so much obliged to you, my dear. And my brother would be delighted to doctor her for nothing – medicines, leeches, and all. I know that he and her ladyship – (my dear! I little thought in the days I was telling you of that I should ever come to be sister-in-law to a ladyship!) – would do anything for her. We all would.'

I told her I was quite sure of it, and promised all sorts of things, in my anxiety to get home to Miss Matty, who might well be wondering what had become of me, – absent from her two hours without being able to account for it. She had taken very little note of time, however, as she had been occupied in numberless little arrangements preparatory to the great step of giving up her house. It was evidently a relief to her to be doing something in the way of retrenchment; for, as she said, whenever she paused to think, the recollection of the poor fellow with his bad five-pound note came over her, and she felt quite dishonest; only if it made her so uncomfortable, what must it not be doing to the directors of the Bank, who must know so much more of the misery consequent upon this failure?[a] She almost made me angry by dividing her sympathy between these directors (whom she imagined overwhelmed by self-reproach for the mismanagement of other people's affairs), and those who were suffering like her. Indeed, of the two, she seemed to think poverty a lighter burden than self-reproach; but I privately doubted if the directors would agree with her.

Old hoards were taken out and examined as to their money value, which luckily was small, or else I don't know how Miss Matty would have prevailed upon herself to part with such things as her mother's wedding-ring, the strange uncouth brooch with which her father had disfigured his shirt-frill, &c. However, we arranged things a little in order as to their pecuniary estimation, and were all ready for my father when he came the next morning.

I am[b] not going to weary you with the details of all the business we went through; and one reason for not telling about them is, that I did not understand what we were doing at the time, and cannot recollect it now. Miss Matty and I sat assenting to accounts, and schemes, and reports, and documents, of which I do not believe we either of us understood a word; for my father was clear-headed and decisive, and a capital man of business, and if we made the slightest inquiry, or expressed the slightest want of comprehension, he had a sharp way of saying, 'Eh? eh? it's as clear as daylight. What's your objection?' And as we had not comprehended anything of what he had proposed, we found it rather difficult to shape our objections; in fact, we never were sure if we had any. So, presently Miss Matty got into a nervously acquiescent state, and said "Yes" and "Certainly" at every pause, whether required or not: but when I once joined in as chorus to a "Decidedly," pronounced by Miss Matty in a tremblingly dubious tone, my father fired round at me and asked me "What there was to decide?" And I am sure, to this day, I have never known. But, in justice to him, I must say, he had come over from Drumble to help Miss Matty when he could ill spare the time, and when his own affairs were in a very anxious state.

While Miss Matty was out of the room, giving orders for luncheon – and sadly perplexed between her desire of honouring my father by a delicate dainty meal, and her conviction that she had no right now that all her money was gone, to indulge this desire, – I told him of the meeting of Cranford ladies at Miss Pole's the day before. He kept brushing his hand before his eyes as I spoke; – and when I went back to Martha's offer the evening before, of receiving Miss Matty as a lodger, he fairly walked away from me to the window, and began drumming with his fingers upon it. Then he turned abruptly round, and said, 'See, Mary, how a good innocent life makes friends all around. Confound it! I could make a good lesson out of it if I were a parson; but as it is, I can't get a tail to my sentences – only I'm sure you feel what I want to say. You and I will have a walk after lunch, and talk a bit more about these plans.'

The lunch – a hot savoury mutton-chop, and a little of the cold lion[140a] sliced and fried – was now brought in. Every morsel of this last dish was finished, to Martha's great gratification. Then my father bluntly told Miss Matty he wanted to talk to me alone, and that he would stroll out and see some of the old places, and then I could tell her what plan we thought desirable. Just before we went out, she called me back and said, 'Remember dear, I'm the only one left – I mean there's no one to be hurt by what I do. I'm willing to do anything that's right and honest; and I don't think, if Deborah knows where she is, she'll care so very much if I'm not genteel; because, you see, she'll know all, dear. Only let me see what I can,[141b] and pay the poor people as far as I'm able.'

I gave her a hearty kiss, and ran after my father. The result of our conversation was this. If all parties were agreeable, Martha and Jem were to be married with as little delay as possible, and they were to live on in Miss Matty's present abode; the sum which the Cranford ladies had agreed to contribute annually, being sufficient to meet the greater part of the rent, and leaving Martha free to appropriate what Miss Matty should pay for her lodgings to any little extra comforts required. About the sale, my father was dubious at first. He said the old rectory furniture, however carefully used, and reverently treated, would fetch very little; and that little would be but as a drop in the sea of the debts of the Town and County Bank. But when I represented how Miss Matty's tender conscience would be soothed by feeling that she had done what she could, he gave way; especially after I had told him the five-pound-note adventure, and he had scolded me well for allowing it. I then alluded to my idea that she might add to her small income by selling tea; and, to my surprise, (for I had nearly given up the plan,) my father grasped at it with all the energy of a tradesman. I think he reckoned his chickens before they were hatched, for he immediately ran up the profits of the sales that she could effect in Cranford to more than twenty pounds a-year. The small dining-parlour was to be converted into a shop, without any of its degrading characteristics; a table was to be the counter; one window was to be retained unaltered, and the other changed into a glass door. I evidently rose in his estimation, for having made this bright suggestion. I only hoped we should not both fall in Miss Matty's.

But she was patient and content with all our arrangements. She knew, she said, that we should do the best we could for her; and she only hoped, only stipulated, that she should pay every farthing that she could be said to owe for her father's sake, who had been so respected in Cranford. My father and I had agreed to say as little as possible about the Bank, indeed never to mention it again, if it could be helped. Some of the plans were evidently a little perplexing to her; but she had seen me sufficiently snubbed in the morning for want of comprehension to venture on too many inquiries now; and all passed over well, with a hope on her part that no one would be hurried into marriage on her account. When we came to the proposal that she should sell tea, I could see it was rather a shock to her; not on account of any personal loss of gentility involved, but only because she distrusted her own powers of action in a new line of life, and would timidly have preferred a little more privation to any exertion for which she feared she was unfitted. However, when she saw my father was bent upon it, she sighed, and said she would try; and if she did not do well, of course she might give it up. One good thing about it was, she did not think men ever bought tea; and it was of men particularly she was afraid. They had such sharp loud ways with them; and did up accounts, and counted their change so quickly! Now, if she might only sell comfits to children, she was sure she could please them!

CHAPTER XV.[a]

A HAPPY RETURN.[b]

BEFORE I left Miss Matty at Cranford everything had been comfortably arranged for her. Even Mrs. Jamieson's approval of her selling tea had been gained. That oracle had taken a few days to consider whether by so doing Miss Matty would forfeit her right to the privileges of society in Cranford. I think she had some little idea of mortifying Lady Glenmire by the decision she gave at last; which was to this effect: that whereas a married woman takes her husband's rank by the strict laws of precedence, an unmarried woman retains the station her father occupied. So Cranford was allowed to visit Miss Matty; and, whether allowed or not, it intended to visit Lady Glenmire.

But what[c] was our surprise – our dismay – when we learnt that Mr. and *Mrs. Hoggins* were returning on the following Tuesday. Mrs. Hoggins! Had she absolutely dropped her title, and so, in a spirit of bravado, cut the aristocracy to become a Hoggins! She, who might have been called Lady Glenmire to her dying day! Mrs. Jamieson was pleased. She said it only convinced her of what she had known from the first, that the creature had a low taste. But 'the creature' looked very happy on Sunday at church; nor did we see it necessary to keep our veils down on that side of our bonnets on which Mr. and Mrs. Hoggins sate, as Mrs. Jamieson did; thereby missing all the smiling glory of his face, and all the becoming blushes of hers. I am not sure if Martha and Jem looked more radiant in the afternoon, when they too made their first appearance. Mrs. Jamieson soothed the turbulence of her soul, by having the blinds of her windows drawn down, as if for a funeral, on the day when Mr. and Mrs. Hoggins received callers; and it was with some difficulty that she was prevailed upon to continue the St. James's Chronicle – so indignant was she with its having inserted the announcement of the marriage.

Miss Matty's sale went off famously. She retained the furniture of her sitting-room, and bedroom; the former of which she was to occupy till Martha could meet with a lodger who might wish to take it; and into this sitting-room and bedroom she had to cram all sorts of things, which were (the auctioneer assured her) bought in for her at the sale by an unknown friend. I always suspected Mrs. Fitz-Adam of this; but she must have had an accessory, who knew what articles were particularly regarded by Miss Matty on account of their associations with her early days. The rest of the house looked rather bare, to be sure; all except one tiny bedroom; of which my father allowed me to purchase the furniture for my occasional use, in case of Miss Matty's illness.

I had[a] expended my own small store in buying all manner of comfits and lozenges, in order to tempt the little people whom Miss Matty loved so much, to come about her. Tea in bright green canisters – and comfits in tumblers – Miss Matty and I felt quite proud as we looked round us on the evening before the shop was to be opened. Martha had scoured the boarded floor to a white cleanness, and it was adorned with a brilliant piece of oil-cloth on which customers were to stand before the table-counter. The wholesome smell of plaster and white-wash pervaded the apartment. A very small 'Matilda Jenkyns, licensed to sell tea' was hidden under the lintel of the new door, and two boxes of tea with cabalistic inscriptions all over them stood ready to disgorge their contents into the canisters.

Miss Matty,[b] as I ought to have mentioned before, had had some scruples of conscience at selling tea when there was already Mr. Johnson[c] in the town, who included it among his numerous commodities; and, before she could quite reconcile herself to the adoption of her new business, she had trotted down to his shop, unknown to me, to tell him of the project that was entertained, and to inquire if it was likely to injure his business. My father called this idea of hers 'great nonsense,' and 'wondered how tradespeople were to get on if there was to be a continual consulting of each others' interests, which would put a stop to all competition directly.' And, perhaps, it would not have done in Drumble, but in Cranford it answered very well; for not only did Mr. Johnson[d] kindly put at rest all Miss Matty's scruples, and fear of injuring his business, but, I have reason to know, he repeatedly sent customers to her, saying that the teas he kept were of a common kind, but that Miss Jenkyns had all the choice sorts. And expensive tea is a very favourite luxury with well-to-do tradespeople, and rich farmers' wives, who turn up their noses at the Congou and Souchong prevalent at many tables of gentility, and will have nothing else[e] than Gunpowder and Pekoe for themselves.[142]

But to return to Miss Matty. It was really very pleasant to see how her unselfishness, and simple sense of justice, called out the same good qualities in others. She never seemed to think any one would impose upon her, because she should be so grieved to do it to them. I have heard her put a stop to the asseverations of the man who brought her coals, by quietly saying, 'I am sure you would be sorry to bring me wrong weight;' and if the coals were short measure that time, I don't believe they ever were again. People would have felt as much ashamed of presuming on her good faith as they would have done on that of a child. But my father says, 'such simplicity might be very well in Cranford, but would never do in the world.' And I fancy the world must be very bad, for with all my father's suspicion of every one with whom he has dealings, and in spite of all his many precautions, he lost upwards of a thousand pounds by roguery only last year.

I just stayed long enough to establish Miss Matty in her new mode of life, and to pack up the library, which the Rector had purchased. He had written a very kind letter to Miss Matty, saying, 'how glad he should be take a library so well selected as he knew that the late Mr. Jenkyns's[a] must have been, at any valuation put upon them.' And when she agreed to this, with a touch of sorrowful gladness that they would go back to the Rectory, and be arranged on the accustomed walls once more, he sent word that he feared that he had not room for them all, and perhaps Miss Matty would kindly allow him to leave some volumes on her shelves. But Miss Matty said that she had her Bible, and Johnson's Dictionary, and should not have much time for reading, she was afraid. Still I retained a few books out of consideration for the Rector's kindness.

The money[b] which he had paid, and that produced by the sale, was partly expended in the stock of tea, and part of it was invested against a rainy day; *i. e.* old age or illness. It was but a small sum, it is true; and it occasioned a few evasions of truth and white lies (all of which I think very wrong indeed – in theory – and would rather not put them in practice), for we knew Miss Matty would be perplexed as to her duty if she were aware of any little reserve-fund being made for her while the debts of the Bank remained unpaid. Moreover, she had never been told of the way in which her friends were contributing to pay the rent. I should have liked to tell her this; but the mystery of the affair gave a piquancy to their deed of kindness which the ladies were unwilling to give up; and at first Martha had to shirk many a perplexed question as to her ways and means of living in such a house; but by and by Miss Matty's prudent uneasiness sank down into acquiescence with the existing arrangement.

I left Miss Matty with a good heart. Her sales of tea during the first two days had surpassed my most sanguine expectations. The whole country round seemed to be all out of tea at once. The only alteration I could have desired in Miss Matty's way of doing business was, that she should not have so plaintively entreated some of her customers not to buy green tea – running it down as slow poison, sure to destroy the nerves, and produce all manner of evil. Their pertinacity in taking it, in spite of all her warnings, distressed her so much that I really thought she would relinquish the sale of it, and so lose half her custom; and I was driven to my wits' end for instances of longevity entirely attributable to a persevering use of green tea. But the final argument, which settled the question, was a happy reference of mine to the train oil and tallow candles which the Esquimaux not only enjoy but digest.[143] After that she acknowledged that 'one man's meat might be another man's poison,' and contented herself thenceforward with an occasional remonstrance, when she thought the purchaser was too young and innocent to be acquainted with the evil effects green tea produced on some constitutions; and an habitual sigh when people old enough to choose more wisely would prefer it.

I went over from Drumble once a quarter at least, to settle the accounts, and see after the necessary business letters. And, speaking of letters, I began to be very much ashamed of remembering my letter to the Aga Jenkyns, and very glad I had never named my writing to any one. I only hoped the letter was lost. No answer came. No sign was made.

About a year after Miss Matty set up shop, I received one of Martha's hieroglyphics, begging me to come to Cranford very soon. I was afraid that Miss Matty was ill, and went off that very afternoon, and took Martha by surprise when she saw me on opening the door. We went into the kitchen, as usual, to have our confidential conference; and then Martha told me she was expecting her confinement very soon – in a week or two; and she did not think Miss Matty was aware of it; and she wanted me to break the news to her, 'for indeed Miss!' continued Martha, crying hysterically, 'I'm afraid she won't approve of it; and I'm sure I don't know who is to take care of her as she should be taken care of, when I am laid up.'

I comforted[a] Martha by telling her I would remain till she was about again; and only wished she had told me her reason for this sudden summons, as then I would have brought the requisite stock of clothes. But Martha was so tearful and tender-spirited, and unlike her usual self, that I said as little as possible about myself, and endeavoured rather to comfort Martha under all the probable and possible misfortunes which came crowding upon her imagination.

I then[b] stole out of the house-door, and made my appearance, as if I were a customer, in the shop just to take Miss Matty by surprise, and gain an idea of how she looked in her new situation. It was warm May weather, so only the little half-door was closed; and Miss Matty sate behind her counter, knitting an elaborate pair of garters: elaborate they seemed to me, but the difficult stitch was no weight upon her mind, for she was singing in a low voice to herself as her needles went rapidly in and out. I call it singing, but I dare say a musician would not use that word to the tuneless yet sweet humming of the low worn voice. I found out from the words, far more than from the attempt at the tune, that it was the Old Hundredth[144] she was crooning to herself: but the quiet continuous sound told of content, and gave me a pleasant feeling, as I stood in the street just outside the door, quite in harmony with that soft May morning. I went in. At first she did not catch who it was, and stood up as if to serve me; but in another minute watchful pussy had clutched her knitting, which was dropped in her eager joy at seeing me. I found, after we had had a little conversation, that it was as Martha said, and that Miss Matty had no idea of the approaching household event.

So I thought I would let things take their course, secure that when I went to her with the baby in my arms I should obtain that forgiveness for Martha which she was needlessly frightening herself into believing that Miss Matty would withhold, under some notion that the new claimant would require attentions from its mother that it would be faithless treason to Miss Matty to render.

But I was right. I think that must be an hereditary quality, for my father says he is scarcely ever wrong. One morning, within a week after I arrived, I went to call Miss Matty, with a little bundle of flannel in my arms. She was very much awe-struck when I showed her what it was, and asked for her spectacles off the dressing-table, and looked at it curiously, with a sort of tender wonder at its small perfection of parts. She could not banish the thought of the surprise all day, but went about on tip-toe, and was very silent. But she stole up to see Martha, and they both cried with joy; and she got into a complimentary speech to Jem, and did not know how to get out of it again, and was only extricated from her dilemma by the sound of the shop-bell, which was an equal relief to the shy, proud, honest Jem, who shook my hand so vigorously when I congratulated him that I think I feel the pain of it yet.

I had a busy life while Martha was laid up. I attended on Miss Matty, and prepared her meals; I cast up her accounts, and examined into the state of her cannisters[a] and tumblers. I helped her too, occasionally, in the shop; and it gave me no small amusement, and sometimes a little uneasiness, to watch her ways there. If a little child came in to ask for an ounce of almond-comfits (and four of the large kind which Miss Matty sold weighed that much), she always added one more by 'way of make-weight' as she called it, although the scale was handsomely turned before; and when I remonstrated against this, her reply was, 'The little things like it so much!' There was no use in telling her that the fifth comfit weighed a quarter of an ounce, and made every sale into a loss to her pocket. So I remembered the green tea, and winged my shaft with a feather out of her own plumage. I told her how unwholesome almond-comfits were; and how ill excess in them might make the little children. This argument produced some effect; for, henceforward, instead of the fifth comfit, she always told them to hold out their tiny palms, into which she shook either peppermint or ginger lozenges, as a preventive to the dangers that might arise from the previous sale. Altogether the lozenge trade, conducted on these principles, did not promise to be remunerative; but I was happy to find she had made more than twenty pounds during the last year by her sales of tea; and, moreover, that now she was accustomed to it, she did not dislike the employment, which brought her into kindly intercourse with many of the people round about. If she gave them good weight they, in their turn, brought many a little country present to the 'old rector's daughter;' – a cream cheese, a few new-laid eggs, a little fresh ripe fruit, a bunch of flowers. The counter was quite loaded with these offerings sometimes, as she told me.

As for Cranford in general, it was going on much as usual. The Jamieson and Hoggins feud still raged, if a feud it could be called, when only one side cared much about it. Mr. and Mrs. Hoggins were very happy together; and, like most very happy people, quite ready to be friendly: indeed, Mrs. Hoggins was really desirous to be restored to Mrs. Jamieson's good graces, because of the former intimacy. But Mrs. Jamieson considered their very happiness an insult to the Glenmire family, to which she had still the honour to belong; and she doggedly refused and rejected every advance. Mr. Mulliner, like a faithful clansman, espoused his mistress's side with ardour. If he saw either Mr. or Mrs. Hoggins, he would cross the street, and appear absorbed in the contemplation of life in general, and his own path in particular, until he had passed them by. Miss Pole used to amuse herself with wondering what in the world Mrs. Jamieson would do, if either she or Mr. Mulliner, or any other member of her household, was taken ill; she could hardly have the face to call in Mr. Hoggins after the way she had behaved to them. Miss Pole grew quite impatient for some indisposition or accident to befal[a] Mrs. Jamieson or her dependants, in order that Cranford might see how she would act under the perplexing circumstances.

Martha was beginning to go about again, and I had already fixed a limit, not very far distant, to my visit, when one afternoon, as I was sitting in the shop-parlour with Miss Matty – I remember the weather was colder now than it had been in May, three weeks before, and we had a fire, and kept the door fully closed – we saw a gentleman go slowly past the window, and then stand opposite to the door, as if looking out for the name which we had so carefully hidden. He took out a double eye-glass and peered about for some time before he could discover it. Then he came in. And, all on a sudden, it flashed across me that it was the Aga himself! For his clothes had an out-of-the-way foreign cut about them; and his face was deep brown as if tanned and re-tanned by the sun. His complexion contrasted oddly with his plentiful snow-white hair; his eyes were dark and piercing, and he had an odd way of contracting them, and puckering up his cheeks into innumerable wrinkles when he looked earnestly at objects. He did so to Miss Matty when he first came in. His glance had first caught and lingered a little upon me; but then turned, with the peculiar searching look I have described, to Miss Matty. She was a little fluttered and nervous, but no more so than she always was when any man came into her shop. She thought that he would probably have a note, or a sovereign at least, for which she would have to give change, which was an operation she very much disliked to perform. But the present customer stood opposite to her, without asking for anything, only looking fixedly at her as he drummed upon the table with his fingers, just for all the world as Miss Jenkyns used to do. Miss Matty was on the point of asking him what he wanted (as she told me afterwards), when he turned sharp to me: 'Is your name Mary Smith?'

'Yes!' said I.

All my doubts as to his identity were set at rest; and, I only wondered what he would say or do next, and how Miss Matty would stand the joyful shock of what he had to reveal. Apparently he was at a loss how to announce himself; for he looked round at last in search of something to buy, so as to gain time; and, as it happened, his eye caught on the almond-comfits, and he boldly asked for a pound of 'those things.' I doubt if Miss Matty had a whole pound in the shop; and besides the unusual magnitude of the order, she was distressed with the idea of the indigestion they would produce, taken in such unlimited quantities. She looked up to remonstrate. Something of tender relaxation in his face struck home to her heart. She said, 'It is –[a] oh, sir! can you be Peter?' and trembled from head to foot. In a moment he was round the table, and had her in his arms, sobbing the tearless cries of old age. I brought her a glass of wine; for indeed her colour had changed so as to alarm me, and Mr. Peter, too. He kept saying, 'I have been too sudden for you, Matty, – I have, my little girl.'

I proposed that she should go at once up into the drawing-room and lie down on the sofa there; she looked wistfully at her brother, whose hand she had held tight, even when nearly fainting; but on his assuring her that he would not leave her, she allowed him to carry her upstairs.

I thought[b] that the best I could do, was to run and put the kettle on the fire for early tea, and then to attend to the shop, leaving the brother and sister to exchange some of the many thousand things they must have to say. I had also to break the news to Martha, who received it with a burst of tears, which nearly infected me. She kept recovering herself to ask if I was sure it was indeed Miss Matty's brother; for I had mentioned that he had gray hair and she had always heard that he was a very handsome young man. Something of the same kind perplexed Miss Matty at tea-time, when she was installed in the great easy chair opposite to Mr. Jenkyns's, in order to gaze her fill. She could hardly drink for looking at him; and as for eating, that was out of the question.

'I suppose hot climates age people very quickly,' said she, almost to herself. 'When you left Cranford you had not a gray hair in your head.'

'But how many years ago is that?' said Mr. Peter, smiling.

'Ah! true! yes! I suppose you and I are getting old. But still I did not think we were so very old! But white hair is very becoming to you, Peter,' she continued – a little afraid lest she had hurt him by revealing how his appearance had impressed her.

'I suppose I forgot dates too, Matty, for what do you think I have brought for you from India? I have an Indian muslin gown and a pearl necklace for you somewhere or other in my chest at Portsmouth.' He smiled as if amused at the idea of the incongruity of his presents with the appearance of his sister; but this did not strike her all at once, while the elegance of the articles did. I could see that for a moment her imagination dwelt complacently on the idea of herself thus attired; and instinctively she put her hand up to her throat – that little delicate throat which (as Miss Pole had told me) had been one of her youthful charms; but the hand met the touch of folds of soft muslin, in which she was always swathed up to her chin; and the sensation recalled a sense of the unsuitableness of a pearl necklace to her age. She said, 'I'm afraid I'm too old; but it was very kind of you to think of it. They are just what I should have liked years ago – when I was young!'

'So I thought, my little Matty. I remembered your tastes; they were so like my dear mother's.' At the mention of that name, the brother and sister clasped each other's hands yet more fondly; and although they were perfectly silent, I fancied they might have something to say if they were unchecked by my presence, and I got up to arrange my room for Mr. Peter's occupation that night, intending myself to share Miss Matty's bed. But at my movement he started up. 'I must go and settle about a room at the George. My carpetbag is there too.'

'No!' said Miss Matty in great distress – 'you must not go; please, dear Peter – pray, Mary – oh! you must not go!'

She was[a] so much agitated that we both promised everything she wished. Peter sat down again, and gave her his hand, which for better security she held in both of hers, and I left the room to accomplish my arrangements.

Long, long into the night, far, far into the morning, did Miss Matty and I talk. She had much to tell me of her brother's life and adventures which he had communicated to her, as they had sat alone. She said that all was thoroughly clear to her; but I never quite understood the whole story; and when in after days I lost my awe of Mr. Peter enough to question him myself, he laughed at my curiosity and told me stories that sounded so very much like Baron Munchausen's[145] that I was sure he was making fun of me. What I heard from Miss Matty was, that he had been a volunteer at the siege of Rangoon;[146] had been taken prisoner by the Burmese; had somehow obtained favour and eventual freedom from knowing how to bleed the chief of the small tribe in some case of dangerous illness; that on his release from years of captivity he had had his letters returned from England with the ominous word 'Dead' marked upon them; and believing himself to be the last of his race, he had settled down as an indigo planter; and had proposed to spend the remainder of his life in the country to whose inhabitants and modes of life he had become habituated; when my letter had reached him; and with the odd vehemence which characterised him in age as it had done in youth, he had sold his land and all his possessions to the first purchaser, and come home to the poor old sister, who was more glad and rich than any princess when she looked at him. She talked me to sleep at last, and then I was awakened by a slight sound at the door, for which she begged my pardon as she crept penitently into bed; but it seems that when I could no longer confirm her belief that the long-lost-was really here – under the same roof – she had begun to fear lest it was only a waking dream of hers; that there never had been a Peter sitting by her all that blessed evening – but that the real Peter lay dead far away beneath some wild sea-wave, or under some strange Eastern tree. And so strong had this nervous feeling of hers become that she was fain to get up and go and convince herself that he was really there by listening through the door to his even regular breathing – I don't like to call it snoring, but I heard it myself through two closed doors – and by-and-by it soothed Miss Matty to sleep.

I don't believe Mr. Peter came home from India as rich as a Nabob; he even considered himself poor, but neither he nor Miss Matty cared much about that. At any rate, he had enough to live upon 'very genteelly' at Cranford; he and Miss Matty together. And a day or two after his arrival, the shop was closed, while troops of little urchins gleefully awaited the showers of comfits and lozenges that came from time to time down upon their faces as they stood up-gazing at Miss Matty's drawing-room windows. Occasionally Miss Matty would say to them (half hidden behind the curtains), 'My dear children, don't make yourselves ill;' but a strong arm pulled her back, and a more rattling shower than ever succeeded. A part of the tea was sent in presents to the Cranford ladies; and some of it was distributed among the old people who remembered Mr. Peter in the days of his frolicsome youth. The India muslin gown was reserved for darling Flora Gordon (Miss Jessie Brown's daughter). The Gordons had been on the Continent for the last few years, but were now expected to return very soon; and Miss Matty, in her sisterly pride, anticipated great delight in the joy of showing them Mr. Peter. The pearl necklace disappeared; and about that time many handsome and useful presents made their appearance in the households of Miss Pole and Mrs. Forrester; and some rare and delicate Indian ornaments graced the drawing-rooms of Mrs. Jamieson and Mrs. Fitz-Adam. I myself was not forgotten. Among other things, I had the handsomest bound and best edition of Dr. Johnson's works that could be procured; and dear Miss Matty, with tears in her eyes, begged me to consider it as a present from her sister as well as herself. In short no one was forgotten; and what was more, every one, however insignificant, who had shown kindness to Miss Matty at any time, was sure of Mr. Peter's cordial regard.

CHAPTER XVI.

'PEACE TO CRANFORD.'[a]

IT was not surprising that Mr. Peter[b] became such a favourite at Cranford. The ladies vied with each other who should admire him most; and no wonder; for their quiet lives were astonishingly stirred up by the arrival from India – especially as the person arrived told more wonderful stories than Sindbad the sailor; and, as Miss Pole said, was quite as good as an Arabian night any evening. For my own part, I had vibrated all my life between Drumble and Cranford, and I thought it was quite possible that all Mr. Peter's stories might be true although wonderful; but when I found, that if we swallowed an anecdote of tolerable magnitude one week, we had the dose considerably increased the next, I began to have my doubts; especially as I noticed that when his sister was present the accounts of Indian life were comparatively tame; not that she knew more than we did, perhaps less. I noticed also that when the Rector came to call, Mr. Peter talked in a different way about the countries he had been in. But I don't think the ladies in Cranford would have considered him such a wonderful traveller if they had only heard him talk in the quiet way he did to him. They liked him the better, indeed, for being what they called 'so very Oriental.'

One day,[c] at a select party in his honour, which Miss Pole gave, and from which, as Mrs. Jamieson honoured it with her presence, and had even offered to send Mr. Mulliner to wait, Mr. and Mrs. Hoggins and Mrs. Fitz-Adam were necessarily excluded – one day at Miss Pole's Mr. Peter said he was tired of sitting upright against the hard-backed uneasy chairs, and asked if he might not indulge himself in sitting cross-legged. Miss Pole's consent was eagerly given, and down he went with the utmost gravity. But when Miss Pole asked me, in an audible whisper, 'if he did not remind me of the Father of the Faithful?'[147] I could not help thinking of poor Simon Jones the lame tailor; and while Mrs. Jamieson slowly commented on the elegance and convenience of the attitude, I remember how we had all followed that lady's lead in condemning Mr. Hoggins for vulgarity because he simply crossed his legs as he sate still on his chair. Many of Mr. Peter's ways of eating were a little strange amongst such ladies as Miss Pole, and Miss Matty, and Mrs. Jamieson, especially when I recollected the untasted green peas and two-pronged forks at poor Mr. Holbrook's dinner.

The mention of that gentleman's name recalls to my mind a conversation between Mr. Peter and Miss Matty one evening in the summer after he returned to Cranford. The day had been very hot, and Miss Matty had been much oppressed by the weather; in the heat of which her brother revelled. I remember that she had been unable to nurse Martha's baby; which had become her favourite employment of late, and which was as much at home in her arms as in its mother's, as long as it remained a light weight – portable by one so fragile as Miss Matty. This day to which I refer, Miss Matty had seemed more than usually feeble and languid, and only revived when the sun went down, and her sofa was wheeled to the open window, through which, although it looked into the principal street of Cranford, the fragrant smell of the neighbouring hayfields came in every now and then, borne by the soft breezes that stirred the dull air of the summer twilight, and then died away. The silence of the sultry atmosphere was lost in the murmuring noises which came in from many an open window and door; even the children were abroad in the street, late as it was (between ten and eleven), enjoying the game of play for which they had not had spirits during the heat of the day. It was a source of satisfaction to Miss Matty to see how few candles were lighted even in the apartments of those houses from which issued the greatest signs of life. Mr. Peter, Miss Matty and I, had all been quiet, each with a separate reverie, for some little time, when Mr. Peter broke in –

'Do you know, little Matty, I could have sworn you were on the high road to matrimony when I left England that last time! If anybody had told me you would have lived and died an old maid then, I should have laughed in their faces.'

Miss Matty made no reply; and I tried in vain to think of some subject which should effectually turn the conversation; but I was very stupid; and before I spoke, he went on:

'It was Holbrook; that fine manly fellow who lived at Woodley,[a] that I used to think would carry off my little Matty. You would not think it now, I dare say, Mary! but this sister of mine was once a very pretty girl – at least I thought so; and so I've a notion did poor Holbrook. What business had he to die before I came home to thank him for all his kindness to a good-for-nothing cub as I was? It was that that made me first think he cared for you; for in all our fishing expeditions it was Matty, Matty, we talked about. Poor Deborah! What a lecture she read me on having asked him home to lunch one day, when she had seen the Arley carriage in the town, and thought that my lady might call. Well, that's long years ago; more than half a lifetime! and yet it seems like yesterday! I don't know a fellow I should have liked better as a brother-in-law. You must have played your cards badly, my little Matty, somehow or another – wanted your brother to be a good go-between, eh! little one?' said he, putting out his hand to take hold of hers as she lay on the

sofa – 'Why what's this? you're shivering and shaking, Matty, with that con-
founded open window. Shut it, Mary, this minute!'

I did so, and then stooped down to kiss Miss Matty, and see if she really
were chilled. She caught at my hand, and gave it a hard squeeze – but
unconsciously I think – for in a minute or two she spoke to us quite in her
usual voice, and smiled our uneasiness away; although she patiently submit-
ted to the prescriptions we enforced of a warmed bed, and a glass of weak
negus. I was to leave Cranford the next day, and before I went I saw that all
the effects of the open window had quite vanished. I had superintended
most of the alterations necessary in the house and household during the lat-
ter weeks of my stay. The shop was once more a parlour; the empty
resounding rooms again furnished up to the very garrets.

There has been some talk of establishing Martha and Jem in another
house; but Miss Matty would not hear of this. Indeed I never saw her so
much roused as when Miss Pole had assumed it to be the most desirable
arrangement. As long as Martha would remain with Miss Matty, Miss Matty
was only too thankful to have her about her; yes, and Jem too, who was a
very pleasant man to have in the house, for she never saw him from week's
end to week's end. And as for the probable children, if they would all turn
out such little darlings as her god-daughter Matilda, she should not mind
the number, if Martha didn't. Besides the next was to be called Deborah; a
point which Miss Matty had reluctantly yielded to Martha's stubborn deter-
mination that her first-born was to be Matilda. So Miss Pole had to lower
her colours, and even her voice, as she said to me that as Mr. and Mrs.
Hearne were still to go on living in the same house with Miss Matty, we had
certainly done a wise thing in hiring Martha's niece as an auxiliary.

I left[a] Miss Matty and Mr. Peter most comfortable and contented; the
only subject for regret to the tender heart of the one and the social friendly
nature of the other being the unfortunate quarrel between Mrs. Jamieson
and the plebeian Hogginses and their following. In joke I prophesied one
day that this would only last until Mrs. Jamieson or Mr. Mulliner were ill, in
which case they would only be too glad to be friends with Mr. Hoggins; but
Miss Matty did not like my looking forward to anything like illness in so
light a manner; and, before the year was out, all had come round in a far
more satisfactory way.

I received[b] two Cranford letters on one auspicious October morning.
Both Miss Pole and Miss Matty wrote to ask me to come over and meet the
Gordons, who had returned to England alive and well, with their two chil-
dren, now almost grown up. Dear Jessie Brown had kept her old kind
nature, although she had changed her name and station; and she wrote to say
that she and Major Gordon expected to be in Cranford on the fourteenth,
and she hoped and begged to be remembered to Mrs. Jamieson (named first,
as became her honourable station), Miss Pole, and Miss Matty – could she

ever forget their kindness to her poor father and sister? – Mrs. Forrester, Mr. Hoggins (and here again came in an allusion to kindness shown to the dead long ago), his new wife, who as such must allow Mrs. Gordon to desire to make her acquaintance, and who was moreover an old Scotch friend of her husband's. In short, every one was named, from the Rector – who had been appointed to Cranford in the interim between Captain Brown's death and Miss Jessie's marriage, and was now associated with the latter event – down to Miss Betty Barker; all were asked to the luncheon; all except Mrs. Fitz-Adam, who had come to live in Cranford since Miss Jessie Brown's days, and whom I found rather moping on account of the omission. People wondered at Miss Betty Barker's being included in the honourable list; but then, as Miss Pole said, we must remember the disregard of the genteel proprieties of life in which the poor captain had educated his girls; and for his sake we swallowed our pride; indeed Mrs. Jamieson rather took it is a compliment, as putting Miss Betty (formerly *her* maid)[148] on a level with 'those Hogginses.'

But when I arrived in Cranford, nothing was as yet ascertained of Mrs. Jamieson's own intentions; would the honourable lady go, or would she not? Mr. Peter declared that she should and she would; Miss Pole shook her head and desponded. But Mr. Peter was a man of resources. In the first place, he persuaded Miss Matty to write to Mrs. Gordon, and to tell her of Mrs. Fitz-Adam's existence, and to beg that one so kind, and cordial, and generous, might be included in the pleasant invitation. An answer came back by return of post, with a pretty little note for Mrs. Fitz-Adam, and a request that Miss Matty would deliver it herself and explain the previous omission. Mrs. Fitz-Adam was as pleased as could be, and thanked Miss Matty over and over again. Mr. Peter had said, 'Leave Mrs. Jamieson to me;' so we did; especially as we knew nothing that we could do to alter her determination if once formed.

I did[a] not know, nor did Miss Matty, how things were going on, until Miss Pole asked me, just the day before Mrs. Gordon came, if I thought there was anything between Mr. Peter and Mrs. Jamieson in the matrimonial line, for that Mrs. Jamieson was really going to the lunch at the George. She had sent Mr. Mulliner down to desire that there might be a foot-stool put to the warmest seat in the room, as she meant to come, and knew that their chairs were very high. Miss Pole had picked this piece of news up, and from it she conjectured all sorts of things, and bemoaned yet more. 'If Peter should marry, what would become of poor dear Miss Matty! And Mrs. Jamieson, of all people!' Miss Pole seemed to think there were other ladies in Cranford who would have done more credit to his choice, and I think she must have had some one who was unmarried in her head, for she kept saying, 'It was so wanting in delicacy in a widow to think of such a thing.'

When I got back to Miss Matty's, I really did begin to think that Mr. Peter might be thinking of Mrs. Jamieson for a wife; and I was as unhappy as Miss Pole about it. He had the proof-sheet of a great placard in his hand. 'Signor Brunoni, Magician to the King of Delhi, the Rajah of Oude, and the Great Lama of Thibet, &c. &c.,'[149] was going to 'perform in Cranford for one night only,' – the very next night; and Miss Matty, exultant, showed me a letter from the Gordons, promising to remain over this gaiety, which Miss Matty said was entirely Peter's doing. He had written to ask the Signor to come, and was to be at all the expenses of the affair. Tickets were to be sent gratis to as many as the room would hold. In short, Miss Matty was charmed with the plan, and said that to-morrow Cranford would remind her of the Preston Guild,[150] to which she had been in her youth – a luncheon at the George, with the dear Gordons, and the Signor in the Assembly-room in the evening. But I – I looked only at the fatal words: –

'Under the patronage of the HONOURABLE MRS. JAMIESON.'

She, then, was chosen to preside over this entertainment of Mr. Peter's; she was perhaps going to displace my dear Miss Matty in his heart, and make her life lonely once more! I could not look forward to the morrow with any pleasure; and every innocent anticipation of Miss Matty's only served to add to my annoyance.

So angry,[a] and irritated, and exaggerating every little incident which could add to my irritation, I went on till we were all assembled in the great parlour at the George. Major and Mrs. Gordon and pretty Flora and Mr. Ludovic were all as bright and handsome and friendly as could be; but I could hardly attend to them for watching Mr. Peter, and I saw that Miss Pole was equally busy. I had never seen Mrs. Jamieson so roused and animated before; her face looked full of interest in what Mr. Peter was saying. I drew near to listen. My relief was great when I caught that his words were not words of love, but that, for all his grave face, he was at his old tricks. He was telling her of his travels in India, and describing the wonderful height of the Himalaya mountains: one touch after another added to their size; and each exceeded the former in absurdity; but Mrs. Jamieson really enjoyed all in perfect good faith. I suppose she required strong stimulants to excite her to come out of her apathy. Mr. Peter wound up his account by saying that, of course, at that altitude there were none of the animals to be found that existed in the lower regions; the game – everything was different. Firing one day at some flying creature, he was very much dismayed, when it fell; to find that he had shot a cherubim! Mr. Peter caught my eye at this moment, and gave me such a funny twinkle, that I felt sure he had no thoughts of Mrs. Jamieson as a wife, from that time. She looked uncomfortably amazed:

'But, Mr. Peter – shooting a cherubim – don't you think – I am afraid that was sacrilege!'

Mr. Peter composed his countenance in a moment, and appeared shocked at the idea! which, as he said truly enough, was now presented to him for the first time; but then Mrs. Jamieson must remember that he had been living for a long time among savages – all of whom were heathens – some of them, he was afraid, were downright Dissenters. Then, seeing Miss Matty draw near, he hastily changed the conversation, and after a little while, turning to me, he said, 'Don't be shocked, prim little Mary, at all my wonderful stories; I consider Mrs. Jamieson fair game, and besides, I am bent on propitiating her, and the first step towards it is keeping her well awake. I bribed her here by asking her to let me have[a] her name as patroness for my poor conjuror this evening; and I don't want to give her time enough to get up her rancour against the Hogginses, who are just coming in. I want everybody to be friends, for it harasses Matty so much to hear of these quarrels. I shall go at it again by-and-by, so you need not look shocked. I intend to enter the Assembly-room to-night with Mrs. Jamieson on one side, and my lady Mrs. Hoggins on the other. You see if I don't.'

Somehow or another he did; and fairly got them into conversation together. Major and Mrs. Gordon helped at the good work with their perfect ignorance of any existing coolness between any of the inhabitants of Cranford.

Ever since that day there has been the old friendly sociability in Cranford society; which I am thankful for, because of my dear Miss Matty's love of peace and kindliness. We all love Miss Matty, and I somehow think we are all of us better when she is near us.

THE END.

THE CAGE AT CRANFORD

The Cage at Cranford appeared for the first and only time during EG's lifetime in *All the Year Round* on 28 November 1863. In 1863 negotiations were in hand for the transfer of copyright for *Cranford* from Chapman and Hall, with whom it had lain dormant since 1855, to Smith, Elder & Co., and this may have brought her earlier work to EG's mind. According to Chadwick, *The Cage at Cranford* was 'just a little comedy that Mrs. Gaskell probably prepared hurriedly, sending it to Dickens, who, partial to anything that savoured of *Cranford*, at once printed it in *All the Year Round*.' Chadwick continues, 'Mrs. Gaskell did not like this little sketch after it was published, and for this reason, by her daughters' desire, it was not published in the Knutsford edition of her works' (*Homes and Haunts*, pp. 295–6). These comments are somewhat speculative, but it is the case that there is no mention of the story in EG's correspondence; furthermore she did not repeat the attempt to return to the scene of her earlier success. Those critics who have referred to the story have been mostly consistent in the view that it was not a success: Sharps, for example, comments that 'literary successes can rarely be repeated, and Mrs. Gaskell rarely endeavoured to do so' (*Sharps*, p. 443). There is no manuscript, and the *All the Year Round* text has been reprinted as it stands.

THE CAGE AT CRANFORD.

HAVE I told you anything about my friends at Cranford since the year 1856?[1] I think not.

You remember the Gordons, don't you? She that was Jessie Brown, who married her old love, Major Gordon: and from being poor became quite a rich lady: but for all that never forgot any of her old friends in Cranford.

Well! the Gordons were travelling abroad, for they were very fond of travelling; people who have had to spend part of their lives in a regiment always are, I think. They were now at Paris, in May, 1856, and were going to stop there, and in the neighbourhood all summer, but Mr. Ludovic was coming to England soon; so Mrs. Gordon wrote me word. I was glad she told me, for just then I was waiting to make a little present to Miss Pole, with whom I was staying; so I wrote to Mrs. Gordon, and asked her to choose me out something pretty and new and fashionable, that would be acceptable to Miss Pole. Miss Pole had just been talking a great deal about Mrs. FitzAdam's[2] caps being so unfashionable, which I suppose made me put in that word fashionable; but afterwards I wished I had sent to say my present was not to be too fashionable; for there *is* such a thing, I can assure you! The price of my present was not to be more than twenty shillings, but that is a very handsome sum if you put it in that way, though it may not sound so much if you only call it a sovereign.

Mrs. Gordon wrote back to me, pleased, as she always was, with doing anything for her old friends. She told me she had been out for a day's shopping before going into the country, and had got a cage for herself of the newest and most elegant description, and had thought that she could not do better than get another like it as my present for Miss Pole, as cages were so much better made in Paris than anywhere else. I was rather dismayed when I read this letter, for, however pretty a cage might be, it was something for Miss Pole's own self, and not for her parrot, that I had intended to get. Here had I been finding ever so many reasons against her buying a new cap at Johnson's fashion-show, because I thought that the present which Mrs. Gordon was to choose for me in Paris might turn out to be an elegant and fashionable head-dress; a kind of cross between a turban and a cap, as I see those from Paris mostly are; and now I had to veer round, and advise her to go as fast as she could, and secure Mr. Johnson's cap before any other purchaser snatched it up. But Miss Pole was too sharp for me.

'Why, Mary,' said she, 'it was only yesterday you were running down that cap like anything. You said you know, that lilac was too old a colour for me; and green too young; and that the mixture was very unbecoming.'

'Yes I know,' said I; 'but I have thought better of it. I thought about it a great deal last night, and I think – I thought – they would neutralise each other; and the shadows of any colour are, you know – something I know – complementary colours.' I was not sure of my own meaning, but I had an idea in my head, though I could not express it. She took me up shortly.

'Child, you don't know what you are saying. And besides, I don't want compliments at my time of life. I lay awake, too, thinking of the cap. I only buy one ready-made once a year, and of course it's a matter for considera-tion; and I came to the conclusion that you were quite right.'

'Oh! dear Miss Pole! I was quite wrong; if you only knew – I did think it a very pretty cap – only –'

'Well! do just finish what you've got to say. You're almost as bad as Miss Matty in your way of talking, without being half as good as she is in other ways; though I'm very fond of you, Mary, I don't mean I am not; but you must see you're very off and on, and very muddle-headed. It's the truth, so you will not mind my saying so.'

It was just because it did seem like the truth at that time that I did mind her saying so; and, in despair, I thought I would tell her all.

'I did not mean what I said; I don't think lilac too old or green too young; and I think the mixture very becoming to you; and I think you will never get such a pretty cap again, at least in Cranford.' It was fully out, so far, at least.

'Then, Mary Smith, will you tell me what you did mean, by speaking as you did, and convincing me against my will, and giving me a bad night?'

'I meant – oh, Miss Pole, I meant to surprise you with a present from Paris; and I thought it would be a cap. Mrs. Gordon was to choose it, and Mr. Ludovic to bring it. I dare say it is in England now; only it's not a cap. And I did not want you to buy Johnson's cap, when I thought I was getting another for you.'

Miss Pole found this speech 'muddle-headed,' I have no doubt though she did not say so, only making an odd noise of perplexity. I went on: 'I wrote to Mrs. Gordon, and asked her to get you a present – something new and pretty. I meant it to be a dress, but I suppose I did not say so; I thought it would be a cap, for Paris is so famous for caps, and it is –

'You're a good girl, Mary' (I was past thirty,[3] but did not object to being called a girl; and, indeed, I generally felt like a girl at Cranford, where every-body was so much older than I was), 'but when you want a thing, say what you want; it is the best way in general. And now I suppose Mrs. Gordon has bought something quite different? – a pair of shoes, I dare say, for people talk a deal of Paris shoes. Anyhow, I'm just as much obliged to you, Mary, my dear. Only you should not go and spend your money on me.'

'It was not much money; and it was not a pair of shoes. You'll let me go and get the cap, won't you? It was so pretty – somebody will be sure to snatch it up.'

'I don't like getting a cap that's sure to be unbecoming.'

'But it is not; it was not. I never saw you look so well in anything,' said I.

'Mary, Mary, remember who is the father of lies!'

'But he's not my father,' exclaimed I, in a hurry, for I saw Mrs. FitzAdam go down the street in the direction of Johnson's shop. 'I'll eat my words; they were all false: only just let me run down and buy you that cap – that pretty cap.'

'Well! run off, child. I liked it myself till you put me out of taste with it.'

I brought it back in triumph from under Mrs. FitzAdam's very nose, as she was hanging in meditation over it; and the more we saw of it, the more we felt pleased with our purchase. We turned it on this side, and we turned it on that; and though we hurried it away into Miss Pole's bedroom at the sound of a double knock at the door, when we found it was only Miss Matty and Mr. Peter, Miss Pole could not resist the opportunity of displaying it, and said in a solemn way to Miss Matty:

'Can I speak to you for a few minutes in private?' And I knew feminine delicacy too well to explain what this grave prelude was to lead to; aware how immediately Miss Matty's anxious tremor would be allayed by the sight of the cap. I had to go on talking to Mr. Peter, however, when I would far rather have been in the bedroom, and heard the observations and comments.

We talked of the new cap all day; what gowns it would suit; whether a certain bow was not rather too coquettish for a woman of Miss Pole's age. 'No longer young,' as she called herself, after a little struggle with the words, though at sixty-five she need not have blushed as if she were telling a falsehood. But at last the cap was put away, and with a wrench we turned our thoughts from the subject. We had been silent for a little while, each at our work with a candle between us, when Miss Pole began:

'It was very kind of you, Mary, to think of giving me a present from Paris.'

'Oh, I was only too glad to be able to get you something! I hope you will like it, though it is not what I expected.'

'I am sure I shall like it. And a surprise is always so pleasant.'

'Yes; but I think Mrs. Gordon has made a very odd choice.'

'I wonder what it is. I don't like to ask, but there's a great deal in anticipation; I remember hearing dear Miss Jenkyns say that "anticipation was the soul of enjoyment," or something like that. Now there is no anticipation in a surprise; that's the worst of it.'

'Shall I tell you what it is?'

'Just as you like, my dear. If it is any pleasure to you, I am quite willing to hear.'

'Perhaps I had better not. It is something quite different to what I expected, and meant to have got; and I'm not sure if I like it as well.'

'Relieve your mind, if you like, Mary. In all disappointments sympathy is a great balm.'

'Well, then, it's something not for you; it's for Polly. It's a cage. Mrs. Gordon says they make such pretty ones in Paris.'

I could see that Miss Pole's first emotion was disappointment. But she was very fond of her cockatoo, and the thought of his smartness in his new habitation made her be reconciled in a moment; besides that she was really grateful to me for having planned a present for her.

'Polly! Well, yes; his old cage is very shabby; he is so continually pecking at it with his sharp bill. I dare say Mrs. Gordon noticed it when she called here last October. I shall always think of you, Mary, when I see him in it. Now we can have him in the drawing-room, for I dare say a French cage will be quite an ornament to the room.'

And so she talked on, till we worked ourselves up into high delight at the idea of Polly in his new abode, presentable in it even to the Honourable Mrs. Jamieson. The next morning Miss Pole said she had been dreaming of Polly with her new cap on his head, while she herself sat on a perch in the new cage and admired him. Then, as if ashamed of having revealed the fact of imagining 'such arrant nonsense' in her sleep, she passed on rapidly to the philosophy of dreams, quoting some book she had lately been reading, which was either too deep in itself, or too confused in her repetition for me to understand it. After breakfast, we had the cap out again; and that in its different aspects occupied us for an hour or so; and then, as it was a fine day, we turned into the garden, where Polly was hung on a nail outside the kitchen window. He clamoured and screamed at the sight of his mistress, who went to look for an almond for him. I examined his cage meanwhile, old discoloured wicker-work, clumsily made by a Cranford basket-maker. I took out Mrs. Gordon's letter; it was dated the fifteenth, and this was the twentieth, for I had kept it secret for two days in my pocket. Mr. Ludovic was on the point of setting out for England when she wrote.

'Poor Polly!' said I, as Miss Pole, returning, fed him with the almond.

'Ah! Polly does not know what a pretty cage he is going to have,' said she, talking to him as she would have done to a child; and then turning to me, she asked when I thought it would come? We reckoned up dates, and made out that it might arrive that very day. So she called to her little stupid servant-maiden Fanny,[4] and bade her go out and buy a great brass-headed nail, very strong, strong enough to bear Polly and the new cage, and we all three weighed the cage in our hands, and on her return she was to come up into the drawing-room with the nail and a hammer.

Fanny was a long time, as she always was, over her errands; but as soon as she came back, we knocked the nail, with solemn earnestness, into the house-wall, just outside the drawing-room window; for, as Miss Pole observed, when I was not there she had no one to talk to, and as in summer-time she generally sat with the window open, she could combine two purposes, the giving air and sun to Polly-Cockatoo, and the having his agreeable companionship in her solitary hours.

'When it rains, my dear, or even in a very hot sun, I shall take the cage in. I would not have your pretty present spoilt for the world. It was very kind of you to think of it; I am quite come round to liking it better than any present of mere dress; and dear Mrs. Gordon has shown all her usual pretty observation in remembering my Polly-Cockatoo.'

'Polly-Cockatoo' was his grand name; I had only once or twice heard him spoken of by Miss Pole in this formal manner, except when she was speaking to the servants; then she always gave him his full designation, just as most people call their daughters Miss, in speaking of them to strangers or servants. But since Polly was to have a new cage, and all the way from Paris too, Miss Pole evidently thought it necessary to treat him with unusual respect.

We were obliged to go out to pay some calls; but we left strict orders with Fanny what to do if the cage arrived in our absence, as (we had calculated) it might. Miss Pole stood ready bonneted and shawled at the kitchen door, I behind her, and cook behind Fanny, each of us listening to the conversation of the other two.

'And Fanny, mind if it comes you coax Polly-Cockatoo nicely into it. He is very particular, and may be attached to his old cage, though it is so shabby. Remember, birds have their feelings as much as we have! Don't hurry him in making up his mind.'

'Please, ma'am, I think an almond would help him to get over his feelings,' said Fanny, dropping a curtsey at every speech, as she had been taught to do at her charity school.

'A very good idea, very. If I have my keys in my pocket I will give you an almond for him. I think he is sure to like the view up the street from the window; he likes seeing people, I think.'

'It's but a dull look-out into the garden; nowt but dumb flowers,' said cook, touched by this allusion to the cheerfulness of the street, as contrasted with the view from her own kitchen window.

'It's a very good look-out for busy people,' said Miss Pole, severely. And then, feeling she was likely to get the worst of it in an encounter with her old servant, she withdrew with meek dignity, being deaf to some sharp reply; and of course I, being bound to keep order, was deaf too. If the truth must be told, we rather hastened our steps, until we had banged the street-door behind us.

We called on Miss Matty, of course; and then on Mrs. Hoggins. It seemed as if ill-luck would have it that we went to the only two households of Cranford where there was the encumbrance of a man, and in both places the man was where he ought not to have been – namely, in his own house, and in the way. Miss Pole – out of civility to me, and because she really was full of the new cage for Polly, and because we all in Cranford relied on the sympathy of our neighbours in the veriest trifle that interested us – told Miss Matty, and Mr. Peter, and Mr. and Mrs Hoggins; he was standing in the drawing-room, booted and spurred, and eating his hunk of bread-and-cheese in the very presence of his aristocratic wife, my lady that was. As Miss Pole said afterwards, if refinement was not to be found in Cranford, blessed as it was with so many scions of county families, she did not know where to meet with it. Bread-and-cheese in a drawing-room! Onions next.

But for all Mr. Hoggins's vulgarity, Miss Pole told him of the present she was about to receive.

'Only think! a new cage for Polly – Polly – Polly-Cockatoo, you know, Mr. Hoggins. You remember him, and the bite he gave me once because he wanted to be put back in his cage, pretty bird?'

'I only hope the new cage will be strong as well as pretty, for I must say a – ' He caught a look from his wife, I think, for he stopped short. 'Well, we're old friends, Polly and I, and he put some practice in my way once. I shall be up the street this afternoon, and perhaps I shall step in and see this smart Parisian cage.'

'Do!' said Miss Pole, eagerly. 'Or, if you are in a hurry, look up at my drawing-room window; if the cage is come, it will be hanging out there, and Polly in it.'

We had passed the omnibus that met the train from London some time ago, so we were not surprised as we returned home to see Fanny half out of the window, and cook evidently either helping or hindering her. Then they both took their heads in; but there was no cage hanging up. We hastened up the steps.

Both Fanny and the cook met us in the passage.

'Please, ma'am,' said Fanny, 'there's no bottom to the cage, and Polly would fly away.'

'And there's no top,' exclaimed cook. 'He might get out at the top quite easy.'

'Let me see,' said Miss Pole, brushing past, thinking no doubt that her superior intelligence was all that was needed to set things to rights. On the ground lay a bundle, or a circle of hoops, neatly covered over with calico, no more like a cage for Polly-Cockatoo than I am like a cage. Cook took something up between her finger and thumb, and lifted the unsightly present from Paris. How I wish it had stayed there! – but foolish ambition has brought people to ruin before now; and my twenty shillings are gone, sure enough, and there must be some use or some ornament intended by the maker of the thing before us.

'Don't you think it's a mousetrap, ma'am?' asked Fanny, dropping her little curtsey.

For reply, the cook lifted up the machine, and showed how easily mice might run out; and Fanny shrank back abashed. Cook was evidently set against the new invention, and muttered about its being all of a piece with French things – French cooks, French plums (nasty dried-up things), French rolls (as had no substance in 'em).

Miss Pole's good manners, and desire of making the best of things in my presence, induced her to try and drown cook's mutterings.

'Indeed, I think it will make a very nice cage for Polly-Cockatoo. How pleased he will be to go from one hoop to another, just like a ladder, and with a board or two at the bottom, and nicely tied up at the top –'

Fanny was struck with a new idea.

'Please, ma'am, my sister-in-law has got an aunt as lives lady's-maid with Sir John's daughter – Miss Arley. And they did say as she wore iron petticoats all made of hoops –'

'Nonsense, Fanny!' we all cried; for such a thing had not been heard of in all Drumble, let alone Cranford, and I was rather looked upon in the light of a fast young woman by all the laundresses of Cranford, because I had two corded petticoats.

'Go mind thy business, wench,' said cook, with the utmost contempt; 'I'll warrant we'll manage th' cage without thy help.'

'It is near dinner-time, Fanny, and the cloth not laid,' said Miss Pole, hoping the remark might cut two ways; but cook had no notion of going. She stood on the bottom step of the stairs, holding the Paris perplexity aloft in the air.

'It might do for a meat-safe,'[5] said she. 'Cover it o'er wi' canvas, to keep th' flies out. It is a good framework, I reckon, anyhow!' She held her head on one side, like a connoisseur in meat-safes, as she was.

Miss Pole said, 'Are you sure Mrs. Gordon called it a cage, Mary? Because she is a woman of her word, and would not have called it so if it was not.'

'Look here; I have the letter in my pocket.'

'"I have wondered how I could best fulfil your commission for me to purchase something to the value of" – um, um, never mind – "fashionable and pretty for dear Miss Pole, and at length I have decided upon one of the new kind of 'cages'" (look here, Miss Pole; here is the word C. A. G. E.), "which are made so much lighter and more elegant in Paris than in England. Indeed, I am not sure if they have ever reached you, for it is not a month since I saw the first of the kind in Paris."'

'Does she say anything about Polly Cockatoo?' asked Miss Pole. 'That would settle the matter at once, as showing that she had him in her mind.'

'No – nothing.'

Just then Fanny came along the passage with the tray full of dinner-things in her hands. When she had put them down, she stood at the door of the dining-room taking a distant view of the article. 'Please, ma'am, it looks like a petticoat without any stuff in it; indeed it does, if I'm to be whipped for saying it.'

But she only drew down upon herself a fresh objurgation from the cook; and sorry and annoyed, I seized the opportunity of taking the thing out of cook's hand, and carrying it upstairs, for it was full time to get ready for dinner. But we had very little appetite for our meal, and kept constantly making suggestions, one to the other, as to the nature and purpose of this Paris 'cage,' but as constantly snubbing poor little Fanny's reiteration of 'Please, ma'am, I do believe it's a kind of petticoat – indeed I do.' At length Miss Pole turned upon her with almost as much vehemence as cook had done, only in choicer language.

'Don't be so silly, Fanny. Do you think ladies are like children, and must be put in go-carts; or need wire guards like fires to surround them; or can get warmth out of bits of whale-bone and steel; a likely thing indeed! Don't keep talking about what you don't understand.'

So our maiden was mute for the rest of the meal. After dinner we had Polly brought upstairs in her old cage, and I held out the new one, and we turned it about in every way. At length Miss Pole said:

'Put Polly-Cockatoo back, and shut him up in his cage. You hold this French thing up' (alas! that my present should be called a 'thing'), 'and I'll sew a bottom on to it. I'll lay a good deal, they've forgotten to sew in the bottom before sending it off.' So I held and she sewed; and then she held and I sewed, till it was all done. Just as we had put Polly-Cockatoo in, and were closing up the top with a pretty piece of old yellow ribbon – and, indeed, it was not a bad-looking cage after all our trouble – Mr. Hoggins came upstairs, having been seen by Fanny before he had time to knock at the door.

'Hallo!' said he, almost tumbling over us, as we were sitting on the floor at our work. 'What's this?'

'It's this pretty present for Polly-Cockatoo,' said Miss Pole, raising herself up with as much dignity as she could, 'that Mary has had sent from Paris for me.' Miss Pole was in great spirits now we had got Polly in; I can't say that I was.

Mr. Hoggins began to laugh in his boisterous vulgar way.

'For Polly – ha! ha! It's meant for you, Miss Pole – ha! ha! It's a new invention to hold your gowns out – ha! ha!'

'Mr. Hoggins! you may be a surgeon, and a very clever one, but nothing – not even your profession – gives you a right to be indecent.'

Miss Pole was throughly roused, and I trembled in my shoes. But Mr. Hoggins only laughed the more. Polly screamed in concert, but Miss Pole stood in stiff rigid propriety, very red in the face.

'I beg your pardon, Miss Pole, I am sure. But I am pretty certain I am right. It's no indecency that I can see; my wife and Mrs. Fitz-Adam take in a Paris fashion-book between 'em, and I can't help seeing the plates of fashions sometimes – ha! ha! ha! Look, Polly has got out of his queer prison – ha! ha! ha!'

Just then Mr. Peter came in; Miss Matty was so curious to know if the expected present had arrived. Mr. Hoggins took him by the arm, and pointed to the poor thing lying on the ground, but could not explain for laughing. Miss Pole said:

'Although I am not accustomed to give an explanation of my conduct to gentlemen, yet, being insulted in my own house by – by Mr. Hoggins, I must appeal to the brother of my old friend – my very oldest friend. Is this article a lady's petticoat, or a bird's cage?'

She held it up as she made this solemn inquiery. Mr. Hoggins seized the moment to leave the room, in shame, as I supposed, but, in reality, to fetch his wife's fashion-book; and, before I had completed the narration of the story of my unlucky commission, he returned, and, holding the fashion-plate open by the side of the extended article, demonstrated the identity of the two.

But Mr. Peter had always a smooth way of turning off anger, by either his fun or a compliment. 'It is a cage,' said he, bowing to Miss Pole; 'but it is a cage for an angel, instead of a bird! Come along, Hoggins, I want to speak to you!'

And, with an apology, he took the offending and victorious surgeon out of Miss Pole's presence. For a good while we said nothing; and we were now rather shy of little Fanny's superior wisdom when she brought up tea. But towards night our spirits revived, and we were quite ourselves again, when Miss Pole proposed that we should cut up the pieces of steel or whalebone – which, to do them justice, were very elastic – and make ourselves two good comfortable English calashes[6] out of them with the aid of a piece of dyed silk which Miss Pole had by her.

APPENDIX A

The following illustrations by Myles Birket Foster are taken from the first edition of *The Moorland Cottage*, published by Chapman and Hall in 1850.

FRONTISPIECE.

THE MOORLAND COTTAGE
BY THE AUTHOR OF MARY BARTON
CHAPMAN AND HALL
193 PICCADILLY

The Moorland Cottage.

CHAPTER I.

IF you take the turn to the left, after you pass the lyke-gate at Combehurst Church, you will come to the wooden bridge over the brook ; keep along the field-path which mounts higher and higher, and, in half a mile or so, you will be in a breezy upland field, almost

Oh, Maggie! look what you 've done! Spilt it all, with not turning quickly enough when I told you. Now you may fetch it again for yourself, for I 'll have nothing to do with it.''

"I did not understand you in time," said she, softly. But he had turned away, and gone back in offended dignity to the house. Maggie had nothing to do but return to the well, and fill

CHAPTER II.

T length they were dressed, and
Nancy stood on the court-steps,
shading her eyes, and looking
after them, as they climbed the
heathery slope leading to Combe-
hurst.

"I wish she 'd take her hand sometimes, just to let
her know the feel of her mother's hand. Perhaps she
will, at least after Master Edward goes to school."

36 THE MOORLAND COTTAGE.

soothe the poor child, who was crying at the thought that Mrs. Buxton would soon die, and that she should never see her again. Nancy loved Maggie dearly, and felt no jealousy of this warm admiration of the unknown lady. She listened to her story and her fears till the sobs were hushed; and the moon fell through the casement on the white closed eyelids of one, who still sighed in her sleep.

CHAPTER III.

N three weeks, the day came for Edward's departure. A great cake and a parcel of gingerbread soothed his sorrows on leaving home.

"Don't cry, Maggie!" said he to her on the last morning; "you see I don't. Christmas will soon be here, and I dare

52   THE MOORLAND COTTAGE.

You 'll have it in your power to help him on in the
world."

But Frank answered, " He is not quite honourable,
sir.   I can't bear a boy who is not quite honourable.
Boys brought up at those private schools are so full of
tricks ! "

" Nay, my lad, there thou 'rt wrong. I was brought
up at a private school, and no one can say I ever
dirtied my hands with a trick in my life.   Good old
Mr. Thomson would have flogged the life out of a boy
who did anything mean or underhand."

CHAPTER V.

CHRISTMAS-DAY was strange and
sad. Mrs. Buxton had always contrived
to be in the drawing-room, ready to
receive them all after dinner. Mr. Bux-
ton tried to do away with his thoughts
of her by much talking ; but every now
and then he looked wistfully towards the
door. Erminia exerted herself to be as
lively as she could, in order, if possible, to
fill up the vacuum. Edward,

CHAPTER VII.

HE next day Mr. Henry came. He was a quiet, stern-looking man, of considerable intelligence and refinement, and so much taste for music as to charm Erminia, who had rather dreaded his visit. But all the amenities of life were put aside when he entered Mr. Buxton's sanctum—his " office," as he called the room where he received his tenants and

CHAPTER IX.

HEN she opened the kitchen-door, there was the same small, mizzling rain that had obscured the light for weeks, and now it seemed to obscure hope. She clambered slowly (for indeed she was very feeble,) up the Fell Lane, and threw herself under the leafless thorn, every small branch and twig of which was loaded with rain-drops. She did not see the well-beloved and familiar landscape, for her tears; and did not miss the hills in the distance

CHAPTER XI.

MAGGIE sat on deck, wrapped in her duffel-cloak; the old familiar cloak, which had been her wrap in many a

182   THE MOORLAND COTTAGE.

Over both old and young the memory of one who is dead broods like a dove,—of one who could do but little during her lifetime ; who was doomed only to " stand and wait ;" who was meekly content to *be* gentle, holy, patient, and undefiled,—the memory of the invalid Mrs. Buxton.

APPENDIX B

Cranford: *Household Words* and *1853* instalment and chapter divisions

Household Words	1853
Our Society at Cranford 4 (13 December 1851)	Chapters I ('Our Society') and II ('The Captain')
A Love Affair at Cranford 4 (3 January 1852)	Chapters III ('A Love Affair of Long Ago') and IV ('A Visit to an Old Bachelor')
Memory at Cranford 4 (13 March 1852)	Chapters V ('Old Letters') and VI ('Poor Peter')
Visiting at Cranford 5 (3 April 1852)	Chapters VII ('Visiting') and VIII ('"Your Ladyship"')
The Great Cranford Panic. In two chapters. Chapter the first. 6 (8 January 1853)	Chapter IX ('Signor Brunoni'); Chapter X ('The Panic') up to 'con- venient and acceptable.' (p. 247)
The Great Cranford Panic. In two chapters. Chapter the second. 6 (15 January 1853)	Chapter X, continuing from break in chapter as above. Chapter XI ('Samuel Brown')
Stopped Payment at Cranford 7 (2 April 1853)	Chapters XII ('Engaged to be Mar- ried') and XIII ('Stopped Payment')
Friends in Need at Cranford 7 (7 May 1853)	Chapter XIV ('Friends in Need')
A Happy Return to Cranford 7 (21 May 1853)	Chapters XV ('A Happy Return') and XVI ('Peace to Cranford')

APPENDIX C

The following four illustrations by George Du Maurier are taken from the 'Illustrated Edition' of *Cranford*, published by Smith, Elder & Co. in 1864.

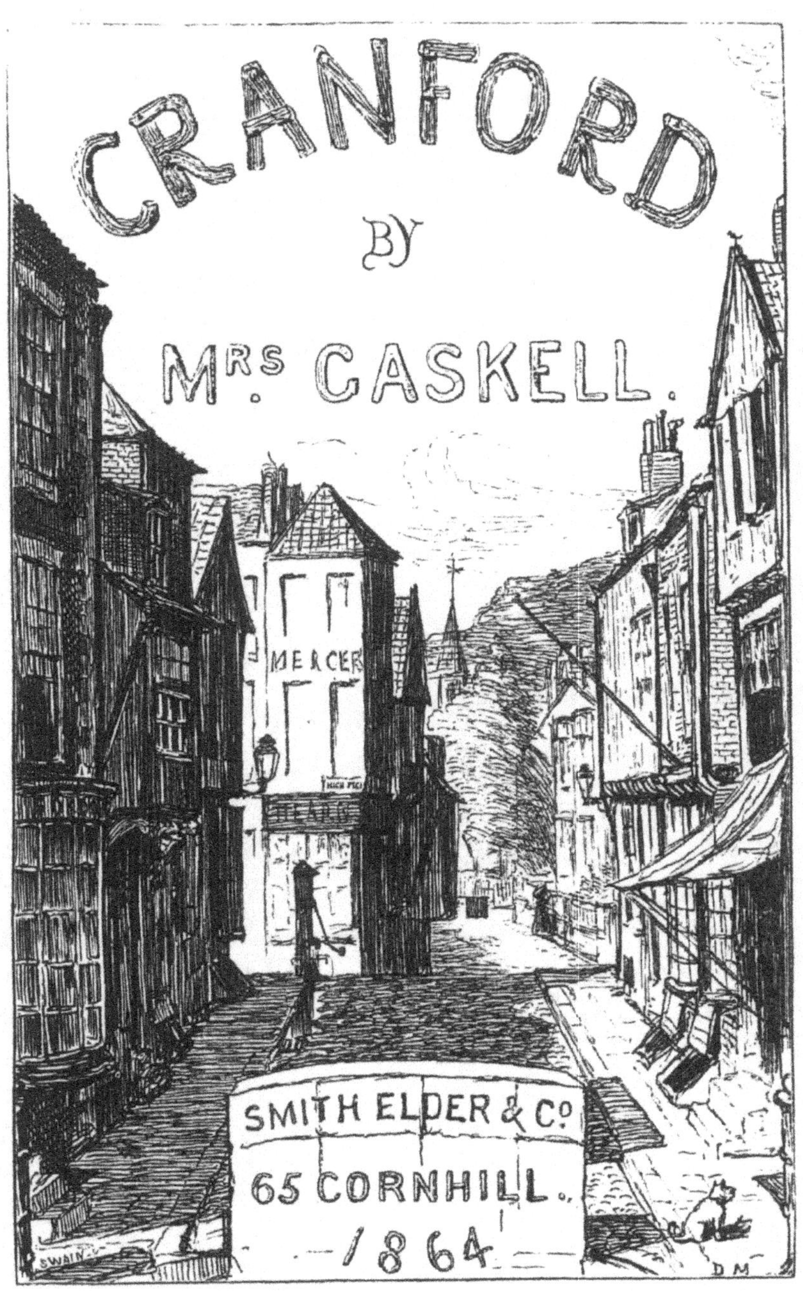
CRANFORD
BY
Mrs GASKELL.
MERCER
SMITH ELDER & Co
65 CORNHILL.
1864
SWAIN
DM

"She looked up to remonstrate."

"Matty—Miss Matilda—Miss Jenkyns!"

" Please, ma'am, he's only Jem Hearn."

EXPLANATORY NOTES

The Moorland Cottage

1   *lyke-gate*] more commonly lychgate: a roofed gateway at the entrance to a churchyard, traditionally the point at which the officiating clergyman at a funeral received the coffin.

2   *German forest-tales.*] Two possible sources have been identified for these stories: either *The Fair-Haired Eckbert*, a fairy tale by Ludwig Tieck (1774–1853), which EG might have read in a translation by Thomas Carlyle, or the *Schwarzwälder Dorfgeschichten* or *Village Tales from the Black Forest* by Berthold Auerbach (1812–82), described by Peter Skrine as 'the German best-sellers of the 1840s' ('Mrs Gaskell and Germany', *GSJ*, 7 (1993), p. 43). A review of the English translation of the latter appeared in the *British Quarterly Review* in 1847.

3   *noisettes … crane's-bill*] The contrast here is between the cultivated and semi-cultivated plants around the house and the wild flowers of the moorland. Of the plants referred to noisettes are a variety of rose, fraxinellas are highly scented species of the shrub dittany, cistus is a shrub also known as rock rose. Cranesbill, of the genus *geranium*, has fruit in the shape of a long slender beak; here it is growing wild.

4   *beau-pot*] a flower vase.

5   *'As founder's line … of presentation';*] i.e., to a place at the school to which Edward is to be sent. Mr Buxton is presumably a descendent of its founder. This seems a more likely explanation at this point than Lewis's suggestion that the presentation is to a church living, although there is a later reference to Mr Buxton having the right of presentation to the living of Combehurst (p. 29).

6   *Abdel-Kadr,*] The Arabic name of the horse suggests its quality.

7   *the man in the Arabian … hard, barren rock*] The story is the familiar one of Ali Baba, who saw a band of robbers disappear into a cave, apparently solid rock, which opened up at the command, 'Open Sesame!' The popularity of the *Arabian Nights* in the Victorian period is reflected by the frequent reprinting of the translation by Edward William Lane (1801–76), first published in monthly parts 1839–40.

8   *cured of a waste by a charm.*] cured of a potentially fatal decline in health perhaps by a folk remedy. The term 'waste' was already an archaism, although *OED* cites an example of 1878.

9   *'ministers of Him, to do His pleasure.*] Psalms 103:21: 'Bless ye the Lord, all ye his hosts; ye ministers of his, that do his pleasure.'

10   *'All may have … a glorious life, or grave."*] from 'The Church-Porch' by George Herbert (1593–1633), the introductory poem to his collection *The Temple* (1633). EG misquotes: the original reads 'all may have/If they dare try, a glorious life or grave.'

11   *those whose names … a genteel education.*] These references interestingly anticipate the contrast between Dorothea Brooke and Rosamund Vincy in George Eliot's *Middlemarch* (1872–3).

12   *'Arma, virumque … primus ab oris.'*] 'Arms and the man who first from the shores of Troy, I sing' (Latin) – the famous first line of the *Aeneid*, by Virgil.

13   *'Infir dealis … eelis, inclay noneis."'*] a joke, with the English words reformed to appear as Latin.

14   *'"Apud in is almi des ire … at restis."'*] see note 13, above. Edward replies in kind: 'A pudding is all my desire / My mistress I never require, / A lover I find it a jest is, / His misery never at rest is.' Edward's rhyme is perhaps slightly improper, given the company; it is certainly misjudged.

15   *Don Quixote,*] the eponymous hero of Cervantes novel (1605, 1615). Sancho Panza is his foil.

16   *'And she shall … pass into her face.'*] William Wordsworth (1770–1850), 'Three years she grew in sun and shower', written in 1799 and first published in the two-volume second edition of *Lyrical Ballads* (1800). Except for the fact that Lucy dies an early death her situation in the poems makes her an appropriate analogy for Maggie in this very Wordsworthian story.

17   *common delf or the best China,*] earthenware, from Delft in Holland, as distinct from porcelain from China.

18   *it's not post-day.*] In remoter parts of the country there would not have been a daily post at this point in time.

19   *turkey red cotton.*] cotton of a bright red dye, used for marking clothes.

20   *as long as … Victoria was unmarried,*] Princess Victoria became Queen in 1837 and married the Prince Consort in 1840. This helps to fix the date of the action. Later Edward takes a steam ship to America; this would not have been possible before 1840. See note 37, below.

21   *charr.*] a small lake-fish, regarded as a delicacy in its preserved or potted form.

22   *I, a 'fool, rush in where angels fear to tread,'*] Pope, *Essay on Criticism* (1709), Part III, l. 627: 'Fools rush in where Angels fear to tread.'

23   gêne,] awkwardness (French).

24   *in standing for the shire;*] i.e., as Member of Parliament.

25   *the 'melodies of the everlasting chime'*] from John Keble, 'St. Matthew', in *The Christian Year* (1827): 'There are in this loud stunning tide / Of human care and crime, / With whom the melodies abide / Of th'everlasting chime; / Who carry music in their heart / Through dusky lane and wrangling mart, / Plying their daily task with busier feet, / Because their secret souls a holy strain repeat.' EG cites the complete stanza as a chapter-motto in *Ruth* (Ch. V).

26   *'Whose faith is fixt … I love.'*'] The lines are from Tennyson's *In Memoriam* (1850), xcvii.33–6, with the opening word changed from 'Her' to 'Whose'. EG was an admirer of Tennyson's poem: 'I have got an In Memoriam of my own, it is a pleasure to me to have what I like so earnestly of *my own*' (*Letters*, p. 130).

27   *'Pleasure digging a Grave;'*] *Lewis* notes that books of engravings were used for entertainment and instruction in polite social circles in the nineteenth-century, but the specific engraving referred to here remains unidentified.

28   *intended to enter … vacation was ended.*] i.e., to qualify for a career in the legal profession.

29   *the widow … her mite.*] Mark 12:42–4.

30   *a story … Transmigration of Indra?*] A story of a man who is magically enabled to experience the lives and feelings of animals. It appears in vol. ii of *Evenings at Home; or the Juvenile Budget Opened. Consisting of a variety of Miscellaneous Pieces, for the Instruction and Amusement of Young Persons,* by Dr John Aiken and Mrs Anna Laetitia Barbauld, 6 vols (1743–1824). (*Lewis,* who points out that EG misquotes the title, 'The Transmigrations of Indur.')

31   *'"What's done we partly … what's resisted,"'*] Robert Burns (1759–96), 'An address to unco'guid or the rigidly righteous'.

32   *breach of promise of marriage.*] an action of breach of promise could be brought against any party who broke off an engagement: such actions were usually brought by women who had been deserted. They usually involved property considerations. Mr Buxton is saying here that any action brought against his son could be defended on the grounds of Edward's exposure. Breach of promise in itself was effectively removed from the statue book by the *Law Reform (Miscellaneous Provisions) Act* of 1970.

33   *hard as a nether mill-stone.*] *OED* cites the Geneva Bible, Job 41:14 for 'nether mill-stone' thus 'His heart is as strong as a stone, and as hard as the nether mill-stone.' The passage does not appear thus in the King James translation. The nether millstone was the lower stone, against which the corn was ground.

34 *half the damages … in any other way.*] i.e., as the consequences of an action for breach of promise. The suggestion seems to conflict with Mr Buxton's statement (see note 32, above).

35 *make assurance doubly sure.*] *Macbeth*, IV.i.83.

36 *some Ariel imprisoned in the thick branches*] In Shakespeare's *The Tempest*, Ariel is a spirit who, prior to the action of the play, had been imprisoned in a tree by the witch Sycorax.

37 *as soon as possible, to Liverpool,*] from where boats to America depart. The illustration at the head of Chapter XI (see Appendix A, p. 315) makes it clear that the packet referred to here is a steamship. Regular crossings of the Atlantic by steam from Liverpool were initiated in 1840: this is thus the first possible date for the action. Edward is to travel by packet-boat, a scheduled service.

38 *shippen.*] or 'shippon', a cowshed.

39 *Botany Bay.*] geographically the bay on the east coast of Australia where captain Cook first landed in 1770. More generally a term used loosely for transportation to the penal colony in New South Wales.

40 *El Dorado*] traditionally the name given to the mythical city ruled over by 'El Dorado' (the Golden One (Spanish)), but used metaphorically for any location believed to have the resources to make men's fortunes.

41 *The Spaniards who went out with Pizarro*] the expedition to Peru led by Francisco Pizarro (1475–1541) which conquered the Incas.

42 *'working his way … hunting-counties,'*] the midland counties of England, notably Leicestershire, Rutland and Northamptonshire, which had excellent hunting facilities.

43 *Esau's craving for a blessing,*] The reference is to the story of Jacob and Esau. Jacob contrived to obtain his father's blessing, instead of his brother Esau, on whom it should have been bestowed. See Genesis 25–3. *Lewis* (p. 293), draws parallels between the biblical story and that of Edward and Maggie.

44 *steerage-passengers*] Steerage was the accommodation provided for the cheapest passages, where there was no privacy or provision for individual accommodation.

45 *Llandudno … the little Ormes' head.'*] on the extreme north coast of Wales. As a young woman EG recorded the effects of a shipping disaster in 1831 off the North Wales coast (to Harriet Carr, 'August the last. 1831 & Sep. 1ˢᵗ', *Further Letters*, p. 7.) EG's personal knowledge of both Liverpool and North Wales is well attested, and it reveals itself in the story in her references to local place names.

46 *'in that new world which is the old.'*] Tennyson, 'The Departure', l. 4, from his poetic sequence, 'The Day-dream', *Poems* (1842): 'And on her lover's arm she leant, / And round her waist she felt it fold, / And far across the hills they went / In that new world which is the old'. Lewis

(p. 294), emphasises the appropriateness of the whole poem to the story.

47 *his mother's diamond-guard,*] a device used to protect a piece of jewellery. *OED* does not record, but offers, under 'keeper' (6c): 'guard-ring: a finger-ring to keep another (esp. the wedding ring) on the finger', citing instances from 1851 and 1858.

48 *their car.*] obviously a horse-drawn vehicle, although the term was also used at this time for a railway-carriage.

49 *'stand and wait;'*] John Milton (1608–74), 'On his Blindness': 'They also serve who only stand and wait.'

The Last Generation in England

1 *an old number ... domestic life.'*] *Edinburgh Review*, 87 (January–April 1848), p. 390. The observation occurs in a review of works relating to Samuel Taylor Coleridge and Robert Southey.

2 *early volumes of the 'Doctor, &c.'*] *The Doctor*, 7 vols (1834–7), by Robert Southey but published anonymously, and described by *DNB* as 'that glorious commonplace book'. A selection in one volume was published in 1848 and thus may have come to EG's attention.

3 *a very old ... of these families,*] The town, though unspecified here, is Knutsford: a number of landed families lived in the area. The most influential of them in Knutsford itself in the nineteenth century were the Egertons of Tatton, although the reference to 'a very old family' and the continuation in the plural may suggest others – for example the Stanley family, descendants of the Earls of Derby, referred to later in the essay, the Leycesters of Toft, close to Knutsford itself, or the Leicesters of Tabley Hall, a few miles further away.

4 *the cadets of these same families;*] the younger sons.

5 ci-devant] former (French).

6 *the Mohawks a century before.*] Samuel Johnson, in his *Dictionary* (1755) defines 'Mohock' as 'the name of a cruel nation of America given to ruffians who infested, or rather were imagined to infest, the streets of London'. There are various literary references to the phenomenon from the early eighteenth century.

7 *'Mrs Grundy's' existence*] Mrs Grundy was a character in *Speed the Plough* (1798), a five-act comedy by Thomas Morton (c. 1764–1838). Her name became synonymous with narrow-minded social and moral disapproval, and in particular with prudishness.

8 *No old lady ... day of its death.*] The same story appears in *Cranford*. See p. 168.

9.   *Lilliputian*] tiny, from Gulliver's voyage to Lilliput in Swift's *Gulliver's Travels* (1726)

10. *Fairly Fair.*] 'Hir silken cords of twirtle twist, / Weil plett with silver schene; / And apron sett with mony a dice / Of needle-wark sae rare, / Wove by nae hand, as ze may guess, / Saif that of Fairly fair.' Elizabeth, Lady Wardlaw (1677–1727), *Hardyknute: A Scottish Fragment*, reprinted in Thomas Percy's *Reliques* (1767). The term is used repeatedly in the ballad as a name for its heroine.

11. *One lady … inside, my dear!'*] another famous *Cranford* episode. See pp. 232–3.

12. *calash and pattens,*] articles of protective clothing. Calaches were hoods that protected ladies' bonnets; pattens were overshoes.

13. *Preference,*] a card game, similar to quadrille, whist and bridge, in that players bid for trumps and for the number of tricks that they will win.

14. *he called the knave … voted him vulgar;*] cf., Dickens, *Great Expectations* (1860–1), ch. 8: '"He calls the knaves, Jacks, this boy!"' The terminology is indicative of social origins. In *Cranford* the solecisim is committed by the Cranford surgeon, Mr Hoggins. See *Cranford*, p. 254 and note 105, below.

15   comme il faut … haute volée.] The two French terms are used with Anglicised inferences. 'Comme il faut' in this context suggests that the tea parties are at a certain level of gentility; 'haut volée' suggests people of superior social rank.

16   *Mr. Rigmarole,*] referred to several times as a fictional persona in the essays of Oliver Goldsmith. See e.g., 'A Reverie at the Boar's-head tavern in Eastcheap' (1760) where 'Mr. Rigmarole' is addressed by Mistress Quickly, and *Essays* (1798), pp. 152, 158, 160, 163.

17   *I remember a card-party … the couch.*] again repeated in *Cranford*. See pp. 166–7.

18   *two earl's daughters … married a General,*] The references are to the Stanley family, Earls of Derby. The 11th Earl (1689–1776) had six daughters, four of whom remained unmarried, and a son, James, who predeceased him. In 1743 Lady Charlotte Stanley, one of the six daughters, eloped with and married the then Colonel John Burgoyne (1722–92), who as General Burgoyne became commander of the British forces in the American War of Independence. He wrote a number of plays.

19   *Lady Jane*] Lady Jane Stanley, one of the six daughters of the 11th Earl of Derby (see note 18, above). The incident of the paving of the footpath is described in *Knutsford Its Traditions and History* (1859), p. 144 by the Revd Henry Green. Green was known to EG, who clearly knew of the story before its appearance in Green's book. According to Green, Lady Jane Stanley 'filled a very important and influential position in

the town, and her memory is still highly respected for her benevolence as well as for her other sterling qualities … but she had very strict notions of the proprieties of life, – and would not have them infringed' (pp. 144–5).

20   *'In my days … the world come to?'*] These conventions of correspondence inform Chapter V ('Old Letters') of *Cranford*.

21   *brobdignagian*] a further reference to *Gulliver's Travels*, this time to the voyage to Brobdignag, the land of the giants.

Mr. Harrison's Confessions

1   *a beautiful case of preparations,*] For 'preparation' *OED* offers, *inter alia*, 'a specimen of a natural object specially prepared for some scientific purpose.' This is the likely meaning here, with the inference that the scientific purpose is a medical one.

2   *in* dishabille.] informally dressed, not dressed for public appearance (French).

3   *Mayence*] the French name of the German city of Mainz.

4   *Hessian boots … top-boots*] Hessian boots were formal high boots named after the German troops of Hesse who wore them as part of their uniform. Top boots were a more conventional riding boot.

5   *"jemmy:"*] spruce, neat (*OED*).

6   *'cut-away,'*] a coat with the skirt cut back from the waist.

7   *Galen or Hippocrates*] Galen (c. AD 130–201) and Hippocrates (c. 460–375 BC) were Greek physicians. Hippocrates was regarded as the father of medicine; Galen's works were current as late as the eighteenth century.

8   *that remark … of Sir Astley Cooper's?*] Sir Astley Cooper (1768–1841) was a prominent surgeon who combined practice with teaching and research. He played a major role in the development of Guy's hospital as the leading teaching hospital. In 1827 he became president of the Royal College of Surgeons and in the following year Surgeon to the King.

9   *Sir Robert Peel*] (1788–1850) Prime Minister (1841–6), famous for his role in the repeal of the Corn Laws.

10   *five-sixths of our householders … are women.*] cf., *Cranford*, Chapter I: 'In the first place, Cranford is a town in possession of the Amazons; all the holders of houses, above a certain rent, are women', p. 165.

11   *an Apollo … Æsculapius combined in one;*] Aesculapius was, in Greek mythology, the god of healing. He was the son of Apollo, god of medicine. Apollo was also the most beautiful of the gods: the implication

here is that beauty and medical expertise are combined in the expected figure of Mr Harrison.

12   *Genoa velvet.*] The richest and best quality velvet was believed to be that from Utrecht and from Genoa.

13   outré] forward, exaggerated (French).

14   *Sir Everard Home*] (1756–1832), President of the Royal College of Surgeons from 1821; also Professor of Surgery and Anatomy at the Royal College.

15   *Abernethy*] John Abernethy (1764–1831), distinguished surgeon and teacher at St Barthomolew's Hospital; he was instrumental in developing its medical school.

16   *manners that make the man*] 'Manners makyth man' is the motto of Winchester College.

17   *Solomon's seal*] *Polygonatum multiflorum*, a plant with drooping green and white flowers.

18   *jargonelle pears*] a mellow variety of pear. EG seems to have liked them: she refers to them in *North and South*, vol. i, Ch. III.

19   mal-àpropos] (mal à propos) inappropriately (French).

20   *the 'Lancet.'*] Founded in 1823, the *Lancet* became the leading British medical journal. It wrote up significant medical cases and histories.

21   *who was to … with two old ladies,*] *OED* cites, 'To ride or sit bodkin', 'A person wedged in between two others where there is room for two only.'

22   *ride and tie;*] a relay system of riding, whereby two riders share the same horse. The first rides on, while the second follows on foot. At an agreed distance, the first rider dismounts and ties up the horse to await the second, himself continuing on foot. The system is repeated until the journey has been completed.

23   *'Oh wie wohl ist mir am abend,' &c.*] 'Oh how well I feel in the evening' (German), from a German traditional folk-song.

24   *Liebig*] Baron Justus von Liebig (1803–1873), German chemist. He began his training as a pharmacist, and then studied extensively in France.

25   *the croup*] an inflammatory disease of the larynx, affecting children.

26   'Sleep, baby, sleep.'] the stanza is from a German original, translated by Elizabeth Payson Prentice (1818–78).

27   *'Peculiar people … made dear.'*] an adaptation of a line from *Letter II: The Church*, a poem by George Crabbe (1754–1832): 'Peculiar people – death has made them dear' (l. 245). The phrase was important to EG because of the early death of her son, Willy, in 1845. She refers to it again in *North and South* (vol. ii, Ch. VI).

28   *a war-horse at the sound of the trumpet,*] Job 40:19–24: 'Hast thou given the horse strength … He swalloweth the ground with fierceness and rage: neither believeth he that it is the sound of the trumpet.'

29   *white love-ribbon*] perhaps ribbon for a love knot, a ribbon tied in an unusual way as a token of love.

30   *hyosciamus*] henbane, a dangerous narcotic drug.

31   *conversation cards –*] See *Cranford*, note 78.

32   *"wersh"*] insipid (dialect). Writing to George Smith about *The Life of Charlotte Brontë*, EG says, 'It is "anything for a quiet life" with me just now; so if anybody objects to anything I am ready to take it out, and leave the Memoir as "wersh and fusionless", as need be' (*Letters*, p. 464).

33   *Stentor's*] In the *Iliad*, Stentor, herald of the Greeks, was known for the power of his voice.

34   *Short's.*] a pleasure gardens in Drury Lane. Popular with young men about town in the eighteenth and early nineteenth centuries, it was also a haunt of petty criminals, and developed increasingly unsalubrious reputation.

35   *the Mermaid.*] a famous London tavern associated with Shakespeare.

36   *minister to a heart diseased!*] cf., *Macbeth*, V.iii.40: 'Can'st thou not minister to a mind diseased … ?'

37   Mens conscia recti,] A mind conscious of the right (Latin). Quoted from Virgil's *Aeneid*, i.604.

38   *'hodie;'*] daily (Latin). Prescription instructions were – and sometime still are – written in Latin.

39   *Consols,*] i.e., 'consolidated annuities', British Government securities. They consisted of a variety of securities brought together as a single stock in 1751; until 1889 they yielded 3% interest.

40   *Corazza shirts,*] a style of sleeveless shirts (from Italian: corazza, a cuirass). They had come into fashion on account of English interest in Italian political movements, although the fashion will not have reached Duncombe.

41   *"like winds in summer sighing,"*] The reference is probably to a poem by Caroline Howard Gilman (1794–1888), 'Asking about sorrow': 'Perhaps our tears are sent like showers / But to refresh the heart, / And sighs like winds in summer hours, / Will make new virtues start.' The poem was published in Gilman's *A Gift Book of Stories and Poems for Children* (1850).

42   *"lo'ed a the better.*] EG was fond of passing references to regional verse, especially relating to Scotland and the north of England. I have been unable to trace this specific example.

43   vi et armis.] by force and by arms (Latin).

44   *Paris*] the son of Priam, King of Troy. Called on to judge between the beauty of Hera, Athena and Aphrodite, he chose Aphrodite, goddess of love. The story became interwoven with the story of the apple of discord in which Eris, personification of strife, offered a golden apple to be claimed by the fairest of the three goddesses.

45   *Meurice's.*] a hotel in Paris popular with English travellers.

46   *the Peace Society*] Founded in 1816, and still functioning at the time of EG's writing. It argued against the use of force in international disputes. There were a number of such societies in the nineteenth century.

47   *gay Lothario,*] a libertine, after a character in *The Fair Penitent* (1703) by Nicholas Rowe (1674–1718).

48   *Bay Maldon,*] possibly an error for 'Bay Malton', a famous racehorse of the 1760s, owned by Lord Rockingham, one of the original Jockey Club members. The name has survived as a public house name, and here is perhaps used as a generic name for a fast horse.

49   *the negro song,*] The line quoted is from a song in *Camaralzaman and Badoura*, an 'Extravagant Arabian Nights Entertainment in two acts' by the brothers Robert (1828–60) and William (1826–70) Brough, first performed at the Haymarket Theatre on 26 December 1848. The song perhaps gained popular currency independently of its source.

50   *Jenny Lind;*] Swedish singer (1820–87), known as the 'Swedish nightingale'. She gave two concerts in Manchester in December 1848, where EG may have heard her (*Letters*, p. 62).

51   *a tallow-chandler?*] a maker and seller of candles.

Cranford

1   *the even tenor of their lives*] an echo of Thomas Gray, *Elegy in a Country Churchyard*, stanza 19: 'They kept the noiseless tenor of their way.' Cf., also Beilby Porteus (1731–1808), *Death*, ll.107–8: 'The venerable Patriarch guileless held / The tenor of his way.'

2   *Miss Tyler, of cleanly memory;*] Anne Tyler was the aunt of Robert Southey who, in a letter quoted in his *Life and Correspondence* (ed. by Charles Southey, 6 vols (London: Longmans, 1849), vol. i, p. 34), wrote that when staying with her as a child he was 'Never allowed to do anything in which possibly I might dirt [*sic*] myself.'

3   *the last gigot,*] 'gigot' or 'leg-of-mutton' sleeves had gone out of fashion by the 1830s; petticoats had increased in width as fuller skirts came into fashion in the first half of the nineteenth-century (*Mitchell*).

4 *the Tinwald Mount.*] on the Isle of Man, the site of the Manx parliament.

5 *a half-pay Captain,*] Army and naval officers who were not on active service, or who had retired, were paid a reduced allowance, informally known as 'half-pay'.

6 *gender,*] The undated edition, assumed to be printed from the cheap edition of 1855, reads 'genber': 'd' having apparently been accidentally reversed. This, together with other minor differences between the 1855 edition and the undated one, suggests that the plates of the 1855 edition were in fact subject to alteration for later impressions. See textual note 167b; *Collin*; *Smith*, pp. 73–4.

7 *to ears polite.*] Alexander Pope, *Moral Essays IV*: 'To Richard Boyle, Earl of Burlington', ll. 149–50: 'To rest, the Cushion and soft Dean invite / Who never mentions Hell to ears polite.'

8 *the Morning Hymn,*] by Bishop Ken (1637–1711): 'Awake, my soul, and with the sun.'

9 *'Preference,'*] See *The Last Generation in England*, note 13.

10 *'Jock of Hazeldean'*] a romantic ballad (1825) by Sir Walter Scott.

11 *numbers of "The Pickwick Papers?"*] Dickens's *Pickwick Papers* was published in twenty monthly parts from April 1836 to November 1837. Dickens was twenty-five years of age at its completion. In the ensuing debate between Captain Brown and Miss Jenkyns, Dickens is referred to as 'Boz', the pseudonym used for his first published work, *Sketches by Boz*, and for *Pickwick Papers* itself. In the *Household Words* text Dickens altered all the references to himself and to his own works to references to Thomas Hood, explaining to EG that 'with my name on every page of "Household Words" there would be – or at least I should feel – an impropriety in so mentioning myself' (to EG (5 December 1851), *CD Letters*, vol. vi, 1850–2, p. 549). He had made the alterations without consulting EG, explaining that he had already sent the copy to the printer.

12 *the 'swarry' which Sam. Weller gave at Bath.*] described in *Pickwick Papers*, ch. 36.

13 *"Rasselas,"*] by Samuel Johnson (1709–84). The work was written in three weeks and published in 1759.

14 *the "Rambler"*] a sequence of literary essays, mostly written by Johnson and published twice a week from 1750–2.

15 *Brutus wig*] a close-curled wig originating in Paris at the time of the French Revolution, and named after the wigs seen on statues of the Roman Brutuses.

16 *'But don't you forget … of the old song;*] the refrain of a song, 'Country Commissions to my Cousins in Town': 'A skein of white worsted from

Flint's'. Flint's was a haberdasher's shop close to the Monument (*Watson, Mitchell*).

17   *the Hebrew prophetess*] Judges 4:4: 'And Deborah, a prophetess, the wife of Lapidoth.'

18   *'plumed wars,'*] *Othello*, III.iii.350–1: 'Farewell the plumed troop and the big wars / That make ambition virtue.'

19   *'the feast of reason and the flow of soul;'*] Alexander Pope, *The First Satire of the Second Book of Horace Imitated* (1733), l. 128.

20   *'the pure wells of English undefiled,'*] Edmund Spenser, *The Faerie Queene*, IV.ii.32: 'Dan *Chaucer*, well of English undefiled.'

21   *them nasty cruel railroads!'*] In that *Cranford* is usually assumed to be a fictional representation of Knutsford in Cheshire, the reference to the coming of the railroads is perhaps prophetic. Captain Brown has been working on the railroad, and it could be assumed that this might be the Manchester to Birmingham line, authorised in 1837, since we are later told that his accident occurred while he was reading the latest number of *Pickwick Papers* (p. 178). However, Knutsford itself was served by the joint line of the Cheshire Lines Committee, on a line running between the Cheshire towns of Altrincham and Northwich, and built in the early 1860s. Captain Brown is described as 'a-waiting for the down train' (p. 178), so the implication must be that the accident occurred at an operative station; however the station at Knutsford was not opened until 1862. This is a case in which the line is not immaterial.

22   *it's mammy, and gave it's*] This paragraph indicates EG's arbitrary use of the apostrophe. Here she uses it to form the possessive of the third person pronoun; later she uses it as a contraction ('it's quite true') and finally she omits it when forming the possessive ('its mammy'). Manuscript of her letters confirms that for her this was common practice, and I have retained the usages she adopted in each case.

23   *where the weary are at rest.*] Job 3:17.

24   *'Though He slay me, yet will I trust in Him.'*] Job 13:5.

25   *'Galignani.'*] *Galignani's Messenger*, an English newspaper published in Paris and named after its publisher. It carried details of the movements of English travellers, as well as articles on English subject-matter, and was read on the continent by travellers and expatriates.

26   *"Old Poz"' –*] a story in Maria Edgeworth's *The Parent's Assistant* (1795). There would appear to have been a dramatised version. Miss Jenkyns confuses the name of the play with Dickens's pseudonym.

27   *the 'Christmas Carol,'*] The first of Dickens's Christmas books, published in 1843. The reference is one of the various literary references that enable us to establish an approximate date for the action in *Cranford*. Given the earlier references to *Pickwick Papers*, about six years have passed since Captain Brown's death. However, over the course of the

novel as a whole, there are a number of inconsistencies. That notwith-
standing, this final paragraph very effectively concludes the original
instalment of *Cranford* in *Household Words* while anticipating the theme
of the passage of time in the chapters to follow.

28   *'Hortus Siccus,'*] 'An arranged collection of dried plants' (*OED*). The
     plants were usually preserved in a book; the literal translation from the
     Latin is 'dry garden'.

29   *Blue Beard?*] from *Histoires ou contes du temps passés*, a collection of fairy
     stories by Charles Perrault (1628–1703). Blue Beard was a sinister
     character who in one of the stories murders his wife.

30   *"Leave me, leave me to repose."*] Thomas Gray, 'The Descent of Odin: an
     Ode' ll. 49–50: 'Unwillingly I my lips unclose / Leave me, leave me to
     repose.'

31   *'pride which apes humility,'*] From a poem, 'The Devil's Thoughts'
     (1799), by Coleridge and Southey: 'And the Devil did grin, for his dar-
     ling sin / Is the pride which apes humility.'

32   *Miss Jenkyns.*] See textual note, 189a. The alteration allows EG to trans-
     fer the snobbery from Miss Matty's mother to her sister.

33   *mousseline-de-laine*] a fine light-weight woollen material.

34   *sarsenet*] 'a very fine and soft material, made both plain and twilled, in
     various colours, now used chiefly for linings' (*OED*).

35   *'As Goethe says, "Ye ever-verdant palaces,"'*] The provenance of this refer-
     ence as a direct quotation of Goethe has been questioned. It may be
     either a conflation, or a misquotation from memory. See Alan Mehen-
     net, 'A Goethe reference in *Cranford*', *GSJ*, 8 (1994), pp. 111–2.

36   *Aminé … her previous feast with the Ghoul.*] In the story of Sidi-Nouman
     in the *Arabian Nights* Amina (or Aminé) is the wife of Sidi-Nouman.
     She refuses to eat with him, taking only a few grains of rice on the end
     of a pin, and he afterwards discovers that in the company of a female
     ghoul she eats the flesh of corpses in a graveyard. (*The Arabian Nights
     Entertainments*, selected and edited by Andrew Lang (London: Long-
     mans and Co., 1898), pp. 331 ff.)

37   *'The cedar spreads … layers of shade.'*] Tennyson, 'The Gardener's Daugh-
     ter', l. 115, first published in *Poems* (1842): 'A cedar spread his dark-
     green layers of shade.' The *Household Words* text runs on two separate
     lines from Tennyson's poem: 'More black than ash-buds in the front of
     March, / A cedar spread his dark-green layers of shade.' See textual
     note, 194b.

38   *the review of his poems in 'Blackwood,'*] The fifth edition of *Poems* (1842)
     in which the poems referred to in this chapter by Thomas Holbrook
     appeared, was reviewed in *Blackwood's Edinburgh Magazine* by William
     Henry Smith as late as April 1849 (65, pp. 453–67). As *Watson* suggests,
     EG may also have had in mind an enthusiastic review of the first edi-

tion of the same collection, by Monckton Milnes, in October 1842 in the *Westminster Review* ('His command of diction is complete, his sense and execution of the harmonies of verse accurate and admirable ...' (28, pp. 371–90)).

39   *Black as ash-buds in March.*] 'The Gardener's Daughter', l. 28: 'More black than ash-buds in the front of March.' See note 37, above.

40   *a long poem called 'Locksley Hall,'*] Tennyson's 'Locksley Hall' was first published in his *Poems* (1842). As with 'The Gardener's Daughter', its subject-matter of love frustrated by considerations of social status is appropriate to the story of Miss Matty and Thomas Holbrook.

41   *dim parties ... the benefit society for the poor,*] The 1853 copy-text reads 'grim parties', as do *1855, 1864*. But the *Household Words* edition has 'dim' and seems more likely to be correct, thus I have amended the text to 'dim' here. Benefit societies were an early form of insurance society. The bulk of the subscriptions were paid by the more affluent inhabitants of the locality who thus controlled the funds; at the same time the poor were encouraged to contribute at their own level. Such societies were common in provincial areas.

42   *Jem Hearn,*] EG's long-serving servant was named Ann Hearn: when Jem and Martha are married she will thus adopt this name. The copy-text has 'Jim' but this is inconsistent with later references and I have amended to 'Jem'. *1855, 1864* confirm Jem as correct, as does the illustration caption facing p. 203 in *1864*.

43   *a Joint-Stock Bank,*] a bank owned by shareholders, who were jointly liable for its debts. *Mitchell* notes that such banks came into operation from 1844, and were confined to the provinces.

44   *'blind man's holiday.'*] a popular term for twilight, or for the night itself.

45   *Tonquin beans*] the seeds of Cumaru (*Dipterix oderata*), a large leguminous tree of South America. Powder from the beans was often added to snuff. The correct term is Tonka beans; EG follows an eighteenth century usage associating the beans with the orient.

46   *'Paduasoy,'*] a thick corded silk. The name suggests that it was silk from Padua, where there was a large silk industry, but according to *OED* it is a corruption of 'pou de soie', a kind of taffeta or glossy silk (French), the three final letters reflecting the eighteenth century English pronunciation of the final syllable.

47   *J. and J. Rivingtons*] The publishing firm of Rivingtons specialised in works with a theological and ecclesiastical emphasis. It was founded in 1711, and was sold to Longman's in 1890.

48   dum ... artus,'] Virgil, *Aeneid*, iv.336. EG has omitted the word 'hos' ('hos regit artus') from this line. It translates as: 'while I have memory of myself, and while breath still sways these limbs' (Latin).

49   *the* carmen] i.e., the love song (from Latin).

50   *the 'Gentleman's Magazine,'*] a prominent periodical in the eighteenth
     century, noted for its emphasis on antiquarian, historical and literary
     subject-matter.

51   *M.T. Ciceronis Epistolæ*] letters by Marcus Tullius Cicero (103–43 BC)

52   *Mrs Chapone,*] Hester Chapone (1717–1801). Her *Letters on the Improve-
     ment of the Mind* (1773–4) had currency as a conduct book.

53   *Mrs Carter! ... Epictetus,*] Elizabeth Carter (1717–1806), translator of
     the Greek philosopher Epictetus. Her *Letters* were published in 1809
     and 1817.

54   *'I canna be fashed!'*] It is not entirely clear who has made this remark.
     The implication is that it can be attributed to Mrs Carter. It means 'I
     cannot be troubled to'.

55   *the old original Post ... twanging his horn.*] The reference is to a type of let-
     ter-paper, then outdated, which carried the watermark, or as suggested
     here, the stamp, of a post-boy blowing his horn (*Watson, Mitchell*).

56   *Miss Edgeworth's ... polite society.*] Wafers were letter-seals backed by
     gum, as an improvement on wax seals. Maria Edgeworth's novel,
     Patronage (1813) tells of an aristocratic character who rejects a letter
     sealed in this way, saying 'I wonder how any man can have the imper-
     tinence to send me his spittle!' (vol. i, ch. 8; Connor Carville and
     Marilyn Butler (eds), *The Works of Maria Edgeworth*, 'Pickering Masters'
     edn, 6 vols (London: Pickering & Chatto, 1999), vol. vi, p. 83).

57   *a means of paying debts ... Parliament.*] MPs could send letters free by
     using a parliamentary frank. Indigent members could thus trade this
     privilege. I am indebted to *Watson* and *Mitchell* for the information con-
     tained in notes 55–7.

58   *crossing.*] Writing both vertically and horizontally across the page, in
     order to save paper and thus postage, which was charged by weight.
     Some of EG's own early letters were written in this way.

59   *Herod, Tetrarch ... of Etruriæ,*] Herod the Great, who was said to have
     ordered the massacre of the innocents. Miss Matty confuses his title
     with other classical names that she has heard.

60   *a visit to some ... Newcastle-upon-Tyne.*] EG herself made one, or more
     possibly two, visits to friends in Newcastle-upon-Tyne as a young
     woman between 1829 and 1831.

61   *the salt-mines;*] There are salt mines at Northwich in Cheshire, approx-
     imately seven miles from Knutsford. These mines are hollowed out in
     a way that would make it quite possible for people to retreat there.

62   *Apollyon and Abaddon.*] Revelations 9:11: 'And they had a king over
     them, which is the angel of the bottomless pit, whose name in the
     Hebrew tongue is Abaddon, but in the Greek tongue hath his name
     Apollyon.'

63   *at school at Shrewsbury*] Shrewsbury School, a noted boys boarding school, was founded in 1552. Its location in Shropshire makes it a likely school for Peter Jenkyns, as EG would have been aware from personal knowledge of, for example, Charles Darwin who was educated there.

64   Bonus Bernadus … *as the Proverbia say.*'] 'The good Bernadus does not see everything' (Latin), a proverb associated with St Bernard of Clairvaux and cited by both Chaucer and by William Cowper in his *Correspondence*, published in 1824, EG's most likely source.

65   *He was to win honours … thick to Cambridge,*] See note 63, above. At the time when Peter would have been at Shrewsbury the school was in a state of some decay. Its academic successes, particularly at Cambridge University, were achieved under the headmastership of Samuel Butler, who was appointed in 1798, but the full effect of whose regimen did not become apparent until the second decade of the nineteenth century. There is thus an element of anachronism in EG's reference to the family's aspirations for their son.

66   *the St. James's Chronicle*] a weekly periodical, initially published more frequently. Of establishment leanings, it was popular with the upper classes and the clergy.

67   *Queen Esther and King Ahasuerus;*] Esther was chosen to be his queen by King Ahasuerus after his wrath at Queen Vashti's refusal to obey his command to appear before the people. The story is told in the Old Testament book of Esther. See especially Esther 2:12–17.

68   *there was war then;*] i.e., the continuing Napoleonic wars. We have earlier been told (pp. 206, 208) that Peter was at Shrewsbury School in about 1805. At a somewhat later date EG's brother, John Stevenson (1798–c. 1828), had sailed for India and failed to return, either because his ship was lost at sea or because he had died after arriving in India.

69   *Dor*] The copy-text has 'Don' but *HW, 1855* and *1864* have 'Dor' which both *Watson* and *Mitchell* accept as a contraction of Deborah. It does not appear at any point elsewhere in the novel, and the supposition seems less than certain, but I have accepted the reading of the majority of the texts consulted and amended to 'Dor'.

70   *some great war in India* –] Probably the First Burmese War (1824–6), given the later reference to Peter's presence at the siege of Rangoon, cf. note 146, below.

71   *Queen Adelaide … King William*] William IV, King of England from 1830 to his death in 1837, and his wife Adelaide of Saxe-Coburg Meiningen (1792–1849). The reference is slightly confusing in that it refers to events that have taken place prior to the narrator's visits to Cranford.

72   *that Marchioness of Exeter … Hoggins;*] an historical figure, a Shropshire woman who became the second wife of Henry Cecil, who succeeded

to the title of Earl of Exeter in 1793. They were in fact twice married, the first time bigamously. Cecil was created Marquess after her death in 1801 (*Mitchell*).

73   '*bombazine*] a dress material of worsted, or cotton and worsted mixture. Its dullness of texture made it appropriate for mourning dress.

74   *a general officer … American war;*] an allusion to General Burgoyne, commander of the British forces in the American War of Independence. Burgoyne (1722–92) wrote a number of plays and was married to Lady Charlotte Stanley, daughter of the Earl of Derby. See *The Last Generation in England*, note 18.

75   *Spadille from Manille,*] terms from the card-games of Ombre and Quadrille. 'Spadille' is the Ace of Spades, and 'Manille' the second best trump.

76   '*basting*'] a technical term used when bidding in the various card games referred to.

77   '*little Cupids,*'] a dessert dish of macaroons and syllabub.

78   *conversation-cards, puzzle-cards*] forms of social entertainment. Conversation-cards carried questions and answers on either side, devised in a way that made it possible to mix them to form conversation. Puzzle-cards usually carried riddles.

79   *a sort of 'A Lord and No Lord'*] Watson cites two possible precedents, *A King and No King* (1611), a play by Beaumont and Fletcher, and an anonymous ballad 'A Lord and No Lord' (c. 1726).

80   *Basto!*] the ace of clubs in Ombre and Quadrille.

81   *the Catholic Emancipation Bill.*] passed in 1829 to repeal laws restricting the civil rights of Roman Catholics.

82   *Francis Moore's … predictions;*] From 1699 Francis Moore (1657–1715) published the astrological predictions which later became known as *Old Moore's Almanac*.

83   *Soon after the events … part of that year.*] This opening paragraph is a fictional explanation of the fact that there had been a gap of nine months between the appearance of this instalment of *Cranford* in *Household Words* and its predecessor (see Appendix A). EG apparently felt no need to remove it from the single-volume edition of *1853*.

84   *Michaelmas to Lady-day,*] i.e., from 29 September to 25 March.

85   *Wombwell's lions*] George Wombwell (1778–1850) was the owner of a noted travelling circus.

86   minuets de la cour!)] Stately formal dances, out of date by the time of the action.

87   *clothes-maids,*] heavy racks, usually suspended from the ceiling, for the drying and airing of clothes.

88   *Thaddeus of Warsaw … Santo Sebastiani;*] Novels of an earlier period: *Thaddeus of Warsaw* (1776), by Jane Porter; *The Hungarian Brothers*

(1780) by Jane's sister Anna Maria Porter, and *Santo Sebastiano, or, the Young Protector* (1806) by Catherine Cuthbertson. In a letter EG described Cuthbertson's novel as 'so funny and so ridiculous, that it carries one on through all that quantity of reading' (*Further Letters*, p. 58). It was first published anonymously in five volumes, and from her account EG seems to have believed its author to have been a daughter of George III.

89   *the Witch of Endor.*] The Old Testament figure who conjured up the ghost of Samuel for Saul (1 Samuel 28).

90   *death-watches.*] a type of beetle which is supposed to prefigure death by the sound that it makes.

91   *'winding-sheets ... roly-poleys!'*] The accumulation of dripping wax on candles was believed to be an augury of death.

92   *one of the Gunnings*] two sisters, Maria (1733–60) and Elizabeth (1734–90) Gunning, famous society beauties of the mid-eighteenth century.

93   chapeau bras] a three-cornered silk hat for fashionable formal wear.

94   *National School boys,*] The National Schools originated in 1816 as a consequence of the awareness of Anglican evangelicals that elementary education was needed for the children of the expanding working class, and that such education should be underpinned by the tenets of the established church. Hence the presence of the Rector.

95   *chinks*] convulsive fits. EG's usage here is cited by *OED*.

96   *General Burgoyne ... the French in Spain,*] For the American war and General Burgoyne see note 74 above. The British fought the French in Spain in the Peninsular War (1803–14).

97   *a print of Madame de Staël ... Mr. Denon*] Germaine Necker, Baronne de Stael-Holstein (1766–1817), always known as Mme de Staël, was a French novelist and essayist whose activities at the time of the French revolution added to her fame; her name recurs in EG's correspondence. The portrait of her referred to here was probably that engraved by J. Thomson and published in 1819. Baron Dominic Vivan-Denon (1747–1825), an Egyptologist, accompanied Napoleon on his Egyptian campaign. No portrait matching this description has been traced (*Watson*).

98   *I had read ... down dead.*] The story originates in John Ford's play, *The Lover's Melancholy* (1628). *Mitchell* notes that the play is quoted in Mary Russell Mitford's *Our Village* (1824), which may be the source of its transference to EG.

99   *a slow dark thread of blood came oozing out.*] *Mitchell* traces this story to the Scottish borders, and suggests James Hogg's *The Long Pack* (1817) as a version of it.

100 *Italian irons,*] crimping irons, as used to iron pleats and frills.

101 *spillikins,*] the small rods or sticks used in the game of the same name, in which the objective is to move each rod one by one without disturbing the others.

102 *'where nae men should be;'*] from the Scottish ballad, 'Our goodman came home at e'en', in David Herd, *Ancient and Modern Scottish Songs*, 2 vols (Edinburgh: Dickson and Elliot, 1776), vol. ii, pp. 172–5. The poem turns on the joke of a deceived husband who believes his wife's improbable explanations of evidence that she has admitted a man to her house in his absence.

103 *cold-pigged*] 'cold-pie, cold-pig' (colloq.): 'The application of cold water to wake a person' (*OED*).

104 *Dr. Ferrier and Dr. Hibbert*] authors of works on illusions and apparitions. Dr John Ferrier (1761–1815) delivered papers entitled 'Of Popular Illusions, and more Particularly of Modern Demonolatry', and 'Towards a Theory of Apparitions', in Manchester. Dr Samuel Hibbert, later Hibbert-Ware (1782–1848), antiquarian and geologist, was the author of *Sketches of the Philosophy of Apparitions* (1824). Born in Manchester, he later resided in the north-west after a period spent in Scotland.

105 *though Mr Hoggins ... call Preference 'Pref,'*] Watson suggests that these are terms from cribbage; the point is that Mr Hoggins reveals his social origins by his use of socially inferior terms when playing cards.

106 *Lord Chesterfield's Letters*] Lord Chesterfield's *Letters to his Son* (1774), regarded as providing a model for social behaviour, but dismissed by Dr Johnson in Boswell's *Life* as teaching 'the morals of a whore, and the manners of a dancing–master', a judgement of which the Cranford ladies were probably not aware.

107 *by birth a Tyrrell ... Princes in the Tower,*] Walter Tyrrell was supposedly the murderer of William II, known as William Rufus, in 1100. The Princes in the Tower, Edward V and his brother Richard, were murdered by Sir James Tyrell who claimed descent from the same family. *Mitchell* notes that in its reference to these crimes the sequence is a parody of aristocratic pretensions.

108 *two pieces of red flannel ... garment.*] *Watson* and *Mitchell* both note that such a device was regarded as a charm against witchcraft.

109 *charges;*] instructions to the clergy of the diocese under his supervision.

110 *I drew a lot to go,*] When a battalion was warned for overseas service a limited number of the wives of non-commissioned ranks, normally six only per company, were allowed to accompany their husbands. The restriction on numbers meant that ballots were held for these places.

111 *every pice*] A pice was the smallest unit of Indian currency at that time.

112 *a little picture ... little Saviour,*] *Watson* identifies this as the *Madonna della Sedia* of Raphael, 'perhaps the most popular of all his paintings in the

nineteenth century', although she says that the story of its being painted on a cask is 'apocryphal'.

113   *Chunderabaddad;*] apparently an invented name.

114   *Aga*] a title of Turkish origin, used as a courtesy title for civilian members of the Indian administration.

115   *As somebody says, that was the question.*] an allusion to the first line of Hamlet's famous soliloquy, *Hamlet*, III.i.56.

116   *a Ladies' Committee … own satisfaction.*] *Pickwick Papers*, ch. 32: 'The chorus was the essence of the song; and, as each gentleman sang it to the tune he knew best, the effect was very striking indeed.' As elsewhere, Dickens changed the reference to himself in the *Household* Words text to a reference to Thomas Hood, but he left the situation described to stand. See note 11, above. Ladies' committees usually met on charitable business.

117   *Lalla Rookh –*] a sequence of four narrative poems on oriental themes (1817) by Thomas Hood. *The Veiled Prophet of Khorassan* is the first of them.

118   *Rowland's Kalydor,*] a popular cosmetic.

119   *Peruvian bonds,*] The Spanish colonies which achieved independence in the early nineteenth century had granted mining concession to the English, resulting in a speculative boom. Dickens makes a similar reference in *Dombey and Son*, ch. 8, where 'the Peruvian mines' are described as having been the death of Mrs Pipchin's husband.

120   *Wombwell*] See note 85, above.

121   *'surveying mankind from China to Peru,'*] From the opening lines of Samuel Johnson's poem, *The Vanity of Human Wishes* (1749): 'Let observation with extensive view / Survey mankind, from China to Peru.'

122   *St. James's Chronicle*] See note 66 above.

123   *Captain Brown's song 'Tibbie Fowler,'*] a traditional Scots song: 'Be a lassie e'er sae black, / An she hae the name o'siller / Set her upo'Tintock-tap, / The wind will blaw a man till her.' A version by Robert Burns was printed in *The Scots Musical Museum*, 6 vols (1803). See *Poems and Songs of Robert Burns*, ed. by James Kinsley, 3 vols (Oxford: Clarendon Press, 1968), vol. iii, p. 1507, for the full text and a discussion of the poem's proverbial content.

124   *new-pieced,*] i.e., mended, newly-patched.

125   *the Queen of Spain's legs –*] From a story in Madame D'Aulnoy's *Mémoirs de la cour D'Espagne* (1690) in which a young Austrian princess having been offered a present of silk stockings, her major-domo returns them with the words 'the Queens of Spain have no legs' (*Watson, Mitchell*).

126   *welly stawed*] almost stopped (i.e., from proceeding on his rounds).

127 *green tea*] unfermented tea, which retains some of its original colour after the manufacturing process. It was believed to have a bad effect on the nerves.

128 *Joint Stock Bank,*] See note 43, above.

129 do on] Perhaps a mistake for 'go on', but all texts consulted and all modern editors retain.

130 *without teeth,*] Miss Pole apparently has false teeth; according to Watson these were first introduced in France in 1774. In a letter to John Forster, EG wrote: 'Shall I tell you a Cranfordism. An old lady a Mrs Frances Wright said to one of my cousins "I have never been able to spell since I lost my teeth"' (*Letters*, p. 290).

131 *the Rubric*] of the Book of Common Prayer. *Mitchell* notes that directions for the services were printed in red.

132 *the Savings' Bank,*] In the first half of the nineteenth century savings banks of this kind were popular in England, the first of them having been founded in 1810 by the Reverend Henry Duncan (*Watson*).

133 Ah! Vous dirai-je, maman?'] a French children's song, a version of which appeared in England in 1795; it was used in the teaching of French.

134 *the branches of a solid English education –*] This paragraph is an extended joke at the expense of the conventions of female education earlier in the century. The accomplishments referred to – piano-playing, drawing, embroidery, the use of the terrestrial and astronomical globes, and the study of geography and astronomy generally – were all aspects of the syllabus of an earlier age. EG herself received a better than usual formal education when she boarded at the school of the Misses Byerley in Warwickshire from c. 1821 to c. 1825–6. See Edward Chitham, 'Elizabeth Stevenson's Schooldays', *GSJ*, 5 (1991), pp. 1–15; J. A. V. Chapple, *Elizabeth Gaskell: The Early Years* (Manchester: Manchester University Press, 1997), ch. 13.

135 *the loyal wool-work*] a style of embroidery incorporating likenesses of members of the Royal Family; it was out of fashion by the time of *Cranford* (*Mitchell*).

136 *the signs of the Zodiac … the Black Art.*] The signs of the Zodiac had legitimate astronomical application and featured on the astronomical globe, but the narrator's train of thought takes her into the realms of sorcery.

137 *the chapter*] i.e., of the Bible. Miss Matty has difficulty with those chapters of the Old Testament which consist of genealogies, often with names that are difficult to pronounce.

138 *a lion* couchant] a heraldic lion, made by a specially shaped pudding mould.

139 *the East India Tea Company … existed?*] The English East India Company was, during the period of its existence (1600–1858), the world's great-

est tea monopoly. The Company was dissolved in 1858, when its powers reverted to the Crown: EG's comment 'which then existed' thus anticipates its demise, but the monopoly of its trade with China, chiefly in tea, had been ended in 1833.

140 *lion*] Later editions (*1855, 1864*) mistakenly correct this to 'loin', failing to recognise the earlier references to a dessert in the shape of a lion.

141 *see what I can,*] see textual note, 286b. The later readings (*1855, 1864*) make sense of the error in *1853*, but fail to restore what was probably the intended reading of *HW.*

142 *Congou and Souchong ... Pekoe for themselves.*] all types of tea. Pekoe was a black tea made from the finest leaf from India, Sri Lanka or China; Congou a black tea from India or China, and Souchong a black tea from India or Sri Lanka. Gunpowder was a superior green tea from China.

143 *train oil and tallow ... but digest.*] Train oil was in fact whale oil, from the Dutch, 'traen'.

144 *the Old Hundredth*] a psalm tune, included in Sternhold and Hopkins's *Psalter* (1562), and used in church services to accompany the metrical version of Psalm 100, 'All people that on earth do dwell'.

145 *Baron Munchausen's*] *Baron Munchausen's Narrative of His Marvellous Travels and Campaign in Russia*, by Rudolf Erich Raspe, was published in England in 1785. The narrative describes fantastically exaggerated exploits.

146 *the siege of Rangoon;*] Rangoon was besieged and taken by the British in 1824 at the outset of the first Burmese War (1824–6). It was returned to the Burmese at the end of the war, but a second Burmese War followed in 1852 which effectively established British rule.

147 *the Father of the Faithful?'*] i.e., Abraham, so described by St Paul in the Bible, Romans 4:9–23.

148 *(formerly* her *maid)*] EG is guilty of a minor inconsistency here; it is Miss Betty Barker's sister who, in Chapter VII, has been described as the Honourable Mrs Jamieson's maid.

149 *'Signor Brunoni ... Lama of Thibet, &c. &c.,'*] The place names are genuine; the titles less reliably so.

150 *the Preston Guild,*] a body dating from mediaeval times. Its charter was granted in 1329, and it held festivals usually at twenty-year intervals. The festival of 1862 lasted for five days; it involved trades processions, religious processions, celebration dinners and concerts, and concluded with a costume ball and fireworks. The most recent Preston Guild was held in 1992.

The Cage at Cranford

1   *since the year 1856?*] The final instalment of *Cranford* appeared in *Household Words* on 21 May 1853. *Watson* suggests that the choice of date here represents a deliberate effort to update the chronology, confirmed by the later suggestion that the narrator is 'past thirty'. EG herself visited Paris almost annually from 1853. See Philip Yarrow, 'Mrs. Gaskell and France,' *GSJ*, 7 (1993), pp. 16–36.

2   *Mrs FitzAdam's*] In *Cranford* this name is hyphenated.

3   *I was past thirty,*] See note 1, above. There is no specific indication of the narrator's age in *Cranford*.

4   *servant-maiden Fanny,*] In *Cranford* Miss Pole's servant is first called Betty, and then Lizzie. She could of course have acquired a new servant, but the inconsistency is more likely a consequence of EG's carelessness with names.

5   *a meat-safe*] usually a box or cupboard with gauze sides, kept in a cool place to keep meat cool.

6   *calashes*] See *The Last Generation in England*, note 12, above.

TEXTUAL NOTES

Cranford

The Chapman and Hall *1853* edition is used as copy-text. The *Household Words* instalments are used as comparison texts and the variants between these and the copy-text are given below. The editions of *1855* and *1864* have also been collated and variants recorded. See the following list for silent corrections made to the copy-text. A first American edition was published in New York by Harper & Brothers on 5 August 1853 (*Smith*). There is no evidence that EG was aware of its existence at the time.

VARIANTS

165a   CHAPTER I.] *HW omits*

165b   OUR SOCIETY.] OUR SOCIETY AT CRANFORD. *HW*

166a   Tinwald Mount.] Tyne-wold Mount. *HW*

166b   my dear, (fifteen … carriage); they] my dear' (fifteen miles, in a gentleman's carriage); 'they *HW, 1855, 1864*

167a   Glenmire,] Cranford, *HW*

167b   gender,] genber, *undated cheap edition* [see explanatory note 6]

167c   walked] walked home *HW*

169a   wondering] wandering *HW*

169b   altogether] all together *1855, 1864*

171a   "The Pickwick Papers?"'] "Hood's Own?"' *HW* [see explanatory note 11]

171b   (They] (It *HW*

171c   them;] it; *HW*

171d   them.'] it.' *HW*

171e   them?'] it?' *HW*

171f   'Aren't they] 'Isn't it *HW*

171g   they are] it is *HW*

171h   the 'swarry' … Weller gave at Bath.] the gentleman who was terrified out of his wits by political events, who 'could no more collect himself than the Irish tithes.' *HW*

171i   Boz] Hood *HW*

172a   Boz.'] Hood.' *HW*

173a   CHAPTER II. / THE CAPTAIN.] *HW has no chapter break and no chapter title*

174a   – knowing, most likely,] feeling, probably, *HW*

174b   Boz] Hood *HW*

174c   *au fait* to] thus, *HW*; *au fait* as to *1855, 1864*

174d   Miss Matty,] Miss Matey *HW* [This is the first appearance of the revised name; it has been adhered to throughout *1853* and following editions.]

175a   honoured] loved *HW*

175b   feelings who is free?'] failings who is altogether free?' *1855, 1864*

176a   Boz;] Hood; *HW*

176b   Miss Matty,] Miss Pole, *HW*

176c   Miss Matty] Miss Pole *HW*

176d   Miss Matty,] Miss Pole, *HW*

178a   it's] its *HW*

178b   in bringing her round:] to bring her round; *HW*

178c   Mr. Hoggins] Dr. Colburn *HW*

179a   a number of "Pickwick,"] Hood's Poems, *HW*

180a   die; what] die! What *1855, 1864*

181a   about] above *1855, 1864*

181b   a-year,] per annum, *HW*

181c   spoke. 'I] spoke. / 'I *1864*

182a   Gordon] Campbell *HW*

182b   Gordon] Campbell *HW*

182c   'Deborah,] 'Caroline, *HW*

182d   Gordon] Campbell *HW*

183a   Gordon,] Campbell, *HW*

183b   Gordon] Campbell *HW*

183c   that book by Mr. Boz … left on the table.] – that book by Mr. Hood, you know – Hood – Admiral Hood; when I was a girl; but that's a long time ago, – I wore a cloak with a red Hood' – she babbled on long enough for Flora to get a good long spell at 'Miss Kilmansegg and her Golden Leg,' which Miss Matey had left on the table.
        Poor, dear Miss Jenkyns! Cranford is Man-less now. *HW*

184a   CHAPTER III.] *HW omits*

184b   A LOVE AFFAIR OF LONG AGO.] A LOVE AFFAIR AT CRANFORD. / 'I AM tempted to relate it, as having interested me in a quiet sort of way, and as being the latest intelligence of Our Society at Cranford.' *HW*

184c   I THOUGHT that … Jenkyns's death;] I thought, after Miss Jenkyns's death', that probably my connexion with Cranford would cease; *HW*

185a and we all tried … the attempt.] and the appellation of Matey was dropped by all, except a very old woman, who had been nurse in the rector's family, and had persevered, through many long years, in calling the Miss Jenkynses 'the girls;' she said 'Matey,' to the day of her death. *HW*

185b that she should give a party,] her to give a party, *HW*

185c related to a shadow … years before.] related to the love affair I am coming to; – gradually, not in a hurry, for we are never in a hurry at Cranford. *HW*

186a The] These *HW*

187a *must*] must *HW*

188a *Esq.*;] Esq.; *HW*

188b *Mr.*] Mr. *HW*

189a Miss] Mrs. *HW* [see explanatory note 32]

190a sarsenet] sarcenet *HW*

191a CHAPTER IV. / A VISIT TO AN OLD BACHELOR.] *HW has no chapter break and no chapter title*

192a Bÿrron,'] Byrron,' *HW, 1855, 1864*

193a most smart things,] most things, *HW*

193b these] things *HW*

193c peas] pease *HW*

194a men.] niece. *HW*

194b 'The cedar spreads … shade.'] 'More black than ash-buds in the front of March / A cedar spread his dark green layers of shade.' *HW* [see explanatory note 37]

194c but] but that *HW*

197a upon me. / 'Dear!] upon me. 'Dear! *HW*

197b all the afternoon,] all afternoon *HW*

200a CHAPTER V.] *HW omits*

200b OLD LETTERS.] MEMORY AT CRANFORD. *HW*

202a 1774.'] 1764.' *HW*

202b 'Paduasoy,' –] Paduasay,' – *HW*

202c 'Paduasoy.'] Paduasay.' *HW*

203a 'Paduasoy'] Paduasay *HW*

204a 1782. / Her letters] 1772. Her letters *HW*

204b grandmother] grandfather *HW*

205a sisters. / By-and-by] sisters. By-and-by *HW*

205b sentence. / The Rector's] sentence. The Rector's *HW*

206a right. / I can't] right. I can't *HW*

206b One day, when … actually given] This warning summons was actually given, one day, when Miss Jenkyns and her hosts were at a dinner-party in Newcastle *HW*

206c   I know I … people talked] My mother has sat by my bed half a night through, holding my hand and comforting me; and many people talked *HW*

206d   an Apollyon] Apollyon *HW*

208a   CHAPTER VI. / POOR PETER.] *HW has no chapter break and no chapter title*

209a   lady that] lady who *HW*

209b   my father] but my father *HW*

209c   now, and we have plenty to say;] now, – the very same advantage we have, and we have plenty to say; *HW*

210a   terribly! – and] terribly! and *HW*

210b   Peter! / 'My dear!] Peter! 'My dear! *HW*

211a   ever after. / 'Presently,] ever after. 'Presently, *HW*

213a   waking. / 'The same] wakening. 'The same *HW*

213b   did not come] never came *HW*

213c   his mother's face.] father or mother. *HW*

214a   her again.] her again.' But Miss Matey was not foolish, poor dear thing! *HW*

214b   liked. / We thought] liked. We thought *HW*

215a   liked it.' / 'Well!] liked it.' 'Well!

216a   comes. / 'That's] comes. 'That's *HW*

216b   aching.' / So she] aching.' So she *HW*

217a   CHAPTER VII.] *HW omits*

217b   VISITING.] VISITING AT CRANFORD. *HW*

217c   Miss Jenkyns's] Miss Jenkyns' *HW*

217d   Mr. Jenkyns's] Mr. Jenkyns' *HW*

219a   she was born a Tyrrell, and] *HW omits*

219b   families. / Soon after] families. Soon after *HW*

220a   disappoint her. / So] disappoint her. So *HW*

222a   it shall!' / In] it shall!' In *HW*

222b   compliment.' / Miss] compliment.' Miss *HW*

222c   home. / The card-table] home. The card-table *HW*

223a   looking] looked *HW*

223b   sorts] sort *HW*

225a   CHAPTER VIII. / 'YOUR LADYSHIP.'] *HW has no chapter break and no chapter title*

227a   the country] — shire *HW*

229a   it. / And with] it. And with *HW*

230a   company. / Miss Pole] company. Miss Pole *HW*

231a   be hurried.' / We] be hurried.' We *HW*

231b   'St. James's Chronicle'] St James's Chronicle *HW*

232a   minnikin] minikin *HW*

232b   her. / The friendship,] her. The friendship, *HW*

233a   for the next half-hour.] that next half hour. *HW*

235a   CHAPTER IX / SIGNOR BRUNONI.] THE GREAT CRANFORD PANIC. / IN TWO CHAPTERS. CHAPTER THE FIRST. *HW*

235b   that year. / Late in] that year. Late in *HW*

236a   turban. / Miss Pole] turban. / Miss Pole *HW*

237a   'Had he a … Did he look' –] 'Had he a beard? Was he young or old? Fair or dark? Did he look' – *HW*

238a   dispatched] despatched *HW, 1855, 1864*

238b   encyclopædia] encyclopedia *HW* Encyclopaedia *1855, 1864*

239a   arts. / We went] arts. We went *HW*

240a   asleep. / At length] asleep. At length *HW*

241a   Dakin,] Dabine *HW*

241b   at ease. / I have] at ease. I have *HW*

242a   CHAPTER X. / THE PANIC.] *HW has no chapter break and no chapter title*

242b   door. / Miss Pole,] door. Miss Pole, *HW*

242c   Hoggins's] Hoggins' *HW*

243a   French. / The last] French. The last *HW*

243b   of course. / Really I] of course. Really I *HW*

243c   to] at *HW*

245a   grease. / We parted] grease. We parted *HW*

246a   he was! / Poor Carlo!] he was! Poor Carlo! *HW*

246b   the sure pursuer, Death. / We] the fell pursuer, Death. We *HW*

246c   awful things! / We] awful things! / We *HW*

246d   health. / Lady Glenmire] health. Lady Glenmire *HW*

247a   Be that as it might,] However, *HW*

247b   her stay] her to stay *HW*

247c   acceptable.] *HW instalment for 8 January 1853 ends here and new instalment for 15 January 1853 headed* THE GREAT CRANFORD PANIC. / IN TWO CHAPTERS. CHAPTER THE SECOND *begins*

247d   a stride. / If] a stride. If Miss

249a   of Cranford. / Having] of Cranford. Having *HW*

251a   home. / In spite] home. In spite *HW*

251b   here.' / 'And] here.' – 'And *HW*

253a   CHAPTER XI. / SAMUEL BROWN.] *HW omits*

254a   inconvenience. / Before] inconvenience. Before *HW*

254b   doctor. We often] doctor. / We often *HW*

256a   the] her *HW*

257a   "*When*] "When *HW*

257b   "*If*] "If *HW*

257c   hers. / If I] hers. If I *HW*

258a   Phœbe. / The Signora] Phœbe. The Signora *HW*

260a   morning, I was so tired!] morning I was so tired; *HW*

260b   head: could] head. Could *HW*

261a   CHAPTER XII.] *HW omits*

261b   ENGAGED TO BE MARRIED!] STOPPED PAYMENT, AT CRANFORD. *HW*

261c   Miss Jenkynses. / In my] Miss Jenkyns's. In my *HW*

261d   Dickens,] Hood, *HW*

261e   satisfaction. So, at] satisfaction. So, at *HW*

261f   Rookh –] Rookh, *HW*

262a   spelt. / The only] spelt. The only *HW*

262b   'surveying mankind from China to Peru,'] surveying, mankind from China to Peru *HW*

262c   the St. James's Chronicle. A few] the newspaper before named in Cranford visiting; a few *HW*

263a   Glenmire!'] Glenmire' *HW*

264a   "Tibbie Fowler,"] "Jibbie Fowler," *HW*

264b   Tintock] Tintorle *HW*

264c   "Tibbie Fowler"] Jibbie Fowler *HW*

264d   pleasant-looking,'] pleasant looking,' *HW*

265a   did not. / Mrs. Forrester's] did not. Mrs. Forrester's *HW*

265b   aristocracy. / When she] aristocracy. When she *HW*

265c   next. / I don't] next. I don't *HW*

266a   Till] Until *HW*

266b   silk. / I must] silk. I must *HW*

266c   a word or two here] a little *HW*

266d   Jenkyns] Jenkyns' *HW*

266e   'poor Peter,'] poor Peter, *HW*

267a   CHAPTER XIII. / STOPPED PAYMENT.] *HW has no chapter break and no chapter title*

268a   At last she spoke:] *HW omits*

270a   'I am … hesitating, 'whichever] 'I am afraid whichever *HW*

270b   my dear?' / And] my dear?' And *HW*

272a   because … said, she had] because she had *HW*

274a   me.' / Miss Matty] me.' Miss Matey *HW*

275a   CHAPTER XIV.] *HW omits*

275b   FRIENDS IN NEED.] FRIENDS IN NEED, AT CRANFORD. *HW*

276a   Rosy,] Jopley, *HW*

276b   the table.'] th'table.' *HW*

278a   loved her? / I had] loved her? I had *HW*

278b   my father. / No!] my father. No! *HW*

278c   person. / I had] person. I had *HW*

279a   involved. / While I] involved. While I *HW*

279b   Jenkyns's] Jenkyns' *HW*

281a   *eleven*] eleven *HW*

283a composure. / 'I don't] composure. 'I don't *HW*
283b writers. / When] writers. When *HW*
283c Miss Pole. / On] Miss Pole. On *HW*
284a comforts. / It was] comforts. / It was *HW*
284b passed,] passed me *HW*
285a failure?] failure. *HW*
285b morning. / I am] morning. I am *HW*
286a lion] loin, *1855, 1864* [see explanatory note 140]
286b see what I can,] sell what I can, *HW*; see what I can do, *1855*; see what I can do, *1864*
288a CHAPTER XV.] *HW omits*
288b A HAPPY RETURN.] A HAPPY RETURN TO CRANFORD. *HW*
288c Glenmire. / But what] Glenmire. But what *HW*
289a illness. / I had] illness. I had
289b canisters. / Miss Matty,] canisters. Miss Matty, *HW*
289c Mr. Johnson] Mr. Wright *HW*
289d Mr. Johnson] Mr. Wright *HW*
289e else] less *HW*
290a Jenkyns's] Jenkyns' *HW*
290b kindness. / The money] kindness. The money *HW*
291a laid up.' / I comforted] laid up.' I comforted *HW*
291b imagination. / I then] imagination. I then *HW*
292a cannisters] canisters *HW, 1855, 1864*
293a befal] befall *HW, 1855*
294a 'It is –] 'Is it – *HW*
294b upstairs. / I thought] upstairs. I thought *HW*
295a go!' / She was] go!' She was *HW*
297a CHAPTER XVI. / 'PEACE TO CRANFORD.'] *HW has no chapter break and no chapter title*
297b not surprising that Mr. Peter] no wonder that he *HW*
297c Oriental.' / One day] Oriental.' One day *HW*
298a at Woodley,] at —, *HW*
299a auxiliary. / I left] auxiliary. I left *HW*
299b way. / I received] way. I received *HW*
300a formed. / I did] formed. / I did *HW*
301a annoyance. / So angry,] annoyance. So angry,
302a have] know *HW*

SILENT CORRECTIONS

109 and he gave me a skull] and gave me a skull
110 so very *mal-àpropos*] to very *mal-àpropos*
116 Miss Tomkinson] Miss Tomlinson

121   Miss Tomkinson] Miss Tomlinson
122   By-and-by] By-and-bye
125   I've had such fun] I ve had such fun
126   Helen] Ellen
138   enough of these] enough of thees
139   CHAPTER XVI.] CHAPTER XIV.
197   dim parties] grim parties
199   Jem Hearn] Jim Hearn
203   she being indisposed] she being undisposed
283   them all off] the mall off

For Product Safety Concerns and Information please contact our EU
representative GPSR@taylorandfrancis.com
Taylor & Francis Verlag GmbH, Kaufingerstraße 24, 80331 München, Germany